NOBLE SANCTUARY

A Novel

Scot Morison
Sept 3/90

NOBLE
SANCTUARY
A Novel

Scot Morison

Doubleday Canada Limited, Toronto

Canadian Cataloguing in Publication Data

Morison, Scot
  Noble sanctuary

ISBN 0-385-25249-8

I. Title.

PS8576.077N62 1990   C813'.54   C89-095347-3
PR9199.3.M67N62 1990

Typesetting: Southam Business Information and
  Communications Group Inc.
Design: Ross Mah Design Associates
Jacket photo: Adriene Veninger

Printed and bound in the USA

Published in Canada by
  Doubleday Canada Limited
  105 Bond Street
  Toronto, Ontario
  M5B 1Y3

This book is for Karen

Acknowledgments

I would like to say thank you to a few of the people who have helped me see this novel finished.

Rudy Wiebe, who put me on the path to begin with and instilled a belief in the worth of such travel.

Bob Harlow, who kept me on the right path for this book when I wanted to stray early on.

My mother, the rest of my terrific family on both sides, and many good and wise friends (Mahmuda Ali and Hart Hanson, in particular).

Issa J. Boullata, for permission to use his English translation of "Don't Sleep" by Mahmud Darwish.

Thanks also to Alberta Culture, the Near East Cultural and Educational Foundation of Canada (NECEF) and the International Center for Research and Public Policy (ICRPP) for their generous assistance.

Don't Sleep

When the moon falls
Like broken mirrors
The shadow grows larger among us
And legends die.
Don't sleep, my darling.
Our wound has become medals,
It has become fire on a moon.

Beyond our window is a bright day
And an arm of satisfaction
When it embraced me and flew
I thought I was a butterfly
In necklaces of pomegranate blossoms.
Lips of dew
Spoke to me without words.
Don't sleep, my darling
Beyond our window is a bright day.

Roses fell from my hand
Without fragrance, without torpor.
Don't sleep, my darling
Birds are committing suicide
My eyelashes are ears of corn
Drink night and destiny.
Your sweet voice is a kiss
And a wing on a string.
An olive branch wept
In exile over a stone
Looking for its roots,
Sun and rain.
Don't sleep, darling.
Birds are committing suicide.

When the moon falls
Like broken mirrors
The shadow drinks our shame
And we hide our escape.
When the moon falls
Love becomes an epic.
Don't sleep darling
Our wound has become medals
And our hands on the darkness
Are a nightingale on a string.

Mahmud Darwish

ONE

THE TALKATIVE ONE IN THE AISLE SEAT NEXT TO GEOFF'S WAS A Texan, a toolpush with Aramco. He was Geoff's age, or perhaps a little deeper into the sucking muck of his thirties, cowboy lean with an outdoors face, and he smelled like polished leather. He said he was on the way back to his rig in the Saudi Arabian Desert after a quick trip home to Lubbock to bury his father. He flashed an enormous signet ring on his right middle finger, sipped Pepsi steadily and cracked his peppermint chewing gum so loud that one of the flight attendants finally came back to investigate.

"Ah'm in training." He grinned at Geoff and scratched his long sideburns with the edge of a glass full of ice cubes. "A guy's gotta make do with soda there. There ain't no barrooms in Saudi.' *Sow-dee* (like howdy) was the way it ambled forth in his drawl.

"I imagine you go through a lot of liquid out there with the heat." Geoff had decided that with no other choices it was preferable to be talked to than talked at.

"Oh, hey, it's hot, all right. Hundred ten, hundred fifteen at this time of year. But it's a dry heat, you understand, like Texas, New Mexico, Arizona. It's a way worse in a place like Singapore or Bangkok on account of the humidity."

Geoff nodded.

"You ever been to Bangkok, buddy?"

"No."

"The name fits, I'll tell you. A fella can really bang it over

1

there." The Texan laughed hard at his own joke. "Say, where you from?"

"Vancouver," Geoff answered. "Canada."

"I heard of it. West Coast, just north of Seattle."

"That's right."

"I been to Canada, you know. Mind, it was years ago. Whole damn family climbed into a trailer and went to see the Rocky Mountains. I never seen so many goddamn American state licence plates in my life as I seen in that one mountain town. What's it called . . . ?"

"Banff?"

"That's it, yeah. Funny-sounding name that–Banff. Don't quite seem finished when you're done saying it. Nice little place, Canada. I'll have to get back there someday. What I'd really like to do is shoot a bear up there for the floor in front of my fireplace."

Geoff turned away and bit his lip; he could scarcely believe this guy wasn't putting him on.

"Did you say this was your first trip to the Middle East?"

"I didn't say. But yes, it is."

"Well, let me tell you, buddy. Them Arabs are friendly dudes. Real so, and their women are definite lookers." He winked. "But listen, that's all you're gonna be able to do–look at 'em, that is. Touch, and you're in big trouble. Know what I mean?"

Geoff turned away again. He stared down at the Mediterranean, cobalt from thirty thousand feet.

"Just some friendly advice from a man who knows whereof he speaks," the Texan went on, chuckling. "Look, look a lot even, but don't touch."

*　　　*　　　*

The salt and seaweed bite of that other, much larger body of water had been stronger than he'd ever remembered it, and its essence stuck with him long after he left the Seawall and jogged back through the moss-choked inner paths of Stanley Park, heading for a steaming shower and the jug of orange juice in his refrigerator. The idea of cold juice made him forget the Pacific Ocean for a moment and instead feel his dehydration. He was hungover, miserably sober: the morning after another night of too much scotch and far too little sleep. It was not an epic–an epic would have kept him off these paths altogether and tucked into bed until noon–but as a midweek hangover it was plenty bad enough. He knew he really ought to try harder to avoid such sessions with the Chivas bottle.

Emerging from under the high canopy of cedar and Douglas fir into a brief clearing, Geoff looked up and saw a blue sky waiting with West Coast patience behind a dawn mist that had lightened some but not yet begun to burn off. It was going to be one of those rare dry days that moved tourists to declare Vancouver one of the planet's most precious cities. Lotusland.

Back in the trees again, he heard the angry honking of some Canada geese announcing his approach on Lost Lagoon. He cleared his throat and spit a reminder of the night into some dew-soaked ferns beside the trail, cut left at the next junction and followed another branch towards the noise, all the while trying to remember his schedule for the day. He could make it only as far as Dan Wilson/9:45/Bedford Block/Richards Street, and gave up. It made his head hurt something awful to concentrate. He arrived in the open beside the little stream that fed the lagoon, grunted hello at a fellow jogger going the other way and shifted gears, suddenly more anxious than ever to get home to the toilet and his jug of juice.

He was running at a fair pace, and a stitch began in his side. He might well have stopped to let it subside anyway, even if he had not seen her there.

She was standing at the edge of Lost Lagoon, tossing out pieces of bread to an assembly of geese and ducks at her feet. She struck him as stunning in a city well-known for its women. Thick black hair hung long over her round shoulders, and her face was olive colored and flawless. She wore a pink sweatsuit and sneakers, but looked more like a simple walker than yet another dilettante runner. Quite unable not to, he pulled up and stopped at the base of a lone cedar nearby and, placing his palms against the rough trunk, leaned through the motions of a hamstring stretch so he could watch her.

He was still watching and stretching when the last of the bread was claimed by the squawking waterfowl. The woman brushed off her hands, dropped the empty plastic bag in a trash can and turned to leave. Walking up the path past his tree, she glanced up.

"Hello," he said. The word was yanked from his mouth. It was her eyes that had done it: sad, green eyes.

"Good morning." She answered him without looking back. He pushed away from the tree and moved into stride beside her.

"Greedy little bastards, aren't they?" He said it as cheerfully as his hangover would allow.

"The birds? Yes, they are," she agreed with a tired smile. "Some of them look very fed well."

"Fat, you mean." He struggled to place her accent. Not Spanish, though the face and hair looked about right. Italian or Greek, perhaps. He was half-considering asking her which when she suddenly stepped away from the path and headed out across the grass. He stopped walking to watch her go.

"Bye."

"Have a nice day," she called back. It was clearly no more than afterthought on her part.

"You too," he replied, and then, "Do you walk here very often?"

"No."

"Oh. That's too bad." But even that did not turn her head his way again.

*   *   *

The Texan had dragged the July 3 *Houston Post* out from under his seat and he skimmed over the front section, flipping the pages with accompanying loud cracks of his peppermint gum. Trying not to be too obvious about it, Geoff looked on over his shoulder. The international section of this paper, like all others lately, was dominated by dispatches from Lebanon. He rolled its pleasant rhythm around his mouth: Lebanon. And to think that only two months earlier, he couldn't even name its capital in a game of Trivial Pursuit.

"Could I have a look at that if you're done?" he asked. The Texan had moved on to the baseball box scores.

"Sure. Just more of the same old thing, though." As if he knew exactly what Geoff was in such a hurry to read, he added with a laugh, "The Jews are some mean motherfuckers when they go to war, huh?"

Geoff ignored him and opened the section to a large photograph of a tank. It had paint-chipped Hebrew characters on its side and was shown rumbling past blocks of shelled-out buildings. The cutline beneath read: Reconnaissance near the Green Line in East Beirut. He stared at the brief wire-service article that accompanied the photo. Phrases like "estimated death toll," "unnamed Israeli military sources" and "dug-in Palestinian guerrilla positions" ran together in a black blur.

This is lunacy, he thought. I can't be doing this, can I?

It felt odd that he should–or perhaps it was not odd at all–but he found himself remembering the night he and Angela went out to see the film *Gallipoli*. It must, in fact, have been just a few days before or after that first almost-meeting in Stanley Park.

He thought the movie, about two young Aussies who travel from their safe, slumbering back country into battle on a hopeless Turkish beachhead, a brilliant one. But the ending haunted him. Raised on a Hollywood diet since childhood, used to the hero staggering on to collect his medals and get the girl in spite of his wounds, he was stunned by the single, perfect shot from a faceless Turk that snuffed out the life of the blond star and brought the closing credits rolling onto the screen. All the way back to Angela's place afterwards, he'd sat silent behind the wheel of his car, seeing that man-boy caught in midstride by a rifle bullet high in the chest, a two-inch sheath of tempered steel that shattered ribs and crushed the heart.

"What's the matter, Geoff?" Angela had finally asked.

"I can't get that damned movie out of my mind," he told her. "It's ruining John Wayne for me."

Angela had laughed–Angela could always be counted on to laugh at his jokes–and, in tribute to John Wayne, sang him the first verse of the "Ballad of the Green Berets."

Later on, tucked into her bed, another shock waited for him. He could not make love. So imprinted on his brain was that stark, vivid image of one man's death that he found himself gazing down at his bewildered girlfriend, and he suddenly realized he'd gone quite soft in her hand.

As embarrassed as he was, though, he could not find the words to explain what had happened in his head and was left with nothing but a mumbled, crimson sorry. Rolling away from Angela, he stared up into the darkness and pulled the latch on the cage that held his crazily tumbling thoughts . . . .

His father had owned a magnificent collection of Time-Life picture books, and the dusty den corner where he discovered them one day as a twelve-year-old became his favorite spot in the house. With the metal register in the linoleum floor pushing hot air from the furnace up the tail of his shirt, a stack of raisin toast and a glass of Strawberry Quick at his feet, he spent hours on rainy winter days flipping through volumes on the pygmies of the Congo, the history of aviation and life on the coral reef. Best of all, though, were the books on war: World War I, World War II, Korea and an odd little job he had never heard of called the Spanish Civil War. That book contained the one photograph he most remembered from all the dozens of books lined up on those sagging shelves. A famous, or so he read, black and white shot by Robert Capa, it showed a Republican soldier dying on his feet on an arid Spanish steppe as one of General Franco's snipers put a bullet through his forehead. Transfixed by this eerie capturing of the faint boundary beween pulsing life and death, he eventually tore the photograph out of the book and kept it folded in his wallet until his mother discovered it one day and called a somewhat frantic parental conference over the psychological health of her son. His father had only laughed. Perhaps he understood. It was one of the questions he now wished he'd asked while that self-contained old man was still alive . . . .

There was a cousin whom he hadn't seen in a decade or longer. As kids, they had been inseparable and for a couple of years got together often to pit their armies of toy soldiers against each other on the rumpus-room carpet. One afternoon, he guessed it was about the time they both began to notice the swelling chests of the girls in their class, they met and hauled all of their plastic Germans and Allies, Apaches and U.S. cavalry troopers down into his father's workroom. Setting them up one last time on the concrete floor–all of them massed together on one vast nonsense battlefield–they made scores of small firebombs out of cotton batting dipped in nail polish remover and melted everything together: the blue cavalry buglers folding from their horses into the bayonets of Rommel's gray Afrika Corps, the red Apache archers flowing into the arms and between the bowed legs of the green Allied commandoes. When the thick, acrid smoke from their flash inferno had lifted, it revealed only a sweeping technicolor smudge on the concrete. They had both stopped laughing long enough then to know how beautiful the product of their destruction looked. He had recently learned a new word in his social studies class, and so, with the same gravity that adults he knew reserved for the term, he called it a *holocaust*.

"It's all right, you know, Geoff," Angela had whispered through the darkness, her hand reaching over to squeeze his. "These things are no big deal."

"I know," he'd answered. And then, after another stretch of silence, he asked, "Ange, do you ever think about death?"

"Yes."

"Good," he'd heard himself say.

"Why is that good, Geoff?"

"Because there are times when I think I'm the only one."

"So, it looks like old Raines there had himself a whale of a game last night."

"Pardon?" Geoff lowered the newspaper to his lap. It was the Texan, chainsawing into his thoughts.

"Timmy Raines. Three for four, with two stolen bases. Your Expos beat the snot out of our Giants again, 10–2. Or are you a Toe-run-toe Blue Jays man?"

"Yankees, actually," Geoff said.

"No shit? Oh, hey, s'cuse me, ma'am," the Texan purred at a passing attendant. "Another Pepsi, if you don't mind."

She looked at Geoff.

"Scotch, please," he added to the order.

"*Shook-ran*," grinned the Texan, taking his soft drink in hand when the attendant returned a few moments later. "That's how you say thanks in Arabic," he explained. "*Shookran*."

"I know," Geoff said, softly.

*   *   *

Geoff left the Texan sprawled across a couch in the Amman

airport transit lounge, waiting for his connection to Riyadh. Collecting his baggage, he cleared Customs quickly, changed some money and went outside to find a taxi into the Jordanian capital. The first thing, Walid had said, was to go to the Ministry of the Interior and arrange for a permit to travel to the West Bank. It was an elaborate formality, the Moroccan had told him, King Hussein's vain posturing of authority over something he had probably kissed away forever a decade and a half earlier, but it would allow Geoff to get back into the other Arab countries later if he needed to. Whatever you do, Walid had warned, don't let the Israelis stamp your passport.

"Amman?" inquired the cab driver he finally chose from among the many who'd immediately rushed over and pressed their services upon him.

"Yes." As Geoff slid into the front seat he winced at the heat of the black leather upholstery on his bare arms. He listened to the trunk lid slam down over his bag.

"Is bery hot, no?" The cabbie bounced in beside him with a laugh. He punched the car into gear and they started away with a squeal of tires.

Swinging in and out of the on-coming lane to get past straining diesel trucks and horse-drawn carts, the cabbie hummed peacefully to himself and tapped his fingernails against the plastic of the steering wheel, leaving Geoff alone to pick up what he could as first impression.

In truth, there was little to impress. The landscape on either side of the black ribbon of highway was flat sand and scrub, interrupted only near the horizon by groupings of low hills that were the same dull boxed-cereal colors. With the mileage clicking away steadily on the meter, they closed on the city and Geoff at last began to pick out the flags of habitation. A canvas-topped military transport of universal green bounced and yawed along the shoulder for a couple of hundred yards, before veering away sharply towards a sheet-metal building standing alone in the middle distance. As it did, he saw a dozen dark young male faces looking back at him between the truck's canvas flaps. Farther on, he watched a boy and his dog pushing along a flock of dusty sheep, though what they could be finding to graze upon out there was a mystery to Geoff. A red Mercedes, piloted by an obese man wearing the familiar white head scarf Geoff associated with this part of the world, sped past them. With both hands on his steering wheel, the Arab stared ahead, not even flicking acknowledgment at their brief presence beside him. Geoff glanced over at the cab driver, who glanced back at him and then sneered.

"Big Saudi," he said, disdainfully lifting his chin after the departed Mercedes.

Geoff nodded his understanding. The have-nots forever being passed by the haves on the highways of life.

"You come here make business?" The cabbie's tone had resumed its pleasantness.

"No."

"Bleasure?" Joking, the driver passed his hand over the barren scene outside the car.

"Something like that, I guess."

"*Ahlan wa-sahlan*-welcome," the Arab said.

Geoff went to mumble thanks but no sound came. Up from his gut, a sick and overwhelmed feeling was kicking hard to resurface. There was business, there was pleasure, and then there was something else that was neither one. What could he call it?

TWO

JOHN AND TOMMY, TWO OF ANGELA'S NUMEROUS GAY FRIENDS, threw generous bacchanals in their large glass house overlooking Kitsilano Beach, along Point Grey. A certain homophobia notwithstanding, Geoff enjoyed their parties because they always provided him with a free drunk of good scotch and an array of easy targets for his cynicism. Whenever Angela went off for a hair consult with John, who owned a high priced salon on fashionable Robson Street, or disappeared with epicurean Tommy to admire the latest additions to his wine cellar and fend off his half-hearted bisexuality, Geoff could always find some would-be rock star or actress to stand with in a corner and pretend to flatter, while out in the center of the sprawling living room couples of all bedding preference bobbed and weaved to the sounds of Latin beat and androgenous Euro-pop under a spinning strobe ball.

That night, his mingling companion during Angela's wandering absence was a playwright named Hal Sims, author of a momentary hit in town entitled "A Dog's Breakfast." Rocking back and forth on his clog-clad feet, while he stuffed his face full of caviar slathered on Triscuits, Sims looked the part of a playwright too, with his green corduroy jacket and wind-whipped sweep of graying hair. Even the bleary eyes and the pock-marked cheeks fit.

"Good caviar," the playwright commented, flipping over his broad palm to catch what fell from his lips. He washed it down with a slurp of Tommy's red wine.

"Doesn't do a thing for me," Geoff said. "I hate the stuff, in fact."

"Hate? A good word. I like it," Sims said.

"You like hate?"

"Yes, because it's strong. There is a distinct lack of strong emotion these days, you know. Our times are miserably cursed by too much equivocation and ambivalence. Of course, it would be better if there was something you hated more than caviar."

"There is," Geoff said, thinking, I hate pretentious artistes.

"Oh, what?"

"Olives." He pointed at a bowl of them next to the caviar.

"Olives? What about nuclear proliferation, violent crime, the breakdown of the family unit, the chasm of roaring silence between the sexes?"

Geoff pretended to think about it for a moment and then he shrugged his shoulders. At that, the two men shared a laugh, and Geoff decided the playwright was perhaps a tolerable sort after all.

"Getting back to hate," the writer went on. "How did you get that terrific shiner?"

Self-conscious out of vanity, Geoff touched the bruise beneath his right eye and the scab over his brow.

"At a hockey game. I play for my office team. We won," he added.

"Did you?"

It had happened earlier that evening. Geoff's team, the Haywood Harris Hurricanes, had played off against the Royalty Realty Royals for the Vancouver Real Estate League championship. The game had been a close one: two equally awful teams of fat-bottomed, pot-bellied smokers and drinkers gasping after each other around the ice and wobbling further onto their ankles as the first period became the second became the third. With the score tied 8–8 late in the game, something had happened to clear the benches, and he'd quickly found himself paired off with one of the stronger, more athletic Royals. For a few moments, the two of them did little more than jerk each other around by their jerseys. Geoff, at least, had no interest at all in fighting. It had been years since he'd last thrown any kind of

punch, and he wasn't even sure he'd remember how.
Unfortunately, his partner in this little waltz around the ice had
no such reluctance. Finally shoving off, the Royals' player tagged
him twice in the eye before he could raise his arms in self-defense.
His battered face throbbing, he had lunged after his attacker,
throwing crazy punches–ridiculous haymakers–and while
missing with most had landed at least one fierce hook to the nose,
snapping it, before the referee and linesman jumped in to
separate them. With blood streaming from both nostrils, the
Royal had struggled back onto his skates and stood there with a
horrible adrenalin grin on his face. And Geoff had grinned too, as
though it was good, clean fun.

"I'd like to write something about hockey," Sims declared.
"Something earthy and wholesome."

Geoff laughed. He looked away for some sign of Angela. She
was still nowhere around. But then, on the other side of the room,
he saw another face that made him smile. Excusing himself from
Sims, he skirted around the dancing and walked over. Stan Getz's
"The Girl From Ipanema" was purring forth from the stereo, and
it felt as if he were walking in perfect time to it. He probably was,
so he slowed down to throw himself off the beat.

"Hi."

"Hello."

"You don't remember me, do you?" The woman was standing
alone. She appeared not to know anyone.

"We have met before?"

"Briefly, down in Stanley Park. You were feeding the
birds."

"I remember you now, yes." She returned a small part of his
smile.

"How have you been?" he asked.

"Fine, thank you."

"Good. I've been fine, too."

"That is good," she said. The green eyes betrayed her
amusement.

"Yeah, I feel the same way."

She nodded. He nodded. They stared silently out at the dance
floor. Geoff sighed and yawned.

"Good party, don't you think?" he said.

"Yes," she answered.

"Would you like to dance?"

"No, thank you."

"Then I guess a walk on the beach or a necking session in the closet is out of the question as well?"

She smiled benignly at him, and said nothing.

"Please, excuse me. I hope I am not interrupting?" A man had slipped through the archway from the kitchen and stood beside them. Geoff was deflated by the other's chiseled Mediterranean looks and the fondness he saw in the woman's eyes as she greeted him.

"Hello." The man spoke easily, reaching out to offer his hand. "I am Walid."

"Geoff."

"Your poor eye." Walid nodded up at Geoff's face. "Does it hurt you much?"

"No, just looks ugly."

"It is not ugly," Walid said, politely. His accent was not as pronounced as the woman's, and his English was better.

"It gives a certain character to his face, does it not?" Walid turned to the woman. She did not reply, but continued to study Geoff's eye.

"Aha, here you are," Angela said. She came up from behind him, her manicured fingers snaking around his elbow, a knee playfully dipping in to the back of his. She flicked her eyes at his company, flicked them twice at Walid.

"Hi there," she said, and then, "Geoff, aren't you going to introduce me?"

"Sure. This is Angela. Walid, and, I'm sorry, I don't think I caught your name?"

"Nadya," she answered, briefly shaking Angela's hand.

"Nadya. That's such a pretty name." Angela smiled. "Are you Russian like that famous gymnast named Nadia?"

"She was Romanian," Geoff corrected.

"No, I am Palestinian," the woman told them.

"Palestinian?" Angela said. "I've heard of that . . . I think. Where is that?"

"My family comes from a village to the west and north of Jerusalem."

"I bet it's beautiful there," Geoff said. "Jerusalem, I mean. A friend of mine spent a few months in Israel once, picking fruit on a kibbutz. He said the old part of Jerusalem is just magic." Geoff saw Walid and Nadya glance at each other.

"I too have heard that it is a magical place, but I have never seen it," Nadya told him. Her voice was cool.

"So, are you friends of Tommy and John's?" Angela asked, moving the suddenly stalled conversation in a new direction.

"I am a stylist in John's shop," Walid said.

"Really? Funny, I haven't seen you there," Angela said.

"I have only been here for a month. I moved out from Toronto."

"Well there you go. I haven't been into the shop for a while," she said. "Speaking of which, I was thinking about making an appointment next week. Any suggestions as to what I should do? Can you see me with a perm?"

Not conscious of doing so, Geoff stared at Nadya. Suddenly, she turned and walked into the kitchen.

"Yes, a permanent would look nice on you. On the other hand, however–"

"Excuse me." Geoff interrupted. "I was just going to fix myself a drink. I'm taking orders?"

"Yes, I'll have another, darling. More ice this time, please," Angela said.

Walid lifted his hand and smiled. "Nothing for me, thank you."

Geoff accepted Angela's empty glass and headed into the kitchen. He saw Nadya leaning over the sink, running herself a glass of cold water.

"That's it?" he teased.

"Pardon?"

"Just water? Nothing for flavor in there?"

"I don't drink alcohol," she said.

"Never mind," he smiled, shaking the mostly empty bottle of Chivas on the countertop. "I drink enough for both of us."

She turned off the water and looked about to leave him standing there.

"Don't go yet. I don't bite. Besides, they're only talking about hair."

She settled back against the counter and, over the rim of her water glass, watched him fix Angela's Grand Marnier.

"You like to drink," she observed.

"I find it improves my vision."

"Somehow, I think it would not."

"Ah, but how can you be sure? You don't drink."

She accepted his point with a strange little nod that served to underscore her foreignness. Geoff remembered why it was he'd really come in here.

"I'm sorry if my staring out there bothered you. It's just that I've never seen eyes quite like yours before. They're very beautiful, you know. . . . Oh, oh, I'm staring again, aren't I?"

She smiled. "We have a saying in Arabic. Would you like to hear it?"

"Yes, I would, very much."

"We say the first look it is for you, but the second look it is on you."

Geoff was astounded to feel himself blush at the elegance of her scolding. But then, just as quickly, she granted him a pardon.

"Do you mean to have them both?" she inquired, gesturing at the two full drinks in his hands.

"No, one of them is for Angela, but I'm only going to take it to her if you promise you'll wait here until I get back."

He got no such promise, only a vague gaze, but she was there when he'd tactfully disengaged himself from Angela and Walid again after an interminable couple of minutes and returned to the kitchen. She wasn't alone, though. Hal Sims' green corduroy jacket was pressed in close beside her along the counter. Too close.

"Quite frankly, I've never been able to understand the appeal of Yasser Arafat," the playwright was saying. "Now George Habash, him I could see as a leader. I think that as a physician by vocation, a saver of lives, he has a certain moral authority. Don't you agree?"

"But Habash is a Marxist, and we Palestinians are free enterprisers," Nadya answered lightly.

"The Palestinian bourgeoisie, you mean, are free enterprisers."

"Perhaps so." Nadya smiled, noticing Geoff's return.

"The terror of the blueline," Sims quipped across his casually folded arms. "A nasty business, this national game of ours, hockey." He'd said that for Nadya's benefit and at Geoff's cost. Thus was a rivalry announced–even though Angela was not twenty feet away, and the playwright had a wife somewhere else in the house.

"Some person did that to your eye at a *hockey* game?" Nadya spoke the word like Geoff might have said jai alai.

"Yes," he replied, "but as the old saying goes, you should have seen the other guy."

"You are proud?" she said.

"No, not exactly proud, but fistfights are part of the game." Why had he said that when he didn't for a moment believe it? This other sport had barely begun and Sims had him whipped already.

"I think I would not like this game of yours," she concluded. The playwright nodded earnestly and smirked at Geoff.

Laughing like old friends, Angela and Walid drifted into the kitchen and joined them. Geoff gradually backed off and stood at the edge of the chatter. Their brief moment of contact gone, he found he had nothing to say to Nadya in a group. Instead, he poured himself another drink that he didn't need and sulked. Twice during the playwright's caustic, well-practiced monologue on the personal quirks of his play's cast, Geoff glanced over to see her looking back at him, but both times she looked away as soon as he went to smile. Not long afterwards, in spite of vigorous protests from Angela and Sims, Walid went upstairs to search for their coats and the two of them left the party.

"Wow." Angela was a little drunk herself after four or five drinks. "He was gorgeous. I wouldn't kick him out of bed for eating crackers."

"No, I'm sure you wouldn't," Geoff said.

"His girlfriend was beautiful too, wasn't she?" Angela added.

"She was all right, I suppose," he said, staring at the front door as Walid pulled it closed after them.

"I've heard it from entirely reliable sources that the Arab man can go all night," Sims said, moving his eyebrows up and down.

"Really?" Angela gushed, then blushed.

Geoff shook his head. He knew this type–*he* was this type; with Nadya gone, the playwright would redirect his percolating lust towards Angela. Strangely, Geoff could not have cared less. Crossing his eyes at his drunk and horny girlfriend, he walked away from them and back into the confusion of the living room.

*   *   *

"Ooo, Raymond Clarkson, you dirty little cretin, you! Mummy, Raymond took hold of my vagina just now."

"Did not!"

"Did too!"

"Not."

"Too."

"Not."

"I say, children, do stop picking at one another, please."

"But, Daddy, it's Raymond doing the picking. He's picking my vagina."

"Am not!"

"Are too!"

"That's quite enough now, both of you. Play together nicely in there, or out you'll come."

Geoff was not comfortable. The sweat dripped off his face and his elbows chafed just a little too hard against the concrete deck. Bunching his shirt into something of a pillow for his head, he rolled with a grunt onto his back. He held his Michelin map of the Middle East six inches above his face, blocking the sun and easing his twisted squint. Better.

Chest-deep in the middle of the hotel pool, a pair of prepubescent English children continued to splash insults and chlorine in each other's faces, alternately breaking into excited summer holiday giggles. As far away as they could possibly get, the children's ruddy parents lay dozing on chaise lounges, disguised under polaroid wraparounds and broad straw hats. Just audible behind the shrieks of the children, from down in one of the crowded concrete valleys of seven-hilled Amman, he could make out the call to noon prayer from a mosque. Staring at his map, he ran a fingertip over the brief span of colored paper that separated Amman from Jerusalem and swore softly.

"Forty-eight hours, sir," the starched and pressed official at the Interior Ministry had droned in that off-handed triplicate.

"It's *very* important to me, can it not be sped up? All you've got to do is sign some form and stamp it, right?"

"Such things take time, sir." The man's smile would not be shaken.

"Can't it be ready tomorrow, then? Surely one day is enough."

"Tomorrow is Friday. The ministry is closed for religious reasons."

"How about this? Does this help?" Geoff slapped an American twenty down on the desk in front of the mulish bureaucrat.

"Thank you," the man said, pocketing the bill with an elegant tuck of his chin. He pulled open his desk drawer and handed over a faded tourist pamphlet: "The Wonders of Jordan."

"Did you know that in the time of Ptolemy, our city was known as Philadelphia?"

"Terrific, the city of brotherly love. Now when will my permission to cross be ready?"

"As I said, forty-eight hours, sir."

Carelessly refolding the map, Geoff fired it to the cement beside his towel. He rolled forward, grasped his knees and stood up. Twisting the tension out of his neck, he paused to let a moment of dizziness pass, then walked to the edge of the pool and dove in. Surfacing as late as he could, he glided caiman-like to the far edge of the pool and held on with the tips of his fingers, quietly blowing bubbles in the water. Throwing his head back, he gazed up through lightly closed eyelids at the Middle Eastern sun and saw everywhere a shuddering blood red. Dizzied again, he kicked out into the deep end, hyperventilated for a while and then took another big chestful of air and dropped to the bottom of the pool. Sitting there cross-legged, he opened his eyes and looked up. He could stare right into the sun now. It rippled for him.

Raymond and his sister were treading water overhead. Pushing off the bottom of the pool to surface for air, Geoff watched the graceless sprawl of their skinny legs. It was too familiar-the gawkiness of all things young. But he was thirty-three, and his own departed youth was suddenly every bit as vivid as the bald climate of this place. He felt old for the first time in his life and tried to remember if the two of them had ever talked of children. They might have; he'd lately begun to want kids. Passing Raymond's legs, he spotted a faint, smoky cloud of urine drift out from between the boy's thighs. Bobbing at the surface beside him, Geoff couldn't help but smile just a little at the defiant smirk he saw. That's right, Raymond, you piss on it all while you can.

*   *   *

Geoff had never been much bothered by bad sleep and dreams, but that night he woke up over and over again, sweating, and kicking the sheets into a damp gray knot around his ankles. He flipped and punched the hard hotel pillows until there was little body left in them, and later, just before dawn, he dreamt about murmurs of concern that turned with the languid gradualness of a summer day into screams. Yes, they were screams, but screams so distant and rhythmic that they sounded like the perfectly pitched cries of a seagull. There is someone drowning out there, mumbled a voice as sun-drunk and apathetic as his own. No, it's just a bird, he replied, eyes shut, stretched out in the grass on his elbows. Just a bird is all, he repeated. Then, in this dream, he fell asleep and began to dream of a naked shoulder so familiar he could describe the exact taste of its salt on his tongue. But strangely, he could put no face to this shoulder. And then he was suddenly jerked from this dream within a dream by a voice now harsh and sober giving him the name of a woman who had just drowned. The name was not one he recognized at all, but he broke down and cried just the same as the voice began shouting at him in fury for the stupidity of having mistaken the earlier screams for a bird.

When he awoke afterwards-when he really did, and not just inside another dream-he found that his pillow was wet, though wet from drool not tears. He got up and walked over to the open window in his room. His fourth-floor view was of an alley that ran between the hotel and the next building, and he leaned out over it. The dead still air was cool for early summer in this part of the world, but spoiled by the smell of diesel exhaust coming from a garbage truck that had turned into the far end of the alley. Geoff watched the truck's creeping approach up the alley and the sideman jogging just ahead so as to heft and pitch the boxes and bags of waiting trash into the side bucket.

The comfortable banality of this small moment ended, violently, with the sideman's discovery of a figure-to Geoff, in the half-light, it looked like an old man or perhaps a cripple-sleeping next to a pile of refuse along the wall of the hotel. Reaching up into the truck, as though this was common practice, the sideman grabbed a heavy stick and began to swing it at the figure's shoulders and back. Geoff had to blink hard a couple of times before he would believe he was seeing straight.

"Hey!"

The hoarse echo of his voice off the tight confines of the alley was what served to make Geoff conscious of the absurd silence of the assault. Neither the attacker nor the attacked made any sound. The only noise, other than the rough idle of the truck, was that horrifying one of the sideman's club walloping against human flesh.

"Stop that!" Geoff shouted. "Leave him alone!"

Pausing in midswing, the sideman peered up at Geoff, then looked away and carried through with his swing. Swearing, Geoff grabbed a glass from the nightstand. Leaning way out the window, he pegged the glass at the front of the garbage truck. It fell short and smashed on the pavement. Again the sideman looked up at the window, and this time he shouted something angry and waved his stick at Geoff. Then, as before, he calmly resumed his flogging of the man at his feet.

Jumping into a pair of walking shorts-the first things he saw-Geoff ran from his room, realizing as he slammed the door behind him that he didn't have his key, and took the stairs two at a time. He sprinted through the empty lobby to the alley side exit of the hotel and burst through the doors, wondering what on earth he could hope to do against the sideman, the driver and the sideman's vicious stick.

But he did not have to do anything. They were gone-all of

them, and the pile of garbage too. The only thing left behind to assure Geoff it had happened at all was the dirty smell of burnt diesel. Turning, he went back inside the hotel to try to find someone who could let him into his room.

THREE

AT EIGHT-THIRTY ON SATURDAY MORNING, WHILE HE WAS still undressed and repacking what little he'd disturbed in his suitcase in two days, there was a knock at the door. He jammed his shaving kit into the bag and called out a hello.

"Mister, is me," came the husky reply.

"Who?"

"Taxi man, remember you, me you tell come today. Today you go Jerusalem."

Geoff checked his watch to be sure it hadn't stopped running while he was in the shower. He opened the door a crack.

"You're an hour early. I thought the Arabs were always late."

"Always me early," the driver replied, beaming.

"All right," he said. "I'll meet you outside after I have something to eat."

Downstairs in the patio dining room near the pool, Geoff rushed through a breakfast of cold scrambled eggs on hard, dry toast. He watched young Raymond, at the next table, use his knife to flip patties of melting butter at his sister's bare legs, then fend off her howls and his parent's scowls with a crooked, eat-shit grin. At one point, the children's mother looked across at Geoff with an exasperated expression.

"Have you any of your own?" she asked.

He shook his head.

"Keep it that way."

Geoff found the cabbie waiting outside on the hotel driveway, chattering with a doorman while he wiped invisible dust from the impressive sheen of his black Peugeot.

"*Sabah el-khair,*" Geoff said, haltingly. Not the least bit interested in "The Wonders of Jordan," he had spent the previous evening trying to absorb some conversational Arabic from a Berlitz book.

"Good morning you too, mister. Is good, you speak the language."

"Ha."

"You will learning more," the driver said, amiably. He abandoned his dusting to toss Geoff's suitcase into the trunk. "We go?"

"Yes, let's go. To the ministry, then to *Al Quds–*Jerusalem."

"See, you speaking good." The driver laughed.

His permit to cross was sitting with several others in the out-basket on the otherwise empty desk of the same smiling official who'd taken his twenty-dollar bill. Without so much as a nod of recognition, Geoff handed over his passport for identification, took it and the stamped document back in return and pivoted sharply to leave.

"I hope you enjoyed our city, sir," the Jordanian said pleasantly.

"And I hope you rot in hell," Geoff told him, every bit as pleasantly but much more sincerely. He turned and almost ran out of the building.

"You like music, mister?" the cabbie asked. He was digging through a shoebox full of dusty cassettes when Geoff returned to the car. Finally deciding on one, he slipped it into the cheap tapedeck mounted under the dash. In a moment, the machine hissed and crackled to life. The driver smiled. Obviously intimate with his collection, he began to sing along at the exact moment the first selection began, then broke into laughter at the tunelessness of his own voice. They pulled away from the curb and out into traffic.

*   *   *

Foreign music of some kind echoed through the empty corridors of the building. He followed it to the source and found a large ghetto-blaster sharing space on top of a lab bench crowded with trays of test tubes, beakers, rolls of masking tape and coiled lengths of rubber tubing. At first, he saw nobody and pictured himself trying to explain his presence here to some zealous campus cop convinced he had caught an equipment thief. But then, from behind another lab bench, she stood up–her dark hair all the blacker for the bleached white of her lab coat.

"So that's what Arab music sounds like." He said it slowly, hoping not to startle her. She was startled anyway, and a small gasp escaped from her lips. She turned and glared at him.

"I'm sorry," he said lamely.

"What are you doing here?" She demanded, moving to turn off the music.

"I came to give you a lift home. That is, unless you plan to work all night, in which case I came to keep you company for a while."

"How did you get in? The building it is locked after six."

"I lied to a janitor. Told him I was one of your professors," he said. In spite of her little start and her anger, he saw that she was unable to suppress a slight smile at his gall.

"You are going home, right?" He walked towards her.

"Yes," she said, "and I when I do so I shall take the bus."

"Oh, come on. I'm right here, and I've got a car. You might as well save your bus fare. Think of it as my contribution to higher learning."

"I have a transit pass. A ride would not save me any money," she countered.

"I'll take you right to your front door."

"Not necessary. The bus it goes very near to my building. The walk is short and I value fresh air."

He wanted to believe she was teasing him with this tough parrying, but he just wasn't sure.

"Aren't you at least a little curious to know how I found you?" he asked.

She narrowed her gaze at him. "A little."

"That's too bad." He shrugged. "Spurned men tell no tales."

She sighed. "All right. If you will permit me some time to clean up the lab and collect my things, I accept your offer."

"Take as long as you like. I'll just poke around here." He reached out to pick up a beaker full of clear blue liquid. She moved quickly to take it away from him, and it very nearly slipped out of her hands.

"Please–do not touch anything," she said, concerned.

Twenty minutes later, he led her to the parking lot. He had her ghetto-blaster in one hand, and it was every ounce as heavy as it looked. He thought about her lugging it to and fro every day on the bus along with her books and papers.

"I'm told you're working on your PhD in chemistry."

"Biochemistry," she corrected him.

"Biology, chemistry–I made a point of not taking either at university."

"You went to university?" she asked. Her tone stung him.

"Don't sound so surprised," he laughed.

She shook her head. "I am sorry. I do not know why I have said that."

"You're forgiven."

"What did you study?" she asked, a little too eagerly.

"I have a Bachelor of Commerce. I took it out here at UBC too, though it was more than a few years ago now."

"Does that mean you are in business?"

"In a manner of speaking. I sell commercial real estate," he said, unlocking the passenger door for her.

"You must be doing well," she observed, admiring the dark interior of his BMW as she got in. She looked up at him, still standing there in her open door, looking down. "If you don't like the work, why do you do it?" she asked.

"The million-dollar question. . . . But I don't remember saying I didn't like it."

"No, that is true, you did not."

Frowning at her quick reading of him, he walked around to his side of the car, unlocked the door (she did not make a move from inside to do that for him) and slid in.

"Okay," he said, draping his arms over the steering wheel. "Where to?"

"Bidwell Street."

"Bidwell? In the weirdly West End." He might have said

more–West End Vancouver was a gay enclave of sorts–but he
cautioned himself that this was a woman who'd already shown
that she had little tolerance for his silly shows of macho.

"No black eye this time, you'll be happy to notice," he said,
examining his mostly healed eye and then her through a corner of
the sharply tilted rearview mirror.

"You have still not told me," she said, ignoring him.

"Told you what?"

"How you found out what I do and where I work."

"I have a spy in John's shop. I bribed the manicurist to ask
Walid all about you."

"With what did you bribe your spy?"

"Top secret," he smiled. "Can't divulge."

He'd run out of things to say to her by the time they crossed the
Burrard Street Bridge. He turned west onto Davie Street, and in
silence both of them watched the dull succession of drug marts,
corner groceries and fast-food restaurants slip past. Her
apartment building was an aging white highrise.

"I'll bet your place is on the other side, about ten floors up,
with a great view of the ocean." He watched her rummage
through her purse for keys.

"Fifteenth floor, and yes, it is beautiful," she said. "Would you
like–"

"I'd love to." He cut her off, making them both laugh. "I was
afraid you'd change your mind," he explained.

"I might have," she acknowledged, pushing open the car
door.

She was right: framed on the far left by the dark shoreline of the
Point Grey peninsula and on the near right by the dense
vegetation of Stanley Park, her view of English Bay was a
postcard picture. The late spring sunset was a cherry-red smear
along the horizon now, and the night sky raced in behind it first
as gray streaks, then as splashes of charcoal and finally as thick
pools of black. Out in the middle of the placid bay, a dozen
freighters sat at anchor under running lights, their crews
probably right now getting drunk in the strip joints along
Granville Street.

He heard the racket she was making in the kitchen come

to an end, and then she stepped out on the narrow balcony beside him.

"It will take a minute for the water to boil," she said.

"You know, even without the downtown skyline, it must have been quite a first sight for Captain Vancouver. I've lived here all my life and I'm still, every now and then, amazed by this place."

"It is something special," she agreed. "Some nights, I feel I am being called to bring a chair out here and write poetry."

"A scientist and poet rolled into one."

"No." She blushed. "I try, but my poetry is louse. No, this is not the right word, I think?"

"Lousy is what you mean. But I doubt it. I'd like to read some."

"It is written in Arabic, and much of the meaning is lost in the translation. Our two languages are very different."

"How so?"

"English, I believe, is a straight language. Most of your words have precise meanings. Arabic is a language of layers. There are many times poems hiding in the poems themselves."

"I'd like to be able to tell you I understand, but I'm not sure I do."

"To express it another way, sometimes what we are heard to be saying is not what we are saying at all." She laughed softly and turned to face him along the railing. "I think that is why the Arabs are so . . . perplexing? Yes, perplexing . . . for you in the West."

Geoff looked at her–she was standing as close to him and seemingly at ease as she had yet been–and he wondered what she was saying to him, really saying to him, now. The evening breeze whipped softly around their faces; he thought he could smell lemon in her hair, and his desire to put his hands on her shoulders was suddenly overwhelming. But something just as quickly told him he must not do that. He must not touch. They both smiled then at the sound of her kettle starting to whistle, and went back inside.

*   *   *

"Nadya, what did you mean that night when you said you'd never been to Jerusalem? Didn't you say your family comes from around there?" Geoff had not forgotten the sudden chill of that particular moment at the party.

They were sitting cross-legged on the living-room floor, facing each other over a low coffeetable. Arabs, she had instructed him, preferred a floor littered with pillows to even the softest couch.

"Our home is there; but it was taken from us in 1948, and we had to leave."

"Leave?" Until now their words across this table had been light and full of smiling.

"My family took what they could carry and walked north to Lebanon. I was born there. Later, we moved to Kuwait."

"But why did you leave? Why was your home taken?"

She frowned and her shoulders sagged. Geoff saw it as frustration at his lack of knowledge.

"I do not understand *why*, none of our people understand why, but you might say it had to do with the trick of words that created the Israeli state. When the Jews of Europe came, it was decided for us that we leave. We have been the ones to pay for the crimes of the Nazis."

"They were terrible, terrible crimes," he said instinctively.

"Yes, of course."

"Those things that were done to the Jews–I mean, that was mankind as the lowest life form on earth."

"Geoff, I too have seen the pictures of the trains and the mass graves and the concentration camp survivors. I do not need a lecture about horror from you. Believe me, I do not," she said emphatically. "The evil of Adolph Hitler is not the point. It is not the point at all when one speaks of Palestine."

He listened to the sharpening edge in her voice and shook his head.

"What?" she asked.

"This heaviness, it's not what I wanted to have happen here tonight. I wanted to talk to you, begin to know you, not have you get angry at me."

"You are right," she said, nodding. "Perhaps it is best if we change the subject." Then, as if to search for that change, she looked around the room. Her face brightened. "Would you like to hear music?"

She was up on her feet before he'd answered yes and heading for the ghetto-blaster. She returned with the coffee pot in hand just as the tape she had inserted began to play. Reaching up from behind a wall of frantic strings and thumping drums, a woman's strong voice filled his ears with an unintelligible but richly melodic tumble of vowels and *h*'s and *b*'s. He rested his neck against the sofa and closed his eyes to listen.

He found her staring at him when he opened his eyes at the end of the song, but held off teasing her with her own Arabic maxim about first and second looks.

"You look peaceful. You like this music?" she asked.

"Quite a voice."

"Her name was Um Kalthum. She was Egyptian. She is dead now, but all over the Middle East she is still famous."

"Kind of the Arab Billie Holiday, eh?"

Nadya frowned. "I have not heard of this person."

"She was an American jazz singer who also had an incredible voice. She killed herself with alcohol and drugs and men."

"Um Kalthum died of natural causes. No drugs or alcohol for her, and only one man." She smiled at her little cultural joke.

"Well, that would never happen here, you see. The brightest stars always go out with a bang," he said. "Anyway, it was beautiful. A free plane ride."

"How do you mean?" She shifted positions to lean out across the coffeetable, and her feet brushed lightly against his. As innocent as it was, they were both very conscious of it having happened. Geoff studied her face for reaction.

"It draws images in my mind. Things I imagine seeing in that part of the world."

"What do you think you would see?"

"No way. You'll laugh at me. And quite deservedly, I'm sure."

"I will not laugh at you," she said sternly. "Tell me."

"Oh, I don't know–mangy camels, lots of swirling sand, veiled women, crowded narrow streets, blind alleys. . . . Should I stop already?" He laughed.

"You could see some of those things, it is true." She looked ready to say something more, but instead settled back with a weary smile.

"Nadya, may I ask you a personal sort of question?"

She nodded.

"Who is Walid?"

"He is a friend."

"Hmm." Geoff scratched his nose, thinking about it for a moment before plunging on. "A friend or *a* friend?"

"Just a friend." She managed to keep a straight face when answering him, but barely.

"And what about you?" she asked.

"Me?"

"You and . . . I have forgotten her name."

"Angela."

"Yes. You and Angela."

He looked at her and wanted to lie, believing it would make things so much simpler. But he was afraid those strong, unhappy eyes would see right through him, and in the end he told her the truth as best he knew it.

"Right now, I don't know what Angela and I are. And things become considerably more confused every minute I spend with you."

"This is not good," she said, flushing and fidgeting.

"Don't run away, Nadya," he said, sensing that she was about to flee to the kitchen. It felt odd that they should still be sitting this far apart after an admission like the one he'd just made.

"I think you must leave," she said suddenly.

Although leaving was the last thing he wanted to do right then, he had almost seen her reaction coming and he chose not to fight it. Without consulting her, he had already decided there would be other nights.

"All right, but I'm going to see you again–soon."

"No, I do not think so," she said, getting to her feet. He stood too and followed her slowly to the door.

"I can't not see you again, Nadya. I have to. There's something happening here. Call it biochemistry."

But she did not smile. "Where I come from this would not be done," she said.

"I understand that, but you're not there now, you're here. And

I am not from there, I'm from here. Different place, different rules."

"Please." She shook her head, her voice uncertain as it pushed him towards the open door.

"I'll call you." He turned to stop the door with the toe of his shoe.

"Goodbye, Geoff."

"I'm going to call you," he repeated before letting her close the door.

*   *   *

It was hot and getting hotter by the minute as they descended a series of long, twisting hills, called the Moab Mountains, that would eventually deposit them at the bottom of the Jordan Valley. Cotton-throated, Geoff wanted to ask the cabbie for a cupful of water or whatever it was in the plaid thermos that lay between them on the front seat, but didn't. Instead, he watched the man riding his brakes where he should be gearing down, and found that this small mechanical carelessness annoyed him greatly. He slumped against the door and leaned his face out the open window into the tepid shear of their movement. He stuck his hand out and let it play in the air like a child might.

Given a further moment to consider it, everything annoyed him today: the cabbie's sandal on that small pad of rubber over steel; the coarse grayness of the man's long, uncut toenails protruding from the ends of the sandals; the raw, functional ugliness of sandals; the relentless howl of this taped music, one tape now sounding just like the next; whatever it was about this place, its food or drink that had pinned him to the toilet seat much of last night; the smirking bureaucrat in the Interior Ministry; the idea of an English wanker's piss washing over him in the pool at an overpriced Amman hotel; the Texan on the airplane who'd fit every laughable stereotype he'd ever held; the crack and smell of the Texan's peppermint chewing gum; the fact that she hadn't told him. Why hadn't she told him? Why? He felt like swearing out loud.

Glancing over at him, the cabbie turned off the music and reached for his thermos.

"You want drink? Is good water."

Taking the plastic cup when it was filled and offered, Geoff swallowed half then handed it back to the driver to finish. Steadying the wheel with the inside of his knees, the Arab replaced the cup with one sharp twist and dropped the thermos back on the seat. The music remained off.

"You no habby, mister?"

It was a few miles farther on. Geoff had returned to his slump against the door, lulled into almost pleasant numbness by the whine of soft tires on soft asphalt.

"No," he admitted.

"*Ma' laish.* Jerusalem will makes you habby again."

There was something unmistakable about the way the Arab had said it that made Geoff sit upright. He took a closer look at the cabbie. He was a man well into middle age, with the typical accompanying slackness of belly. His tangled mat of hair had begun to salt over, and so too had the heavy stubble on his fleshy cheeks. Knowing what little he did about these people, Geoff would have guessed him to have a wife ten or fifteen years his junior and half a dozen adoring but strictly obedient children. The eldest daughter was probably already married now and would have a child or two of her own.

"You're Palestinian, aren't you?"

The reply was a tired nod.

"When did you leave?"

"Since long time–Six-Day War," the cabbie answered.

"And you miss it."

"Yes, I miss."

"What do you miss most of all?" Geoff wondered if he really ought to be asking. But then again, the cabbie had felt free enough a moment earlier to intrude on his private gloom.

"Blease, I sorry, my English is no bery good."

"Your English is fine." He remembered what she'd once told him about the Arab's struggle with *p*'s and *v*'s. *Hockey buck*: it still made him want to laugh at the way she said it.

"I miss Dome of the Rock," the cabbie said. "To look it at once more times make me habby."

In his own mind, from films and photographs he had seen, Geoff recreated the gold-topped Dome of the Rock. As infuriating as it must be for the Israelis, there was no more immediately recognizable symbol of Jerusalem than that Muslim shrine. Visible from every modest promontory in the city, it was said to be the single most beautiful thing inside the old walls. Slowly, something occurred to him.

"You can't take me to Jerusalem, can you."

"No, only to bridge," the cabbie admitted. "But you no worry, mister. My cousin, him he be there on other side. He take you."

"Your cousin lives on the West Bank?"

"Yes, he will waiting at bridge for you. Him I haf telephone."

Geoff nodded.

"Is there anything I can give him for you? A letter or something?" he asked.

"You can touch Dome of the Rock for me. This is enough."

"I'd do that for you, but I'm not stopping in Jerusalem." He suddenly felt the need to confess to this man.

"Ah. You got to kibbutz?" the cabbie asked, placidly enough.

"No, no." Geoff shook his head. "I'm going to Lebanon."

"Lebanon?" The Palestinian stared at him for a long moment, so long that Geoff was afraid the unattended car might leave the narrow road. "You go Lebanon fight for us, maybe?" He said it in a voice filled with such sudden contempt that Geoff felt himself starting to redden, and he had to look away.

*　　　*　　　*

The cabbie's West Bank cousin was a slight and sullen man by comparison, with no interest in talking at all beyond quickly settling on an equitable price to drive as far as the Lebanese border. This was fine with Geoff, because he was still absorbed by the frontier crossing he'd just made; with attempting to sort and understand certain mental snapshots, the fragments of briefest observation.

The first of these were the differences: the sense of half-hearted temporariness in the simple bare bivouacs employed by the

Jordanians, set against the resolute permanence of the concrete footings and solid wooden frames constructed by the Israelis. It was as if the former were saying that the current affront to their dignity would not be permitted to last much longer–not too much anyway; all this while the latter were sending down the deep, sprawling roots of fait accompli, and smirking: You lost it–it's ours now, this place is ours forever more.

And then there was the bridge itself, another source of difference. Heading from east to west as he had just done, it was the King Hussein Bridge. Going the other way, as he might do later, he would find it called the General Allenby Bridge. Two impressive names for a span that was anything but.

Yet it was not the small bridge at all. No, it was what the bridge crossed that had surprised him with its physical insignificance. Another kind of snapshot: his passionately Methodist father using a wiener stick to stir embers in a summer campfire twenty years before, and singing out in his crystal baritone.

"The river Jordan is deep and wide, Hallelujah. Milk and honey on the other side, Hal-lel-u-jah."

Back then when his father sang about it and he was reasonably certain he would never see it himself, this chalky little dribble, this entirely forgettable stream, had been the rushing, tumbling equal of the Nile and the Amazon, had been the breathless subterranean stuff of some greatness of deed and spirit that would be waiting for him, and him alone, when he was no longer a child. It had, of course, never happened. There were no great deeds–he hawked commercial real estate–and his spirit had grown more black and pocked each day of adulthood. The mighty Jordan was a metaphor for the one important thing he'd discovered about life: most of it was overrated.

Why then was he here? He thought he knew the answer, but could hardly believe he truly believed it. He was here because he had successfully convinced himself (duped himself?) that the one small thing he'd found that was not overrated was somewhere on this side of the bridge and its piddle of a river.

"Milk and honey on the other side, Hal-lel-u-jah."

It was funny, in a way, that he should have thought about his father again just now, because in the moments before they had reached the Jordanian frontier post he was remembering the uncanny way the old man had managed to insinuate himself into this whole thing from the grave. That balmy afternoon when he'd gone to tell his mother about his plans had been exactly one year to the day since the man had died.

He had parked on the street out front and walked around to the back of the house, expecting to find her, as he did, sitting legs askew on the lawn at the edge of one of her flower beds. She was tugging up weeds.

"Geoffrey," she said, with a mix of surprise and pleasure. She was careful to keep her dirty hands off his suit jacket when he bent to take her kiss on his cheek. "This is a nice treat."

"I was at a property in the area. Thought I'd stop by." He started off with a lie. His knees cracked loudly, as always, when he sank to a squat.

"Have you had your lunch?" she asked. "I've got some nice smoked salmon."

"Not hungry, thanks. Your flowers look nice." They both admired the neat rows of red salvia, daisies and marigolds for a moment. There were honeybees flitting everywhere, and the very dirt seemed to hum with life. The earth's white noise. In fact, his father was probably right now complaining about the endless racket down there.

"Well, I try to keep up, but it's getting harder."

"I know it is, and I've been meaning to come over and help."

"It's okay, dear. I know you're busy."

"Right," he mumbled.

"How's work?" she asked, with a cheerfulness that Geoff found forced.

"Work's work."

The dog bounded over from its shaded run next to the garage. Geoff slapped its black muzzle a few times, then scratched its belly when it flopped over and whined for attention. Its hind legs twitched and stretched when rubbed in a certain spot.

"What's the matter, Geoffrey?" she asked him.

"I guess I was just wondering what you're supposed to say on a day like this. Happy anniversary doesn't quite fit, does it?"

His mother said nothing; she merely returned to picking at the weeds. He thought about offering to drive her up to the cemetery.

"I'm going out of town for a while," he told her instead.

"You've taken holidays before. You're old enough to go without my permission," she teased. "Angela going with you?"

"It's not a vacation, and no she's not."

"No? What, then?"

"I'm not sure."

"Where are you going?'

"To the Middle East. Lebanon."

His mother stopped clawing at the dirt. She turned on one hip to peer into his eyes. He presumed they must be bloodshot from lack of sleep lately.

"Lebanon. Why?'

He could hear her straining to keep her voice calm.

"There's something I have to do. A personal matter."

"A *personal matter*? This is your mother here." In an awkward reach for playfulness, she rapped his kneecap with the back of her hand spade.

He nodded, then reached into his breast pocket to extract the long, expensive envelope his lawyer's secretary had given him.

"Here, this is just a precaution. You know, in case the plane crashes or something." He grinned woodenly.

"Your will?" She held the envelope in front of her and stared at it.

"Yes."

"But why, Geoffrey, why today?'

Her buttery mother's eyes suddenly brimmed with tears. He lurched over from his squat and put an arm around her shoulders.

"Come on, nothing's going to happen to me, Mom." I'm numb to life, immune to death, immortal, he thought.

Just at that moment, the dog, with energy beyond its twelve years, jumped up on his chest and tried to lick his face. Geoff shoved it away much harder than he needed to, and yelping in pain it limped back to its run. His mother, dabbing her eyes with the back of her silly floral-print garden gloves, noticed.

*   *   *

"Whoa," he heard himself saying, and realized in the same instant that the idiom would mean nothing at all to his driver. Half an hour over the border, they had just flashed past a road sign indicating Jerusalem eight kilometers away. But the cabbie had paid it no attention and instead turned onto a new road.

"Please, would you go to Jerusalem?"

"But this the road to the Lebanon," the driver complained. Only very reluctantly did he begin to apply the brakes.

"Don't worry, I'll pay you for the extra time," Geoff said. "I need a few minutes there, that's all."

Still agitated, but saying nothing more on the matter, the Arab swung around from the gravel shoulder and headed back to the junction. Minutes later, they had reached the eastern outskirts of quite possibly the most famous city of them all.

Built low to the ground, and as lumpy and cereal-colored as Amman, Jerusalem was, at least outwardly, no more attractive than the Jordanian capital had been. But something about it made Geoff's breath catch high in his chest. Having long ago affixed the doubter's label to himself, it was a discomforting surprise to find that a place this unashamedly godly had so suddenly (and so easily) grabbed hold of him.

With a final, jerky downshift of gears, they crested a modest hill and the view became panorama. Geoff leaned through the window on his elbows and stared down the slope at the Old City, nestled in the middle distance at the base of another hill. Rising above the time-weathered walls near its heart was the Dome of the Rock. The late morning sun glinted off its gold plate. Unexpectedly accommodating, the driver slowed right down to let Geoff's gaze linger.

"Mount of Olives."

"Where?" Geoff asked.

"This." The Arab pointed straight down. He then threw his arm out in a lazy arc to indicate a grove of green shubbery and stunted trees on the downslope to their right. "Garden of Gethsemane."

To which Geoff nodded, because that one he knew. The garden of the great betrayal. So, he hadn't completely forgotten his Sunday school lessons after all. For a moment he pictured a dozen antsy little boys, brush-scrubbed clean and trying to outdo each other for farting noises made into copies of the King James Version behind the teacher's–his earnest father's–back. Gethsemane. He thought about smaller, more recent betrayals.

After parking in a grassy lot outside the Damascus Gate, the cabbie made arrangements with Geoff to meet back at the car in half an hour, then wandered off with a couple of friends he had run into. They disappeared, chattering, into a busy cafe.

Armed with a tourist map, Geoff headed into the Old City. From the moment he'd passed through the centuries-old Damascus Gate portal, however, he was sorry he hadn't asked the driver to come with him. Standing in a clutter of noisy Arab commerce, he had already lost sight of the Dome and he felt a mild panic welling up. To his right was a row of money-changers' booths, the operators perched on high stools behind their glass partitions, trading dollars for Israeli shekels and shekels for Jordanian dinars and dinars back again for dollars. To the left were farmers, displaying callused hands and wearing dirt-stained djellabahs, hunched over rusted iron scales behind nearly symmetrical piles of apples, oranges, scallions, potatoes and carrots. Farther up the sloping cobblestone road, he saw souvenir vendors beckoning him insistently from the sunken doorways of their shops. A pair of fatigues-clad Israeli soldiers approached from the same direction, Uzis slung casually over their shoulders, yarmulkes pinned to the back of their heads; but they passed him and disappeared into the thick, buzzing crowd, pressing out towards the Damascus gate before he could think to ask them for directions.

Just then, hearing the lazily drawn-out inflections of American English behind him, he turned to see a tall, reedy blond man step away from one of the money-changer's booths with a knot of faded shekels in his hand.

"Excuse me. Which way do I go to the Dome of the Rock?"

Casually, the American buttoned his money into the breast pocket of his shirt. He smiled down at Geoff.

"Straight on from here. As they say, you can't miss it."

"Thanks."

"Don't mention it."

As the American had said, it was indeed straight on from there, five minutes' walk through narrowing streets, streets that were more exactly lanes or alleys, past hookah-lined tea rooms and dozens of souvenir shops, all selling the same olive-wood chess sets, onyx Christ and Mother figurines and T-shirts with Coca-Cola emblazoned in Hebrew. Stepping through a soldier's cursory security check at a final portico, Geoff emerged into the sunlight of a broad, open square. His eyes immediately reclaimed the golden dome, jutting up from behind yet another set of walls on the plateau of a small hill. At the foot of the hill, directly adjacent to the stone-and-concrete pathway leading up to the plateau, a solemn gathering of men, most dressed in black, some with long beards and ringlets, stood facing a high, ocher-colored block wall–this city was rife with such barriers–reading aloud to themselves from small books and occasionally nodding and bobbing forward.

It was, of course, the Wailing Wall. Somehow, Geoff would never have expected to find it right here. But then that would certainly explain the security check on the way in and the numerous Israeli soldiers navigating the square amongst the middle-aged Western tourists, the young kibbutz-bound backpackers, the khaffiyeh-wrapped Palestinians heading up, singly or in pairs, to pray at the mosque beside the Dome, and these self-absorbed Jews right now doing the same thing beside their own holy site.

An unarmed Arab guard at the top of the pathway studied Geoff curiously and cautiously before allowing him to pass through the low-cut entrance to the plateau enclosure. Straightening up on the other side of the green wooden door, he stopped and took in his first full view of the Dome and its surroundings. Below its golden cap, the structure was octagonal and ornamented above its marble base with mosaic tiles of robin's egg and royal blue, yellow and white.

The nearby mosque, marked Al-Aqsa on his tourist map, was

less ornate but larger than the Dome, and busy where the Dome was quiet. A crudely painted sign, written in Arabic and English but conspicuously not in Hebrew, was jammed into a piece of deepest-green lawn. It proclaimed the enclosed plateau in its entirety to be the Noble Sanctuary. Taking in its aging olive trees and blooming rose bushes, stunted palms and marble archways, the sounds of birds and of water's soft splash, and the reposeful expressions on the faces of the many old men strolling through the courtyard, Geoff was inclined to agree. This was peace, by the piece. Incarnate. For the first time in many, many days, the knot of his body began to relax.

He walked right to the base of the Dome and reached out to touch its coolness for the Palestinian cabbie he had left on the other side of the Jordan River. He stepped away, was about to start back for the car, when something made him turn again. Reaching up, he touched the wall of the shrine once more, and this time with the full flat of his palm. He closed his eyes, and soon, warming to his touch, the marble felt like a flawless cheek.

<u>FOUR</u>

HE WAS STANDING NAKED IN THE KITCHEN, HIS MOUTH FULL OF
overripe banana, when the telephone rang. Holding a damp tea
towel over his crotch, he hurried into the living-room to answer it.
Naturally, all the lights in his condominium were on, all the
curtains pulled wide open. He imagined the burn of someone's
binoculars on his backside.

"Hello," he mumbled, struggling to swallow the last of the
suddenly adhesive banana.

"Thank you for the rose. It is lovely."

"How did you know it was from me?"

"A guess," she said, her pleasure jumping right through the
line.

"It was going to be my last . . . *overture*, you know," he told her
pointedly.

"Yes. How did you get into my apartment building?"

"I just hung around the doors waiting for someone to
leave."

She laughed. "You would make a good bugler, I think."

"Burglar." He grinned at another of her precious assaults on
the English language. "I hope the scotch tape I used didn't do
any damage to your door."

"No damage," she answered.

He sucked some banana from between his teeth to fill the
silence.

"Nadya, why didn't you return any of my calls? Did the

41

secretary in the biochemistry department not pass on my messages?"

"She gave me the messages."

"I see."

From different sides of the city, they were groping for the edges of this shapeless thing between them.

"How is Angela?"

"Angela is fine."

"Oh," she said. "That is good. I am glad."

He couldn't help but smile at her oblique approach to this (for her, anyway) delicate and important subject.

"To answer the question you're really asking, or at least the one I hope you're really asking, Angela is history."

"History? What do you mean?"

"I talked to her–about you."

"*Oh.*"

"Oh," he mimicked to tease. "So–you called, finally," he said, loud and pleasant.

"Geoff, I am not a very good cook, but I do not think I could kill you."

"That's reassuring."

"What I mean–" she started again, suddenly sounding very self-conscious.

"You wouldn't happen to be trying to invite me over for a meal or something, would you?"

"Yes. Yes, for dinner."

He took two bottles of wine–a red Bordeaux and a Moselle (chilled all afternoon in the office refrigerator)–and only remembered that she didn't drink after he stepped off the elevator and was standing outside her door. He knocked once and fussed with the knot of his tie, all the while trying to think of something funny to say about the liquor. Nothing came to him. When Walid opened the door and grinned, it was like someone had yanked the plug on his air mattress. He sagged.

"Good evening, Geoff. It is very nice to see you again."

"Yes, you too," he replied quietly.

"Come in. Nadya is fighting with a couple of chickens in the kitchen."

Geoff discovered that his twosome turned three's company was in fact a full dinner party. Spread out on the living-room floor and on the couch and chairs were five more people, sipping wine and talking.

With Walid's help, he bobbed and smiled through introductions. It was an assembly of the United Nations: there was Seamus, full-bearded and irrevocably Irish; Prettima, pretty, yes, an East Indian; blonde Brigitta, looking solid, stolid and probably German; Abdullah, a scarred black face with an Arab's name; and Danielle, French, short-haired and passionate if the way she attacked a glass of red wine and smoked a home-rolled cigaret was any indication.

"You and I, I fear, may be out of our league," Walid confided as the conversation turned back in on itself. "Graduate student types, all of them." He tapped his forehead.

"Marhaba, Geoff." Nadya's voice spun him around.

"Hi."

"Marhaba is Arabic for hi." She was drying her hands on a towel.

He held out the wine and shrugged.

"I forgot you don't drink."

"But the others do," she said.

"Ah, yes, the others." He smiled. She returned his smile, improved it immensely, then accepted the wine and took it into the kitchen. He followed her, picking up the pleasant smells of garlic and onion fried in oil.

"You look nice tonight," he said with deliberate under-statement. "Is that something Palestinian?" He admired the brocaded trim of her loose-fitting red robe. Though the garment gave him nothing, he saw her body beneath its lightweight cotton.

"This?" Absently, she picked up a fold of the material while scanning the countertop for a corkscrew. "It is called a caftan. Very simple. Common in the Arab countries." Locating the corkscrew, she handed it to him and turned her attention to the stove.

"Smells terrific. What are we having?'

"A chicken dish called *musakhan.*"

He tried without success to repeat the name. She did not laugh at his efforts.

"I am so happy you came tonight," she said.

"Me too, though I have to tell you I didn't quite expect you'd invite other people."

"No?"

"But it's all right, really. I don't mind, of course," he added quickly.

She forked a pot of rice and smiled.

"That is good, Geoff, because I invited them first."

*   *   *

With knives, forks and naked chicken bones spoking from their edges, the dinner plates were haphazardly stacked on top of each other and shoved into an empty corner of the living-room. Geoff stared at them from his place on the couch next to Abdullah and made a dessert of feeling sorry for himself. Nadya, down on the floor, with most of her back to him, was leaning into some obscure, esoteric subject with Seamus and Danielle. Walid and Prettima were comparing nouns in Arabic and Hindi and flirting like bedmates soon-to-be. Brigitta, head down, was flipping through an atlas she'd pulled from Nadya's little brick and plank library, and Abdullah was smiling at everyone but had yet to say much all evening. He was an Ethiopian mathematician and extremely self-conscious about his English, although it was really not that much worse than Nadya's.

Not that Geoff had exactly been an engine of excitement driving the evening along either. Gatherings like this had always been his Achilles' heel, and he allowed himself to resent Nadya a little for not guessing this in advance. His forte–if he had one–was the stand-up-and-mingle party, where he could drink a lot without people noticing and then swoop in with quick and witty one-liners. Tonight, with only a couple of glasses of wine behind him, and forced to sit still, and to eat with a plate on his lap, he felt like the inarticulate dullard he feared he was. Every time he'd begun to open his mouth during dinner, he heard a small inner voice calling back; bor-ing.

"Antagonistic moralities have nothing to bloody do with it." Seamus' insistent brogue demanded attention. "Morality has never been a major player on the world stage. With the possible exception of the abolition of slavery in the 1800s, when a few real people in Europe may have splashed enough piss and vinegar to help overturn a system. Nah, I take that back; that was just cosmetics. No, the only force in play, *ever*, has been economics. The Christ-almighty ducat."

"What about Hitler?" Danielle said.

"What about that regrettable fellow?" Seamus snorted.

"Was it not morality that finally brought the Allies to fight him?"

"Nah, purely economics. It was the Nazi threat to the Western industrialists' ability to make money that brought them into the war."

"And the Russian Revolution?" Nadya said.

"Ah, well there you've got a lad where his heart is," the Irishman smiled. "But, yes, even there it was economics and nothing more. Look, all this high-minded chatter about the aesthetic right and wrong is just so much mental masturbation, as I see it. It's money: if you've got it, I want it, and I'll be as nice or nasty as I have to be to wrest it away from you."

"I cannot accept that," Nadya said. "I care nothing at all for money, and I know I am not alone in feeling that way."

"It's just a well-known defense mechanism," Seamus said. "If you haven't got, you pretend you really don't want. Go on with ya."

"No, you go on with you," Danielle countered, missing the twinkle in Seamus' eye. "What Nadya wants is not money, and you know it. She wants what all her people want, a home of their own. A free and sovereign state called Palestine."

"Yes," Nadya said, solemnly. "That is it in an eggshell."

Geoff's brittle laughter turned everyone's head his way. He registered their faces: the astonishment on Walid's, the instant contempt on Seamus' and Danielle's. And Nadya's, shining with hurt.

"Nutshell. It's just that the right word is nutshell," he corrected her, weakly, then stared down at the empty wine glass in his hand.

The public shunning that followed did not reach the level its very keen leader, Seamus, had hoped for. That was because Nadya, with ferocious magnanimity, would not stand for it. She insisted that Geoff be treated better than he had any right to be and took the lead there by paying more attention to him than she had since he'd arrived. Geoff believed she was much too ingenuous to know what a weapon she had in forgiveness.

"*Keef halak*? How are you?" She turned from her place on the floor to ask him for about the fifth time in five minutes.

"I'm okay. Nadya–" He was about to apologize, but he stopped and shook his head. Seamus was listening in, shamelessly. "Later," he whispered to her through a strained smile.

The forces of erosion are relentless. Eventually, the back and forth rub of Nadya trying far too hard to keep him involved in the party and everyone else subtly resisting her will built a tension that drove him away. He got up from the couch and wandered into the bathroom, where he stared at his face in the small, discolored mirror over the sink. He leaned close and examined the pores on the skin of his nose, the darkening shadow of his day's growth of beard and the high cheekbones that a married woman at some party–a stand-up-and-mingle party–had once flirtingly described as haughty. It was a word whose exact meaning he'd had to look up later, but from that point on he liked to think of his face as portraying pride on the verge of arrogance. Tonight, though, all he saw looking back at him was the ugly expression of his petty mean-spiritedness.

In passing the kitchen on his way back to the living-room, Geoff heard Seamus and Nadya.

"The man is a loser. That's what happens when you invite a cretin to dine with you. What was it you said he sold for a living, used cars?"

"Oh, Seamus. Do you not see that you can only make it more unhappy this way."

He did not slow down to hear any more. When, after a considerable while, the two of them returned to the living-room, Nadya refused to meet his gaze, but Seamus more than made up for it with his unfettered expression scorn.

At some point during the fuzz of smothered rage that was the next half hour, the conversation swirling around Geoff moved to the Munich Olympics of 1972 and then, inexorably, to the hostage incident that had ended with the killing of eleven Israeli team members by Palestinian gunmen.

"Cook the damned crow," Seamus said. "I'll eat it."

"What do you mean?" Walid asked with a laugh.

"Antagonistic moralities do exist. You've just identified one here that opens the door to scores more. I'm chastened."

"I like this. Do go on, Seamus," Danielle said, rolling another cigaret.

"Must I? I mean it is so simple as to make me sound moronic."

"Yes, you must. It is all part of being chastened," she insisted.

"You mean like a demonstration of my understanding? Like writing 'I shalt not' lines on the chalkboard for the headmaster?"

"Yes," Danielle laughed. "I like this analogy."

"Fine then." He cleared his throat for emphasis. "There are people, lots of people, the vast majority of people here in North America, for instance, who would label Black September's Munich operation an act of pure, cold-blooded terrorism. That said, there are also people–more of them in Europe than here, of course, and many, many more still in the Third World–who would call it justifiably desperate means in a desperately just struggle."

"The sum of these two parts being . . . ?" Danielle anticipated.

"Yes, all right, rub it in. Antagonistic sensibilities about right and wrong."

"I believe there is some hope for this opinionated friend of ours yet," Danielle told the group. There was comradely laughter.

"You know something," Seamus said, looking right at Geoff but talking to everybody else. "I've just now realized that among this gathering of bright minds, we have only one North American. I wonder what he, as a resident of this side of the pond, thinks about Munich and the like."

It was a clear setup, of course, but Geoff did not care. He walked right into it with a plastered-on grin. "Oh, I think a couple of things, Seamus. First of all, I think *you* would make a good used car salesman, because you're just about the biggest bullshit artist I've ever run into." A quick glance at Nadya told him she understood he'd overheard them talking. "The second thing I think is that bastards who commit murderous acts like the one at Munich should be lined up against a wall and shot with their own guns. There, does that tell you what you wanted to know?"

The Irishman smiled. "Let me put it to you this way. It merely confirms what I expected to find out."

"Geoff," Nadya broke in, "can I see you in the kitchen?"

"The *kitchen*? Sure, why the hell not?" he said, still grinning at Seamus. "It seems to be the place tonight for important little tête-à-têtes."

When they were alone, she moved in close to him. But there was nothing close about it.

"This is cozy," he said, humorlessly.

"I think you should leave."

"My, this is getting a bit monotonous isn't it, Nadya? I've been to your place twice, and both times you've given me the boot."

"Please, I am tired of this. Just go, Geoff."

He nodded. "Fine."

As he headed for the door, unaccompanied, he said, "I'll let you say goodbye to your charming friends for me, if that's all right. Tell them I thought it was swell getting to know them, eh."

*   *   *

If it happened a different way, if the circumstances were not these right now skidding through his mind, this picking at sores might even have been therapeutic. He couldn't remember a period in his adult life when he'd had so much time to think–to do nothing, in fact, but think. These hours spent by himself in the departure lounges of airports, on foreign streets and in dusty taxis whose drivers he could not even talk to about the wicked summer heat. It was a kind of purgative, just as surely as this rough road rumbling under his bowels would prove to have been a purgative the next time they stopped at a place with bathroom facilities. Thinking, a purgative? Sure thing, shit for brains.

That was just the sort of curare-tipped dart Linda was fond of firing at him during their short, though hardly brief, six months of marriage. Linda. He smiled to think that eight years later he would remember her mouth but not her lips, her various expressions but not her face. He had no idea at all where she might be now, nor did he care. She had very nearly ruined him with that mouth, had almost created another misogynist. He considered it his one victory over her that she'd failed there; in spite of her best attempt at it, she had not been able to make him hate women, only her. And that made it a double victory, because Linda had never taken failure well–hers or his.

If Linda was the first benchmark–assuming that all who came before her were insignificant others–Angela was the second. Where Linda, then articling with a law firm in Vancouver, had been hard and bright, Angela, his frosted blonde fashion buyer for Sears, was soft and dull. It was the first time he'd ever directly compared the two women like that, and therefore the first time he'd been conscious of their perfect oppositeness. But, of course, magazine-stand psychology would assure him it only made sense that he had swung from one pole to the other.

Linda fired poison darts, and Angela was a sponge in the sweetest possible sense of the word. Takes a licking and keeps on ticking. In their three years–years that were usually casual, only occasionally more than that–she'd absorbed every bit of ugliness he could dump on her without a flinch: sleeping around, condescension, lies, and an emotional fickleness so erratic it often amazed even him. It occurred to him that he had not once mentioned marriage to her, even though he had no doubt she would have roped her arms around his neck and said yes in an instant. Perhaps, if she had only flinched a little.

And now she too was gone, and better off for it. For Angela, to be rid of him was a good career move (even if he'd made it for her).

Which brought him to the last benchmark in the triumvirate: Nadya. This was a woman bright and soft, brighter than Linda, but thankfully not as soft as Angela. When he'd hurt her, the welts showed red and angry at the surface, as they should.

But he found he could appraise Nadya no further. Reliving the dinner party fiasco yet again, he felt that now-familiar fear returning. A question calling out for an answer he just didn't have. *What was in this for her?* He knew only that if he couldn't answer it, he had no business being here. There could be no half-baked gestures. Here, he had to believe it all the way, or he must right now turn around and go home.

*   *   *

Geoff heard the frustrated honking of someone's horn. Opening his eyes, rolling his tongue over the sour film on his teeth, he pulled himself upright away from the door. When had he begun to sleep? he wondered. He focused slowly and looked up the stretch of coast highway in front of him, and realized the honking had been his own driver's. Strung out for at least a mile, and moving at a diesel crawl, were scores of Israeli tanks and personnel carriers, jeeps and transport trucks.

"Are we getting close?" He had to shout over the grating of the tanks' steel treads on the pavement. It was like being trapped inside the barrel of a cement truck.

The driver nodded once and jerked his car hard into the other lane to pass a single tank, before jerking it quickly back again to avoid the line of almost equally heavy traffic rolling south.

"There's no rush," Geoff suggested, realizing it was futile. He found himself staring at the impassive men seated on top and inside the vehicles they passed as the cabbie continued to honk and curse and leapfrog up the line. Most of them were young and dark-haired as he expected, but there were also blonds and redheads, and even some gray with middle age. He had difficulty picturing many of these faces sighting down a rifle, much less being part of what was reported to be one of the world's crack armies. But he also knew that was a dangerous underestimation: these were people who had repeatedly proven they took the making of war very seriously.

Back across the highway, the Mediterranean shuddered in appealing little swells beneath the sun and the cloudless July sky. Juxtaposed against the column of battle-green hardware creeping north were lollipop-colored umbrellas stabbed here and there into the sandy beach, and families, temporarily ruled by young children, splashing in the surf, building castles and picnicking on towels and blankets. In other places, skinny, bare-chested boys stood up near the edge of the road, watching the armor move and waving at the soldiers, some of whom waved back.

It was not long afterwards that a jeep they had previously passed sitting at the shoulder raced up behind them in the on-coming lane. As the jeep pulled even with them, a hard-faced officer riding in the passenger seat snapped his arm straight out and signaled the cabbie to pull over. At the same time, Geoff saw a blur of twisting dust, hovering helicopter and flapping canvas tent just ahead, and comprehended that they had reached the border.

"What do they want?" Geoff asked after the cabbie had stopped. He felt for the reassuring edge of his passport in the travel pouch strung around his neck.

"Is maybe problems," the cabbie replied, looking neither especially surprised nor terribly troubled. He turned off the ignition and reached over Geoff's knees for his own documents in the glove box. Geoff heard the crunch of gravel under booted foot.

"What are you doing here?" Following, as it did, an initial exchange in heated Arabic with the driver, the officer's easy fluency in English took Geoff by surprise. The Israeli leaned through the driver's window, waiting for an answer. Geoff looked into the man's polaroid sunglasses and saw himself looking back, his features grotesquely pinched and stretched at the same time.

"I'm going to Lebanon."

The Israeli looked down at the cabbie and screwed up his face.

"There is a war going on," he said. "You cannot go into Lebanon." His voice was incredulous, almost amused. Geoff saw large hoops of sweat under his armpits.

"I don't see how that's any of your business, quite frankly. It's up to the Lebanese authorities to decide." Without being asked for it, he shoved his passport at the officer, flipped open to the page with a Lebanese visa stamped on it. The Israeli stood up, thumbed the passport briefly, then leaned back in to return it.

"Very nice, but there are no Lebanese authorities here. *We* are the authorities now, and we say you will turn back."

Geoff had shoved open his door, was standing half out of the taxi by the time the Israeli finished talking. He strode around to the front of the car and was met there by the officer and his noncom driver. The two men positioned themselves on either side of him and moved in close. The noncom had garlic and tobacco on his breath.

"Yes?" the officer invited.

"You've got to let me in. I've traveled all the way from Canada—" He tried to say more, but his voice cracked and he realized he was on the edge of tears. He stopped speaking and shook his head. To keep the two Israelis from noticing his struggle, he turned away from them and stared up the road after the departing convoy. The officer finally spoke up, this time almost kindly.

"Lebanon is in flames, sir. Do you not understand, there is nothing for you there?"

*   *   *

The scotch was an old friend met on some street corner, and Geoff embraced it with desperate affection. Slumped at a table for two in the darkened back end of the lounge of the King David Hotel in West Jerusalem, he found himself folding into blessed drunkenness. One, two, five, six drinks/like blinks. He smoked cigarets for the first time in years and scribbled nonsense on the white paper cocktail napkins the waiter brought with each new glass. He even tried to remember the lines to one of the poems Nadya had read him, couldn't, then made up a verse of his own and wrote it down on a napkin with such force that the lead tip of the pencil snapped off.

Roses are red, violets are blue,
Now what the fuck am I going to do?

There was Syria—but not likely. He'd been told he could probably get a seventy-two-hour transit visa at that country's embassy in Amman, then fly to Damascus. But Walid, for one, had strongly doubted the Syrians would ever let him cross their frontier with Lebanon, because it meant traveling right through their lines in the Bekaa Valley and on into Israeli-held territory. He'd be seen as a spy.

Which left Cyprus. Provided he could find a flight from Tel Aviv or even Amman to Nicosia, there was apparently a shipping line running between there and Beirut. But would the ships be going anywhere near the Lebanese coast with the Israelis currently shooting at anything that was not flagged with the blue and white Star of David? No one he talked to knew for sure, but they all said they doubted it. Still, even if the ships were not going, there would be fishermen and other Cypriots with small boats for hire. He had money, and money, he was reasonably certain of it, could get him to Beirut even now.

He sat up, crumpled the napkin with his verse on it into a ball and dropped it in his ashtray. Lighting an edge of the flimsy paper with a package of hotel matches, he watched it flame up and burn out black. What a crock, he thought. This renewed courage of his was only as deep as his glass, and it would be gone with the arrival of tomorrow's hangover. After all, hadn't he almost started crying at the border?

He wanted another drink. Waving at the waiter, he pulled out his wallet and counted the Israeli currency inside, and tried to remember the exchange rate between shekels and dollars. The money made him wonder once again if it had been pigeon or rat shit all over the floor of the bank earlier.

It was a branch of the Arab Land Bank. He had found it just outside the Damascus Gate after discovering, upon his unhappy return to Jerusalem from the border, that the money-changers inside the walls of the Old City had all packed up and left for the day. Hoping he might be able to get a better rate on his traveler's cheques there than here at the hotel, he'd gone inside the building and climbed the unlit staircase to the mezzanine entrance. The bank was closed; had been for some time. It had been abandoned, he deduced, when the Israelis captured East Jerusalem during the Six-Day War. A sheet of heavy-gauge tin plate had been sloppily wedged into place in front of the doorway. Peering through a small hole in the tin, Geoff saw a portrait of a young King Hussein hanging crookedly on the farthest wall. Sitting on the countertops where Palestinian tellers had once taken in and handed out cash, there were what appeared to be files and other bank records piled into cardboard boxes. Someone had obviously taken the trouble to pack them, but there they sat still waiting to be hauled away fifteen years later. But hauled where? The floor, he noticed last, was covered in dried-out animal droppings, but it was impossible to tell if they were the work of the pigeons he heard cooing in the ceiling, or of the rats he imagined scurrying back and forth across the wooden floor after dark. In any case, whatever had left them there had done so with an almost perfect symmetry of distribution. Was this territoriality, Middle Eastern style?

The soft bang of glass on wood announced his fresh drink. Without bothering to look up, he reached for his wallet on the table.

"Tell me, did you find what you were looking for?"

Twisting sharply in his chair, Geoff saw that the bearer of his drink was not the waiter but a tall, sun-battered man with thinning blond hair. He was smiling, and he held another glass, his own. Pulling out the unoccupied chair with his foot, he sat down across the table from Geoff.

"Didn't mean to startle you. I just wanted to know if you'd found your way up to the Dome of the Rock all right."

"Yes. Thanks. Your directions were perfect." Geoff glanced around the American and tried to catch the waiter's eye.

"I've already paid him. If you feel like it, you can buy the next one."

Geoff nodded and mumbled another thank you. Through his own fog, he picked out a slur in the other man's voice. What was he mourning tonight?

"It is kind of nice up there, isn't it?" The American laughed. "Even for a religious site."

"Yes," Geoff said, haltingly. He thought: if this guy only knew how little I want to make small talk with him tonight.

"You know, this is just a guess, but I figure you must be a Canadian for all the talking you do."

Geoff felt himself smile.

"Aha. From where?"

"Vancouver."

"Another *nice* place, and not the least bit religious either."

Without troubling Geoff for a handshake, he introduced himself. "Thomas Dix."

"Geoff Andrews."

"I knew a fellow named Geoff once. He was gay. Are you gay, Geoff Andrews?"

"No."

"I am. I'm gay. Carefree and gay, whee." His voice was deadpan. "How does that line go? I'm not as think as you drunk I am."

"I'm betting you're not as gay either," Geoff said.

"You're right, you know." Dix spoke thoughtfully. "I don't spend one minute more with man than I have to."

"Why are you spending time with me?"

The American smiled. With the plastic stir stick from his drink, he probed at the black remains of Geoff's napkin.

"I was destroying some incriminating evidence," Geoff said.

"A spy, huh?"

"But my cover is real estate sales."

"No harm there. People have to have a roof over their heads in rainy Vancouver, I understand."

"What do you do, Thomas?"

"I drink."

A man after my own heart, Geoff thought.

"It's good work if you can get it."

"And steady."

"That too."

"Do you do anything part time? On the side, so to speak?"

The American took a long swallow of his drink and swirled the ice cubes around the bottom of the glass. "Yes. When I'm not drinking, you can usually find me out watching man get fucked by man. It's my own version of the gay lifestyle: I watch."

Geoff twisted uncomfortably in his chair.

FIVE

"I'M A JOURNALIST, A CORONER FOR THE LIVING," DIX FINALLY told him.

"Someone had a bad day at the office," Geoff said.

"No, a pretty typical day at the office, actually." Dix stopped in thought for a moment. "But tell me, what brings a real estate man to Jerusalem? I know the market demand for this piece of property is hot, but–"

"A personal matter."

Dix waited through the arid pause that followed, then shrugged. "Fair enough," he said.

Geoff smiled: no offense intended. The American smiled back: no offense taken. The waiter drifted past and they ordered another round. Dix turned in his chair to watch the waiter carry off their empties. He waved briefly at two other Western-looking men standing at the bar.

"Friends of yours?" Geoff asked.

"We're convivial. They're fellow coroners."

"Do you want to ask them to join us?"

"No, not unless you want to treble a dubious pleasure." Dix reached into his shirt pocket and extracted a tube of chap stick. He ran it over his lips.

"That's quite a tan you've got there. Spending your days off at the beach?" Geoff asked.

"It is a good one, isn't it?" Dix stroked his brown cheeks with the backs of his hands. "I did some fine work on it today, as a matter of fact."

"Really?" Given Dix's mood, this surprised Geoff.

"I had a whole afternoon to soak up rays. I even did some sightseeing across the border in Lebanon. Would you like to know what I saw?"

Geoff nodded.

"I saw an eight-year-old boy with an Israeli bullet hole the size of a silver dollar in the center of his forehead."

Dix stopped while the waiter set their drinks down and Geoff paid.

"I saw his blood and brains like spilled jam on the front seat of an otherwise very nice car."

"Do I really want to hear this?" Geoff asked.

"That's entirely up to you," the American answered. "They'll never get that guck out of the upholstery. It's worse than ragout sauce on a tablecloth."

Between the scotch, the cigarets and now this, Geoff was not feeling well. He must have looked it too because Dix made a suggestion.

"Some fresh air would help. Care to take a walk?"

Geoff nodded hard. Yes, please.

They got up from the table and weaved out of the bar. Dix's colleagues had already left, but the Arab bartender addressed him by name in saying goodnight.

"Ma' salame. Sleep well, Thomas."

Dix smiled back tightly.

A full moon was slung low in the sky. The stars looked much closer and more plentiful than they ever did back home in Vancouver. Stopping at the sidewalk, Dix licked a finger, held it up in the muggy air and jokingly pointed to the other side of the street. They crossed and stood alongside the wall that fronted the large YMCA building with its impressive belltower.

"Speak ye comfortably to Jerusalem, and cry unto her that her warfare is accomplished," the American said in a loud stage bass. His voice echoed down the deserted street.

"What's that–Shakespeare?" Geoff asked, twigged by something familiar in it.

"Isaiah. Old Testament," Dix said. He leaned back against the wall and assumed roughly the arms-spread, head-slumped death pose of Christ on the cross. When he tried to put one foot on top of the other and complete the impression, however, he lost his balance and stumbled to the ground. Picking himself up, he tried again and this time managed to hold the pose while he spoke.

"Do you know anything about the history of the hotel you're staying in?" Dix asked, lifting his chin towards the King David.

"No." Geoff found himself watching this odd American very closely.

"During the Palestine Mandate, the British kept their military and administrative offices in one wing of the hotel. A good move, to my thinking. Left them handy to the bar. In the summer of 1946–I can't recall the exact date–a group of Jewish extremists called the Irgun blew up that particular wing as part of their campaign to drive the Brits out of here. A hundred people died."

Geoff frowned. It felt necessary to insert some sort of punctuation.

"There were Brits, Jews, a few loose Europeans and lots of Palestinian Arabs among the dead."

"An unprejudiced bunch of killers."

"Quite. Anyway, the story goes that one of the Brits, I don't know if he was of any real importance or not, was blown right out of the hotel and all the way over here against the wall of the YMCA." Still in his crucifixion pose, Dix slapped the pale stone wall behind him. "They say the impect left a perfect silhouette of his body in blood. Can you feature that?"

Dix pushed away from the wall. "I guess you'd have to say he left his mark, huh?"

Geoff was drunk after all: he laughed.

"Do you know who it was that planned the King David bombing–the leader of Irgun?" the journalist asked.

Geoff shook his head.

Dix licked chapped lips and stared at him for a moment. There was an outburst of giggling. Both men turned to watch a young couple striding hand-in-hand up the sidewalk towards them. From her high-heeled feet and long, blue-jeaned legs on up, the woman was attractive.

"*Shalom,*" her lover mouthed as they passed.

"You were saying?" Geoff asked.

"Never mind. It hardly matters anymore," Dix said, dully. He stared after the woman. "Come on, let's go."

"Go where?" Geoff said.

"Where? How about to great lengths, and for no good reason at all?"

They walked in silence for some blocks, with Geoff struggling to keep Dix's horrific imagery from overwhelming the simple pleasantness of night in this now quiet city. After a while, certain corners, store fronts and street signs began to look familiar. Then Geoff saw the floodlit walls of the Old City coming into view, then the Damascus Gate and then, once again, tucked in shadow, the facade of the building that had housed the Arab Land bank. Just for something to say, he told Dix about the abandoned bank. The American's eyes widened, and he immediately insisted they go inside and have a look.

"Rats–I knew there'd be rats," Geoff said, watching and hearing them scatter away from the weak glow of Dix's match held up to the hole in the tin plate.

"Somebody once told me they like the binding glue in books and things like that," Dix said, ushering Geoff out of the way so he could see too. "Could be that if you picked up a box of those files in there, the whole thing would just come apart in your hands." He laughed. "Palestine gone as a handful of dust."

"Are you sure you're not thinking of termites?"

"Termites? They eat wood. Hey, I thought you were from British Columbia?"

"I sell square footage, not board length," Geoff said.

They left the rats to their binding glue and went back downstairs and outside. When Dix stopped to remove a stone from inside one of his desert boots, Geoff sat down on the curb beside him. He felt his legs give thanks for the rest. Shortly, Dix sat down as well and went to work retying his boot. He glanced back over his shoulder at the bank building.

"This city has plenty of neat little secrets just waiting to be discovered."

"Thomas." Geoff had been waiting to say this ever since Dix's story about the boy. "Is there any way for a guy to get to Beirut these days?"

"Certainly. Enlist in the Israeli army."

"I'm serious," he said. But the American ignored him.

"Hey, have you seen the T-shirts they're selling in the souvenir shops here? The ones that say 'Join the Army, See the World, Meet Interesting People–and Kill Them'?" This broke Dix up, and it was a long time before he stopped chuckling.

"Are you finished?" Geoff asked coolly.

The American's laugh lines softened.

"No, there is no way for you to get to Beirut," he said, rising to his feet. "Now, I'm tired, and worse yet I'm starting to sober up."

A token protest: Geoff watched the journalist walk away and cover half a block before getting up himself. In the end, he saw there was no point to it; Dix was only restating known fact for him. Tomorrow, he would just have to find that flight to Cyprus and take his chances with the boats.

Dix stopped and waited for him to catch up. Just as he did, a low-riding army personnel carrier with a large-caliber machine gun mounted on a turret wheeled around the corner and lurched up beside them. The beam from a powerful flashlight darted across their chests and shoulders once, but was courteously kept out of their faces.

"*Shalom,*" said a voice behind the flashlight. It was a security check.

"Of that we can only hope, can't we," Dix half-muttered.

The flashlight was turned off and the vehicle moved on for a block, then it swung right down the next street and disappeared into the night.

"Thomas."

"What now?"

"Tell me who planned the bombing of the King David Hotel."

"Tell me who the prime minister of Israel is," Dix said.

"Menachem Begin . . .?"

"Surprised? Don't be. That's the way of the world, guy."

*   *   *

The ceiling had started to spin, an unpleasant portent, and a clinical thought intruded as he lay there on his back, slowly losing ground in a tug-o'-war against nausea: you, friend Geoff, have developed quite the little alcohol habit in recent years.

It was a realization, but far from a great revelation. Another kind of realization: disgusting was the way he must have smelled when he showed up at her door that night. It was two days after the dinner party debacle and, after getting himself good and cut, he was finally ready to apologize. As if the twin odors of cigaret smoke and spilled beer that he'd carried out of the bar . . . bars . . . in his hair and on his clothing were not bad enough. Witless, he had parked in front of a 7-Eleven store a block from her place and run inside for some breath mints. Instead, he'd bought grape bubblegum, because he liked the taste of it better, and a large white cooking onion, which he peeled and took two good bites of to the delighted horror of the store clerk.

Nadya was not amused this time when she answered the knock at her door and discovered that he'd once again circumvented the building's security intercom. She simply stood there and looked at him. Her long hair was tied back with a white scarf, and she was wearing the same pink sweatsuit as on that first, mist-framed morning down in Stanley Park.

"May I come in?" He pulled the roses, half a dozen red ones purchased from some peddler in the evening's last bar, out from behind his back and handed them to her. She took hold of them, but he had the feeling it was only to prevent them falling to the floor.

"It is late and I have much reading to do."

"I promise it won't take long. Ten minutes. You can even put a stopwatch on me if you want to." He discovered that in spite of his best efforts at faking sobriety, he couldn't quite stand still. No doubt he was slurring his words too.

She moved aside at last to let him in. He followed her into the living room and was initially surprised to see her choose the couch instead of the floor. But then he understood: she was not eager to prolong his stay. The couch was more formal; cool and structured, it was a thing with limits to it. She offered to make him coffee, but he recognized it as rote polite and cultural, not sincerely meant, and said no thank you. He saw some biochemical journals spread out open on the coffeetable. The text, broken up by symbols and equations and jagged graphs, looked complicated. He watched her set the flowers, unopened, down beside the journals.

"Nadya, I feel like hell that I laughed at you."

"It is not important," she said. "I know my English is not as good as it should be."

"Please, don't say that." He could hear the added care in her words and the guilt leveled him. He pointed at her journals.

"Look, your English has to be much better than mine. I couldn't begin to decipher that stuff." He went to touch one of her hands, but she pulled it away–not sharply, just away.

"Apology number two. I'm sorry I got obnoxious with your friends. Seamus pushed all the wrong buttons, I'm afraid."

"Seamus was a guest in my home. He should not have insulted you."

"He's a charmer, all right, but I suppose I deserved most of what he dished out. Most." He smiled a little at the thought of it. "I might even have laughed at his crack about used cars myself if I wasn't so mad."

But Nadya would not let the moment be buoyed. She sat as stiffly as a matron and stared down at her hands, one laid over the other across her lap. Her fingers were long and slender, with strong, unpainted nails. Feeling something quite different than physical want right now, Geoff ached to be free to take one of those hands in his own.

"Nadya, I'm sorry. I was a stupid ass. I don't know what else to tell you."

"You do not need to say anything."

"Then will you tell me how to back this reel up so we can start over?"

"What do you mean?"

"I mean–" With a memory severely impaired by drink, he forgot her earlier, very clear message to him on this score and suddenly stole one of her hands in between both of his. "I mean how do the two of us move on from here? Where is the bridge to take us away from this mess?"

"There is no bridge," she said. "Nowhere we can go."

"Come on, Nadya, is the harm I did the other night that irreparable?"

She extricated her hand and shifted her position on the couch to look at him straight on. Her face was a strange, tight mask of pain and resolve.

"It is not what you did, Geoff. It is what you are, it is what I am. We are too different. I knew this from the beginning."

"Nadya, what are you talking about? Of course, we're different—and I don't mind telling you that's part of the attraction for me."

"But for me, it is not," she told him.

This unpadded declaration hit hard. Gradually, though, it came to him that she might not necessarily be saying what it sounded very much like she was saying. He dusted off his ego and set it back on its feet to find out.

"I'm still scratching at the surface. You know, a man from the West, a woman from the Middle East, the exotic charge they . . . *he* feels. As usual, you're already talking about something deeper, aren't you?"

"I am talking about the thing that matters more than anything else to me, Geoff. My identity and my dignity as a Palestinian."

"But what does that have to do with me? Or, more to the point, what do I have to do with it?"

"You do not remember what you said when we were talking about the incident at Munich?"

"I don't remember my exact words, no, but I think I said something to the effect that they ought to take all terrorists like the sons of bitches that did that and shoot them. I was in a blind rage at Seamus at the time, but I meant it."

He saw her flinch.

"That bothers you?"

"It offends me," she said. "I am a Palestinian, just like those you condemn so easily."

"Oh, for crying out loud, Nadya, there are Canadians I'd recommend for exactly the same fate. I can't believe you'd ever excuse the murder of innocent people."

"The innocent are murdered every day," she told him. "Why is it you in the West will only see them when you want to?"

"I thought we were talking about Munich," he said, because he knew there was no answer to such a question.

"We are talking about Munich. And about the very great difference between us."

"Well," he said, verbally throwing up his hands, "then you're going to have to walk me through this one."

"Walk you?" she said.

"Explain it to me."

She watched him closely as she began. "When you think of the Palestinians who took the Israeli hostages at the Olympic Village, who do you see? Hooded killers with strange accents and stone hearts?"

"If I think about them at all, yeah, that's about right."

"For you they are faceless, nothing." She made a sweeping gesture with her hand.

"No, not nothing," he corrected her. *"Nothing* is completely benign. Those guys were hardly benign."

"Whatever," she said impatiently. "Now, shall I tell you what I see?"

"Please do."

"These who are no more than terrorists to you are for me the sons of old men and women who spend their days doing nothing in the refugee camps of the Middle East. I have seen them and I know, they sit and do nothing but stare into their memories of a lost home and wait for an end to waiting.

"After the thirty-four years of our diaspora, most of these old people have given up. They believe that death is the only thing that will bring an end to their waiting. It is their sons, and their daughters too, Palestinians who like me have never seen Palestine, that cry loudest at this terrible injustice."

"Cry and occasionally kill," Geoff was quick to point out.

"It is very easy for you to sit in judgment, isn't it?" Nadya snapped at him. "You who have been blessed to know so little about any kind of oppression or suffering."

"I'm quite aware of my blessings, thank you," he said, suddenly thinking of his father's irritating penchant for drawing attention to more or less the same thing. "I never claimed to be speaking from a position of authority. You asked for my opinion and that's what you're getting. I was sickened by the deaths of those Israelis in Munich. The fact that you're a Palestinian and I happen to have certain feelings about you changes nothing," he said. To this he carefully added, "I am trusting you want me to be honest and straightforward about everything."

"Yes, I want you to be honest," Nadya said. "Ten years ago, eleven Israelis were killed at Munich and you are outraged to this day. Last summer, on July 16, more than one hundred and thirty Palestinians and Lebanese died when Israeli airplanes dropped bombs on West Beirut. Did you feel the same outrage about that?"

His inability to respond straightaway was response enough for her.

"You are not even aware this happened, are you? But you know, I am not surprised."

"I'm not sure that's a fair comparison."

"No? Why? Because Arab blood spilled does not have the same value as Jewish blood spilled?"

"That's not fair either, Nadya. That's not fair at all, in fact," he said. "You're an Arab."

"I am."

"Then how can you say such a thing to a man who is practically down on his hands and knees at the moment trying to fix the botched-up beginnings of what he hoped could be a relationship with you?"

Nadya's expression softened; her words did not.

"You talk about fairness. Tell me what is fair about this thing people in the West still have for Munich–this . . . this. . . ."

Geoff knew the word she was trying to find. "Pre-occupation?"

"Yes, this preoccupation. What is fair when a decade later more than ten times the number of people can die and nobody even notices?"

Geoff looked at her face, at the smooth and perfect slope of her cheeks. He looked and the selfish little boy, the good time party guy, the lonely and misunderstood man inside him, all called out for an end to this: I don't want to talk about it anymore and I really don't care about your issue; I came here tonight to talk about *us*.

"The reason I said it was not a fair comparison, if you'll hear me out, is because the eyes of the whole world were on Munich. The Olympic Games were underway. Every journalist and his dog was there. It's pretty hard to forget something like that when you had a whole American T.V. network on-site giving you a play-by-play, practically, of the incident as it unfolded."

Nadya did not appear to be the least bit impressed by his point, but she waited for him to finish it.

"As for this bombing last July in Beirut, you're right, I don't remember it. I should, but I don't. All I can say in my defense is that I see and hear so much of that kind of stuff in the news. At some point comes sensory overload and I just stop recording it."

"If this is the case, why then do you remember so much and so long a very small thing like Munich?" she persisted.

There was something uncomfortable about hearing such a violent episode described thus, but in forcing himself to step back from indignation Geoff could see her perspective. At least insofar as death tolls went, Munich was a small thing.

"I don't know why," he had to conclude.

Nadya seemed intent on some thought but holding herself back from sharing it.

"Tell me?" he pressed her.

"It is just that I wonder if Munich would be remembered the same way if the hostages had not been Jews."

Geoff felt his insides tightening and a part of his infatuation with this woman undergoing a rapid freeze.

"That's quite a question, Nadya. Maybe I should answer it with one of my own. How do you feel about Jews?"

Nadya laughed: a single, sarcastic *ha*.

"Did I just say something funny?" Geoff asked, hearing the edge in his voice. He knew it was one of life's peculiar little ironies that Linda, whom he could barely bring himself to even be civil to by the end of their marriage, and who let it be known that she herself was born Jewish only when it was somehow to her advantage, had cultivated in him, as a sort of lasting memento of their wholly unholy union, a hair trigger for anti-Semitism.

"It is as well quite a question you ask," Nadya said.

"Can you answer it?'

"Seamus has sometimes used a saying. I think it to be appropriate here . . . I will not dignify such a question with an answer."

"Why not?"

"Because it is a ridiculous question, and it shows how little you know." Then, as an echo of him just a few moments earlier, she added, "You want my honesty also, no?"

"You're telling me you're not anti-Semitic, then?" he said, trying to bury her put-down.

"First of all, I *am* a Semite, Geoff. Jews and Arabs are both Semitic peoples, and you would know this if you had ever looked the word up in a good dictionary. But no, I do not hate Jews. We are cousins. We share, as it is said, the blood of Abraham. What I hate is Israel, and what that state has done to my people. I am anti-Zionist, not anti-Jewish."

"Then what was all that about Munich being remembered differently, or less, if the hostages had not been Jews?"

"Guilt."

"Guilt? What are you talking about? Whose guilt?" Geoff was sorry he hadn't accepted her offer of coffee, as insincere as it had been. He was beginning to feel dizzy, but he wasn't sure which was more the reason: a potful of liquor on an empty stomach or the crazy, loose-armed spin of an argument he had not voluntarily entered into.

"Will you answer your own question?"

"Which one?"

"How do you feel about Jews?"

"Me?" he said, caught off-balance.

"Yes."

At first, he rejected telling her about Linda. It seemed to be the absolute pinnacle of stupidity, something that could only drive a permanent wedge between them. Slowly, though, it sunk in that avoiding such loud truths was just as big a mistake, bigger, if–as he believed, as the simple fact that he was even sitting here attempting to run this issue out should have proved–he genuinely wanted something more than just to take this woman to bed.

"I was married to one, once."

"So you once loved a woman who was Jewish. Do you think that answers the question? I think not."

"All right then," he said, surprised by her answer, and forming the words slowly in vain hopes of hiding the slur in his voice. "I think that the Jews are a people who are most noteworthy for how badly they've been treated through history, and who now cling with some justifiable paranoia to what they feel is their first and only safe harbor–Israel."

"And just who has treated them badly?"

"Who hasn't? That's the shorter list. What are you getting at, Nadya?"

"I am trying to get you to see the way I see, to see this issue like a Palestinian sees it. Who has treated them badly?"

"Well, everyone knows about the Nazis, but their persecution of the Jews was only the latest if the most horrible. As I've read it, from at least the time of the Inquisition they were essentially spat upon by everyone in Europe."

"Here in North America?"

"This place was initially colonized by Europeans, so here too, naturally–at least until recently. The Holocaust changed everything."

Nadya nodded. "Yes, the Holocaust. And out of it the guilt."

"Here we go again. What guilt?" he demanded.

"*Your* guilt, Geoff. Can you not see it? The guilt you and people like you all over North America and Europe carry around because of what happened to the Jews."

The truth of what she was saying took shape for him abruptly in a strangely refracted, strangely displaced anger.

"Yes, you're right, you know. Absolutely right. Whenever I see those pictures of the death camps, I think about my father, who fought in that war, and about the policial leaders of his generation, and I can't understand *how* it was allowed to happen. Yeah, I do feel a sense of shame and guilt. We must have known what was going on, and we could have stopped it long before we did."

The calm look on Nadya's face was like that of someone who had just had a piece of private speculation confirmed for her.

"I want you to know this about me, Geoff. As any human being with feelings would, I think what happened to the Jews under the Nazis was a terrible and sad thing. But as a Palestinian, when I think about this guilt you have, it is as close as I come to hating you."

"Why?"

For the briefest instant, the green eyes lit up like an angry cat's.

"Because for the past thirty-four years, you in the West have rested your guilt on our backs," she said. "In 1948, you carved up our land like a piece of meat and gave the Zionists the best and largest piece of it. In 1967, you stood by and did nothing to stop them when they took the rest of it. And in the years since then you have covered your eyes and given the Israelis a licence, because they are Jews and you feel this guilt, to do to us whatever pleases them."

"At the very least, I would say that's a gross oversimplification, Nadya."

"No," she said firmly. "You would like it to be more complex than this, but it is not. It is as I told you before–we Palestinians believe that we have been the ones made to pay for the crimes of Hitler. You have used us to make better your guilty consciences."

Geoff opened his mouth to object, but stopped short when he realized he could not do so with any conviction. It was then that an image–a snippet of memory–came to him. It seemed ridiculous, but the perfect rightness of it made him laugh. Nadya looked stunned.

"I was just thinking about the time I broke my ankle," he explained.

"Your ankle?" she said, sounding like she suspected there had been some permanent brain injury as well.

"I was ten or eleven or so, and I had gotten up on this really high and wobbly wood slat fence that separated our yard from the neighbors'. I don't know what I was doing up there, but I couldn't get down–or at least I couldn't make up my mind which side to jump down onto. Either way, it looked like a hard landing. It was only a few minutes, I'm sure, but it felt like I was up there for hours. In the end, the decision was taken out of my hands. I lost my balance and fell. My foot got stuck between the slats coming out the top of the fence. I can still remember the cracking sound of the bone giving. I must have looked really funny dangling there upside down and howling for my father."

He could tell that Nadya did not recognize this for what it was.

"What I'm trying to say is that I feel like I'm up on top of that damned fence again."

"I see. Will you be able to make a decision this time, or will you fall again?" she asked.

"I'm afraid I've already started to fall," he confessed.

Averting her gaze, she bit down on her lower lip.

"Nadya, don't hate me."

She shook her head.

"Jesus," he blurted, looking at his watch. "My ten minutes were up twenty minutes ago. I'm sorry." He stood up to leave, and in his sudden rush to escape something it was too late to escape he stumbled against the edge of the coffeetable. Her journals and the unopened roses slid onto the floor. Red-faced, he stooped to pick them up. Then he felt her hand on his arm.

"Stay a little longer," she said.

"No, I have to let you get back to your reading. I've been here too long already. I've said too much."

"Please, I do not want you to go. Not like this. Let me make coffee."

"Nadya–"

"*Please?*"

So he stayed; stayed to sip several small cups of thick, sweet, cardamon-flavored Turkish coffee–a bribe for someone stuck on the fence, she teased. Eventually, and at his insistence, she moved back to her preferred spot on the floor and took up her reading again. He remained on the couch, finishing one last demitasse of coffee while he flipped through a couple of her journals, trying, when he wasn't looking at her, to make some sense of the long chemical equations and techno-academic language. Soon, the fine print on the pages and the loud silence in the room ganged up to remind him of all the scotch he'd consumed, and he had to put down the journals. He kicked off his shoes and sprawled across her couch, thinking to take just a short rest before leaving, just a little one. The ceiling had started to spin–he'd drunk that much?–and he shut his eyes to stop it.

When he woke up, the lights were off and Nadya was gone from the room. He checked his watch: 4:00 a.m. Rising on his elbows, he discovered that the roses were now sitting in a vase on the coffeetable. He also discovered a quilt tucked neatly around him, and a note under his cup and saucer on the edge of the table. He picked it up and read it.

You had been drinking (how else to explain your words, correct?) and I did not think you should be driving so I let you sleep. If you can wait, I will make you breakfast in the morning.

Nadya

He went into the kitchen for a drink of water, then walked down the hall and stood in the open doorway of her bedroom. Although it was too dark to see, he listened to her breathing in her sleep and imagined himself slipping between the covers to press his body against the warm "S" formed by hers. After a while, he went back to the couch and quickly dropped off again.

The sound of the television woke him up shortly after eight. Nadya was sitting at the end of the couch near his feet. Her face looked drawn and strained and she worked her teeth mercilessly up and down against the edge of her thumbnail. Seemingly unaware of his waking, she stared at "Canada A.M." on her small black and white set.

Geoff pulled himself upright–she still didn't appear to have noticed him–and took her hand in his to stop the attack on her thumbnail. He turned then to see what it was that had so completely absorbed her. The news was on. From what he could pick up out of context, the Israeli ambassador to Great Britain had been shot and critically wounded in London, and Israel had unleashed its air force on a number of Palestinian guerrilla bases and refugee camps in Beirut and other parts of Lebanon in retaliation. In closing his clip over scenes of the destruction wrought by the bombing raid, the reporter noted that it was June third–almost fifteen years to the day since the start of the Six Day War.

"I'm dreaming this, right?" Geoff said.

Nadya finally looked at him.

"This is too weird for words," he mumbled.

*   *   *

The telephone beside his bed rang. Without lifting his head off the pillow, he reached over and fumbled the receiver to his ear. He knew it could be nobody else but Dix.

"My ceiling's spinning. How about yours?" he said.

"Have you ever heard of a place called Malloullah?"

"No. Should I have?"

"It's a small Greek Orthodox village, just a little ways north of Damascus. According to the Syrians, the Malloullahians . . . Malloullahites? . . . the inhabitants of Malloullah are the last people on earth who speak the Aramaic dialect that Christ supposedly spoke."

"Is that so," Geoff said.

"I took a drive out there once."

"You did. And what did you find?"

"Nothing."

"Nothing?"

It was some time before Dix spoke again.

"Why the hell do you want to go to Beirut anyway?"

"I told you, it's a personal matter. A personal fuck-up. Anyway, does it really make any difference at this point, Dix?"

"Not to me, no. To the Israelis, yes."

"Now tell me something I don't already know."

"I've got a bottle of bourbon down here. Did you know that?"

Geoff tried to decide what this meant. "What's your room number?" he asked.

"I'm in 306. It isn't locked."

When Geoff pushed open the door to Dix's room a few minutes later, he found the American stretched out flat on his back on the carpet, knees up and eyes closed. Turning to leave, he heard Dix clear his throat and roll over onto his belly with a pained grunt. His eyes opened and he looked up at Geoff.

"I thought you'd passed out."

"Lumbar troubles," Dix said, with effort. "That position is supposed to help." He picked at the threads of brown carpet below his chin.

"Shall I slip into a kimono and walk up and down on you for a while?"

"Would you?"

Geoff smiled weakly and sat on the edge of the bed. With

another grunt of discomfort, Dix reached over and dragged a bottle of Jack Daniels and two bathroom glasses out from beneath the bed.

"Uh-uh, I'm done with that for tonight," Geoff said.

The American shrugged and sat up to pour his own. He took a deep drink, set the glass down and returned to his back. Geoff watched his knobby Adam's apple still bobbing against the bite of what he'd just swallowed.

"You know, I was thinking about the oddest thing before you got here."

"Which of course you're just about to tell me."

"When I was a kid back in Minnesota, we had this dirt poor Indian family living in a two-room shack on the edge of town. It was fertile ground for eight-year-old imaginations. We used to sneak up through the underbrush and look in the windows to see if they were eating their meat raw, or if they kept any scalps tacked on the walls."

Dix stopped to laugh at himself. "One day, a bunch of us got it in our minds to give the Indians a hostage to torture, or whatever it was we thought Indians did to hostages. Naturally, we picked the class zero, right–a frail-looking kid with thick glasses and this wispy mama's-boy voice. After we'd sucked him into thinking he was at last going to get to play with us, we tied him up with plastic skipping ropes and fixed him to a tree near their shack. Then we took off into the bush to watch.

"I'm telling you, what with his screaming and crying and bleating, it didn't take but thirty seconds for the Indians to come racing outside and untie their terrified prisoner. Then, much to our shock and disappointment, they let him go."

"You bastards. The poor kid," Geoff said.

Dix snorted and sat up. "Poor kid, indeed. Poor little Jacob Feinstein. I'm pretty sure it was his first exposure to anti-Semitism too, though I don't think any of us even knew he was Jewish, or what a Jew was. We must have absorbed it through the skin from our parents. Anyhow, last I heard through the hometown grapevine, old Jake was pulling in about six hundred grand a year performing triple bypasses in upstate New York, and packing a mean, Arab-bashing mouth on behalf of Meir Kahane's charming Jewish Defense League."

"Don't you ever talk in a straight line?" Geoff said.

Dix sat up to drink again. "What for? Over the years, I've discovered there are no beginnings and ends to things, in other words no straight lines. Life is just an exercise in running around circles and loop-the-loops. And you know, we all pass exactly the same scenic points eventually. In fact, most of us, if we live long enough, pass them over and over again."

"Yeah, I know, whatever comes around goes around," Geoff said wearily.

"No, that's someone else's theory. Mine is more like this: whatever comes around comes around and comes around again. It's like the circulation of B-movies through a small town theater chain. Either nobody catches on or nobody gives a damn that they've already seen the same shitty pictures half a dozen times."

Geoff stood up and shook his head.

"Very interesting," he said. "I'd love to be able to sit here and listen to these philosophical treatises of yours until dawn, but I've got a plane to find in the morning."

He was still chewing the sarcasm in his mouth when Dix called him back from the door.

"Do you know how to tell a convincing lie, Geoffrey?"

Geoff frowned.

"Well, do you?"

"Come on, I sell real estate. Sometimes I sell a lot of it."

Dix smiled. "Good, then listen. Forget about Cyprus for now. Stick around Jerusalem for a couple more days."

"I haven't got time to waste."

"You said you wanted to go to Beirut."

"And you said I couldn't get there from Israel."

"That's right, you can't, at least not as Mr. Vancouver, the sullen real estate man."

"But?"

Dix downed what was left of the bourbon in his glass. "Can't we save something for the next chapter? Just hang tight for a couple of days until I see if I can work the details of something out. Practice your bullshit delivery or something, and check for a message at the front desk. I'll be in touch. Oh, and you'll have to get me a photo of yourself. A passport black-and-white will do in a pinch."

"Do I thank you now or later?" Geoff said.

"Thank me? If I get you to Beirut, I won't have done you a favor, believe me."

"Why, then?"

"Why help you? Who knows, maybe I just have this thing for deflowering the innocent? Occupational obsession." With another groan, Dix rolled onto his back again. "Now, are you going to slip into that kimono and walk around on me? Cause if you're not, get the hell out of here so I can get some sleep."

SIX

HER MESSAGE WAS THERE AMONG SEVERAL OTHERS WAITING on his desk when he dawdled back to the office after a lengthy client lunch. There was no request that he phone her at home or the university, just that he meet her, if he could, outside the Robson Street steps to the Vancouver Art Gallery at four o'clock. Geoff dialed the numbers to her lab and apartment anyhow. There was no answer at either place.

At four o'clock, having managed with some difficulty to bump his last appointment over to the following day, he thumbed his tie loose, flung his suit jacket over his shoulder and set out to walk the short distance to the gallery.

He should have been in better spirits. After a stumbling gray start, the day had shaped up a fine one and it looked like half of downtown had fled work early and were out in the streets shedding layers of clothes and exhilarating in the warmth and brilliant sunshine of late June. But he could only enjoy them enjoying it to a very prickly point. The tanned shoulders and delicately muscled bare calves of women sweeping past on the sidewalk made him much too aware, much too quickly, of what was missing from his days, and especially from his nights.

At the age of thirty-three, he would have liked to believe he was well past such single-track hormonal thinking. He would have liked to believe that. Nadya had managed, however, to transform him into a repressed, obsessed post-adolescent again; why, he'd even discovered a pimple that morning. What's more, she'd done it without doing anything at all. Which was exactly the point.

Having acknowledged to himself (to her too, though as yet with no equivalent or unequivocal return acknowledgment . . . nobody could call him a quitter) that this inscrutable Palestinian biochemist had become an extremely important entry in his life–one worth even, say, offering himself up as a pile of political clay for extensive reshaping–and that he wanted something more than just to take her to bed, he nonetheless did want to take her to bed. How could he not want that; just the look of her looking at him from across a room made him hard. And anyway, it seemed to him the perfectly natural next step in any adult relationship. After all, in the three weeks since their big talk and his equally unplanned sleepover on her couch, had they not spent part of just about every single day together?

Ha, but that meant almost nothing at all, for this wasn't *any adult relationship*. It was a source of considerable bemusement for Geoff to know that he'd had what he thought were serious affairs in the past that had burned themselves out and ended in only slightly more time than it had taken him to bring Nadya even as far as a meaningful kiss.

Their first kiss. That tiny summit had been conquered last night, at her apartment, on the famous couch. Oh, sure, he had been able to physically press his lips against hers a number of times before then: once, no twice, in goodbye when he'd dropped her off near her lab on campus following a quick lunch, and two or three times maybe when he'd dropped her off at her apartment after picking her up from the lab late in the evening. But it was not until last night that she had actually responded.

"Nadya, you know you're killing me, don't you? This is a slow death I'm dying."

They had been kissing, finally kissing, for a few minutes, when she suddenly broke his clench and pulled far enough away from him to make the meaning quite clear.

"I am killing you?"

"Yes, you are. I'm not used to this. Tell me, how *do* Palestinian children get conceived?"

"Their parents become husband and wife."

"Oh, so that's it. Okay. Nadya?"

"Yes?"

"Marry me. Marry me soon. Marry me now. . . . Hey, I'll bet

you didn't know I'm a notary public. That makes me practically
a justice of the peace. I can hear our vows and then we can run
down the hall to your bedroom and make things official. What
do you say?"

She was not laughing; he expected that he'd at least be able to
pull a good-natured laugh out of her.

"This is not a very good time for me, Geoff."

"I'm not having all that good a time either."

"I am talking about the situation in Lebanon. I do not mean
you and me."

"Yeah, well—" He had stopped himself just short of dismissing
her preoccupation with that place. "I know."

*   *   *

Crossing Howe Street, Geoff spotted Nadya among a small
crowd of placard-wielding demonstrators in the square below the
art gallery steps. Local gripers of one kind or another often
gathered there to whine, and he began to wonder why she did not
simply move out of their way when another familiar face
appeared beside hers. It was Seamus, holding up a hand-painted
sign. Geoff read it and swore under his breath.

Begin and Reagan share a bed over the graves of innocent dead.

"Geoff, you came." Nadya grabbed his hand and pressed it to
her cheek, a little habit that he ordinarily found quite touching.
Seamus, whom he'd had the good fortune not to see since the
dinner party, looked on disapprovingly.

"So, George ... I mean Geoff ... can I find you a sign?
Something tastefully simple?" The Irishman's mocking tone said
he already knew just what the reply would be.

"No, thanks," Geoff answered, with badly forced pleasantness.
"This isn't my kind of statement. I'll just watch from the sidelines
if it's all the same to you."

Nadya blinked at him.

"Watch? You will not walk with us?" she said, trying at the
same time to turn her face away from him. He saw the tears
anyway.

"All right," he relented, conscious that there were others
around them listening in. "But no sign."

Blinkering himself against all the discreet glances and contemptuous stares of passersby, Geoff shuffled along behind Nadya in the scanty procession around and around the square. He allowed himself to see nothing but her back and the crudely finished cardboard signs joggling up and down in front of him. There were a few clever sounding ones like Seamus', but most were just blunt demands for an immediate Israeli withdrawal from Lebanon and for Ottawa's recognition of the PLO as the legitimate representatives of the Palestinians.

Mercifully, this pointless circling ended after fifteen or twenty minutes. The ring of demonstrators collapsed in on itself and reformed as a loose knot in front of the gallery steps. It was speech-making time. Defensively edging backwards towards the rear of the crowd, Geoff moved in close to Nadya and slipped his arm around her waist. In front of them, Seamus had found a babysitter for his sign and mounted the steps. That figures, Geoff thought.

"How's your day been?" he asked her at the same moment Seamus began to speak.

"*Yanni*–fine." She leaned forward on the balls of her feet to listen.

Yanni: that non-committal Arabic term of hers that could mean anything from "more or less" to "you know." Though Nadya had become increasingly distracted during the three weeks since the Israelis had entered Lebanon, she had never seemed quite this upset or on edge before. He wondered if he might perhaps have missed some major new development in the news that day, but decided that asking her what was wrong would only set her to thinking that much harder about it.

Reaching for his acerbic best, Seamus had just seized Ronald Reagan by his septuagenarian jowls and was shaking him up and down for the crowd. Somewhere on the sidewalk behind them, Geoff heard a woman heckler just beginning to warm up. He badly wanted to leave this scene before the news cameras showed up.

"Nadya, you already know all of this. Why don't we go and have ice cream?" he whispered in her ear, nipping the lobe playfully. "Better yet, let's buy a quart of the stuff and rub it all over each other's bodies."

She shook him off with a dark frown. Her lack of humor snuffed out his.

"Goddamn it, Nadya, you don't need this. You're already worked up enough as it is." He could feel the tension in her body when he tried to pull her closer to him. "See, you're strung tighter than a squash racket."

"Geoff, please just stop. Just *stop*." She turned on him irritably. "I know this means nothing at all to you, but it is very important to me."

"Sorry," he snapped right back. He dropped his arm from her waist and walked away.

Feeling hurt, he went and stood at the edge of the square, determined to wait for her to come over and apologize. She did not; she did not even turn around to see where he'd gone. Just then, someone hustling by on the sidewalk stopped and punched him on the top of his arm. He turned to see two of the other agents from his office.

"Andrews, what did you do, pack it in early so you could come and hang around here with the comrades?" Fat Harry Packard laughed, winking at slight Leonard Wong standing next to him.

"Dental appointment," Geoff said, scrabbling for a suitable lie. "The jerk overbooked, so I left."

"They do that," Leonard sympathized, unconsciously picking at his own teeth with a finger.

"Now you're making *my* mouth hurt," Harry complained. "Let's go, Wong. I'm thirsty."

"Since when were you ever not thirsty, Harry?" Geoff said.

"Ha, ha—and look at the fish that talks," Harry shot back.

"We're headed for the pub, Geoff. Want to join us?" Leonard invited.

Nadya had now moved up near the front of the crowd to listen to Seamus. Geoff looked at her. He gave her one last chance to turn around.

"Why not," he told Leonard. "I've got time for a quickie."

A quickie indeed. If he was to be honest with himself, he knew as soon as he heard Leonard's invitation that there was a better than even chance that the faded, after-work crowd leaning into draught beer and shooters and filthy jokes in the smoky pub would include Angela. It was there that the two of them had first met on a similar afternoon, she sliding over from her table to challenge him to a game of darts, and it became something like the old sneakers they liked to slip into whenever they did not care to dress up to go out.

Chatting away with some coworkers of hers, she did not notice him come in, and through the first drink he managed to leave it alone. By the second round, he was bored with Wong and Packard, who between them made real estate feel less like living than it was. Excusing himself, he stood up, but then instead of walking over to say hello to her he tossed down his share of the bill and headed straight for the door.

The self-congratulatory mood he had worked himself into disappeared the moment he rounded the front of the art gallery and discovered an empty square. A pair of teenaged punk girls sat defiantly on the top step where Seamus had spoken. Geoff looked at his watch and realized how long he'd been gone.

*   *   *

I, who have gladly clambered into every capsule available and so often flown to the backside of my heart, have finally opened my eyes there and found nothing but this darkness. . . .

Geoff remembered that line verbatim, simply because it was the oddest string of words he had ever put down on paper. The rest of the note that she had never got to read, though, blurred in his memory as one long, pathetic apology. Sorry, oh so sorry, darling. He really was some kind of pig.

When the call came, he was halfway back from the bathroom, sponging out the stickiness around his groin with a warm facecloth. Jumping straight back into old habits after only half an hour in his bed, Angela set down her glass of wine and turned her soft, broad buttocks to answer it.

"Don't, Ange," he said, tossing her the facecloth and hurrying over to pick up the phone himself.

"Hello?"

"Where did you go, Geoff?"

"I forgot all about an appointment back at the office, Nadya. You know how work is–I had to go." The wine glass shuddered in his hand.

"You could not tell me you were leaving?"

"You were busy," he said. "Anyway, I thought I could get back before the speech-making was over, but you'd left. All I found were a couple of punk rockers." He heard an idiot's chuckle–his own–and he knew he wasn't fooling anyone.

"You are lying to me," she said flatly.

"Can't we talk about it?"

This time it was her turn to make a sound that might have been a chuckle.

"The saddest thing is that I really did need to talk to you tonight, Geoff."

"Come on, Nadya, I'll be right over. Put the coffee on."

"I am not at home."

"Fine, no problem, I'll pick you up. Where are you?"

"I am with friends," she said. There was silence for a moment. "I just wanted to say goodbye to you, Geoff. I hope you will have a good life. Truly, I do."

"Wait. What is this? Wait, Nadya."

The click of her receiver was a gut-shot. Dizzied, he sat down heavily on the edge of the bed. Angela's movement behind his back turned him around. With her glass of wine in one hand, she was running the palm of the other back and forth over the fitted sheet.

"What are you doing?" he asked her, without interest.

"Looking for our wet spot," she answered, locating it with the tips of her fingers.

"What on earth for?"

"For this," she said, eyeing him carefully as she tipped her glass over the spot. The red wine spidered wide across the white cotton then settled in deeply and forever. He didn't say a word as he watch her get dressed and leave.

*   *   *

As seen from the gusty heights at Ras Naquoura on the Lebanese border, the coast road running back to Haifa was a pale, crimped ribbon dropped between the sea and sprinkler-spit acres of sugar cane and orange and lemon trees. Leaning against a wire fence strung along the edge of the sharp, south facing bluff, Geoff was able to look down and pick out the exact jog where he'd been stopped before and made to turn around. Today, there was not the deafening battle of steel scraping stone. The road was quiet.

Yawning, he walked back to the car and sat down on the trunk to wait for the return of Dix and his photographer-driver, a mop-haired young Israeli freelancer named Amos who cheerfully professed not to have a single political opinion in his head. A concrete distance marker beside the road caught his attention. It revealed that while Jerusalem lay 205 kilometers behind them, Beirut was now only half that far north, and it reminded him of something Dix had said on the drive up that morning. Once, it had been physically possible to get up at dawn in Jerusalem, drive north to Beirut for a late breakfast, east to Damascus for lunch, south to Amman in time for supper, and finally west to sleep once again in your bed in Jerusalem. Armageddon waiting on the head of a pin was how the American had laughingly described it.

Geoff felt the car bouncing under him, and he looked over his shoulder to see Dix and Amos both leaning over the hood watching him. Dix's smile was close-mouthed and crooked.

"Remember your lines?"

Geoff nodded.

Leaving Amos behind to fiddle with his camera gear, Dix led Geoff up the road. They passed the concrete marker–the journalist wordlessly pointing it out–walked through a heavy iron gate and up to the open door of an unlit, single-room building. Dix rapped on the door frame and an Israeli officer sitting in shadow behind a desk waved them in. An electric fan set on a box on the one other chair in the room coaxed the air into motion at half-speed. The thick dust on the fan's horizontal surfaces looked to have the consistency of mud.

"Mr. Dix," the Israeli said. "Back again so soon?"

"What can I say? I missed your smiling face, Captain Levy." Dix grinned down at him and placed his passport and press accreditation politely on the desk. Geoff did the same.

"And today you've brought a friend. Tell me, does he write as well as you do? Another compassionate correspondent?"

Geoff fidgeted with some change in his pocket.

"Ask him," Dix suggested.

"A very good idea, Mr. Dix," Captain Levy replied, just as pleasantly. He slid the journalist's papers back at him and picked up Geoff's.

After a terrible minute's scrutiny of the fabricated documents, he asked, "How long have you been with the *Vancouver Sun*, Mr. Andrews?"

"Couple of years, I guess." Geoff was conscious of Dix's advice that he not say very much or appear too eager. Remember: we are the most tired of men.

Captain Levy chewed on his upper lip. "I do not believe I have encountered your paper here before."

"Well, we're Canadians. We don't make much noise." He watched for Dix's reaction, a grin. "People hardly know we're around."

"Unlike your American friend here," the Israeli said.

"Right," Geoff smiled, hoping it was the right sort of response to make.

The Israeli leaned back in his chair and tapped Geoff's passport against his chin. Suddenly, he squealed the chair forward, picked up the phone on his desk and, without even dialing, began to speak in brusque Hebrew. Dix snorted and shook his head.

"What's wrong?" Geoff said.

"Ours is going to be a crowded little car."

Levy hung up the phone. Dix did not explain.

"All right, you may proceed. Have a good trip, gentlemen. Lebanon is your oyster." The Israeli got to his feet, tossed Geoff's papers back onto the desk, put his arms over his head and stretched.

"I hear oysters put lead in your pencil," Dix quipped. With Levy not looking, he closed his fist to make a jerk-off sign for Geoff's benefit.

"At the rate you are going, this oyster might put lead in your chest someday, Mr. Dix," Levy said. "Do take good care."

"What was that all about?" Geoff demanded. He was forced to walk hard to keep up with Dix's quick strides back to the car.

"Oh, you could say I've had a spot of trouble lately with the

Ministry of Information back in Jerusalem," the American said. "Word eventually trickles back down to plebes like Levy. No big deal, but we're going to have to put up with the company of a soldier for this trip."

"What sort of trouble are you talking about? That little exchange sounded nasty."

"Well, you see, Geoffrey, it's like this," Dix began, his tone sharply patronizing. "I am a foreign correspondent on assignment in Israel. As such, I am required to submit everything I write and intend to dispatch about this little conflict in Lebanon to Israeli military censors before I can call it kosher and file it."

"And the trouble?"

"You really don't have a clue, do you?" Dix said. He had stopped in front of the distance market, and was picking at its rough, white-washed surface with his fingernails. Sun-hardened flecks of paint cut into the soft skin beneath and made him wince.

"Just where is it that you think you're going?" Dix snapped. He reached out and stabbed at the black-lettered Beirut on the market with a finger now dripping blood.

Geoff nodded. "That's where I'm going, all right. Is that symbolism?"

Dix pulled his finger back and stared at it, then he flicked the bubble of blood into Geoff's face and made a move to walk away. Grabbing hold of his sleeve, Geoff spun him around and shoved him back against the marker.

"What's wrong with you anyway, Thomas?"

Dix pushed Geoff away and straightened up. He made a great show of readjusting his shirt.

"You're what's wrong with me right now, you myopic moron," he said. "Now shut up, or you'll be hitchhiking back to Jerusalem from here."

Captain Levy had wandered out of his office. He stood by with crossed arms and waited expressionlessly while the iron gate was pushed open for them and the soldier he'd assigned to accompany them, a tough-looking sergeant with a boxer's broad nose and chin, climbed into the backseat beside Geoff. The soldier placed his rifle, butt down and barrel up, on the floor between them and

smiled faintly at the anxious glance his seat-mate gave it. Geoff
had an urban North American's fear of guns.

"Welcome to Lebanon," Dix said, snapping a crisp military
salute at Levy as they passed through the gate and sped away
north.

"Listen, I'm sorry, Thomas," Geoff said. He leaned over the
seat.

"Yeah, fine."

"No, really." He pressed it, feeling equal parts guilt and
gratitude.

"Forget it already–it's forgotten on this end. Now sit back and
enjoy the ride. You'll have no other like it." Dix flipped on the
small tape player he had brought along. Simon and Garfunkel's
"59th Street Bridge Song" came on in mid-chorus.

"Oh no," Geoff groaned.

"Ha-ha, the perfect *muzak* for this," Dix laughed, jumping into
a singalong with Amos. Geoff and the soldier–who had informed
Amos and Dix in Hebrew that he didn't speak English (though
when Dix had turned around to relay this to Geoff, he did so with
his tongue planted in his cheek as a warning that the man was
surely lying)–just looked at each other and shrugged.

It was a short distance south of Tyre, about fifteen miles up
from the border, that they ran into the heels of the war. As Amos
pulled out wide to pass a column of slow-rolling army supply
trucks, Geoff saw a sprawl of makeshift cardboard lean-tos and
ragged canopies in a stony field beside the road. Disheveled
chickens and black and brown goats ran free, kicking up dust,
while in a square near the center of this junkyard campground,
next to a mountain of garbage, a trio of shirtless Israeli soldiers
stood straddling the top of a water tanker, surrounded by
dirt-streaked children begging for a hosing and sturdy but
exhausted looking women holding aloft plastic pails and
five-gallon jugs. With the exception of a few white-haired old
shufflers, there were no other men to be seen.

"At least they've been given some water today," Dix said.
"Sometimes a little shit hitting the media fan gets results."

"Who are they?" Geoff asked.

"Palestinians mostly, but there are a poor Lebanese there too.
They're from the Rachidieh and Bourj el-Shemali refugee

camps, back there and over that way," Dix said, pointing south and east.

"What are they doing out here?'

"They have to be somewhere. The Israel Defense Force chased them out and flattened their camps. This is just a few hundred of them. There were fifteen thousand people living in Rachidieh alone."

"What the hell was that done for?" Geoff asked, almost surprised by the pique in his voice. Dix heard it too.

"Makes you mad, does it, Geoffrey?"

"These people are harmless." Then he remembered the sergeant sitting beside him. He looked over, but there was no reaction; if the man did speak English, he certainly owned a good poker face.

"No," the journalist said, gravely. "Haven't you heard? They're going to push Israel into the sea."

*   *   *

The car overheated while they were picking their way through the cratered and debris-filled streets of Tyre. Having neglected to pack anything more than a little fruit juice that morning, Amos yanked an empty jerry can from the trunk and disappeared, cursing himself fiercely, in search of relief for the hissing radiator. Dix watched him leave and mumbled something about maybe going off himself to look for an interview. But a headache changed his mind, and he stretched out in the backseat and promptly fell asleep. This struck the IDF sergeant as a good idea, but with bucket seats in the front and the backseat already claimed, he had to settle for a shaded patch of dirt and weeds by the side of the road. He stripped off his tunic, bunched it up as a pillow and lay down with his rifle.

Left to entertain himself, Geoff took a seat in the front but soon grew hot and bored. He marked the location of the car and decided to wander for a little closer look at this half-ruined city. He'd walked down the road only a short distance before he gave in to an impulse to climb into the concrete and twisted steel of what had been a four-story building. As he clambered on hands and knees over blocks of shattered stone as large as delivery vans, he felt a strange excitement. It was the small boy in him back playing war with plastic soldiers on the floor of his father's workroom. Jumping down off the edge of another broken-off block of concrete that was almost as high as he was tall, he hit the ground as casually as a cat and zigzagged like he was under fire into the gaping superstructure of the building.

For a few moments, he stood there just inside, content to have the shade and relative coolness. When he began at last to explore, he quickly discovered that the building had been an apartment complex. Although there was little of it still around, and all of that either worthless or irreparably damaged–looters and residents having long since departed with anything even slightly valuable–there were bits of several households tucked here and there in the rubble. He saw an aluminum cooking pot, perfectly flattened by the impact of something either very heavy or very powerful. Incongruous beside it sat a green paper lampshade, perfectly intact. The four screw-in legs of a sofa were neatly laid across each other like a boy-scout fire awaiting a match, but the sofa itself was gone. There was one plain black man's shoe–there was always a solitary shoe in such landscapes–and the shredded pages from books and magazines had been blown around by breeze or bomb concussion.

Towards the center of the main floor, Geoff found a staircase, and he peered up through the shaft of black and gray inside towards daylight on the roof. Judging the steps sound underfoot, he kicked a twisted tricycle frame away from the landing and headed up.

Though he had braced himself for it, the heat and the thick dust that seemed to be a constant in the air here nearly made him turn around in immediate retreat after he'd stepped out onto the roof. Walking gingerly, he went and stood as near the edge as he dared and looked down over the city.

Pictures from a trip. Like an animal casualty on the side of the road–run over by the Israeli war machine speeding north–Tyre's gray entrails had dribbled slowly down its flanks and congealed. Here and there, from one crumbled block of the city to another, the homeless poked and probed with sticks through the stone and concrete viscera. They gave the appearance of flies on a carcass. Overhead, the largest gulls Geoff had ever seen soared and stalled, their sharp eyes fixed on the carcass as well.

His bladder was full. Turning away from the edge of the roof now, he unzipped and aimed at one of the many small mounds of stone debris on the roof, wondering how an explosion could have deposited such material all the way up here. Shaking himself finished, he zipped up again and decided to head back to the car. On the ground next to the entry to the staircase, he noticed a photograph of a woman on the torn-away cover of a glossy Arab magazine. Although the resemblance was not close, the model in the photograph did have the same long black hair. He stooped to pick it up for a better look. Then he stopped–

Initially, perhaps because it was so grotesquely foreign to them, Geoff's eyes glassed over and refused to acknowledge what they were seeing in the rubble scant inches away from that torn magazine cover. But curiosity is a much stronger pull than horror, and finally they had to take in and register the child's hand, torn off at the wrist. Many, many days into decomposition already, the veins, tendons and shards of bone protruding from the shriveled little glove of skin looked like tangled electrical wiring.

Geoff could taste the bile rising in his throat. Lurching off the roof into the darkness of the stairwell, he lost his footing and tripped down the first step, dropping hard on his knees, elbows, shoulder, again and again, collapsing at the bottom over the tricycle frame he had kicked aside on the way up. When his mind finally caught up with his battered body, it coolly pointed out just whose tricycle this had likely been.

Perhaps he had emerged from a different side of the building, or perhaps he'd come out the right side but in his frantic state had gone the wrong way up the street, but he got lost, and it took him long minutes of sprinting up and down and around the block, turning the heads of the probing homeless of Tyre as he passed, before he found the car again. Leaning breathless across the blazing hood, he heaved at the limp, wretched air and watched Dix toss a baseball high overhead and then catch it with a dusty glove he had carried to the Middle East from home.

"Mine," the American called, waving off imaginary teammates as he stepped beneath another pop fly.

The IDF sergeant was sleeping fitfully in his patch of shaded dirt when Amos returned with water. This gave Dix an idea. Quietly, he unlatched and opened the hood so Amos could refill the parched radiator. Geoff kept watch; the soldier did not stir. When they were done, Amos returned the jerry can to the trunk and Dix carefully lowered and latched the hood. The three of them then slipped back into the car and, after waiting a moment to be sure the soldier was still out, pulled away. Dix and Amos howled with laughter at the thought of him trying to explain their escape to Captain Levy, but Geoff was still in the rubble on top of that rooftop.

Dix turned to him. "So what's with you?"

SEVEN

THE WARM SUMMER RAIN DRIBBLED DOWN HIS WINDSHIELD along many arbitrary and shifting courses, Mick Jagger begged some sympathy for the Devil through the radio speakers, and the Denman Street neon glowed wetly through the dusk as he watched a pair of tall black women striding up the sidewalk. They laughed together under a shared umbrella, their arms affectionately linked.

Thinking that he had begun to see something of her in just about every woman these days, he returned his gaze to the salon door in time to see Walid step outside and pop open his own broad umbrella. Easing his foot off the brake, Geoff rolled along the curb beside the Moroccan for a dozen yards. Finally, he leaned against the horn with his palm, and pushed the power window switch. Walid stopped, turned, recognized the face behind the wheel of the BMW and slowly walked over.

"*Marhaba.*"

"Hop in, I'll give you a lift."

"You needn't bother. This rain is wonderful to walk in."

"Please, Walid," he said with difficulty. "I want . . . I need to talk to you."

With a nod, Walid folded up his umbrella and ducked into the car. Almost immediately, Geoff could smell a day of mousse and gel and hairspray on his clothes.

"How are you?"

"Where is she, Walid?"

"She? You mean Nadya? I do not know."

91

"I don't believe you."

Walid looked half-amused. "You know, I am not at all sure I care if you believe me."

"She hasn't been at her apartment for three days."

"How do you know that? Perhaps she is just not answering her phone."

"I know it because I sat and waited on the floor outside her door all of last night. She has not been home."

"No sleep, then?" Walid rubbed his own cheeks to indicate Geoff's heavy stubble.

"None," he said. "Now, please, where is she? I know she'd tell you."

"Have you tried the university? Maybe she has an important experiment running and must stay there at night to chart the results. She has done that before, you know."

"No. Her department head told me she's taken some sort of leave of absence."

"Oh, well, that is good. She was very tired. Perhaps she has gone away to rest, to the mountains or across to Victoria. She is fond of Victoria."

"No, I don't think so." He shook his head.

"Well, Geoff . . ." Walid shrugged.

"We had an argument—sort of. It was a strange thing." His voice trailed off in remembrance of certain details of its aftermath.

"How do you mean strange? What happened?"

"All kinds of things happened," he said. "But it was basically about this damned war in Lebanon. I couldn't compete with it."

"Compete? You were not in some sort of competition for her attention or affection, Geoff. The Israelis are killing her people over there," the Moroccan said sharply.

"Fine, she's passionately political, a sincere Palestinian nationalist. But what good does it do to make yourself sick worrying about something you're ten thousand miles away from and can't do anything about?"

"Exactly so."

Walid's reply sounded cryptic; Geoff watched him fingering the black leather of the glove box in thought. The humidity in the car was suddenly choking.

"You *do* know where she is, you son of a bitch."

"And what if I do, Geoff? Will you drag me out of your car and beat me up if I refuse to tell you? Judging by what I have seen of you, it would be your style."

"Walid, listen, you and your friends don't like me. That's fine. But this is about Nadya and me. It has nothing to do with any of you."

"You feel very strongly about her, don't you?" Walid said as if he'd just now come to realize it.

"Nobody is more surprised by it than me, because in most respects there's been no relationship at all between us, but I can't stop thinking about her. I've never met anyone who stopped me in my tracks the way she does."

"Did you tell her how you feel?"

"Christ, I've been trying almost since we met," he said. "Please tell me where she is, Walid."

"Geoff, Nadya and I are close friends–as close, anyway, as she has let herself be to anybody–but I have to say that I have learned more about you and her in these last five minutes than I ever got from her."

"That's because the feelings are almost entirely one-way," he admitted, unhappily.

"I am not so sure about that, but it does not matter now."

"I have to talk to her."

"You can't. It's too late. She is gone," Walid said quietly. He returned to fingering the glove box. "It is strange. Nadya is gone, but her leaving has much less to do with you than you think, and yet at the same time perhaps more to do with you than any of us thought."

"For Christ sake, Walid, *where* is she?"

"She is with her grandmother. Did she never talk to you about her grandmother, Geoff?"

"What grandmother? She told me her only living relatives were an aunt and uncle in Kuwait. They raised her after her parents died."

The Moroccan screwed up his face as if he and Geoff were talking about two different Nadyas.

"There is no aunt and uncle in Kuwait, only her grandmother."

"What?"

"Geoff, believe me, you could not have stopped her going. Nobody could have. We tried, all of us–Seamus, Danielle, Prettima. That night when she called you, we were there trying to talk her out of it. But there was no way to talk her out of it."

"Where? Where does her grandmother live?" He grabbed at Walid's sleeve.

"Beirut."

Geoff's ears began to ring, and he felt the blood quit his face. Fearing himself about to black out, he stopped the car right there in the center of the lane. He slumped forward, banging his head lightly against the steering wheel.

"When is she coming back?" he asked weakly.

"I don't know," Walid answered. "Quite truthfully, I don't know if she will come back. The night before she left, she told us that she had finally realized there could be no running away from it."

Geoff sat up. "*It?*"

Walid shrugged and shook his head. "Her Palestinianness, I suppose. I don't know."

"Whereabouts in Beirut? Give me an address."

"I don't know that either, Geoff. Honestly. She would not say. Nadya was extremely private about her life over there. All she ever told any of us was that she had grown up in Beirut. And that is all she said when she left us–'I must go back to Beirut.' "

*   *   *

Geoff had noticed but not given much thought to the faintly rotten smell of the air in Tyre. Here in equally shattered Sidon, twenty-five miles farther north, it was worse, and he couldn't ignore it the way Dix and Amos seemed to be able to.

"What the hell is that smell?" he finally asked, pressing his nostrils into the leather back of Amos' seat for relief.

"Don't you know?" Dix was peeling an orange. He reached back to hand Geoff a third of it. Suddenly, Geoff knew.

"That smell is you, and me, and him," Dix said, pointing around the car for effect. "Why, it's the very perfume of mankind."

Amos laughed through a mouthful of orange.

"It's getting worse," Geoff said.

"Yes, I should say with every passing day of the twentieth century."

"No, I mean as we go north." If this was an incremental thing, worse in Sidon than Tyre with worse still to come, how could anyone possibly bear it in Beirut, where the dying was abbattoir-warm?

"Hey, Geoffrey?" Dix called. "You're from Canada, land of long drives. I'll bet you played car games when you were a kid, didn't you?'

"What are you talking about?"

"You know–car games. I Spy was the best, I think. I spy with my little eye something that is blue."

Geoff could only shake his head. Here they were, looking out at the smashed remains of an occupied city from the stifling hot cocoon of a car that would soon become (if it was not already) the object of one very angry IDF captain's all-points-bulletin, and Dix was talking about a stupid kid's game.

"Well?" Dix was staring at him with his mouth open and fun crouched in the corners of his bug eyes.

"Well what?"

"I spy with my little eye something that is blue. What is it?"

"Be serious, Dix. This place is horrible."

"You're right it is and I am serious, Geoffrey. Dollar a round–real dollars, mind you, not those pastel-colored Canuck bucks. Now guess," he insisted.

Geoff scowled, sucked air through his teeth (he was trying to avoid breathing through his nose) and looked outside for something blue. He understood why Dix had started this game just now and he had to admit he was coming to quite like the man.

"The sky." He wasn't really trying.

"Wrong, bucko–and that's a buck to me. Guess again. You get three of them."

"The sea."

Geoff looked at it and was suddenly struck by just how perfect and transcendent a thing it was. It had been here long before the lunatic primacy of the human race and would still be here long afterwards. Lingering over this moment of unexpected detachment, he decided that given all the possible options it would probably be one of the nicer forms of disposal to be rolled in a shroud and buried at sea. Dropped and plopped, wearing anklets of lead. No doubt it had something to do with the human animal's subconscious longing to return to the safe, salty waters of the original womb.

That ridiculous little thought broke the spell. He heard Dix's voice again.

"Come on, come on—that's two bucks. One more guess, then it's your go."

Holding fast to the Mediterranean, half-wishing to be borne along with it as it rippled away towards Gibraltar, he saw a small Israeli warship. It was surprisingly close to shore and cutting heavy wake as it steamed along in the same direction as they were headed. Beirut: downhill from everything.

"The Israeli flag on that ship out there has two blue stripes in it."

"Well, shit . . . good for you. Okay, but you still owe me a dollar. Your turn." Dix slipped a stick of Juicy Fruit gum into his mouth and dropped the wrapper onto the floor.

"Yellow," Geoff said, immediately.

"No, you have to play the game right. You have to start it the way it's supposed to be started. I spy. . . ," Dix scolded him.

"Jesus, all right. I spy with my little eye something that is yellow."

"Yellow, huh?" Dix twisted all over the place in a hunt for something that color. "The sun."

"No and now we're even. Guess again," Geoff challenged him.

"I don't see anything else that's yellow."

"There is."

"The whites of my jaundiced eyes?"

Geoff shook his head. Dix turned and peered at him.

"The whites of your jaundiced eyes?"

"There, that's three guesses and two dollars for me."

"Wait a second," Dix protested. "Where is the yellow?"

"Look at the gum wrapper on the floor beside your feet."

"Oh, you sly SOB, you. I spy with my little eye something that is gray."

"Gray? What isn't gray in this mess? Sidon is gray."

"Does that mean you give up?"

"Yeah, I give up, and I quit too. It was at this point in our road trips that my dad always stopped for burgers. Where are the golden arches in Sidon, Thomas?"

"Hush up, you're making me drool." But Dix sounded tired of his own manufactured cheer. "Turn here," he muttered to Amos, directing him away from the seafront and east towards a series of bare, shimmering hills.

"You ever been married, Thomas?" Geoff asked after a bit.

"No. You?"

"Once, for a few months. They were the worse years of my life."

Dix snorted at the joke, and then they both stopped to listen to the sound outside. It was the time of afternoon prayers, and from the city's mosques–most of them left untouched by the Israelis–the taped muezzin were beckoning the faithful in their peculiarly melodic whine. *Allah 'u akbar:* God is great. Bits and pieces of Nadya's attempts to teach him her language continued to find their way to Geoff's tongue.

"I guess there isn't much to say about them. Women, I mean," Dix said when the subject did not get picked up again after the muezzin had faded out.

"Not much, no."

They came upon an old woman on the side of the road. She was dressed in the widow's white of Islam and was struggling to heft an enormous cloth sack onto one shoulder. Insisting that Amos stop the car, Dix jumped out. He spoke and gestured with the woman, watched her shake her head hard at everything he said, then ignored her protests and helped her place the sack on her shoulder. When he returned to the car, he was upset about her refusal to accept a ride from them.

"I wonder, Geoffrey," he said, staring back at her as they pulled away.

"You wonder what?"

"Do you think women would ever do this?" He waved at the destruction all around them. "Maggie Thatcher excepted."

"No," Geoff answered straight away. "Women would never do this. Maggie Thatcher and my ex-wife excepted."

Dix nodded. "I find it important to cling to that," he confessed.

"All of which goes to the defense of your earlier point, I guess."

"Which point was that again?" Dix asked. "I mean I make so many that I sometimes forget."

"The point about there not being much to say about them."

"Yeah." Dix smiled. "This is it, turn here," he told Amos.

This last turn put them on a short stretch of road that had been meticulously bulldozed clear of rubble. IDF vehicles were neatly parked along both shoulders, and Israeli soldiers wandered about helmetless and at ease, their heavy assault rifles held more like tennis rackets than weapons. Looking to the end of the road, which was marked by barricades, Geoff could see bulldozers jerking back and forth across a vast, flat pan of ground. It looked like the beginning of some major construction project.

"What are they building?"

"How about a collective memory," Dix replied.

"Sorry I asked." Geoff was getting more than a little tired of the man's rhetorical riddles.

"They're not building anything, they're getting rid of something. This place is called Ein Hilwie. It was the largest Palestinian camp in Lebanon outside of Beirut. Thirty-five thousand refugees–all gone."

"Gone where?"

"North, mostly. North with a memory. For all their firepower, it took the IDF six full days to take this camp. I think it left a sour taste in their mouths, hence the bulldozers."

"Why are we here?" Geoff asked.

"I want to say a quick hello to a friend of mine," Dix said. "Park over there," he directed Amos, pointing to an opening along the shoulder.

The friend had seen their arrival, because as soon as Dix pulled himself out of the car and unfolded his large frame, he was caught in the happy hug of a very unsoldierly Israeli officer. Thick through the middle, with Popeye forearms and a balding head of gray curls, he looked more like a pastry chef, in fact. He was almost a full foot shorter than Dix too, which made their embrace look comic.

"They have let you into their tea party again, have they?" the Israeli laughed, slapping Dix on the shoulder as he released him. Though he had long ago discovered how poor he was with accents, Geoff thought he was probably right this time in guessing the man to be originally from somewhere in the Eastern Bloc, likely the Soviet Union.

"Yes, but it was made plenty clear that they aren't happy with me back in Jerusalem." Dix made no effort to hide how much this fact pleased him. He cocked his head at Amos and Geoff.

"Yuri, this is Amos, my pics shooter for today." The two Israelis exchanged a couple of pleasantries in Hebrew.

"And this is a new friend of mine, a colleague from Canada. Geoff Andrews, Lieutenant Yuri Gavron."

"A pleasure," Gavron smiled, surprising Geoff with the strength of his handshake. "Please, join me for some refreshment." Stepping between his visitors, he led them down through the dry ditch beside the road and up towards one of several carelessly pitched tents.

"Beer?" Gavron asked, making straight for an ice chest at the back of the tent. Other than it, a small table and a pair of military cots, the tent was bare.

"Perfect," Dix answered for them all.

Shifting from foot to foot, Geoff listened to the lieutenant fishing for cold glass in his cooler. He emerged with four dripping bottles and used the edge of the table to bang the caps off each before passing them around. Settling down on one of the cots, he invited Dix to sit beside him. Geoff claimed a seat on the other cot, while Amos sank to a cross-legged squat on the ground and downed half his beer in one long swallow.

"So, what's new, Yuri?" Dix asked, rapping his bottle against the soldier's. "I must say you seem some happier than the last time I saw you."

"That is because they are finally sending me back, Thomas. You have helped me get out of here."

"Well, that is good news. Congratulations." Dix bumped his drink against Gavron's once again, then looked at Geoff, who was studying the label on his bottle and soundlessly mouthing the brand name.

"Maccabee Lager," Dix said. "Not bad, huh?"

"Sounds like a Scottish brew," Geoff said.

"Scottish?" Dix and the two Israelis laughed like it was about the funniest thing they'd heard all day.

Dix explained. "The Maccabees were a family of Jewish zealots who led a revolt against the Syrians and took control of Palestine for a hundred years or so before the Romans showed up."

"I knew that," Geoff said, laughing at himself.

"Actually, this stuff really makes me hoot," Dix said. "I grew up thinking of national heroes in terms of postage stamps, paper money, baseball cards. To me, this is a little like us having Abe Lincoln bourbon."

"Or Louis St. Laurent rye."

"Who?" Dix said.

Geoff smirked and took another swallow of beer.

Dix turned back to Gavron. "Did they put you on report for taking me inside?"

"Yes, but they know I do not care. I am certain, in fact, that is why they are sending me home. Get this soft-hearted fool out of our road."

"That's right, they're scared. Soft-hearted fools like you are really screwing up Ariel Sharon's precious war. Did you hear? Last week, Peace Now drew a hundred thousand to a demonstration in Tel Aviv. They even called for Sharon's resignation."

"Sharon does not care what the people think. I doubt that bull can be stopped with anything less than a bazooka shot to the heart," Gavron said.

"You think the general even has a heart?" Dix scoffed.

"If he does, it is only a device for the pumping of blood through his fat body." The lieutenant smiled at Geoff.

"As a journalist, perhaps your friend would also like to see the remains of Ein Hilwie?"

"No, Yuri, it's not worth it. You don't want to risk a court martial, do you?"

But Gavron was inspired. "Thomas, if a hundred thousand Israelis can march against this war in Tel Aviv, this Israeli can risk a court martial. You know me, I would be happy for the opportunity to speak out in court."

Dix sighed hard and threw up his hands.

"Why not, it'll probably do him good," he said and stood up. "The more material we have to work with the better." He took a close look at Geoff. "Besides, my friend here doesn't notice things until he sees them lying at his feet in the rubble. Isn't that so?"

"I thank you very much for reminding me of that," Geoff said miserably.

"But perhaps *you* should not come this time, Thomas," the lieutenant said as they were leaving the tent. "They cannot hurt me, but they could cause big problems for you."

Geoff nodded in agreement. Dix had explained to him that the camp was off-limits to foreign correspondents and that it had been an unauthorized visit like this one a week earlier that had gotten him into trouble, thus explaining the behavior of Captain Levy at the border.

"Hell, it doesn't matter. I've already got big problems. We ditched the escort they insisted on giving us back in Tyre."

"No, you did not?"

Dix nodded, and Gavron burst into doughy laughter.

"You are marvelous, Thomas. Very stupid, but marvelous."

If the sentry posted to the barricades at the end of the road wondered who these three civilians were strolling past him into the camp, he did not let on. Saluting Lieutenant Gavron, who merely waved back, he hardly gave them a second look before turning his attention up the road once more.

"He is another likely recruit for the Peace Now forces," Gavron told them. "And there are others here also. Perhaps we could organize a mutiny?" He chuckled.

"I want an exclusive if you do," Dix said.

"What about your friend here?"

"Fuck him. Let him find his own sources for stories," Dix said, winking at Geoff.

Scooting between two loud, smoking bulldozers, which cruised like marauding sharks in search of new things to seize hold of and tear apart, the four men walked until they were at the center of Ein Hilwie. Here the dozers had much left to do, though they had clearly done plenty already. Mounds of masonry and concrete piled fifteen to twenty feet high loomed overhead, periodically sending tiny avalanches shivering across the narrow footpath they were navigating. Poking out from the banks of these mounds and growing more prominent with each new avalanche were the ends of steel reinforcing bars, pieces of wood and furniture and strips of cloth and clothing that took Geoff back yet again to the rooftop in Tyre. But he felt certain he would not see anything like it here. The sharks would have found and quickly done away with anything fleshy.

"Here," Gavron said, leading them off the footpath now and up one of the more climbable mounds. Standing on top, they squinted through the dust they had whipped up and looked across the core of the camp. It was roughly half a square mile in area, Geoff calculated with a realtor's eye, and it was all just like this: ridges and hummocks of nothing; a moonscape of man-made destruction. Just as in Tyre, Geoff spotted sea gulls again, looking for food, and he thought he could have heard them cry if not for the bulldozers.

"Lovely," Dix mumbled.

"Ein Hilwie. It means beautiful view in Arabic," Gavron noted.

Geoff laughed.

"What do you make the death toll now, Yuri?" Dix asked.

"Six hundred here, perhaps more. We still find a few bodies every day."

"Add that to a thousand or so in Sidon itself. A nice piece of work, Herr General."

Geoff looked over at apolitical Amos, firing shot after shot with his Nikon. He lowered the camera for a moment, and Geoff saw him reach up and smudge away a tear from his cheek.

A sharp bark in Hebrew spun all four men around in the same instant. Glaring up at them from the footpath, his hands square on his hips, was an officer of obviously higher rank than Gavron. Behind him stood the embarrassed IDF sergeant they had left in Tyre.

"Oops," was all Dix said.

They were marched out of the camp and across the road to a different pitching of drab tents beyond the barricades, and then into the most official-looking of these tents.

"I'm sorry, but we may have messed you up good here," Dix muttered, ducking through the canvas flaps ahead of Geoff.

The drill that followed was obviously a familiar one because the sharp words took wing as soon as the commanding officer strode into the tent after them. It sounded like, and probably was, an old fight renewed. Pacing back and forth through his swelling lather, the major shouted at Gavron in Hebrew, but saved all of his hateful glare for Dix. Dix, who apparently understood most of what was being said, laughed out loud once or twice but otherwise bit his sarcastic tongue. Evidently, this was serious.

And then it was over. The major, who had stopped most of his yelling a few moments earlier, suddenly ended discussion altogether with a calm declaration. He called for someone outside the tent, and a pair of MPs immediately stepped inside.

Gavron shook his head. Dix turned away and kicked a metal folding chair halfway across the tent. "Fuck off and die," he said, peering around as if in search of another chair to kick.

"Tell me what's going on," Geoff demanded, clutching at Dix's elbow.

"There's nothing to tell. We're out of here. Back to Jerusalem with our asses tied to a rail. He's kicking us out of Lebanon."

"No way—he can't do that," Geoff cried.

"Well he's doing it," Dix said with a sudden sharp tilt towards resignation.

"But I have to, absolutely *have to* go on to Beirut."

"Why?" Dix snapped. "Don't you think it's time to tell me why?"

Geoff said nothing. To get into it here and now would be to risk an even larger problem, namely that the major might well understand enough English to sniff out their little ruse. He frowned and hoped his meaning was clear: give me a break.

Dix scowled. "Go wait outside," he said.

Twenty minutes later he emerged from the tent: twenty minutes that had begun with more of the major's shouting but ended with Gavron's quiet, placating voice.

"You're an unlucky man today," Dix said, steering Geoff away from the tent.

"What?"

"Yuri's persuaded the major to give you a break. First offense, good public relations and all that crap. The guy should be a lawyer."

"That's great," Geoff said numbly.

"Not that great. You're all alone from here on, bucko. Amos and I are headed back to Ras Naquoura under escort."

Geoff must have looked like a whipped pup.

"No, you won't have to walk there. They'll find you a ride the rest of the way with one of their local collaborators. Whatever you do, though, keep your smart mouth shut. If clowns like that'll sell out their own for money, they'll happily hang you out to dry quicker than spit. By the way, whoever it is they line up will probably try to charge you a couple of hundred dollars."

"I'll pay it," Geoff said. "Thomas, I owe you."

"You sure do," Dix agreed. "Do you know where you're going to stay?"

Geoff shook his head.

"Oh, man," Dix groaned. "Come back with me. Go to Cyprus and find a boat. I don't want to be responsible for this."

"You're not. I'm a big boy."

"Yeah, and *boy* feels like the operative word at the moment. All right, listen. Go to the Hotel St. Michel. I haven't been there in several years, but I remember it being comfortable, and it's far enough into East Beirut to be relatively safe."

Gavron and the major had emerged from the tent with Amos. The MPs were waiting. Geoff thrust out his hand to Dix.

"Some day, Geoffrey, you'll have to look me up and tell me your reasons," Dix said. "I'm a journalist—it's damn near killed me not to know."

"I will, but there's really not much to say about them," Geoff said, wondering if Dix would remember and make the connection.

"Yeah." The American nodded. "Yeah, somehow I thought as much too."

EIGHT

WITH ITS LEADED WINDOWS AND HEAVY RED VELVET DRAPES, its oak panel walls and softly creaking floor boards, the worn leather couches and the crystal chandelier in its lobby, the Hotel St. Michel offered to save Geoff ever having to visit Europe. The only concessions he could see to its geography were the various signs in Arabic–in addition to English and French–around the registration desk, and a sallow old man with a carmine fez and a magnificent gray slash of waxed mustache, seated stiffly on one of the couches, his lips around the bit of a gently bubbling waterpipe and his bony hands folded over the quartz knob of an elegant black walking stick. He stared impassively at Geoff, or perhaps he stared right through him.

The St. Michel's concessions to war were less understated. Outside the leaded windows, sandbags stacked fifteen high blocked sun, moon, streetlight and, with luck, shrapnel and shell concussion. The polished tables in the lobby all had fresh candles ready for lighting in the event of a sudden blackout, and there was a notice tacked over the archway to the small dining room. Its English version said:

In a most unhappy case of bad bombing close, please to proceed to the basement as fast as is comfortably so. Thanking you so much–

The Management

105

The management, like its notice, tripped all over itself trying to be polite while concerned. As soon as Geoff's suitcase was dropped on the sidewalk outside the hotel by the driver the Israelis had reluctantly provided for him—at a cost to him of $175—he and it both had been rather clumsily whisked inside by a pair of young houseboys.

"It is better not to be outside when one has a place to go inside these present days," said the nervously grinning, heavily perspiring desk manager as he took Geoff's passport and slid him the ledger in exchange. Geoff saw that the ledger, and hence the hotel, was mostly empty.

"I guess this means I'm staying," Geoff said. In truth, he was exhausted in most of the ways it was possible to be exhausted and did not mind being swept up like this and tucked into bed.

"My dear friend, you must stay," the desk manager said, pressing down the ends of his trim black mustache. "Today it was quiet, so tonight and tomorrow it will be bad."

"What will?" Geoff watched his suitcase disappearing with one of the houseboys into a cage elevator on the far side of the lobby.

"The *bom-bing*. One day the Israelis they bomb much, the next day little, then much, then little. They are clever," the desk manager chuckled.

"Clever? They're pounding your city into the ground."

"No, no," the manager said, shaking his index finger. "They are bom-bing the west, not the east."

"But the sign over your dining room," Geoff said, pointing.

"The Palestinians. They bomb the east because the Israelis are here."

This Geoff knew to be true. He had started to see the first IDF tanks and artillery pieces when his twisting route up from Ein Hilwie at length brought him into the villa-dotted eastern hills overlooking Beirut. The sun pitching into the sea along the horizon had splashed pink back into the dusk behind the highrise skyline on the western side of the city, and it reminded him, in an uncanny way, of Vancouver looking out towards the island. Even the Israeli collaborator, a Shiite from southern Lebanon, had been affected by the view.

"How late do you serve dinner?" Geoff was aware he had not eaten since breakfast.

"We are at your service," the desk manager smiled, cocking his head.

"Good. I'm just going to wash up, then I'll be right down."

"The boy has your key. You are in room 22. It is on the safe side of the hotel."

"Facing east," Geoff said.

"Yes, facing east," the desk manager nodded. "Away from that most horrible place."

The houseboy was still in the room, playing at a little final tidying. Geoff tipped him with his last one-dollar bill, locked the door after him, then dropped his clothes on the floor and climbed into the shower. There was good pressure and plenty of hot water, and he nearly fell asleep letting it pelt his shoulders and back. He rubbed and rinsed through two shampoos before the brillo pad on top of his head was cleaned of the day's dust.

After his shower, he stood in front of a small clearing in the steamed mirror over the vanity and shaved. The popcorn pop of small-arms fire a long way off brought him over to the open bathroom window. He toweled off and listened, pleased in a certain way that the firing of guns hadn't frightened him. His father, after all, had lived through the blitz of London. This was nothing, though his father of course would also be the first to tell him that.

"Are you *refleshed* now?" the desk manager asked when Geoff returned to the lobby.

He smiled at the unhappy memory of Nadya's periodic destruction of words, and his own inability to keep his mouth shut about it.

"Yes, thank you, I am."

Alone in the restaurant, he had the full attention of the cook and waiter while he ate. Twice the cook pushed the waiter over to see if he was satisfied with his pepper steak. He was, and if the waiter had only spoken more English he would have asked him how such meat was available here now. He drank most of a Beaujolais with his meal and afterwards, unordered, cognac and a Cuban cigar were brought with his coffee. When he tried to explain that he had not asked for them, the waiter just stared and smiled uncomprehendingly.

He was walking back across the lobby to the elevator afterwards when the aroma of cigar smoke made him stop and turn around. Smiling at him from the same leather couch where the old man with the fez still sat pillar-stiff and sucking on his waterpipe was a powerful-looking younger man with straight white teeth and carefully combed black hair. Strangely, the feature that had led Geoff to see him straightaway as powerful was not his size–though he had a broad chest and could be seen as quite tall even while seated–but the fact that he was an Arab without a beard or mustache. In a part of the world where the cosmetic accoutrements of maleness were worn like campaign medals, it was rare to find a man who chose not to sport facial hair of some kind. Geoff could tell that in this man's case it was something intended to draw the attention of men and women both: a challenge.

"Thank you for the brandy and the cigar," Geoff said, setting his tiredness aside to walk over and say hello.

In a gesture of utmost courtesy, the man placed his cigar in an ashtray and got to his feet immediately. He extended his hand and smiled warmly.

"You are most welcome," he said in English that was more accented by French than Arabic, Geoff thought.

"I'm not much of a smoker, and I don't want to see a good Cuban go to waste," Geoff explained, trying to return the foil-wrapped cigar. But the Arab would have no part of it.

"Please, keep it," he insisted. "Anyway, you are in a very funny place now, this Beirut of ours, and you may soon enough wish to begin smoking."

Geoff smiled at the dark joke.

"Please, sit down, join us."

"Okay, thank you, I will for a moment."

"You are sleepy? Then, please, do not let us keep you up."

"No, no, it's all right. I'd like to sit for a while." He sat.

"Good."

"Good," the old man echoed the younger. He had turned away from his waterpipe to grin at Geoff, who could suddenly tell these two were blood-related.

"My name is Camille Haddad, and this is my father, Pierre."

"Geoff Andrews," he said, reaching past the son to shake hands with the father.

"Yes, we know. And you are from Canada," Camille said.

"How do you know that?" Geoff asked, feeling afraid.

"The guest book. I looked."

Tight-lipped, Geoff nodded. Camille laughed.

"Do not be offended. I did not go spying. We own the hotel."

"Oh—well, you have a very nice place."

"Thank you," Camille said. "It is a hobby now more than a business. No guests." He shrugged and laughed again.

The father asked the son something in Arabic.

"My father is curious why someone from Canada comes to Beirut now."

"I work for a newspaper," Geoff stumbled, afraid that Camille's gray eyes would see the lie.

"A reporter. Ah, then you are needed here," Camille said, turning to his father to translate Geoff's reply. The old man puffed out his bottom lip and nodded.

"That's quite a mustache your father has. Does he have to spend a lot of time taking care of it?" To Geoff, it could not have mattered less; he only hoped to change the subject.

"My father is an old Lebanese man," Camille answered with rough affection. "Old Lebanese men have nothing but time to do as they please."

Geoff gestured at his own clean-shaven upper lip for Camille's father. The old man laughed and twisted a handlebar of his mustache.

"Will you be in Beirut long?" Camille asked.

"I don't know. My employer doesn't tell me much of anything in advance," Geoff said.

"This is the nature of bosses," Camille commiserated.

"Yes," Geoff said. "You're right, it is." He slapped his knees lightly, body English, and was just about to stand and say goodnight when one of the houseboys appeared, carrying a tray of tea. If he hadn't learned anything else from Nadya, he knew about the offense that could be taken at the rejection of an Arab's hospitality. He accepted a small glass of clear tea when it was offered to him.

"Thank you, again," he said.

"It is nothing," Camille replied. He fingered some sugar off the rim of his own glass and blew across the hot tea. Geoff watched him, then chose to direct the conversation himself before any casual interrogation could continue.

"Your man at the registration desk said the fighting would be heavy tonight."

"My baby brother, Samir. He worries and sweats too much."

"Does that mean it won't be?"

Camille's smile was the spreading crack in a sheet of ice.

"They will fight, but then this is why you are here, is it not?"

"I suppose it is," Geoff had to say.

"Anyway, it will not be nearly so bad here as in the west of Beirut. The Palestinians and Mourabitoun do not have what the Israelis have to fight with."

An important question occurred to Geoff, a question that a journalist could also ask. "Is it still possible to get around in the city these days?"

"For a reporter, yes. Provided he is prepared for certain risks and has the money to pay for a good driver. I am surprised your bosses did not arrange a driver for you. A foreigner alone in Beirut–it is not a good thing."

"Yes, I'm a little surprised as well." Geoff hurried over it. "You know something, your English is superb. Did you learn it here?"

Camilla laughed. "Here–impossible. I was a student in Paris, and I went often to England."

"So you speak French too?"

"*Certainement.*"

The coals had fallen off the densely packed clot of tobacco in the old man's waterpipe, and he was having difficulty replacing them with a pair of metal tongs. When Camille turned to help, Geoff took advantage of the interruption to swallow what was left of his tea and get to his feet.

"You are leaving?" Camille asked. He was holding a glowing coal in the tongs, and looked about to drop it.

"No, no, don't get up. I'm just heading off to bed."

Camille ignored him and stood up anyway, dropping the hot coal in the pipe tray. They shook hands, then Geoff leaned over to do the same with the father. The old man twisted a handle of his mustache again and guffawed.

"I would like you to come to my house for dinner tomorrow evening."

"That's a nice offer but not necessary, Camille."

"I insist. You are a guest in my family's hotel, and you are here by yourself."

"I might be working," he said, thinking fast.

"But you still must eat, so tomorrow you will eat with us. My wife is an exceptionally good cook."

Geoff looked at Camille's hard, handsome face—at the gray eyes, the heavy blue shadow of his cheeks—and could do nothing but nod consent.

"Excellent. I will fetch you here at half-past six."

"Fine." Geoff managed another smile and started to move away. "If you'll excuse me now."

He was standing in the elevator, had just pulled closed the manual door, when Camille got up from the couch and strode across the floor towards him. Geoff pressed the stop button and peered out from the polished brass cage.

"Have you any sleeping pills?" Camille asked.

"Sorry, no."

"Would you like some?"

"I never take them."

"The noise when there is fighting—it can be rude."

Geoff shook his head and released the stop button. With a shudder of oiled cable, the elevator started up. "I'll be fine," he called down.

Camille merely smiled back.

*   *   *

The fighting began an hour later, and when it came it jarred him from nothing except his own battleground of thoughts. The initial flush he'd felt at arriving here had been overrun by hard facts as he now realized both that this lunatic search had only started, and worse, that it could end in several different shades of failure. Lying naked on his back on his still-made bed, he opened his eyes and listened in darkness to the first Israeli artillery shells thundering over the rooftops of East Beirut and then to their havoc-landing somewhere in the west. As the IDF assault gained momentum (if momentum was the right word for it), changing like rainfall from patter to pour, he counted their steel howling over and smashing down at a rate of close to thirty shells a minute.

When the Palestinians at last answered back, it was as if the thunder had been moved not inside his room but right in through the bone walls of his skull. A pair of small oil paintings dropped from their hooks to the floor, as did the large wooden crucifix above the door. It bounced, then skidded beneath his bed. After another too-close explosion, he joined it there, feeling a bit foolish but safer. Soon, the acrid smells of detonation slipped under the bed as well: acetone, something else quite ammonious, and something else again with the greasy odor of petroleum jelly. Though he had never smelled the substance before, something told him this unpleasant cake mix was cordite. Had she been there under the bed with him, Nadya the biochemist would no doubt have informed him for sure.

The dueling went on for the rest of the night: the Israelis, with superior weapons and numbers of weapons, would lay it on thick for long minutes at a stretch; the PLO gunners would fire back when they could, providing the punctuation points at the end of strung-out sentences and paragraphs. But if the Palestinians could only muster punctuation, they were angry exclamation marks that were enough to keep Geoff under the bed. He emerged just long enough to grab his pillows and drag them beneath to soften the floor. He did not sleep.

Shortly before seven that following morning, the shelling eased and then ended after the Palestinians had lobbed out a final volley. Almost immediately, the sounds of morning traffic drifted up from the streets around the hotel. Geoff heard the rich resonance of a Mercedes-Benz car horn and then the shouts of children. Pulling himself out from beneath the bed, he got up stiffly and walked to the bathroom window. Feeling sore and gummy-eyed, he poked his head outside and saw some of the life responsible for this wonderfully banal noise. He could not spot any damage from the Palestinian guns.

A few moments later came a rap on his door. He pulled on his pants and opened it to find one of the houseboys standing with croissants and a steaming pot of coffee. Geoff beckoned him in, then hurried over to make some room for the breakfast tray on the vanity. While scrabbling around for a tip, he remembered that he had given away his last small bill the previous evening. Apologizing with gestures, he tried to explain that he'd catch up when he had change, and the youth seemed to understand. He nodded at Geoff and turned to leave, but stopped when he saw that the bed had not been slept in. Then he noticed one of the pillows sticking out from underneath. He glanced back at Geoff once more, smirked, and left the room.

"You have been scared by the bom-bing." The desk manager appeared to be a little less jangle-nerved himself with the knowledge that Geoff had passed a bad night. He smiled plastic sympathy and smoothed the ends of his mustache as he waited for Geoff to sign a couple of traveler's cheques at the registration desk.

"Better safe than sorry," Geoff said defensively. "Some of that *bom-bing* came awful close." He pushed the cheques at Samir Haddad and scowled past him at the houseboy, now slouched on a chair and puffing a cigaret in the small office behind the desk.

"Not so very, I think." Samir grinned, counting out the Lebanese lira for Geoff. "They bom-bed Rue Sassine, in Ashrafiya. Two hundred and fifty metres away, maybe more."

"Yeah, well it was close enough to shake the bloody walls. All the pictures fell down."

"No problem, my dear friend. They fall down every night. If you become scared again, I will have one of the boys take you down to the basement."

Geoff let the remark pass and took his money after Samir had counted it a second time. Slapping down his key, he went out into the street, feeling miserable and overwhelmed. What he needed right now was to be starting this behind a full night's sleep, not with a head full of wool; what he needed was a plan, something

that said X marked the spot; what he needed was somebody to
take him by the hand, much as Thomas Dix had, and lead him
through the first turns of this maze. As it stood, he was an
Occidental rat facing an Oriental puzzle.

With his hands jammed in his pockets, he walked around the
block hoping for a *deus ex machina*. Dozens of pairs of curious dark
eyes tracked him in succession. The most ardent watchers,
naturally, were children, and when he began a second, agitated
circuit of the same block a small platoon of them followed at a safe
distance. Finally, the boldest of the bold, two boys about ten years
old, approached until they were just off his heels. They chattered
at each other in Arabic a while, then one of them addressed
Geoff.

"*Parlez-vous français?*"

Geoff ignored him.

"Speak English?" the other tried.

"Yes," Geoff answered, knowing that once they had come this
close they would not just quit and go away. He stopped and
turned to them, and immediately the rest of the kids ran up to
gather round him. With hardly an exception, they were darkly
gorgeous–all thick-haired, silk-skinned and saucer-eyed. Some of
them had bad teeth, but it stopped none of them from smiling up
at him. Where, he wondered, had *they* spent the night before?

"American?" the first bold boy asked.

Geoff shook his head.

"England?" said a dimple-cheeked girl.

Geoff shook his head again. "Canada," he told them.

The children looked about at each other for help, a few of them
even shrugged like old men, and this made Geoff smile a little
through his gloom.

"America," he said, holding his right hand up and horizontal.
"Canada," he continued, placing his left hand above the
right.

There was a murmur of understanding, but before another
geography question could be asked of him a harsh male voice
scattered the children. Geoff watched them go, then turned
around as casually as he could–it wasn't easy.

The voice belonged to a youth who could not have been any
more than seventeen or eighteen. He was dressed in faded

fatigues, wore the requisite heavy black boots and carried his automatic rifle as if he knew how to use it. But at the same time, he owned a face that was still patchy with beard and acne, and there was more colt than studhorse in his swagger as he moved down the sidewalk towards Geoff.

"*Shalom*," softly and conspiratorially mouthed, was all he said to Geoff as he passed. Geoff stared at a pistol jutting out loose from the back of his pants, thought about the crucifix he'd seen hanging from a silver chain around his neck, about the crucifix in his own room at the hotel, and suddenly understood that Dix–though it was his own fault, not Dix's–had put him in front of the wrong entrance to the maze. He would not find Nadya in East Beirut.

*   *   *

Camille Haddad's red-haired wife, Genevieve, was a Parisian, and when she looked at Geoff–who had never been to Paris–he knew all there was to know about the legendary aloofness of that city. That she was pouty-lipped and moved her body as if it had extra joints made it worse. He had always had trouble accepting the disdain of a beautiful woman. She was, as promised, an exceptional cook, and she even smiled a little once when Geoff went on about the sherry sauce in her Coquilles St. Jacques. But that was all.

One byproduct of the wife's chill was that it made the husband that much more appealing by contrast. From the moment he'd arrived at the hotel at six-thirty to fetch Geoff–who had spent most of the day sleeping after his short but telling walk around the neighbourhood–Camille was an attentive and charming host, and he had not picked up the thread of the previous day's interrogation. Driving east out of the city, towards his villa in the same moneyed hills that Geoff and the collaborator had come through the evening before, he had pointed out historic landmarks, poorly-camouflaged IDF positions, and areas of PLO shell damage with equal measures of authority and good humor. He told jokes about the Palestinians, made fun of the Israelis, but saved the real ridicule for his fellow Lebanese, the central government of President Elias Sarkis in particular. When

Geoff, slipping carefully into journalist's garb, asked for *his* prescribed remedy for the woes of Lebanon, he'd only smiled and insisted it would take his wife's good food and many drinks before he could possibly tackle that one. But we will get there, he had laughed, treading on the gas pedal as if for emphasis, we will certainly get there. The effect of all this on Geoff was reassurance: his experience with Dix had made cynicism a place of relative comfort.

When dinner was over, and Genevieve made a restless move to begin clearing the table, Camille picked up a decanter of cognac and two snifters and suggested a tour of the house. Without bothering to wait for Geoff's answer he got up from the table, smiled at his wife and headed out of the dining room. Geoff dropped his napkin on the table and stood.

"*Merci,*" he said, his ego unable to resist a final try at Genevieve's glacial countenance. She looked up from her stacking of plates as he passed, looked up like the Seine, Notre Dame, the Louvre and all the rest he'd never seen, but she still had nothing to say to him. Now it baffled him beyond mere vanity. If she were an Arab woman, he might not like it but he could at least understand it as a result of acculturation. But Genevieve was a European, and he'd seen enough to know there was nothing demure about her.

"Lovely, no? And look at the way the cognac illuminates the edges and corners of the pattern."

Camille was waiting in the hallway, admiring the cut of the crystal in his decanter. He thrust it even higher, into better light, so Geoff could see it too.

"My kind of sunshine," Geoff said.

"Mine as well," Camille smiled. He lowered the decanter and bobbed his head down the hallway. "Shall we?"

Sprawled over three floors, the Haddad villa was at least three thousand square feet in area, Geoff estimated, stuck like Velcro to his only real skill in life, and with the exception of the doors and the dark, rich French Provincial furnishings, almost entirely devoid of wood. The building material of choice here and all around the Mediterranean, from Portugal east, Camille explained, was quarry stone. Cut into blocks and set by masons, it was cool in the summer and cheaper and much more plentiful than lumber. What's more, Camille added, only half-joking, it refused to go up in flames when you hit it with a rocket. Very frustrating for the rocket, he laughed.

"I see a lot of rooms here, but they're empty. You don't have children?"

"We can't have children—I can't have children," Camille said candidly.

"Sorry."

"*Ma' laish*," Camille said, speaking what seemed like the first Arabic Geoff had heard from him. "Never mind."

"There are other ways, of course," Geoff said, trying to be sympathetic.

"Yes." Camille nodded. "But this is Lebanon, and in Lebanon there is only the one way."

They had reached the top floor of the villa, and here Camille was especially eager to show off his library study to a visiting journalist. Smiling, he pushed open a set of double doors and invited Geoff inside.

The room was long but fairly narrow and felt narrower still because of the floor-to-ceiling bookshelves along its walls. The shelves were three-quarters filled with hardcover volumes, many of them leather-bound and looking quite old. Expensive Oriental carpets covered the marble floors, and down at the far end of the room sat a leather couch and two leather armchairs like those in the hotel lobby. Leather was the dominant smell in the room, but close behind it the only slightly paler aromas of stale cigar and aging paper. Geoff had a vague gone-to-seed feeling about the place that made him suspect that Genevieve Haddad rarely ventured in, even just to tidy: it was almost oppressively male.

"Go ahead, look at the books if you wish," Camille said. "Not many in English, I am afraid, but there are some." Leaving Geoff to browse, he walked down to the end of the room, set his snifters and cognac on a table, and dropped into one of the armchairs with a contented sigh.

Most of the books were in French and Arabic, but scattered here and there were a few in English, some classics, some popular novels. Haddad was an eclectic reader.

"Do you see anything you would like to borrow?" Camille asked when Geoff at last came to join him.

"Thank you, I'll think about it."

"Take anything," Camille said, pouring cognac. Picking up one of the snifters for himself, he handed the other to Geoff, then offered his glass in a toast. "To Lebanon."

"Cheers," Geoff replied, and sipped.

"So, you asked me earlier for my views on this country."

Geoff forced himself to sit still and think; it was show time. He took a deep breath and thought: break a leg. "Uh, if you don't think much of the present government, have you got any alternative in mind?"

Camille nodded once. "I believe there is a man in my country who can do the things that are necessary, yes," he said.

"Who is that?"

"He is Bashir Gemayel. You have heard of him, I trust."

"Oh yes, some. But as I told you, I've only been posted here in the Middle East a short while."

"Bashir is, of course, the son of Pierre Gemayel, founder of our Kataeb, or as you in the Western papers call us, the Phalangist Party. He is the military commander of the Lebanese Forces here in Beirut, but next month, after the elections, he will be our president." Camille looked closely at Geoff and laughed softly.

"When Bashir becomes president, there will be something interesting in it for me," he said.

"Oh?"

"We are friends, good friends, he and I. We were boys playing together." Camille's eyes widened with a thought. "I can arrange an interview with him for you."

"That'd be great. Let me check my schedule and I'll let you know as soon as I'm free."

Camille was suddenly restless. "I have one more place to show you," he said, jumping to his feet. He picked up his cognac and waited for Geoff. "Bring your glass—we will drink some more."

Geoff pushed himself up out of the soft chair and, glass in hand, followed Camille once more. In passing, he glanced at the small area of shelfless wall directly behind his chair, and then he froze. The whole of his life suddenly filed into this narrow library as he moved straight to the wall.

"Quite a picture, no?" Camille smiled, coming to stand and look with him.

"Where did you get it?" Geoff said it with a voice more demanding than questioning.

"Bashir gave it to me. His father, you perhaps know, modeled our party after General Franco's Falange. He spent time in Spain during the 1930s and came to be a very great admirer of the general. This is a photograph from Franco's great war."

"Yes, I know."

It was during those next seconds, as he stared at that grainy enlargement of the Republican soldier, crumpled by a fascist bullet, stared at a picture that had once been so inexplicably, viscerally important to him, that something else Thomas Dix had said came into his head: We all pass the same scenic points eventually. We pass them over and over and over again.

Finally allowing himself to be coaxed away from the photograph on the wall, Geoff followed Camille onto a large, semicircular terrace off the third floor. Here, he realized immediately, was the ultimate measure of Haddad's wealth: from here you could look down on things. Railed off by linked miniature colonnades—a statement in themselves—the mosaic-tiled terrace was slung above several acres of manicured lawns and gardens. Geoff could smell damp soil, could hear water running hard; there was even a floodlit tennis court snugged into a small stand of Lebanon's famous fragrant cedars. This was not, Geoff thought, in correcting his earlier assessment of Haddad, the home of a cynic. No, life would have to be very black and white for one to possess all of this.

Excusing himself, Camille stepped over to some nearby switches and flipped off the floods in the tennis courts and gardens. It was as if someone else at that same instant had switched on the night. Why, Geoff wondered, reminded of his strange walk with Dix in Jerusalem, did the stars hang so low in the sky in this part of the world? Maybe it was true after all; maybe people here in the Middle East really were that much closer to whoever or whatever it was watching from up there.

"Here." Camille ushered him to the other side of the terrace. He took Geoff's snifter and set it down on the railing beside his own, then poured more cognac into both. Taking up his glass, he gestured with it at Beirut, spread out and glimmering below them. It was perfectly quiet tonight; another ceasefire had been called, fitting exactly the on-off pattern that sweaty Samir had described. Sign of the times: war on a four-day week.

"So, what do you think of my home?" Camillle asked, grinning because he knew what he'd hear.

"Magnificent is a word that comes to mind."

"I only wish we were a little closer to the city."

"Why, because you'd like to frustrate some rockets?"

Camille laughed. "No, because I would like to play."

"It looks to me like you could play pretty nicely at most things right here," Geoff said.

"Most, but not all things." Camille sipped his drink, then continued. "You see that big area over there?" He pointed to an expanse of open ground several hundred yards below the villa.

"Yes. It looks like somebody is waiting for the land values to go up so he can put in a housing project."

"A housing project?" Camille laughed. "You could say it has already been the site of a housing project."

"Oh?"

"There was once a Palestinian camp called Tal al-Zaatar on that land. It is gone now, which is sad in one respect. We used to have such good fun with that camp."

"Fun? How?"

"In many ways. For example, after a nice dinner like tonight's, we would bring our cognac and tobacco out onto the terrace and fire a few mortar rounds down into Tal al-Zaatar."

"*What?*" It was as if someone had just thrown a sheet over his head and spun him around in tight circles. He was losing his balance and becoming nauseated.

"We would watch them run, we would watch them bleed, and if we were very, very fortunate, we would watch them die."

"Is this a joke, Camille? If it is, you ought to know I'm not laughing."

"Funny, yes, but a joke, no." Haddad's smile had been permuted into a sneer of hatred. "Those evenings out here brought me much pleasure."

"To kill gives you pleasure?" In an attempt to stop himself

shaking, Geoff put his glass down and gripped the railing with both hands. Unable to stomach the sight of Camille just now, he turned and stared without seeing through the blackness at the city in the distance.

"Yes, to kill *them* gives me pleasure. They are disgusting in their camps, and they breed like animals. They must do nothing but fuck, for their children run everywhere like packs of filthy little dogs."

So that's it, Geoff shuddered: children.

"Good God, man, they're people just like you."

"No, there you are wrong–dead wrong, as our American friends are fond of saying. They are not at all like me."

Yes, quite right. Geoff changed his mind. They are not at all like you. "I think I'd like to go back inside now," he said.

NINE

IN THE TENSE AFTERWARDS OF THEIR EXCHANGE ON THE terrace, it had not been difficult to convince Haddad the evening was over. His hostly protests about it being too early were so transparently hollow that for a moment Geoff feared he might even have to find his own way back to the hotel. He need not have worried, for Haddad was trapped by the conventions of his upbringing: it was his duty, he had insisted with terribly forced niceness, to drive Geoff back. It was not his duty, however, to talk if he did not care to—and he clearly did not care to. The ride down from the hills was wordless, and the only thing Geoff said was a cold goodbye as he stepped from the car. The interview with Bashir Gemayel was not mentioned.

Samir Haddad, who appeared to have nothing else to do in life but stand behind the registration desk, welcomed Geoff back to the St. Michel and asked why his brother had not at least stopped off long enough to come in and say hello. Geoff pleaded ignorance. He took his key, but then he changed his mind about going straight up to his room. He had to know more, and he also had to work out both an exit and an entrance.

"It's late, but I wonder if I could still get tea?" he asked.

"No problem, my dear friend," Samir said, pinging his bell for a houseboy.

"Will you join me?" Geoff leaned across the desk, smiling.

"Me? Thank you."

As Geoff had correctly guessed he might be, the younger Haddad brother was flattered to have a foreign correspondent pitching him questions about the war, and he pondered then answered them all as if it was an interview.

Beirut. Samir, Geoff learned early in their chat, had studied biology in Paris while his big brother was out haunting Left Bank cafés with his political philosophy friends. Beirut, he said, was a city in mitosis, but it would not be a wholly successful division, for while one of the halves was vital the other was choking to death. When Geoff sought to probe what he thought was figurative rhetoric, Samir came straight to the guns and butter. The Israeli army and Phalangist militia had linked up here in the east to pinch West Beirut shut, and now they were squeezing it. Water, food, electricity–it was all selectively cut off. All the Lebanese trapped inside were free, of course, to come out, provided they were not members of the Mourabitoun or some other leftist group, but the Palestinians–children, women, old men, all of them–had to stay right there. Any who tried to flee into East Beirut were forced back at gunpoint. When Geoff casually inquired about the possibilities of going the other direction, of crossing into West Beirut, Samir screwed up his face to laugh. Why? he asked, sounding like someone ready for a good punch line.

The Palestinians. Of the Palestinians, Samir's hatred was neither as pathological nor as absolute as his brother's. It also reflected a good deal more actual political philosophy than Geoff had heard at Camille's. At first, Samir said, they were only a nuisance here in Lebanon, but as a nuisance they were tolerable, and for a time they even helped to fill a shortage of street labor in Beirut. It was only later, when their fanaticism about education made them clever, that they became dangerous. They began to speak ideas that did not belong in Lebanon, that the Muslim Lebanese especially did not need to hear. They became socialist and communist troublemakers, and they were threatening a system that had worked very well in Lebanon for a long time. For pests like this–he moved back to his study of biology–a strong pesticide was now called for.

The Israelis. When Geoff asked about the IDF, Samir took on the look of someone caught coming out of a brothel by his nextdoor neighbor. He smirked, but there was sheepishness, not arrogance, behind it. We use each other but do not like each other, and we certainly do not trust each other, he said. He shrugged at Geoff's suggestion that Israel was the original root of the problem, that its creation had made the Palestinians refugees. There are half a million Palestinians here in Lebanon, Samir told him tersely, not half a million Israelis; therefore, our problem is the Palestinians, not the Israelis.

Camille. Samir was surprised to have Geoff suddenly break away from the war to ask about his brother. Part of it, no doubt, was jealously, a reluctance to share Geoff's stage with someone whose shadow was larger than his own. Eventually, perhaps realizing he had a rare chance here to analyze and caricature, he opened up. Camille was a clever man–Samir was extremely fond of *clever* and brandished the word as if it were his invention–but not as clever as he often thought he was. He was both blessed and cursed by great passion in all things, but he was further cursed in a personal matter that Samir could not really speak of but which caused the entire family much sorrow. (Geoff did not let on that he knew about Camille's sterility.) Camille, Samir concluded cryptically, was successful and well connected to power in East Beirut, but he was not happy or fulfilled as a man.

Tell someone who cares, Geoff kept thinking as he listened. He was so choked with loathing right now he wished he could say it aloud, wished he could stand on the roof of the family hotel and yell the family secret until it echoed through those hills and found Camille sitting all alone under that horrible photograph in his stinking little library. He added to that picture the image of Camille and his wife perpetually looking for opposite corners of the house to be in.

When he decided he had all he wanted from Samir–including a crudely sketched route map to the Green Line demarcation separating the two Beiruts–he went up to his room and packed his suitcase. His impulse was to leave now, but he knew he could not attempt a crossing after dark, even if he really had the courage to do it. Slapping off the light, he crawled onto the bed fully clothed and was soon rolling back and forth trying to smother the burn of a furious insomnia.

*   *   *

The dawn broke hot, cracking open a sky that was brilliant and breezeless. In the knowledge that it might be his last opportunity to do so for a long time, Geoff lingered over a shower and shave. It was absurd, given the circumstances, to be concerned at all about a bathroom ritual, but he was the same guy who had always resisted weekend camping because it meant he couldn't start his day with a hair wash. This bit of self-knowledge struck him as funny at first, but then he thought of Nadya, somewhere over there, and the moment outside Tyre when he had ridden past the women and children gathered around the IDF water tanker. Ashamed, he hurried to finish.

The houseboy left to overnight duty was asleep on one of the couches in the lobby. He got to his feet groggily when Geoff poked him awake; was so groggy that he didn't register any surprise at seeing the hotel's only guest about to check out. Yawning as he totaled the bill, he showed the final figure to Geoff, made change for the money handed him, then stared on placidly as Geoff walked down the steps and out the door with his suitcase.

In contrast to the houseboy, the cab driver, who raced his car honking up the empty streets and leapt out athletically to toss Geoff's bag into the backseat, looked surprised indeed when shown the spot on Samir's map where he was to go. When it appeared he was about to protest, or even decline the fare, Geoff produced a thick wad of lira.

"*Le musée?*" he asked, seeking confirmation of their destination. Geoff nodded. They pulled away.

According to Samir, it was about a mile to the Green Line. Geoff traced the penciled route as they drove. Two blocks east of the hotel, he saw the Beirut River. The right turn they made there put them on the Corniche Pierre Gemayel, a broad avenue winding southwest. It ran into the Place Palais de Justice, and five hundred yards straight west from there the National Museum crossing point. It was at the museum, Samir had said, that one could try to get into West Beirut.

As he exited the Palais de Justice square, the driver suddenly slowed down. Reaching under the front of his seat, he yarded up a strip of white bedsheet. He thrust it out his window, shook it clean, then held it clear above the roof of the car. At almost the same moment, Geoff began to pick out the first sandbag fortifications along the sides of the road. Crouched low and peering up at the inching taxi from behind these walls and bunkers were Israelis. They were turtled beneath their flak jackets and steel helmets and looked to have not the slightest intention of coming out to check the identity or credentials, or even the destination, of those inside the car.

The reason was soon made clear. They had only traveled a few dozen yards farther west when a single shot skipped off the pavement in front of them. The driver instantly hit the brakes, pitching Geoff against the dash. Grumbling to himself, he stretched his arm even higher out the window and waved his white flag hard for almost half a minute. When no second shot came, he started forward again, still waving. Geoff closed his eyes and tried to recall a clam sauce recipe he liked.

The car stopped again, this time gently, and Geoff opened his eyes. There was a green and red oil drum in the middle of the road ahead of them and a stop sign sticking out the top of it. On the driver's side, he saw the colonnaded façade of a large, important-looking building. A handful of uniformed and well armed men stood together talking on the stone steps, shielded by the facade from the snipers firing out of the west. Some of them wore Israeli uniforms, others looked like they belonged to the same group as the youth who had addressed him in Hebrew on the street the day before. Geoff assumed they must be Phalangist militiamen.

"Museum?" He pointed towards the building.

The driver nodded yes, but he was much more interested in the group of men. Finally, they looked up from their discussion. One of the Israelis motioned for him to come over.

"Passport," the driver said. Geoff handed over his passport, plus the press credentials Dix had given him, and the man got out of the car. Holding his white sheet aloft until he was out of sniper-view, he crossed the road and joined the huddle on the museum steps.

Geoff stayed low inside the car, wishing he too had a piece of bedsheet to hold up. He watched his documents being passed around from Israeli to Phalangist and back to Israeli and wondered what he could say if they challenged him–if they wanted to know what he planned to report on in West Beirut, how and where he would file his stories. He was reasonably certain that some Dix-style belligerence would not get him past this checkpoint.

After several minutes and what looked like angry talk, the driver turned away from the group of uniforms and headed back to the car, scowling. Geoff pumped himself up to take the white flag from him and charge across to the steps for a fight. Sliding in behind the wheel, the driver returned him his papers, started the engine, backed up just a little, then punched into first and steered around the oil drum.

"It's okay?" Geoff asked.

The driver nodded and lit a cigaret. Remembering his manners after the fact, he turned and offered his pack to Geoff, who took one and smoked it hard.

Just beyond the museum, also on the left side, they approached an area of ragged parkland; in the foreground was a heavily shelled racetrack. Samir had included this on his map and called it the Hippodrome. On the road, next to the Hippodrome, was the first in what Geoff could see was a series of house-high hills of sand and clay. They were arranged in a skew: one mound took up the left half of the road, then, just beyond it, one took up the entire right half, then left again and so on. The car could get through this tight chicane, though it would have to be maneuvered slowly and sharply. Geoff looked at the driver and shrugged a question. The driver smiled through a mouthful of exhaled smoke, made a gun with his hand and a popping noise with his tongue. Geoff understood: it was sniper-proofing.

A small sentry box was set against the base of the first mound, and as they inched near it a Phalangist came out with his rifle and directed them to pull over. The driver stepped out, and this time he indicated that Geoff must get out as well.

Surrendering his papers again, Geoff followed the militiaman and driver around to the rear of the car. There the cabbie opened his trunk, and the Phalangist leaned in to poke at the contents with the barrel of his rifle. Satisfied with what he saw—or did not see—in the clutter of oily rags, spark plugs and wrenches, he instructed the driver to close the trunk and then peered inside the car. He spotted Geoff's suitcase on the backseat, and told the driver to bring it out. Geoff stepped between them and pulled out the bag himself. He set it down on the hood and opened it. The militiaman felt around inside for a moment, then nodded. He handed their documents back to the driver and told them they could pass through.

They emerged from behind the last of the mounds and drove onto a stretch of deserted, exposed road. Here the driver waved his white flag with extra enthusiasm, while Geoff again did his best to look short and not worth shooting. The driver noticed his shrinking act and laughed, though not cruelly.

The end of this no-man's land was signaled by another set of sand and clay mounds. As they drove into them, Geoff thought about Samir's mitosis analogy and began to wonder in what ways the choking of West Beirut would first show. Would the guardians of the gate on this side, for instance, be leaner and more desperate looking?

A barricade of bald tires and barbed wire stretched across most of the road beyond the last mound, and once more the driver stopped and got out of the car. As Geoff opened the passenger door and stood up he was met by two young gunmen wearing around their necks the black and white khaffiyeh of the PLO. They pointed their rifles at his chest, gestured and grunted at him to raise his arms above his head, then they stepped around behind and walked him towards a sandbag hut. Though it was ridiculous, he was peeved by this welcome. (As if: I've come to look for one of your countrywomen, so you ought to treat me well.) It also scared him.

When he hesitated too long outside the low entrance to the hut, Geoff was shoved hard from behind, and he scraped the top of his head as he stumbled inside. Fingering his scalp where the skin had been broken, he stooped to avoid the roof and found himself staring through bad light at another man staring at him from a cot in the corner. This hovel smelled terribly of sweat and mildew and pissed-in sand.

The man on the cot was older than the two who had delivered him, but he was still younger than Geoff. Clad only in his underwear, he had obviously just been woken up to deal with this new arrival. His fatigues were folded over an ammunition crate and his automatic rifle rested against the sandbag wall next to the cot. Swinging his legs around to sit up, he took Geoff's papers and glanced at them, paying closest attention to the likeness of Geoff's passport photo to the real item. Finally, he returned them, mumbled something in Arabic to the others and swung around to lie down again.

Back outside, the message was relayed to the driver, and Geoff followed him to the car.

"Hey, wait," he cried when it was clear they were heading back through the configuration of mounds.

The driver ignored him.

"Stop." He reached over and placed a firm grip on the steering wheel. The driver put a foot on his brakes.

"What the hell is going on?" Geoff demanded, knowing his question was clear enough.

"*Ce n'est pas possible*," the driver said, peeling Geoff's hand off the wheel. Geoff clamped it back on.

"Bullshit it's not," he said. Throwing open his door, he jumped out of the still rolling cab, yanked open the back door, dragged out his suitcase and lugged it towards the barricade.

The two young Palestinians watched his approach with facial weather that changed from anger to amusement and back to anger when he strode right past them. Sprinting around in front of him, they aimed their guns at him. Then, the taller, stronger-looking of the two stepped up and kneed Geoff square in the gut. He fell to the ground. His suitcase popped open and a pile of his underwear tumbled out. When he tried to get up, the tall Arab shoved him back down and pinned his face to the pavement with the barrel of his rifle.

"*Bas! Halas!*" came a forceful shout from behind. It was the half-dressed guerrilla commander, standing in the doorway of the hut. The young Palestinian on top of Geoff lifted his weapon and stepped away to let him up. He was marched back into the hut again.

"What are you trying to do?" the commander asked in competent English.

"I'm a journalist—I have to get into the west to do my job," Geoff said, struggling to stuff his clothes back into his bag.

"No, what you are is a fool. These boys could have shot you right there where you lay, and would not that have been a story for your newspaper."

For the briefest moment, Geoff considered telling this man the truth. He decided against it mostly because of the disdain he had heard in the word *fool*.

"I'm sorry. I know I shouldn't have done that–it was stupid, all right. It's just that it's important that I be allowed through."

The fighter was unmoved. He scratched his crotch and dug around in the pockets of his folded clothing for a cigaret.

"There are enough journalists here in West Beirut. There are even enough journalists here with hearts for the Palestinians," he said, lighting up and inhaling deeply. "We do not need you. Goodbye."

There was finality in this, and Geoff realized there was nothing else left to him.

"Then I need you."

The Palestinian laughed. "And how may I be of service?" he said cuttingly.

"The truth is I'm not a journalist. I came here to find someone."

"In West Beirut?"

"Yes. A woman, a Palestinian."

"Here?"

Geoff had said enough. Now he only nodded.

"Whatever reason you have for seeking a Palestinian woman here, I will tell you you have wasted your time."

"Why?"

"Because she has left long ago when she could, and if she did not leave, she is dead. Or she will be soon."

"How do you know that?"

"How do I know she will be dead? It is simple. The Israelis mean to be done with us here, all of us. *Halas.*" He stuck his cigaret in his mouth and brushed off his hands to emphasize the point. "This is our Warsaw."

"I can't believe that," Geoff said. "Even the Americans are against this invasion and siege."

"You think so?"

"I read the papers. I watch the news."

"The news as it is told in America?"

"Yes."

The Palestinian was silent for a while. He finished his cigaret rather with obvious leisure, then tossed away the butt and surprised Geoff with a little smile.

"I will change my mind, I think. What is one more dead Westerner?" he said. "Come. Come be with us if that is what you want."

*   *   *

The boy did not speak and he hardly smiled, but Geoff was fond of him immediately and stood watching him. He was about the same age as the two bold kids who had talked to him near the Hotel St. Michel. He was dressed in a blue-and-white-striped T-shirt and knee-patched jeans, and he wore a pair of plastic sandals on his grubby feet. Like almost all the children here, he had that mat of thick black hair and dark probing eyes. He was sitting on the curb, making a game of tossing pebbles at his big toes, when Geoff climbed out of the taxi in front of him and looked around. Beside him, roped together at the neck and tied up to the base of a streetlight, were three emaciated sheep. They were down on their forelegs and trembling, eyes wide with fright. Geoff felt sorry for them. When he reached out to try to comfort one of them, the little boy stiffened, and Geoff realized it was his job to guard them. With a smile, he turned instead to muss the boy's hair. Then he stepped by him and moved away down the sidewalk, past an abandoned movie house. Faded by age and the daily blaze of sunlight, the preview posters in the glassless display case by the entrance showed a heavily made-up man and woman staring at each other at a party. It was an Arab movie, and Geoff saw that Arab paradox of passion and chastity on their faces. His thoughts drifted to Nadya, and he wondered if the film had managed a run here before the theater closed, or if this was as near as the man and woman in the poster ever got to touching in Beirut.

He was on Rue Hamra, the major commercial street in West Beirut, according to Samir Haddad, who had marked it on his map. Because it was the closest thing he had to a specific address, he'd asked the driver to drop him here. Anywhere here. The driver, who could not be very surprised by anything Geoff wanted now, was eager to oblige, to collect his fare and get straight back to East Beirut.

As he walked along, watching and listening to the bang-and-rattle opening of shop doors, Geoff was struck by the apparent normality of the city. It was as if the Israeli bombardment the other night had never happened. The buildings were standing; there were no gaping holes in the walls, no craters in the pavement; this was not a Tyre or a Sidon. Where, then, had all that IDF artillery fire been directed–into the sea?

But Geoff soon noticed something else. Although merchants were arriving for work and doors were being opened, they were only the essential doors: a pharmacy here, a bakery there, a few grocers. The insurance company offices, currency exchanges, cafés, jewelry and clothing shops, travel and airline agencies whose signs and facades dominated Hamra remained closed. There was a Sunday feel at midweek.

Hungry for breakfast, Geoff crossed the street and went into a small grocery. He nodded good morning to the proprietor, who looked bored on a high stool behind the front counter. He sniffed the pleasant soap smell, common to all such stores, while he stood and shopped with his eyes.

Quite suddenly, there it was: that first thumbprint on the throat, as Samir might have put it. Misled for an instant by some deceptive shelving on the part of the shopkeeper, Geoff now saw that except for a few canned items there was almost nothing edible available. There was all the detergent one could want, but no produce of any kind: no eggs or milk, no fruit or vegetables. The stand-up cooler at the rear of the store contained one item only–a dozen or so bottles of Pepsi-Cola.

Geoff changed his mind about eating a can of lentils. He settled for a bottle of Pepsi–paying the equivalent of two dollars American–then left the store and hurried back up the street towards a bakery he had passed earlier. He found a crowd of thirty or forty women now waiting to buy bread, where before there had been only a handful. Annoyed with himself for not having stopped the first time, he joined their disorderly queue. Though it was not easy, he endured their stares for almost half an hour, but before he was three-quarters of the way to a purchase, a cry of angry despair went up from the women still ahead of him and the lineup disbanded. He pulled the word *bookra* from their upset chatter—tomorrow.

Geoff banged the cap off his Pepsi against the edge of a windowsill and swallowed the pop on the spot. Then he decided to continue on in the same direction. He was leg-tired and sore-shouldered from lugging his suitcase around, and he wanted to ask the little boy guarding the sheep for directions to a hotel.

But the shepherd and his flock were no longer at the corner. In their place was another long lineup of women waiting to get into a shop that faced the corner. Hoping for another bakery, Geoff walked to the front of the queue and stuck his head inside the door. He saw the boy, standing off to one side in the darkened room, and suddenly knew what kind of shop it was. In the same moment, he heard terrified bleating coming from the back of the shop, bleating that sharpened and swelled then turned pathetic and tremulous before stopping altogether.

Simply because he had nowhere else to go, Geoff stood and listened as the second and then the third sheep were slaughtered. Long minutes afterwards, a splatter-smocked butcher emerged from the back with a first armload of bloody meat on a bed of newspaper. He plunked it down on a countertop with a weighty thud, and the women from the front of the line immediately closed in around it and began to place their orders, all of them speaking at once in staccato bursts of Arabic. Disinterested, the boy hung back and noticed Geoff watching from the doorway. He crossed his arms, adult-like, and smiled.

In the frenzy of sound and motion, Geoff was not sure which he heard first, though it was obvious what must have come first. A woman's cry of warning, a screaming jet, people yelling, the sonic boom, sandal-slap on pavement. Abandoning their orders, the women came rushing from the shop and brushed and bumped past Geoff as they ran off in every direction. The boy and the butcher came out last—son and father? —and worked together on their knees, slipping large padlocks into two hooks in the sidewalk to lock a pull-down metal door in place. The boy looked at Geoff, still watching, then pointed at the sky and made a gesture that meant run. Geoff would have liked to, but he didn't know where, so he waited until the boy and the man ran and then he followed, taking the ridiculous trouble to keep a polite distance.

The jets kept coming as he chased up the street after the man and boy, but he was aware that he had yet to hear a single shell land anywhere during this strange slow air raid. Squinting up at the planes' white streaks across the sky, he saw hundreds of sheets of paper floating down like gargantuan snowflakes. In contrast to absolutely everything else at the moment, they were in no hurry to get anywhere. Their languid drift had slowed him to a near jog when something just ahead exploded, belting him heels over head backwards.

The force of the blast dazed him and his ears were useless. He carefully pulled himself back to his feet and counted four limbs still attached. His vision was blurred and there was thick black smoke pouring out over the street, but beneath it he could make out the sprawled and motionless figures of the butcher and the boy. Beside them, he saw the source of the black smoke: a burned-out car. That was what had exploded; there was no bomb from above.

Something kissed off his cheek as he hurried into the smoke towards the boy, and he reached out instinctively to grab at it. It was one of the airborne papers. He stared blankly at the Arabic written on it, then stuffed it in his pocket and kept going, conscious that his run was more a drunkard's weave.

He was numb. He was someplace else, off-screen, watching himself in action. This sense of ethereality gave him hope that it might only be a dream, that he would wake up shortly and find himself still in bed at the St. Michel. After all, it was not really possible–was it?–that he could be down on one knee like this, on a street littered with shattered glass, with gasoline rainbows trickling escape in the gutter, with fingers, his fingers, searching for a pulse in a little boy's wrist, finding none. Staring amazed at the amount of blood on his pulse-taking fingers, at the blood falling from somewhere, he had no idea from where, to splash across the boy's restful face. Then realizing, how rude: it was his own blood falling on the boy.

His traumatized ears had failed to notice an approaching siren, so when one of the ambulance attendants came up from behind and placed a hand on his shoulder Geoff nearly screamed, thinking it must be the butcher resurrected. With gentle insistence, he was pulled to his feet and led over to the ambulance. There, the first attendant left him in the care of the second and ran back to check on the boy and butcher. He returned, at a walk, a few moments later, while Geoff was having a gauze pad bandaged around his forehead. Slumped on the road, his back against a rear tire of the ambulance, Geoff watched him approach and shake his head at his colleague and felt quite certain he had already seen that blood-spattered smock once already today.

TEN

GEOFF'S BACKFLIP ONTO THE PAVEMENT HAD LEFT HIM WITH A mild concussion and a cut good for close to thirty stitches. The East Indian doctor who had made that diagnosis was tugging through the last of them when Geoff remembered his suitcase and went into a shock induced panic. He mumbled, babbled and then, ignoring the doctor's pleas that he calm down, began to shout. He demanded that the ambulance attendants go back to the bombing site and retrieve his bag, demanded a ride back so he could get it himself, and finally accused them of stealing it. The doctor called out for assistance, and a handful of nurses and orderlies hurried into the treatment room. Close behind them came a second doctor. His severe North European accent cut right through the placating voices swirling around Geoff.

"*You.*" He placed a fine-boned hand on Geoff's chest and leaned in close. "You be quiet now. We do not have time for this foolishness."

"My suitcase. I have no clothes–nothing." Geoff spoke quietly.

"You have the clothes on your back, do you not?" the doctor said. Sensing that Geoff was under control again, he nodded to the Indian doctor and left the treatment room. The nurses and orderlies followed him out.

"But–"

Geoff gave up, beaten into submission by the club of a massive headache, and dropped back onto the table. His temples throbbed. He lay there in cooperative silence, begging the headache to give him peace and watching the Indian doctor squint down at the last stitches in his forehead. Shutting his eyes, he listened to the hum of an electrical generator somewhere nearby and tried not to hate the ambulance attendants any more than he did.

Which was not at all easy because when he was sufficiently bandaged, they had placed him in the back of their ambulance for the ride to the hospital, only to shatter his dim refuge there a moment later by shoving in the bodies of the boy and the butcher. Left alone with two dead and battered faces, he became frantic. Sliding to his knees on the clot-crudded floor of the vehicle, he pounded his fists on the thin steel partition separating front from back. The attendants pounded back for a while, like it was a game he'd invented, and then they ignored him—left him to hammer on unanswered all the way to the hospital, while the butcher's thick leg swung across and bumped lightly against his own at every sharp turn the ambulance took.

The explosion that brought him around again initially made him think he'd been dreaming about the car bomb. Opening his eyes, he realized he was still in the treatment room. He heard someone moving about below him and pushed himself up onto his elbows, expecting to see the East Indian doctor there. Instead, he saw a nurse. Fair-haired and pale, just like the no-nonsense doctor, she was busy pulling bandages and other medical paraphernalia from a cupboard beneath the examining table. Geoff cleared his throat, but his request for a glass of water was lost in the rumbled roar of a whole series of explosions. The nurse stood up, arms laden, and looked at him.

"What's going on?" he asked.

"Israeli air raid." Her accent, too, was like the blond doctor's. She freed a hand from beneath her bundle and checked Geoff's sutures with long, cool fingers. "Headache?" she asked, raising her voice over another shell blast.

"Smashing."

"We have shortages, but I will see if I can get something for the pain."

"Thanks," he said.

He was still waiting for her return when he heard ambulance sirens outside the hospital, and seconds later the cries of incoming wounded in the corridor. He recognized the hard voice shouting out triage instructions, and then the head that owned that voice appeared in the doorway of the treatment room. The doctor's face was tight and strained in concentration.

"Get up, please. We must have this room," he said.

Geoff had scarcely found his feet and begun wobbling towards the door when the doctor and two orderlies pushed past him and tossed a woman onto the examining table. Her stomach was rent wide open, and one of the orderlies was using his bare hand to hold onto coils of spilled intestine. Geoff focused on the lines between the floor tiles to keep from throwing up. The nurse at last reappeared and foisted a couple of tablets in his palm. She pressed him out into the corridor.

"Go. Sit down somewhere," she said, then she hurried to help with the woman.

There was nowhere to sit. Already, the hallway and waiting area were jammed with casualties, their families and hospital staff losing the struggle to tend to both. Shuffling along in a daze, Geoff crossed and then recrossed the main floor, trying both to stay out of the way of the doctors and nurses and to avoid intruding on scenes of private anguish. He came upon a thick smear of blood on the tiles in the center of the waiting area; there were lines of bloody footprints radiating from it like spokes on a wheel. He smelled antiseptic and charred flesh, heard moans and whimpers, sobs and yells, and far away–though not far away at all–the dull thump-thump of anti-aircraft fire and the much louder crash and splinter of shell-struck stone.

It took death to finally find him a seat. After quite some time inside, the grim-looking doctor emerged from the treatment room, wiping his hands and forearms on an already filthy towel. He called an Arab nurse, and Geoff saw her answer his question by pointing out a man sitting with young twin girls on either knee on a nearby bench. The doctor pivoted away then, and the nurse walked over to the man, who got up to meet her. Relieving him of one of the toddlers in his arms, she touched his shoulder and relayed the doctor's bad news. The man said nothing, gave away none of his grief. He simply took back the other child and left, cradling the pair of them high on his chest. As soon as he was gone from sight, Geoff claimed the vacant spot on the bench before anyone else could. He felt like a scavenger.

Accompanied by wild shouting that momentarily over-whelmed the pandemonium of the hospital, an old man was carried through the doors like a rolled-up carpet and deposited on the floor in the waiting area. He was slipping in and out of consciousness and gagging with pain from a chest wound that spewed forth stinking white smoke. He coughed, and more of the smoke escaped through his nostrils and mouth. The East Indian doctor knelt at his side, but Geoff saw his probings and pokings as half-hearted. He knew the old man was already marked down as dead.

"Do you find this all very interesting?"

Geoff turned towards the sarcastic voice. It was the blond doctor. He had stopped in passing to watch Geoff watch the old man.

"What is it?"

"He has fragments from a phosphorus shell inside his chest. The phosphorus will keep burning as long as there is oxygen to feed it. A charming piece of work, no?"

Geoff frowned, but when he began to ask another question he found that the doctor had already left.

*   *   *

The Israeli jets were gone in minutes, yet with predictable geometry it took the staff more than six hours to get through all the casualties who had been brought or brought themselves to the hospital. Those with minor hurts, like Geoff's, were patched and sent straight off again, though they'd had to wait to the end to be seen at all. The seriously injured, those who required surgery or a close watch, were either lined up for an operating theater or assigned to a bed in the wards. The dead went downstairs.

It was midafternoon and Geoff was still on his bench, folding and refolding an airplane he had made from the sheet of paper he'd stuffed into his pocket after the car bombing. The nurse came over and sat down beside him. She was exhausted. There were dirty streaks of perspiration down the sides of her neck, and a thick wetness in her blouse below the hollow between her breasts. Her cropped hair was limp and her uniform more gray now than starch white.

"I'm dying for a cigaret–can you help me out?" she said.

Geoff shook his head.

"What have you got there?" she asked.

"I don't know, it's in Arabic. There were hundreds of them floating through the air." He unfolded the paper airplane and held it out.

"But of course," the nurse said, affecting an official-sounding voice. "Another humanitarian gesture from General Sharon. Good citizens of Lebanon, we appeal to you again to evacuate West Beirut. There are irregular forces here which must be expelled. Do not permit these terrorists to hide behind you."

"Is that what it says?" Geoff asked.

"Something like this," she said, not bothering to read it. "They are fond of these things. They will fly fast and low, as if to attack, but instead they drop such as these."

"But they did attack."

"Yes," she said. "They do that also."

That is because they are clever, Geoff could almost hear Samir Haddad interjecting through those fingers that were perpetually at his mustache. He watched an orderly, down on his knees on the floor, scrub vigorously at the pattern of bloody footprints, now dry and tenacious.

"How many people died?" he asked, knowing of two.

"Seven. But there is a woman who will go soon, so you can say eight."

"Still," Geoff suggested. "With all they dropped, it could have been worse."

There was no ridicule in the nurse's voice, but her response was hard and immediate. "We are only one small hospital. If each of the hospitals and clinics in West Beirut had seven or eight dead today, would you still say it was not bad?"

It was nothing he wanted to argue about, but Geoff felt it important that he not be misunderstood. "I didn't say it wasn't bad. All I said was, it could have been worse."

The nurse nodded, conceding the point. "Your head, how is it?" she asked.

"Better, thanks."

"Did you take the pills?"

"One. I saved the other. Would you like it back?"

She smiled just a little at this. "You may want it later," she said. "Anyway, it is not strong enough to help most who come here."

The blond doctor glanced down at them as he hurried by.

"A busy man," Geoff observed.

"He is in charge of the hospital."

"I don't think he likes me very much."

"You flatter yourself," she said. "I am certain he does not even notice you."

Geoff thought about the old man with phosphorus smoke pouring from his chest, but he kept quiet.

"I must go back to work," the nurse said. "I think it would be all right if you left now, but come back immediately if you begin to feel disoriented."

Geoff watched her get up, but he remained sitting.

"You want to stay?" she said.

"I have nowhere else to go," he admitted.

"Then stay." She shrugged and walked away.

Through the rest of the afternoon and into the early evening, the nurse came back periodically to sit and talk with him, and once to bring him a small plate of food. Her name, he learned, was Grete Johannssen. She was a Norwegian volunteer with the PLO's medical service, the Palestine Red Crescent Society, and she had been in Lebanon for a year. The unfriendly doctor was also a Norwegian, it turned out. Perhaps he was only flattering himself, as Grete had put it, but Geoff speculated privately about a little green demon that he was quite well acquainted with. When he considered it further, it made him want to laugh. That a doctor, a surgeon no less, doing emergency work in a besieged city should feel he might have something to fear from a peddler like him was incomprehensible.

*   *   *

As Grete had predicted, Geoff's head began to hurt again and he swallowed the other painkiller. He was still awaiting the drug's

comforting fingers on his temples when the Israelis attacked once
more at nightfall. From the start, it felt like a much heavier
pounding than the morning's had been, and this was confirmed
by the number of people coming into the hospital. IDF artillery
positions in the East Beirut hills and warships offshore were
adding low trajectory fire to a second aerial bombardment. The
effect was the shearing of whole buildings from their foundations,
the toppling of structures that could not be satisfactorily crushed
from above. The East Indian doctor had warned him that nausea
was one of the companions of concussion, but Geoff knew that the
pitching in his stomach that began as he heard the chorus of sirens
starting up again had another cause. It was fear. Not for his
safety, not even just now for Nadya's, but fear of what he was
about to see. Fear because there was no getting away from this, no
turning the page to the sports section, no flipping the channel to a
cartoon. This was real and really happening. The guerrilla at the
Green Line had granted him admission, and he was locked in
now for the entire performance.

The doctor stood near the receiving doors, awaiting the arrival
of the first ambulance, when Geoff approached him.

"What can I do?"

"What?" The doctor cocked his head and pulled up his mouth
like he hadn't understood the language, much less the question
asked.

"I want to help," Geoff said. "Tell me how I can help."

ELEVEN

THE BEIRUT SUMMER WAS HOT BUT NOT A SHIRT-STICKING, humid hot; it was more like the grape-growing climate of southern California. Baking hot might be the best way to describe it, Geoff thought. The hills above the city in the east stood brown (baked brown) and begging for a rain that was still months away, although there were afternoons when the dancing shimmer off the earth almost looked wet enough to swallow and slake. The dust in the streets, both the real dust from real dirt and that other dust from crumbling buildings, was ready at the faintest whisper off the Mediterranean to get up and scatter. But it never scattered far; like the two hundred thousand Beirutis who had ignored Ariel Sharon's airborne handbills, it clung to the shell of a half-city with remarkable tenacity.

Also clinging to ten square miles of West Beirut by the third week of July were several hundred thousand Lebanese and Palestinians from the south, from Tyre, Nabitiya, Sidon, Damour and the refugee camps like Rachidieh and Ein Hilwie. Driven homeless up the coast by the Israelis, they either had no resources or no strength left to continue farther north. They would make their stand here, bedding down in parking garages and building lobbies, or under United Nations Relief and Works Agency canopies in open parks, defended by what remained of an original force of eight thousand PLO fighters and two or three thousand loosely allied militiamen from various points along the Lebanese political left.

It had been almost two weeks since his arrival at the hospital,

143

and Geoff had built himself a routine. At night, by mutual agreement, he was an orderly, doing whatever the blond doctor, whose name was Thommie Musli, Grete Johannssen, or just about anyone else in whites instructed him to do. He washed bedpans, carried dead to the morgue, scrubbed floors and walls, lugged sandbags, delivered meals, cooked meals, donated blood, and even worked in the ambulances when extra help was needed there. In return for this volunteer labor, he was allowed to sleep and eat in the hospital, meaning that he slept on the floor wherever there was space to spread a mat and got one meal a day, and that in the evening because it was Ramadan, the Muslim holy month of dawn-to-dusk fasting. We can't very well eat if our patients are not eating, was how Dr. Musli introduced him to his new diet. Not that Geoff cared: between the summer heat and the constant chill in his eyes, he had little enough want of food anyway. He lost weight, grew a beard, washed and wore the same set of clothes over and over.

During the daylight hours, he searched. Holding his breath against the smell of garbage, piled and putrefying on every other corner, added to daily but uncollected for the six-plus weeks since the invasion began, while trying to ignore that other, omni-present smell he couldn't hold his breath against, he walked the streets from the American University campus in the north to the airport road in the south, and from the beaches in the west to as near the Green Line as anyone dared go towards the east. He was stopped and questioned, he was followed, he was ignored, he was caught without shelter in air raids and he was shot at by Phalangist snipers, and he saw a hundred Nadyas every day. Occasionally, one of them would stop whatever she was doing and eye him so hard in return that he'd begin to wonder, to question his own memory until, at last, another stranger looked away.

By turns he was filled with hope and then despair. Hope came with his growing knowledge of the city, and how small it was becoming as this siege went on. In concentrating most of their static fire on the perimeter of West Beirut, the Israelis were taking patient little bites, each bite forcing a few more homeless into the downtown core around Hamra Street. It was like a cattle drive, with Geoff the indirect beneficiary; his search area was shrinking as the city emptied inwards on top of itself. One hundred Nadyas became two hundred. *Soon*, he tried to believe.

Despair, on the other hand, was the carnage. Whether by design or carelessness—and right here, right now, it didn't matter which it was—the IDF was killing as it conducted its roundup. Ten thousand fatalities was the figure currently being thrown around. Each dead Nadya could be his Nadya, and it had become an obsession to check the morgue every evening when he returned to the hospital. But that was only one morgue, and there were so many in this city. For Geoff, rising from his mat on the floor with the sun in the morning, the pink-sky end to each day arrived like a shell burst in his spirit. *Never*, he knew.

The one area of West Beirut where the IDF was not succeeding in its strategy to drive and squeeze towards the center was the refugee camps. There Geoff's hope and despair ran against each other hardest. In Sabra, Chatila and Bourj el-Barajneh, three squalid shantytowns sprawled kitty-corner to each other just north of the airport, the bombardment (and death toll) was heavier by far than anywhere else. It was there, he'd finally figured out, that all the artillery fire whistling over the roof of the Hotel St. Michel that first night had landed. Thirty shells a minute. Since then, he had seen the damage that kind of onslaught did. He had seen blood enough to fill bathtubs and fingerpaint walls.

Yet the people of the camps refused to yield. When Geoff was among them, wandering through labyrinthine streets that were often no wider than the span of his arms, whole families would stand in the doorways of their one-room shanties and watch him pass. Their faces, from the young to the old, sometimes a full dozen of them framed in a single doorway, were defiance set in granite, and Geoff knew why it had taken the Israelis almost a week to finish Ein Hilwie. He also knew why they had laid siege to West Beirut for more than a month but would not come in on foot behind their tanks. They were afraid; yes they were, and these people knew it.

At first, Geoff too was afraid; afraid of those tough stares and of the agitated young fedayeen who followed him, rifle-ready, everywhere he walked. The first time he went to the camps, he wandered through the cratered alleys of Sabra for ten uncomfortable minutes, got lost, and left without ever asking his question.

The next time, Sabra again only because it was the closest of the three camps to the hospital, he was recognized as a return visitor. The stares softened a little, the young fighters hung back and relaxed, and he began to ask his simple question. Nadya Karameh *houn*? Nadya Karameh here?

Eventually, the camp grapevine located someone with enough English to find out what this stranger wanted. Geoff was hustled off to the interpreter's home and there made to drink glasses of sweet mint tea and fend off packages of Marlboro cigarets while the accompanying entourage of mostly elderly men, all dry-lipped and devoutly fasting, sat around him and watched. And then the questions began. Where are you from? Why are you here? How do you know this woman you look for? Does she know that you look for her? Why do you want to find her? He answered what he could, jumped over what he could not or would not tell them, and then pressed with his own questions. Is she here? Has she been here? Have you heard of this woman?

Nadya had once told him that there were words in English that Arabs had great trouble saying. At the time, he hadn't suspected she meant anything more than pronunciation. As it was, Geoff had had to return to Sabra three more times, three different days, before he finally figured out that *maybe* and *it is possible* were only efforts to put off disappointing him. Nobody was checking around, as he thought they were, between his visits. Everybody knew everybody else in this camp, though it sheltered thousands, and a woman named Nadya Karameh was not now and never had been among them.

*   *   *

It was a morning when he just couldn't make himself get up, when the hopelessness was huge and black, and all he wanted was to go home. He lay on his mat well past dawn, listening to the breathing of others sleeping on the floor around him, and compiled lists of the things he could be doing if he weren't here. Such as. . . . He could get drunk, reeling, joyously drunk, and laugh until his jaws hurt. Or he could watch his drinking a little, talk some stranger up and then go home with her. (Sex—it was funny how seldom he thought about it anymore.) He could go down to Wreck Beach and peel his clothes off and swim naked in the ocean, feeling cooled and cleansed. Hell, he could eat Cheezies and drink cream soda for breakfast, stay in his king-size bed and watch golf on T.V.

"Should you not be gone by now?"

Geoff sat up to look at Grete. She was dressed in a loose summery smock. Loud green flowers scattered over the light cotton fabric giggled at his gloomy mood. It was the first time he had seen Grete out of her nurse's uniform.

"You're not going out today?" she asked, squatting like a tomboy beside him.

He shrugged, then realized he was staring rather openly at the few inches of milky thigh between her knees and the hem of her dress.

"What are you doing up so early?"

"I need a day away from this place. I was thinking to go with you," she said.

"It's a hell of a way to spend a day off. You've heard that expression, searching for a needle in a haystack?"

"What else am I going to do–go shopping?"

"You could stay in bed, eat Cheezies and watch golf."

"What?"

"Never mind." Geoff smiled, rolling forward off his haunches and onto his feet.

When they got outside, he offered to hire a taxi for the day but Grete refused, insisting they walk if walking was how he was used to conducting his search. She opened her shoulder bag then, glanced back at the entrance of the hospital to see if anyone was watching, and pulled out two scrolled-up loaves of flat Arab bread. "Continental breakfast," she said, handing him the larger of the two loaves.

"There's a green onion in here," he said, thrilling at the mildly spicy taste.

"Stop chewing and hide it quickly." Grete shoved her own crude sandwich back in her purse and held it open so Geoff could toss his in too. Bolus-cheeked, they both looked up and smiled crooked hellos at a Lebanese orderly walking to his shift at the hospital.

"He knew," she said after the orderly was out of earshot.

"Do you think he doesn't cheat once in a while?" Geoff said, not so patiently waiting for his sandwich.

"It is not a question of cheating." Grete opened her purse at last. "We're not Muslims. But it is considered great disrespect to eat in front of those who do fast."

"All this piety in the middle of a war," he said, biting with an atheist's certainty.

"I should think Islam will outlast this war."

"I should think," he repeated after her.

"Bad or worse, the war will end. It has to." She offered him the last half of her sandwich. He would have liked it very much, but he shook his head, knowing she'd want it later.

"Bad?"

"Bad is already here," she said. "The PLO has lost. They may concede this fact and agree to leave."

"Worse?"

"They may not concede."

"And if they leave, what happens then?"

"Nothing that is good," she said. "Lebanon—who knows what becomes of Lebanon. There will be a vacuum, and a vacuum must always be filled. It is true, you know, there are many Lebanese, and not only the Phalange and the Maronite people, who do not like the PLO here. But I wonder if any of them know just how bad it could get when the PLO are no longer here."

"Fighting?" Geoff said.

"Lebanese killing Lebanese in ways and numbers that will make 1975 and 1976 look like a children's argument," she said.

"What will this do to the Palestinians?"

"I don't know, but it may well bring out the extremists: the bombers, the hijackers, the *terrorists*," she said, growing caustic.

"If that happens, the Israelis will be losers too," Geoff argued. "This war will come back to haunt them."

"No," Grete said. "This war may come back to haunt them, but not for that reason. The radicalization of the Palestinians is exactly what people like Sharon and Begin want. Arafat may lose influence, the radicals will attack this and that, and then the

Israelis will be able to say see, these people are not interested in any peace–"

"They want to drive us into the sea," Geoff completed.

"*Us?*"

Geoff laughed at himself. "I've come a long way this summer."

Grete smiled. "That is good. A small victory for our side is still a victory."

They walked in silence for a time, the early sun already hot on their backs. Geoff began to whistle, and then to sing. It was an old Drifters song, "Under the Boardwalk," one of the few tunes he could almost carry. He stopped abruptly.

"That is nice. Please, go on," Grete said, watching him.

"No. It doesn't feel right."

"Geoff, the object in a place like this is to do what we must to survive."

"I know that," he said.

This time their silence was punctured not by a song but by an exchange of small-arms fire from the vicinity of the Green Line. They stopped and listened, but when the shooting came no closer they continued on their way. It was just a wake-up call.

"Tell me about her," Grete said at last.

"I'm not sure I can," Geoff said.

"You will excuse me when I say that sounds very much like a typical man's answer to such a question."

"I'm certain it does."

"But you know, you must try," she pressed. "Consider it the cost of my company today. I will even help you start. Is she pretty?"

"Very."

"Perfectly beautiful?"

"Beautiful, yes–perfectly, no. One of her top front teeth overlaps a little across the other. And one of her eyes, the left I think, gets a bit lazy when she's tired."

"That's it?"

He thought about it for a second more and nodded.

"Okay, so I hate her," Grete joked. "Now tell me about the important part. Inside."

"There's the rub," he said.

"Pardon?"

He shook his head: forget it.

"I am waiting," she said. "Talk to me."

And suddenly he did. Unstoppered, it tumbled out of him like BB shot spilled on a floor, catching Grete flat-footed to grab for it as it bounced past in crazy directions. He told her about the morning jog in Stanley Park and about the much more significant second meeting at the party. There was the rose taped to her door and the miserable way he'd ruined the dinner that flower had earned him an invitation to. He described the night when he'd more or less passed out drunk on her couch and how he'd wakened to find her sitting at his feet, fixed with fear on the T.V. news that had announced the beginning of the invasion. He told her about the rally at the art gallery and how he'd made a mess of that too, but he didn't tell her the part about Angela. There were closets he would open for nobody.

"You are quite right. You have come a long way this summer, haven't you?" Grete observed when he was through. She was looking him up and down. "What you have done in traveling here seems both mad and wonderfully romantic in this age of the cynic."

"Romantic? No, I'm beginning to think it's more like a snowball rolling down a hill. Something about Nadya gave me the push all right, but once I got started I couldn't have stopped. Momentum or something," he said, looking, as ever, for a refuge in flippancy.

"And so here you are at the bottom of the hill. What now?"

"I sit and wait and swear at the sun. There's nowhere left to roll," he replied.

Grete nodded gravely. "Tell me, do you really believe you can find her, wandering around like this?"

He was once again set to say something self-protectively glib, but he stopped himself. "Grete, I don't know what else to do." And he thought: but she's right–this is hell, and I've a snowball's hope.

*   *   *

One man's terrorist is another man's freedom fighter. Where had he heard that? Another Dixism? Perhaps it had come up following that weird episode outside the King David Hotel, when Dix had finally pointed out for him that it was Menachem Begin who had planned the bombing there. And why this current fixation of his on photographs? First, there had been Camille Haddad's little surprise on the library wall, and now this similarly-grainy portrait of a man-boy, a gossamer-lipped eldest son, gone fedayeen to fight the modern David, a David–twist on twist–with the physique and the weaponry of Goliath.

But of course there was another photograph, a photograph that did not exist, and because it did not it was, in a sense, the most vivid photograph of all. Therein the current fixation.

You do not even have a snapshot of her? Grete had said, managing to sound both annoyed and amazed.

No, he had answered, wishing she could understand that he would claw through rock to have such a possession.

You know you make it most difficult for these people to help you, Grete had complained.

Exasperated, he'd snapped back at her. Listen, I would *draw* a picture of her for you if I could.

One man's junk is another man's treasure. It occurred to him as he moved from the photograph, proudly mounted on the wall, to scan the rest of the room that everything owned by the family of eight crowded into this fifteen-by-fifteen-foot space could be shoved into the large storage closet at his condo. It was a pathetic inventory, a pile of nothing: half a dozen elbow cushions (you could hardly call them pillows); a pair of threadbare rugs laid over the concrete floor; a pile of rolled-up sleeping mats in one corner; a plywood cupboard full of dishes and cooking pots; a cardboard calendar, placed in decorative balance to the lone photograph on the opposite wall; a punctured rubber soccer ball; another plywood cupboard, this one full of folded clothing; a wobble-legged coffeetable; and a third plywood cupboard containing a miscellany that included school books, dog-eared sheets of looseleaf paper and a jar of pencils, rattail combs and worn-out toothbrushes.

Geoff ended his sulk at Grete with a question. "Do they know where their son is?"

"No," she answered. "He was in the south when the invasion began, but now—who knows?"

"At least they have a photograph," he said, nodding and smiling a little for the mother and father and five young children who sat staring at them from a tight knot on the other side of the room. Grete caught on immediately.

"I am sorry, Geoff," she said. "I was not being fair."

It had been her suggestion that they come here to Chatila in the afternoon after spending the morning downtown looking among the new arrivals in the temporary shelters around Hamra Street. At noon they had slipped into the bar at the Commodore Hotel, where most of the foreign journalists in West Beirut were these days snugly tucked, and guiltlessly devoured clubhouse sandwiches under the beady gaze of Cocoa, the resident parrot who had taken to mimicking the sounds of shelling. Geoff had intended to search Bourj el-Barajneh during the afternoon because it was a larger camp, but he agreed to the change in plan after Grete told him she was better known in Chatila and that he might as well take advantage of that fact on a day when she accompanied him.

And she certainly was known too. Almost from the moment they had crossed through the north entrance of Chatila, they were surrounded by refugees with a cabin-fever desperation for company and others seeking a nurse's advice for infant diarrhea, colic and bronchitis.

While the adults talked at Grete, the children tugged at Geoff. If it were possible to be overwhelmed by children, he was overwhelmed. Dark and rheumy-eyed, they emerged from every crack and corner, every dirt pile and doorway, to come running and tripping towards the visitors, kicking up an impressive fuss of dust with their hard, bare feet. He watched them dance around and wondered why he hadn't seen them like this in Sabra camp, realizing then that Grete hadn't been there with him. *Baksheesh, baksheesh*—he listened to their voices, resilient through all of this, challenging more than begging him to dig for coins. Sadly, he thought about the boy guarding his sheep on Hamra Street, and then about a much blacker memory, Camille Haddad's ugly venom: they must do nothing but fuck, for their children run everywhere like packs of filthy little dogs.

Eventually, with the various medical questions all answered, those with the greatest claim to acquaintanceship with Grete stepped in to compete for hosting privileges in an afternoon of house-to-house visits. After checking with Geoff, Grete consented to this. But she apportioned their time very carefully, allowing no more than twenty minutes per stop. This was just long enough for the ritual courtesies so important here–the questions: your health? your family? The answers (whether true or not, typically the same one): good, praise be to God, *el-hamdu lillah*–and for Geoff's query. He is looking for a friend, a *sadiqi*, a Palestinian woman named Nadya Karameh, who has been studying in Canada. Have you heard anything of such a woman?

"*Haram.*" A sin. Grete shook her head at the end of a long and angry speech by the missing young fedayeen's father. She turned to Geoff.

"He feels his son is either dead or a prisoner at Ansar, and he thinks Ansar would be the worst of the two. The Israelis say that the men and boys they hold there are not prisoners of war, so they are not obliged to obey the Geneva Conventions," she said. "The conditions are atrocious. Prisoners are being tortured and beaten, some of them to death."

"I've heard stories about Ansar too," Geoff said. "It must be terrifying."

"*As salam alaikoom.*"

"*Alaikoom salam.*"

Peace be with you, and with you be peace. Geoff listened to the exchange as another man–older, perhaps in his late sixties, though it was often hard to know with these life-battered people–entered the house. Gaunt and gray-faced beneath his white khaffiyeh, he walked with what must have been a painful stoop. If not already, he would soon need a cane. He shook hands with the four adults, then sat by himself in an empty corner and fingered the punctured soccer ball lying on the floor. One of the older children jumped up and took him two cushions to lean on, which he accepted with a grateful nod.

"Who is he?" Geoff whispered, although he needn't have bothered to.

"I don't know, but I do not think he is a relative of these people," Grete said. She began to speak to the man.

Geoff's vocabulary of Arabic was at most twenty-five words, so it wasn't comprehension that made his pulse jump as soon as this Palestinian opened his mouth to answer Grete. Even before the pitch of surprise in her voice gave it away, he knew. Grabbing Grete's arm, he held on tight until she'd heard everything the Arab had to tell.

"What? Where is she?"

"Geoff–wait." Grete spoke slowly and softly, and this frightened him.

"What's wrong?" he demanded.

"He says she is not here. She was here, yes, but she left when it was still possible for Palestinians to get out of the city."

"Left for where?"

"He thinks she may have taken her grandmother to Tripoli in the north, or to the Baalbeck area in the Bekaa Valley."

"Which one does he think is more likely?"

"He doesn't know," Grete said. She looked uncomfortable, but he had no time to probe that now.

"Never mind. I'll go to both places. I'll leave today." What was he to make of the ambivalence grabbing hold of him at this moment: anger, of all things, that she had left; relief that she had left; and screaming frustration at being so many steps behind her once more.

"Geoff, there are hundreds of thousands of people in both of those places. You will *not* find her," Grete said, most vehemently. Too vehemently, as far as Geoff was concerned. He looked at her sharply.

"What, then? What would you have me do?"

"Stay here in Beirut. It is best for now. She may come straight back to Chatila as soon as this is over."

"Exactly–she *may*. Which also means she may not."

"Have you lost all the hope that brought you this far? You now know she is alive, and that is more than you had for certain even ten minutes ago."

"Does he at least know where she was staying? Does he know where her grandmother's house is?"

Grete relayed his question, and Geoff recognized the first word of the answer as yes.

"I want to go there. I want him to take me to the house."

For reasons that Geoff cared not a bit to wonder about, the Palestinian was clearly not eager to show him where Nadya's grandmother lived. But after some firm coaxing by Grete, he reluctantly agreed. Because she was not interested in such sightseeing, she said, Grete elected to stay behind and carry on with the visits she had promised. (Geoff wanted to feel mildly hurt that she did not share his eagerness, but he knew that was ridiculous.) They agreed to meet back at the entrance of the camp in a half hour.

It was only when he and the Palestinian were walking alone across the camp that Geoff began to consider Grete's admonishment and realized she'd been quite right. No, he would probably not find Nadya if he began wandering all over north Lebanon. And yes, it was true, she should indeed come straight back to Beirut once this madness was ended. Even if she didn't, where would she go afterwards if not back to Vancouver? He remembered but chose to ignore Walid's strange lack of belief that she would go back to Vancouver. She had to go back.

"*Hoonack.*" The scowling old man had stopped and was pointing to the open doorway of one among a squeeze of tiny block-and-tin hovels. Although this particular house looked undamaged, several near it had been crushed by IDF shells.

"Nadya's?"

The man nodded. "*Na'am.*"

Smiling, in part because he suspected that what he was about to do would annoy his unpleasant guide, Geoff strode right past him and into the house. The smile faded immediately, chased from his face by a tightening in his stomach. It was odd, he thought, to be so anxious entering the home of an absent lover. But then that was it, wasn't it? They weren't lovers. In fact, they might be nothing at all.

He might have turned around and left right then if he had not noticed the splash of hot pink on the far well. He walked right to it and lifted Nadya's sweatsuit top off the bare nail on which it had been left hanging. He pressed it to his face and breathed it, but any smell of her was long gone.

"*Yallah!*" Hurry up. The old Arab quickly stepped up and snatched the sweatsuit top away from him. At another time, in another place, Geoff might have reacted by wheeling around and shoving him, but not here and not now. Leaving it be, he carried on with his poking around the room. Not that there was much poking to be done. This house was as gloomy-small and impoverished as the one he'd just left, even more so because Nadya and her grandmother had evidently taken their essentials with them. The cooking utensils had been picked over pretty well and with the exception of the sweatshirt and a few other odds and leavings, their clothing was gone too.

Which left their junk and possibly–did he dare to hope?–his treasure. With the single-mindedness of a jewel thief in a suburban bedroom, he rifled through cardboard boxes and plywood cupboards, overturning everything without a second's pause to tidy the dishevelment. *Bass! Waqqif!* He ignored the Arab's insistence that he stop what he was doing.

And suddenly there it was: glass in a wood frame at his fingertips. Dragging it out of the box, he held the photograph in front of him. No, it was not a great picture–this Nadya was several years younger, perhaps even still a schoolgirl–but it was a picture just the same, and he nearly pulled it to his lips and kissed the glass.

"*Waqqif!*"

Imbued with fresh patience for the man, Geoff looked up to discover that his cranky old Arab was no longer alone. While this crazy foreigner was tearing the place apart, he must have slipped outside to recruit help because facing Geoff now was a young fedayeen with a pistol.

"*Shu biddak?*" the PLO fighter demanded. What do you want?

"*Ana biddi . . .*" I want . . . Jesus Christ, Geoff thought, how do I say photograph? How do I say girlfriend? In the end, he had to pantomine a camera.

The fighter was unimpressed with Geoff's attempts at charades. "*Imshi, rooh min houn. Yallah.*" Waving the barrel of his gun, he ordered him out of the house.

"*Min fadlak,*" Geoff said. Please.

"*Yallah!*" the old man yelled, rushing over to pull the photograph out of Geoff's hand and place it back in the cardboard box.

"*Yallah*," the fighter said, and Geoff could tell this was a final warning. He did as he was told.

They were about halfway back across the camp when the air raid sirens shrilled to life. Right behind them came the first useless salvos of anti-aircraft fire: Chairman Arafat shaking his fist at the sky. Abandoning Geoff on the spot, the two Palestinians hurried off in directions of duty or self-preservation. Once he was sure they were gone for good, Geoff turned and hurried too.

By the time he got back to the entrance of the camp, the Israeli jets had begun their first pass. He heard them bank out wide over the sea, then swing in low and fast—low enough now to be hit by anti-aircraft fire, but much too fast for anything but the luckiest of shots. In his mind, he could see them breaking formation as they reached the shoreline, each jet heading for a different target: the Fakhani and Corniche Mazraa neighborhoods, the remains of the municipal sports stadium and, of course, the refugee camps. Always the refugee camps.

He must have looked particularly stupid standing there in the open, he realized, waiting as if for a bus while cannon fire from a pair of streaking planes chewed up the buildings around him.

"Grete!" he shouted, but under the roar from above, his voice was a piss in the sea. "Grete!"

Through a veil of drifting smoke, he saw a fedayeen charging up the main camp road towards him. Snagging Geoff by the elbow, the fighter dragged him off the road down a narrow lane, then again down some concrete stairs into the blackness of an unlit cellar. Geoff tripped and fell at the bottom and skidded across the floor into someone's outstretched legs. The owner of the legs grunted. Someone else struck a match; that match lit a lantern. In the amber glow he made out Grete and perhaps two dozen other people. All eyes, for the moment, were on him.

"Are you all right?" Grete asked, coming towards him.

"Yes. You?"

"You've cut your hand," she said, holding his palm to the light so she could examine the laceration.

"Oh, that. It's nothing," he said. "Look, look what I've got." Reaching inside his shirt, he pulled out the photograph. There was some blood on it from the cut he'd given himself smashing the glass, and with his thumb he wiped a half-dried streak from the edge of her face. "It's an old picture, but it's her," he said. "That's Nadya. See, she is beautiful."

But Grete said nothing; she only looked at him.

TWELVE

GRETE HAD FOUND HIM SOME PAPER AND A PEN THAT WROTE well enough between skips, so whenever Geoff could he worked at something that had started out as a letter to his mother. It was no longer that, though; now, it was just a souvenir.

Last night, I went out with one of the doctors to trade for some supplies at a few of the other hospitals. For some reason, we have more plasma than we need at the moment, but an acute (acute–I'm even talking like them now) shortage of morphine and sterile bandage. In other places they are dying, bad joke, for our plasma. I told you about the massage parlor and the hotel bar that have been converted into makeshift hospitals. Well, they had nothing to work with, so we ended up leaving them plasma and even some of the morphine we'd already collected just so they could carry on for the next day or two.

Another stop that needed plasma was an Armenian theological institute very close to the Green Line. Considering that they only have two operating tables there, this particular hospital does an incredible number of amputations. Forty-nine last week alone. They have an orthopedic surgeon who is supposed to be very good, but then how good do you have to be to saw off a leg mid-thigh? I even saw the bin where they toss in what they've just cut off. Saving for a rainy day? Maybe we'll be trading in spare parts soon.

Understatement unavoidable: this is an education I'm getting here. Did you know (I didn't) that in ordinary warfare the statistical balance between killed and wounded is generally about 1:4? Here, it approaches 1:1. The Israelis cannot, however, claim this superior productivity as solely attributable to the expertise of their air force pilots–although, believe me, nobody on the ground in West Beirut would argue that they're not very good at what they do. No, but as impressive as the deliverer looks screaming overhead in his F-15 or F-16, it is the package delivered that counts. That package might be a phosphorus shell, or a cluster bomb, or something else the people here have taken to calling a vacuum bomb. I don't know much about the latter, no one here seems to, except that it's a large shell which implodes rather than explodes. How is that possible, I wonder. The net effect is that whole buildings collapse on top of themselves, story on top of story, family on top of family.

There is nothing so mysterious about phosphorus and cluster bombs. The phosphorus shell, in fact, is old as weapons go; armies have used it since the Second World War. Not like the Israelis use it, mind you. Its traditional deployment, I am told, is as a smokescreen or artillery marker in open battlefields: the cloud of white smoke from an explosion hangs heavy and thick for a long time because phosphorus ignites when exposed to air, and keeps burning until either the air or the phosphorus is exhausted. In urban Beirut, where the artillery targets are obvious enough (everything) and the besiegers have no need of a smokescreen, the phosphorus shell is used as an incendiary. Given that nearly all the significant structures here are concrete and stone, there is only one thing left to burn.

Which brings up cluster bombs. I've been told by some journalists I've run into here that there is quite a ruckus, at the moment, over the use of these things. Washington is quite upset–publicly, anyway–that the Israelis are violating a purchase agreement by using this particular American-made toy in Lebanon. A slap on the wrist seems to be forthcoming. I am sure that knowledge of that scolding will bring big satisfied grins to the faces of all those who've experienced these bomb-filled bombs. You know what they call the little bombs inside the big ones? Bomblets. Kind of cute, don't you think? A mother bomb with her brood of bomblets. Imagine the family photos. I learned a Lebanese card game called busra the other day. The young kid, Mohammed, who taught me the rules plays one-handed now. He lost his legs, too, but he doesn't need them to play busra. I know because I haven't been able to take a game from him yet.

Geoff was up on the hospital roof collecting clean gowns and bedding from the laundry lines when Dr. Musli came to fetch him.

"Good evening," he greeted the surgeon's wordless appearance beside him. He thrust a tangle of sheets into the man's arms.

"Tonight, you will come with me," Musli said in his inimitable way. The Norwegian did not make requests; he issued orders.

"And where will we be going?" Geoff asked, adding more to the load in Musli's arms.

"There is a sick man I must see."

Geoff took the rest of the sheets himself and followed Musli to the stairwell. "He can't come to the hospital like everyone else?"

"No."

"A housecall. I didn't think doctors did that sort of thing anymore."

Musli stopped walking for a moment. "This is all reduceable to a joke for you, isn't it?"

"The object is to find ways to survive," Geoff pointed out, more or less quoting Grete.

"Yes, but preferably with one's dignity intact."

Geoff choked on a laugh of disbelief. From a bad beginning, their relationship had proceeded to deteriorate a little further with almost every encounter. "You know something, you take full advantage of every opportunity you get to convince me you're a pompous ass."

The surgeon ignored Geoff's insult and headed downstairs. "I will meet you at the front entrance in ten minutes," he said. "Grete will be coming as well."

Geoff's job, he discovered when he met the two of them at the front doors, was to carry a heavy canvas duffel that contained medical equipment. This was strange enough, but then they climbed into an unmarked car instead of the ambulance parked outside. Being obvious about it, Geoff placed his palm on Grete's knee and leaned over the seat. "What is this? Why aren't we taking the ambulance?"

"A precaution," Musli said, turning around far enough to see an orderly's hand on a nurse's knee.

"What kind of precaution? Against what?" There was no safer way to travel through Beirut than by ambulance.

But Musli was explaining nothing more. "Okay, *yallah*," he instructed the driver. They pulled out of the driveway and headed north towards the Hamra area, traveling slowly.

"I thought this was a medical emergency," Geoff said.

"It is," Grete replied, pushing his hand off her leg. Geoff was aware that she'd waited until Musli was no longer watching.

Geoff rolled down his window and drank in the tepid air and unusual silence outside. After several days of failure, Phillip Habib, Ronald Reagan's shuttling envoy, had just that afternoon managed to secure another temporary ceasefire from the Israelis. This had brought an end to a period of intense bombardment that saw IDF fire directly aimed, for the first time since the siege began, at predominantly Lebanese neighborhoods, not just Palestinian enclaves. Until now, Geoff had not been able to leave the hospital since his afternoon of important discoveries in Chatila a full week earlier.

"Good for him." Musli and the driver nodded at each other. They had been listening to some news on the radio. With his comment in English, it was apparent that Musli had deigned himself open to a question from Geoff.

"What's good for who?"

"A report on the radio. The Canadian ambassador here, a Mr. Theodore Arcand, has condemned Israel's attacks on civilian targets."

"I can't tell. Are you inviting me to feel proud of him?" Geoff said.

"I invite you to feel nothing. It is a piece of information, that is all."

Grete tried to position herself between the two of them. "He must be a brave man," she said. "They say he is the last Western diplomat left in West Beirut."

"A national character trait. That kind of courage courses though the veins of all of us," Geoff joked.

They were not far now from the campus of the American University of Beirut. Without any apparent instruction to do so from Musli, the driver suddenly pulled over to the curb and turned off his headlights.

"Bring the bag. Let's go," the doctor said. They got out, and as soon as they did the doors were slammed closed behind them and the driver sped off.

"I don't suppose there's any point in asking you where we're going," Geoff said. He struggled to find a more comfortable position for the duffel over his shoulder.

"You know where we are going," Musli said. "I told you. And do not jar the bag any more than you must."

To Geoff's dismay, he found himself walking the remaining three blocks to the American University. They crossed onto the campus at Rue Bliss, made a nonsense circuit around the shadow-skirted exteriors of several faculty buildings, then left the campus via a sidestreet that brought them out to the seafront near the British Embassy. A second car awaited them there.

"Save your breath," Musli advised, directing Geoff to follow Grete into the backseat.

Now they traveled fast, speeding out from the sidestreet onto the Avenue de Paris, west past the Riviera and Sunset hotels, and the Ras Beyrouth amusement park with its inexplicably unscathed high ferris wheel. They swung south with the Avenue de General de Gaulle, past the black-and-white-striped lighthouse, the Military Beach and the Sporting Club. A pair of proud monoliths known as the Raoucheh Rocks loomed up from the water in a small bay just beyond the Sporting Club. At night, they had the eerie profile of icebergs.

Musli pointed towards them. He turned to Geoff with what was almost a friendly question. "I do not suppose you are a rock climber?"

"No," Geoff said.

"Over one year in West Beirut, and every time I see them I think I would like to climb them," the surgeon said.

"Why don't you, then?"

"My staff is afraid I will fall. They will not let me go," Musli said, looking at Grete.

"We're all afraid of something, aren't we?" she replied, staring right back at him.

Not far past the rocks, the driver angled off to the side of the road and stopped.

"Don't tell me—bring the bag," Geoff guessed.

"Quickly now," Musli snapped. "We must hurry."

With long-legged strides, the surgeon led them down a steep path to the beach. Burdened by the heavy bag over his shoulder, Geoff had difficulty with the sand underfoot and would have stumbled to his knees if Grete had not been there to catch him. He smiled at her, wondered at her strange distance this evening—her strange distance, in fact, all this last week since their visit to Chatila—and heard Musli calling back to him.

"Drop that and break anything inside, and they will likely shoot you for your clumsiness."

"Yeah, and who the hell are *they*?" Geoff fired back.

He had his answer when in a moment the three of them were met in the dark by a group of seven or eight fedayeen. These guerrillas were all heavily armed, and they looked older and, if it were possible, harder than most of the PLO men Geoff had come across. Wordlessly falling in among them, he and the two Norwegians were led across the sand to an outcropping of black rock near the base of the slope. Geoff spotted a cave and inside the cave more men squatting and seated in a faint lantern glow. He could see someone stretched out on his back and speculated that it might be the sick man they had played their little game of spooks to reach.

Here the group stopped. There was a brief exchange in Arabic between Musli and one of the fedayeen, and then Geoff was relieved of the duffel bag by a Palestinian.

"They do not want you to come inside," Musli explained unapologetically.

Geoff shrugged. "I'll be out here somewhere."

He watched the group clamber around and over the rock, and duck into the cave, then he wandered away towards the surf. Stopping at the high-water mark, he sat down, grateful, after a week in the crowded and oppressive confines of the hospital, for the vastness before him and the solitude. Death takes a holiday. It was a movie title, wasn't it? He tried to remember for sure, but couldn't. That was happening a lot lately: an uncertainty in his remembrances.

He had been there on the beach for some time, spending his *holiday* on the smallest of pleasures—dragging up mounds of cool, damp sand between his thighs—when he heard voices behind him. A group of Arabs had just come down from the cave and were cutting across the sand on an angle that would put them thirty or forty yards away from him along the water mark. Although he could not make out faces, he could tell that one of the men, the shortest of the group and the only one wearing a khaffiyeh had the rapt attention of the others. This man walked with fast small steps, unhindered by the sand as he led the group down towards the sea.

What was this, Geoff wondered, a team swim? As soon as the idea occurred to him, it appealed to him. Stripping off his clothes, he waded into the water, gasping a little at the chill, and then flung himself forward and dove in.

In spite of a faintly greasy odor at its surface, the cold salt water felt wonderful. He made a long crawl straight out, feeling the accumulated layers of grime wash away from his skin, then somersaulted around and breaststroked back in. It had been a long time since his last real exercise and he was out of breath, so he rolled onto his back and floated for a while, drifting slow yards with the current and light years with his eyes on the night sky.

Finally, he rolled over to tread water and see what had become of the group of Arabs. They were still there, but it was not to swim that they had ventured down to the beach. Bicycling his legs to stay afloat, he watched their ritual of prayer: the careful orientation towards Mecca, southeast from here, and the succession of deferential body positions–head bowed and standing, kneeling, then down on all fours, forehead pressed to the ground, then head bowed and standing again. This show of devotion provoked the cynic in Geoff. Tell me, he wondered, what has *He* done for you lately?

He had returned to the beach and his sandcastles when the prayer session broke up. He heard their voices re-engaged in conversation and assumed they would go back to the cave the same way they had come. They did not. Led again by the darting little man with the khaffiyeh, they started along the water mark towards him. He got to his feet, but did not remember until it was too late that he was standing there naked.

At first, the little man's face did not fully register. As the group of Arabs passed by on either side of him, scarcely acknowledging his presence at all, his initial thoughts were relief at not having been laughed at for his state of exposure. It was only as the last members of the group were going by him that he realized just who the individual leading them on their little walk was.

"Hello."

Geoff pulled his stare away from the back of the departing figure to see that one of the dawdlers in the entourage had stopped beside him. This face was familiar too, albeit for a quite different reason. It was the guerrilla commander he'd had to plead with to be allowed into West Beirut.

"Arafat?" Geoff asked, pointing, though of course he knew it was.

The guerrilla nodded. "Abu Amar is the name we call him. Father who builds."

Geoff again watched the chairman of the PLO moving up the beach. He was gesticulating this point and that as he talked with his followers. A slightly built, middle-aged man with a pinched, salt-and-pepper-bearded face, he was not at all what Geoff would describe as imposing or impressive. The irony of his nickname was not missed either: the father who builds holed-up and planning in a city under destruction.

"Your search, how goes it?" the Palestinian asked.

"I'm still here, if that's an answer," Geoff said.

"The doctor told me you are working very hard at his hospital. This makes it a good thing I permitted you to enter West Beirut."

"The doctor told you that?" Geoff asked with surprise. "You don't mean the nurse?"

"I think the doctor," the guerrilla said. "Yes—it was the doctor. He was complimentary."

The Palestinian had said his goodbye and was heading away to catch up with his compatriots when Geoff felt compelled to ask him much the same question he had once asked Camille Haddad. "Your English is good. Were you a student somewhere?"

"Yes," the Palestinian answered, walking backwards. "In Tucson. I studied business and real estate at the University of Arizona."

"*Real estate?*" Geoff said.

"Land and property, you know." He laughed. "Funny, no, a Palestinian studying about real estate?"

By the time Grete came down to the beach to collect him for their return, Geoff had constructed an elaborate fortress, complete with a moat system and several drawbridges made of sticks. She smiled at his plaything and squatted for a moment to inspect it.

"Well done, little boy," she said, patting him on the head.

"And you, a job well done up there?" he asked, thumbing back at the rocks. He could make out the silhouette of a figure standing near the mouth of the cave, watching them. It was too tall to be anyone but Musli.

"The man has a heart condition, but for now he is all right," she said.

"I know, at least I think I know, why all the secrecy to get here.

I saw him." Geoff could tell that Grete was aware of Musli watching them from a distance too.

"You mean Arafat?"

"Yes," he said.

Grete nodded. "The man with the bad heart is one of his closest advisers," she said. "Do you now understand why we had to come here to him?"

"Not really, but–"

"It is because of spies and informants, of which there are many. Someone would have recognized this man in the hospital, and when he was discharged they could have followed him back to Arafat. Soon after that, the Israelis would know where Arafat was and they would send assassins or an air raid to kill him while he slept."

"But why down here? The beach doesn't seem like an especially safe place to me," Geoff said.

"But, you see, at night it is," she disagreed. "For one thing, the Israelis bomb buildings. They are not interested in blowing up sand. And he never sleeps on the same beach; a different one each night. If he is to survive, Arafat must keep moving."

"You know, after he was gone, I had this image of myself running up the beach after him."

"Why?" Grete asked.

"So I could tell him . . . so I could ask him to quit Beirut and leave. So it would be over," he said, getting to his feet.

"I can tell you this much," she said. "He is thinking about it." She stepped behind him and gently brushed the sand off his backside. They were about to start back up towards the cave and the trail leading to the road above when Geoff turned abruptly and kicked a vicious hole in his sandcastle. He kept kicking until it was all gone.

*   *   *

Geoff had learned that there were certain life courses in Lebanon that even war could not impede for long. The coming together of men and women was one such inexorability. If anything, the constant hover of death here made the drive to create new life that much stronger, and after the passing of the Ramadan fast in late July the season of summer marriages began with urgency.

One of those about to be married was a young Lebanese orderly named Jamal, whose betrothed and family lived in a Sunni village in the Bekaa Valley, about forty miles southeast of Beirut. With a sudden, impetuous flourish, Jamal had decided to invite the entire hospital staff to his weekend wedding. The entire staff could not go, obviously–somebody had to keep the place running, and the Palestinians who worked there could not safely leave West Beirut at all–but Grete and Geoff were among a dozen Lebanese and foreigners (Norwegian, Canadian, Indian, Italian and French) who piled into two white-flagged cars and started out from the hospital on a Friday afternoon.

Dr. Musli was not with them. He had refused to leave his post, and he'd almost succeeded in silently inducing a guilt-stricken Grete to do the same. Almost. There were elaborate games going on between the two Norwegians that Geoff was becoming determined to sort out for himself. There was little doubt in his mind that they had once been lovers, and it was just as clear that they no longer were, but he could not even guess who had done whatever to whom to end it because they both seemed so completely miserable in each other's company.

Azure and hot, it was also a day of undeclared ceasefire following a day and night of unremitting artillery duels. Virtually until the moment they'd actually left, the party of wedding-goers was not sure they would be able to. Traveling south to start with, they crossed the siege-front beyond the airport, running hard into arguments first with the PLO and then, barely a hundred yards farther on, the Israelis. With groom-to-be Jamal in the lead car, however, they were not about to be denied by either side. Geoff, in the second car, imagined an impassioned Jamal demanding: Let me go or kill me here now.

A short distance south of the airport (they were in Israeli-held territory now and would be all weekend), they turned east and began to climb the progression of higher hills that would take them up into the Druze-dominated Chouf Mountains. From these first hills, Geoff discovered a similar sort of panorama to the one he'd had from the terrace at Haddad's villa. He listened to Grete and Dr. Patal, the Indian who'd stitched up his head after the car bombing, mourning the moribund city they saw below them. The airport runways glinted silver in the sunshine: neat and angular slashes marking the entry to a deep and terrible wound.

"Paris of the Middle East. That is what they once called Beirut," said Dr. Patal, who had a trace of the pedant in him. Grete nodded at this piece of non-news. It was an indulgent gesture that Geoff had experienced with her more than once himself.

"And yet," Patal laughed, "at the same time, they once called Lebanon the Switzerland of the Middle East. Look what this crazy little country does to the map of Europe."

Grete looked over at Geoff and rolled her eyes. "I expect that Jamal is getting very excited," she said.

"Yes, probably in more ways than one," Geoff joked. "With all the repressed energy he's got stored up, maybe there is something to be said for this chastity-unto-the-marriage-bed tradition. A bigger bang to the buck."

"Pardon," she said, "I do not entirely understand you? A bigger bang?"

"Nor should you. I'm being crude," he confessed.

"Oh. *Oh*," Grete said, beginning to smile.

"Sex, sex, sex. It is nothing but the physical drive to procreate," Patal said, trying to pretend clinical indifference. "Much more important and wonderful than sex is romance," he continued. "One of the nurses at the hospital was telling me—"

"Would that nurse be Leila?" Grete cut in mischievously. In a place as insular as a small hospital in a blockaded city, there were no secret flirtations.

"Yeah, don't tell us you wouldn't like to have sex with Leila," Geoff teased. Patal squirmed and fidgeted, trapped between his antagonizers in the backseat. At last, he broke down under their amused stares and conceded with a shrug.

"Just the same," he said, "romance is the most wonderful thing. Leila was telling me that many loves have begun this summer between people forced together in the underground garages and shelters by the bombing."

"Next thing you know, Begin and Sharon will be pumping the Americans for more foreign aid to defray the cost of their new matchmaking service," Geoff said. But the laughter ebbed quickly, draining him as it retreated.

It was axiomatic that his stream of one-liners was symptomatic of something. He was jealous of Jamal, and for that matter even of Patal. Despite the fact that he was quite conscious of just how long it had been since he'd made love to anyone, he knew the Indian was right: you could not even begin to compare the pelvic motion to the emotion.

And didn't that mark a turnabout of 180 degrees? He thought about the last thing Angela had said to him in her humiliated state, as she stomped around his bedroom collecting her trail of clothes after Nadya's phone call that night. *You really are just a cock with a person stapled to the back end of it, aren't you?*

"You smile–sort of. Another joke?" Grete was staring past Patal at him.

"No," he said, "I was thinking about something somebody once said about me."

"What did they say?" Patal chipped in on Grete's behalf.

"It wasn't especially flattering. I think I'll keep it to myself," he said in understatement.

"Was it Nadya who said it?" Grete guessed.

He half laughed and shook his head. "No, now change the subject, please."

His requested change of subject came a moment later as their tiny caravan slowed to a creep and entered the outskirts of the Chouf Mountain town of Aley. At this strategic watershed on the Beirut–Damascus highway, they found the Israelis garrisoned in force.

It made sense that they would be. From points in Aley, they could see for miles in all directions. Having asked enough questions over the past month to recreate the entire June invasion for himself, Geoff knew that this town and surrounding area had been the scene of major tank battles between the advancing Israeli and retreating Syrian armies. The Syrians were long gone now, pinned to the east and north, while the IDF's armor was either somewhere nearby under camouflage or down below as part of the garrote tightening around West Beirut, likely both, but the battles they had fought here could still be seen. Stone houses with walls that must have been a full foot thick had been reduced to piles of gravel between olive trees. Other homes and buildings that had been fortunate enough to be hit just once or twice stood bleeding invisibly from cannon holes large enough to run both fists through.

The importance of the place to its occupiers was underscored by the fact that there were roadblocks at both ends of town and that it took the better part of an hour before they were clear of them and underway again. Jamal, of course, was nearly apoplectic by the end of all the body searches–human and automobile–and questions, and, for one tense moment, it looked as if the Israelis were going to take him away for further interrogation. That they were convinced not to in the end was due entirely to the verbal heroics of Dr. Patal. The Indian coaxed and cajoled the two junior officers in charge of the outbound roadblock to the point of distraction until they finally gave up and waved the whole group through.

"Well done," Geoff said, shaking Patal's hand as they drove on. Ahead of them, Jamal leaned out a window of the other car and raised his fist in thanks.

"The resistance goes on with whatever weapons are available," the Indian said, looking pleased with himself.

"Leila will be proud of you," Grete said, offering a wink.

"You think so?" Patal beamed.

Farther east, the Chouf ran into a range of higher mountains called the Barouk. In contrast to the former, with its fertile terraces and orchards, the exposed and bald Barouk offered little more than grazing for sheep and goats and was correspondingly uninhabited.

From the backside of the Barouk, the Bekaa Valley at last came into view: a long green belt of agriculture running north-south between the Barouk and another line of bare hills to the east, towards Syria. Geoff was instantly reminded of British Columbia's Okanagan Valley, minus all the lakes, and that thought led him back to the surprise Jamal had had for him just before they left from the hospital. There is a woman in my village, he had struggled to explain with his few words of English, an old red one from Canada. *Red?* Geoff had asked.

They'd had to seek out Grete for a translation. Red meant Indian, that other kind of Indian. The woman was eighty-some years old and originally from a tribe somewhere in the north of the province called Alberta, Jamal explained through Grete. As a very young woman, she had met and married an intrepid young man from the village who had gone to Canada and opened a general store in the north, where he traded goods for furs with the natives. This man had made a lot of money from his furs, enough so that one day he'd been able to travel home to Lebanon, build a big house in the village and never work again. He was dead now, but his widow lived on in the big house, cared for by her children's children.

"I was just thinking about the story of the old red one," Geoff said.

Grete, staring out her side window, nodded.

"It reads a little bit like a Harlequin novel maybe, but it is pretty stuff just the same. A man and woman from opposite ends of the earth, utterly different cultures." He stopped speaking then, in part because he'd just recognized the parallel with him and Nadya, but mostly because he could tell Grete was crying. He leaned in front of Patal, who was sitting between them, and touched her arm. "Okay?"

"Yes." She glanced up at him only briefly.

Patal, who knew the story of the old red one too, was happy to carry on for them. "Northern Canada, Brazil, Zaire, everywhere that a merchant is needed you will find the Lebanese. They are great travelers, but then what do you expect from a people who sometimes claim ancestry from the Phoenicians?"

Though they were not far from Jamal's village now, the remainder of the trip was the slowest going of all. The reason was the nearness of the Syrian and Israeli forward positions–the Syrians being less than half a mile away in places along the road–an attending air of uneasy standoff, and repeated Israeli checkpoints set up because of it. In truth, it was no standoff at all: the IDF would win any battle they chose to fight with the Syrians. It was just that the cost would be high; the Syrians had drawn an imaginary chalk line at this point and they would fight hard in losing if the Israelis advanced on it. Damascus was too close for comfort now, as Patal put it.

"You know what I think?" Grete said.

"No, Grete, what?" Geoff asked solicitously. It had taken a long time to rouse her from that earlier sadness.

"I think the Americans have told the Israelis they must allow Hafez Assad to save face. I think they have been told to leave the Syrians alone."

"Possibly," Patal conceded.

For his part, Geoff was far more interested right now in Norwegian intrigue than any Syrian-American-Israeli entanglement. When they at last arrived in the village, heralding themselves in with honking horns, he sought Grete out in the crowd that formed around their cars in welcome. "We should talk," he said.

"Tomorrow," she answered.

"What's wrong with tonight?"

"Tonight they will feed us and want everyone happy." With that, she squeezed his arm and walked away.

*　　　*　　　*

In the morning, with some time before the wedding, Grete came to find him. He had not seen her at all the previous night after supper. In what must have been a local variation of the bachelor stag, he'd been hustled off with Jamal and the other men to smoke and play cards. Furthermore, they had been billeted in homes at opposite ends of the village: he rooming with Patal; she with two other women, a French nurse and an Italian X-ray technician.

"You look tired," she said. "Not accustomed to this country air?" She climbed the steps and took a chair beside his on the small terrace at the front of the house. The man of the house and a friend sat nearby, leaning into a slow game of backgammon while they fiddled with worry beads. At the other end of the vine-roofed terrace, the man's wife used a stick to beat the dust out of an old carpet draped over the steel railing. Somewhere in the distance, a donkey brayed as if it too was being hit by a stick. "Or perhaps you now need the lullaby of bombs dropping in order to sleep?"

"I slept all right. It just wasn't long enough. They kept us up

playing Forty-one until two in the morning, and then the
muezzin started at five, and then the roosters."

"Where is Dr. Patal?" she asked.

"Still sleeping. That man snores something awful, by the
way. Perhaps you'd better warn Leila when we get back
to Beirut."

Grete smiled and exchanged a few words of Arabic with the
backgammon players.

"Do you feel like a walk? Jamal told me that the view from
beyond the orchards is very nice," she said, indicating a series of
hills that backed the village.

"Won't people talk?" he joked.

"Let them."

The trail leading up to the orchards had been mutilated by
tank tread, a reminder of the larger state of things here. Geoff and
Grete watched an old farmer coming down from some chore in
the orchards nearly fall when the donkey he was riding stumbled
against one of the hard ridges of torn-up earth. The angry
peasant muttered *calb*–dogs–and then raised a brown, weathered
hand in greeting as he passed.

"Hope he wasn't talking about us," Geoff said. Cusses and
curses: he now knew most of those in Arabic.

"I don't think so," Grete said. She stooped and picked up a
flattened motor oil can. It was khaki-colored and marked with
Hebrew print. She shook off the dirt and handed it to Geoff. He
took a brief look and then tossed it away like a frisbee.

"Where are they?" he asked, scanning the area.

"They are around," she answered. "When they want us to see
them, we will see them."

Apricot, almond, peach, cherry, apple, pear and fig: Grete
identified the trees for Geoff as they climbed up through the
orchards. She told him that in spite of the apparent free-for-all in
planting, the owner of each one would be known to every resident
of the village. And that made a certain amount of sense, because
judging by the gnarled limbs and thickened bark, many of them
were generations old. Family heirlooms. He jumped up to steal a
couple of ripe peaches from a failing branch and remembered
something Nadya had said about fruit trees being the only land
title her family had ever had–or needed, they thought–in
Palestine.

"I saw you talking with the 'old red one' last night at dinner," Grete said, ending a lengthy silence as she tossed away her peach pit.

"We were trying, but she's been here almost fifty years now. There's not much English left." He sensed that this was Grete announcing her readiness to begin talking about the day before. "So. What happened yesterday?" he asked.

"I cried a little is all. It is an easy thing to do in Lebanon."

"Of course," he said, patiently.

They reached the crest of the hill above the orchards, only to discover that there was a higher hill yet tucked behind it. Not that they had any intention of climbing farther. Geoff motioned towards a large, flat rock where they could sit down. He stopped and held out his hand to help Grete negotiate the rough, hummocky traverse.

"Jamal wasn't lying about the view." Geoff stood atop their smooth gray bench of rock and took in the valley. A hot breeze stirred the dry grasses and wildflowers on the near-slope. Farther down, beyond the canopy of the orchards, the houses at the center of the cream-colored village appeared to be scrambling all over each other to get close to the minareted mosque. Below the village were vegetable plots and more orchards and a small, iron-fenced cemetery. Someone had shrewdly herded his sheep and goats inside the fence, and they could be seen working down the high grass around the headstones.

He looked down at Grete now, stretching herself out to sun on the rock. Presumably in deference to their Muslim hosts, she had dressed modestly that morning in a long denim skirt and a loose white blouse that could have been a man's shirt. Up here, though, away from the ever-curious eyes of the village, she obviously felt freed. She had already hiked her skirt well up her thighs and unfastened all but the bottom few buttons of her shirt. Geoff could see she was braless.

"So?" He dropped to his haunches beside her.

"What do you know about impotence?" she suddenly blurted.

"Impotence? Do you mean like sexual impotence?"

She nodded. When she craned her neck to hear his reply, he saw most of her small, pert breasts.

"I know it happens." He thought about the two or three times it had shot him down over the years.

"That was a very odd question, Grete. Why do you ask?"

"Because my husband finds himself so."

"Your husband? You're married?" And then it hit him squarely between the eyes. "You and Musli?"

"Nine years."

"My God, Grete, I must be brain dead. I would never have thought that."

"Perhaps it is because neither one of us has given you any reason to think that." Grete opened her sack purse and pulled out Marlboros and a plastic water bottle. With his lungs still burning from the previous night's card game, Geoff declined her offer of a cigaret but gratefully took some water.

"Jesus," he said, replacing the cap on the bottle.

"Geoff, this amazement of yours does not make me feel any better."

"I'm sorry. It's just that I was thinking about that night in the car when I put my hand on your leg."

"Yes, that did hurt him, and I was happy for it," she admitted.

"How long has he had trouble?"

"Almost from the first day we arrived in Beirut. More than a year now."

"Which might have something to do with it," Geoff suggested. "Being in *that* place, I mean."

"Possibly everything."

"Mutilated bodies are not much of a turn-on for most people."

"I understand that."

"But?"

"But in the last months, he has withdrawn from me completely. Now I get nothing from him. We are strangers."

"It's got to be a kick in the gut for him. Would be for me."

Grete scoffed and tossed her cigaret away.

"He is a doctor, and I am a nurse. If two people such as us cannot talk about it—"

"Physician, heal thyself? If only it were as easy to understand and fix as appendicitis. It's not. At least, I don't think it is."

"Geoff, I know that. He does not have to push me up against a wall and screw me like some satyr. I just need to feel that he still wants me."

"I'm sure he does." He looked at Grete closely and was aware that this was really the first time he had acknowledged that she was an attractive woman.

She laughed.

"Mmm?"

"A question. What do you think as you see me half-nude?"

"I guess I think you're taking advantage of some relative privacy for a little sun."

"That is maybe what it has become."

"What do you mean?"

"Has a starving woman never tried to seduce you before?"

"You were not," he said, smiling.

"Oh yes, I think I was."

He laughed. "I'm pretty slow on the uptake, in that case. Are you terribly offended?"

"No. It is clear that your heart belongs to someone else. You must be in love."

After a long pause, he said, "Am I, though? You know the time I spent with her is best measured in hours?"

"Important hours, though."

"We never even went to bed together, speaking of starvation. Maybe I've just come all this way because I haven't *had* her."

"You do not believe that, Geoff."

"No," he said.

Grete cleared her throat. She looked away and plucked at a loose thread in the hem of her rolled-up skirt. Geoff uncapped the water bottle for another drink. Grete shook her head when he held the bottle out to her. She kept shaking it.

"Life is a terribly unfair sentence we serve."

"You've got that right," he muttered, deep in his own thoughts.

"Geoff, I have been trying to think how to tell you this. There is something you should know."

"Hey . . . What the hell do you suppose *that* is?" he said, not hearing as he cut her off. She turned her head, and he pointed towards a sharp flash of reflected sunshine on the hill above theirs. She shielded her eyes.

"Binoculars. The bastards are watching us," she said.

"Who, the Israelis?"

"Yes. Look closely."

He squinted through the reflection and made out the side of a jeep.

"Out looking for cheap thrills, are they?"

"Let us really give them something to watch, then," Grete said. Abruptly, she undid the remaining buttons on her shirt and pulled it off.

"I've heard about you Scandinavians." He stared at her.

"Take your clothes off too." She got to her feet and wriggled out of her skirt, then she tugged off her panties and stood before him naked.

"What are you doing?" he said.

"Come on." She stepped towards him and reached out to his fly. "Trust me."

"I trust you. It's me I'm worried about."

"This is just a game to be played for their benefit. Kiss me," she said, "and try to be convincing."

He did as she asked—it was not that difficult—and allowed himself to be gradually pulled down to the earth just below the rock. Here, he understood, they were mostly out of view. Grete reached back onto the rock and grabbed the water bottle. She opened it and poured the remaining water into the ground.

"Now, take your clothes off," she told him again. He did as told, then lay on his side, propped on an elbow, watching her mix and squeeze the earth between her fingers to make mud.

"This must be old Viking foreplay," Geoff said. Grete, on her knees, giggled.

"Roll over. Onto your belly," she ordered.

"What?"

"Just do it, Geoff."

"Okay, but don't get kinky on me." He gasped as the first cold mud met his skin.

When he finally figured out what Grete was up to, Geoff could not stop laughing. It was stupid, and at the same time it was perfect. Completing his mud tattoo, she spanked him once on his bare cheeks and then lay down to trade places.

"Do you want punctuation between the letters?" he asked,

taking advantage of the situation to admire the cut of her buttocks for a moment.

"Is there room? Be sure to make the letters big," she said over her shoulder.

The glint of glass was waiting when they finished mucking and got to their feet. Geoff helped Grete up onto the rock, and they stood there holding hands as they faced the voyeurs.

"What a waste if they don't read English?" Geoff said.

"Even if they only speak Hebrew, they will recognize this," she assured him.

"Are you ready?" he asked.

"Yes," she answered. "*Now.*"

Gasping with suppressed laughter, they turned around, leaned forward and mooned the hill above them, reaching back to point at the initials PLO finger-painted on their backsides.

"What was it Patal said yesterday?" Geoff smiled across at her from knee-level. "The resistance goes on with whatever weapons one has."

"Yes, and you've got a nice weapon, I can see," Grete said, making them both burst into laughter.

*   *   *

But the joke was too soon over for Grete. By the time they reached the orchards on their return walk down to the village, she had slipped back into her previous gloom. Geoff put a comradely arm around her shoulders and squeezed.

"It'll be all right, you'll see. One of these days soon, the man will be up to it," he said sounding more glib than he meant to be.

"Oh, Geoff, this is crazy," she cried, rolling away from his arm. They stood facing each other in the silver-leaved shade of an olive tree. Grete scratched at the rough bark of this peace tree with her fingernails. She winced, and Geoff watched her withdraw her hand. The index finger bubbled with blood from a sliver.

"I didn't mean to sound insincere, Grete. I know it's a hard thing for you," he said. "For both of you."

She shook her head to hush his apology. "Geoff, I should have told you this long ago, but I didn't know how."

"Should have told me what?"

"You know that old man in Chatila camp, the one who knew about Nadya?"

"How could I forget him? He nearly had me shot."

"He told me . . . Geoff, he told me that Nadya is engaged to his son."

At first, Geoff screwed up his face and scowled at her: very funny. But Grete, like her impotent husband, was no kidder. It showed in her face; she was genuinely stricken. In the end, he could only think his way clear to say one limp thing to her.

"Go away."

THIRTEEN

THE VOYEURS MUST HAVE LEFT THE AREA ALTOGETHER, GONE on to another high hilltop someplace else, because if they had not left they would surely have raced back with their binoculars to see who it was flinging his hurt across the valley. As it was, Geoff's cry turned the head of a farmer who had gone into the village cemetery to fetch his sheep and goats and drive them home. The Arab cupped his eyes and peered up at the hill above the orchards.

Geoff had made Grete tell him all she knew, everything she had held back from him until now, and then he had simply turned and walked up the hill away from her. She was wise enough not to try to stop him. He returned to the same flat rock again and, after his single angry cry at the unfairness of it, had sat there into the heat of the day, left with the energy to do nothing more than stare at a creased, pilfered photograph.

"What do you mean, she's engaged to his son? Who the hell is his son? Where is he? Where is Nadya?"

He heard her labored explanation; he even understood why she'd felt unable to tell him before, but the rage was there and it had to be aimed somewhere. He was not equipped to choke on it all by himself.

"Just save your goddamn sorries, Grete, and tell me what's going on."

She reported what the old man had told her. Nadya was in Baalbeck; she and her grandmother were in one of the temporary camps set up there by refugees made refugees once more. Her

181

fiancé was not with them; he was PLO, a fedayeen with George Habash's Popular Front.

There was more detail, but he stopped her. He'd heard enough to believe it was true. He'd heard enough. He left her standing in the orchards.

Sweat ran down his spine, adding itch to the drag of dried mud on his behind. He stared at the black-haired phantom in the photograph, she staring back with schoolgirl innocence. He poked himself with darts: Nadya and her guerrilla husband damply entwined on a straw-filled mattress atop a cold stone floor; Nadya's afterwards smile; Nadya on her back, legs spread, knees up, gasping happy through the birthing moment; Nadya older and gone a little soft about the hips, and surrounded by dark, gorgeous children. . . .

Funny, but in his imaginings, he saw her with everything but fruit trees.

It was late afternoon before he returned to the village. He suspected he had missed the wedding, hoped so, but as he neared the main street the sounds of rhythmic hand-clapping and women trilling with joy informed him that something important was underway. Rounding a last corner, he saw the back of a large crowd moving slowly up the road. Someone banged a drum.

"We were thinking we would have to form a searching party for you." Dr. Patal greeted him as he fell into step with the group, which looked to comprise most of the village. At the head of the procession, he could see Jamal and his wife walking hand-in-hand up the rutted, gravel street. The teenaged bride's long white gown was quickly turning dusty gray at the bottom, but neither she nor anybody else appeared to notice or care.

"Where are we going?" Geoff asked. "To watch the consummation?"

"No, to eat." The answer came back in Grete's stern voice, not Patal's. Geoff had failed to see her coming towards him through the crowd. "That was you I heard up on the hill?" she said.

"Primal scream. I feel so much better now."

"Do you." She stared at him.

He did not reply.

When they reached the house where the wedding feast lay spread out on tables on a back terrace, Geoff found he had little appetite. Though he had not eaten since breakfast, the piles of lamb kebab and the bowls of rice, tabouleh, hommous, pickled turnip and fried eggplant did not much interest him. Taking a bit of salad and rice and a single skewer of meat, he sat down in the garden with Dr. Patal, making it obvious to Grete that he did not want to eat with her. (He supposed he was not done slaying the messenger.) For this, he was subjected to a rambling lesson on the rituals and customs of the contemporary Hindu wedding. He offered a nod every few minutes, but otherwise let Patal's voice wash over him like lukewarm water. Chickens and cats wandered past, ignoring each other, and the smell of stabled livestock hung about with the insects in the soupy air.

When the eating was finished, half a dozen women emerged from the house and swept across the terrace and garden, trading dirty plates and cutlery for steaming glasses of sweet tea stuffed with fresh mint leaves. The men pulled out their Marlboros and lit up, and their voices buzzed softly under a blue-gray veil of cigaret smoke in the pink-gray wash of dusk.

The women had just returned with refills of tea when Jamal stood up on the terrace and urged everyone to pick up and move the party out to the street. It was time for music and dancing. Geoff felt sick, but he could not very well run away again.

A quartet had set themselves up on chairs at the edge of the road. There was the tabla player who had drummed the wedding procession to the feast, a violinist, a third man cradling an oud finished with inlaid mother-of-pearl, and a heavy-set singer who appeared even larger than she was because of the ornately brocaded blue velvet caftan she wore. As they emerged from the back of the house, the guests took up positions in a loose semicircle in front of the musicians and waited while the players tuned their instruments and reviewed their repertoire.

Geoff actively avoided Grete. When she began to move towards him, he went to congratulate Jamal. He wondered if he shouldn't also shake hands with the bride, but when she made no move of her own in that direction he settled on a simple nod and smile. After a month and a half in the Middle East, the male-female strictures of Islam continued to baffle him.

The music began with a violin prelude that reminded Geoff less of Arabs than gypsies, but when the drummer and oud player

jumped in the music became very Middle Eastern. Frantic
syncopation. When the singer started, so did the dancing. The
semicircle of wedding guests became a length of chain, became a
charmed snake. Suddenly, men and women were holding
hands–and not just holding hands but actually linking fingers.
Hip pressed tight to hip, arms held straight down at their thighs,
the line of dancers began to lean and bob to the left. Caught up in
the watching, Geoff once again failed to notice Grete coming. She
stepped in beside him.

"They call it *dabke*. Want to try?"

"No thanks," he said, without looking at her. She certainly was
thicker-skinned than he, he'd have to give her that. He watched
her slip away after a moment and join the end of the line.

As the dancing went on, the arrangement of dancers changed.
There was a jockeying of positions, almost competitively towards
the front, that eventually left the head of the line mostly young
and all male. Hooting and dipping at the knee and pirouetting
comically, the men took turns showing off for each other and,
more importantly, Geoff surmised, for the women who were
certain to be watching. Someone produced a knotted white
handkerchief, and soon the dancer in the front position was
cockily twirling it overhead.

When this first frenzied song ended after twenty minutes the
tired dancers disbanded. The men smoked, the women fanned
themselves, and the reconstituted semicircle moved in a little
closer to the quartet to listen to the female vocalist sing a love
ballad especially for the newlyweds.

Geoff thought he recognized the song and leaned towards a
villager to ask about it. "Um Kalthum?" The famous Egyptian's
was the only name he knew.

The Arab smiled but shook his head. "Fairouz. *Min Lebanon*,"
he explained.

"*Shookran*," Geoff thanked him and stepped back.

After the ballad had ended, the same villager caught Geoff's
eye and called out to the singer. There was pleased laughter from
the crowd, and then the man stepped in close to Geoff. He held up
his hand and pinched his fingers together. It was a gesture that
Geoff had come to understand as *shway*: slowly, or wait a minute.

The music started again, this time led by a delicate and mournful violin.

The villager listened for a moment, then he flashed a delighted grin at Geoff. "Um Kalthum," he explained as the vocalist started.

If pain could ever be something exquisite, it was music alone that could render it thus. Geoff stood and listened to this sad song, the words to which he could not possibly understand, and felt the emotion in the singer's voice beginning to cut him. He bled gladly.

"My darling, we are parted."

He turned and stared at Grete, now back at his side once more.

"The name," she said. "That is the name of the song she is singing."

He nodded. For half an instant, he had actually thought she was rubbing it in.

"How do you know Um Kalthum?"

"Nadya used to play some tapes," he answered dully.

The young men were eager to get moving again, and the band was happy to oblige. When they had finished with the mournful Um Kalthum, they launched into another spirited *dabke*. Grete reached for Geoff's hand and tried to coax him into joining the dance, but he refused again and she left him alone. He watched her go and recruit Patal. The Indian quickly showed himself to be a smooth dancer.

When the banging and popping sounds began, Geoff, despite all his time in Beirut, assumed firecrackers were just another part of the wedding fete. It was only after others had heard it too and the quartet abruptly stopped playing that he realized it was gunfire. The line of dancers dissolved in midstep, and soon everybody was packing up and heading towards home. Nobody ran, but neither did anyone dawdle.

"We must go inside," Grete said.

"What is it?" He followed her and Patal.

"An ambush. They are saying that some men from the local resistance have attacked an Israeli patrol up the road."

"Listen. The shooting has already stopped," he said.

"Then we must hurry, because the soldiers will be here very quickly."

Grete was right–they were. Because it was nearer, she led him and Patal to the house where she was staying. Partway there, they were joined by the other two houseguests, the French nurse and Italian X-ray tech. The group had barely crossed over the threshold, ushered in by the host family, themselves just back, when the darting beam of a powerful light on the main street behind them signaled the arrival of the first IDF vehicles.

The family and their five refugees stood in silence at the windows of the darkened house and watched the Israelis drive slowly through the village. Geoff counted four jeeps and a personnel carrier rigged with a spotlight and machine gun.

When they reached the end of town, the Israelis turned around and drove back in again. They stopped in front of the mosque and got out of their vehicles. One of the soldiers spoke Arabic through a megaphone: the voice was harsh but even. Geoff heard Grete talking quietly with the family.

"What do they want?" he asked her.

"They are saying they want all the males between thirteen and sixty-five to go to them at once."

"What if we all just refuse to go?" he said.

Grete gave him a sharp frown but turned to the family and relayed his question anyway. She nodded at the answer she heard. "If the boys and men do not go," she explained, "the Israelis will probably call in one of their tanks and blow up some of the houses."

"What do they want us for?" Geoff was puzzled by the strain in his voice. It was as if everything were different now that Nadya was engaged to another man. It was almost as if before, bombed and shot at in West Beirut, the threat to his life was somehow Zhivagoesque. But now, should he be killed by this nonsense, he would only die a fool far from home.

"They are after the men who planned the attack. You have nothing to be afraid of. You are not an Arab."

"I'm not afraid," Geoff said. "Just annoyed." From outside the open window, he heard the sound of fathers and sons mumbling to each other as they walked slowly up the road towards the soldiers. He heard the brave voices of boys and felt ashamed, and so when Patal and the man of the house headed for the door he quietly went with them.

It was a most peculiar honor system, but when the IDF commander was assured by the village *muktar* that all the men and boys were gathered before him in the square, he took the old mayor's word for it. There were perhaps eighty or a hundred of them, Geoff guessed. He drew strength from their collective calm and especially from the sight of Jamal in his black wedding suit, stonily enduring this affront on his wedding night.

Calling on a Sephardic soldier again to translate his order into Arabic, the IDF officer now lined the group up and marched them single file across the village to the cemetery. There they were made to sit down on the ground in the shadows of the gravestones. A dozen Israelis stood over them, the broad butts of menacing M-16s braced against their hips. The spotlight on the personnel carrier lit everything up, and scores of field mice instantly scattered. Geoff was furious. There had been plenty of room for whatever questioning the Israelis had planned right there in front of the mosque. This move to the cemetery had been made for nothing else but its considerable intimidation value.

"Scum." He said it loud enough so that all of them heard it, even if none of them understood it.

They were kept there like that for more than an hour—no smoking allowed, no getting up to relieve themselves—until the headlights of a jeep came bouncing down the gravel trail. The jeep skidded to a stop in front of the cemetery gate, spraying rocks against the wrought-iron fence, and Geoff saw a hooded figure in the passenger seat next to the driver. For the first time since they'd been brought here, the stoic Lebanese around him broke their silence with a swell of angry muttering and cursing. The soldiers shouted for quiet. They were ignored.

Escorted by the commander, the shrouded collaborator was brought into the graveyard. The Arabic-speaking soldier barked another order and the villagers got to their feet, followed by Patal and Geoff. One of the younger boys spat in the direction of the traitor, and an Israeli immediately poleaxed him on the collarbone with the barrel of his rife. The youth cried out in pain and was hushed by his father.

Another order, and now the villagers aligned themselves side by side, as if for inspection. The officer spoke, and a soldier directed Geoff and Patal to step away from the lineup. Protected by a soldier on either side of him, the collaborator walked slowly past the villagers. A third of the way down the line, he stopped in front of a tall, well-built man, whom Geoff recognized as the most enthusiastic of the *dabke* dancers. He nodded, and one of the soldiers, using his rifle as a prod, turned the villager around. The collaborator pulled a piece of chalk from his pocket and drew a big "X" across the man's back.

Two more villagers were spun around and marked the same way, and then the anonymous accuser stopped in front of Jamal. Dumbstruck, Geoff watched the white chalk slash across the black cloth of Jamal's jacket.

"No." Geoff suddenly found his voice. He ran across the graveyard towards the Israeli officer, his quisling and the four villagers now being led away towards the jeeps. A soldier stepped in front of him, but Geoff feinted left and slipped by on the right. The officer registered the commotion behind him and stopped.

"Where are you going?" Geoff demanded. "What are you doing with these men?"

The Israeli said nothing, but the look on his face told Geoff he'd understood the question perfectly.

"It's this man's wedding night. How the hell can he be involved?"

The Israeli stared at Geoff a moment longer, then dismissed him with a wave of his hand and turned away.

Something triggered inside him. It happened quickly, with no forethought on Geoff's part. As the collaborator stepped past him to follow the Israeli commander and his prisoners out of the graveyard, Geoff snagged him by the collar. He dragged the man back towards him, then ripped the cloth hood off his head. There was a cry of alarm from the now exposed collaborator, a cry of anger from the officer, and then cries of hatred from the four prisoners at seeing the face under the hood. A name was shouted to the rest of the villagers, and suddenly they too were all shouting. Rifles were fired into the air in an attempt to quiet them, and a soldier on the personnel carrier swung the spotlight towards the disturbance. Caught in the center of the blinding beam, the collaborator dropped to his knees and desperately buried his face in his hands. The officer screamed at his unthinking soldier to shut the light off, and the area was immediately plunged into blackness.

For a moment, nothing was heard at all but the continuous murmur of the man's name repeated over and over, from father to son to uncle to nephew to neighbor.

FOURTEEN

CRUSADER: A EUROPEAN CHRISTIAN IN THE MIDDLE EAST, seeking to wrest the holy and cherished away from the infidel. Not quite a dictionary definition, but I don't have one of those handy just now so we'll call it close enough for horseshoes, or dancing, or grenades. This is Lebanon, after all—let's make it grenades. Yes, why don't we do that: grenades at twenty paces; the guy left standing gets the girl? Nah, on second thought, forget it. Real estate pedlar versus fedayeen: pedlar loses.

She was mostly joking, but Grete once called this little adventure of mine a crusade, which would make me a crusader. Hunkered down in mail, lance at my side, I've come trotting in on horseback to reclaim Jerusalem the Golden. My Jerusalem. Richard the Lion-Hearted, make way for Sir Geoffrey the Gutless.

I used to love those old black and white television movies. You know, where the long column of fresh-faced knights comes riding over the hill, buglers trumpeting a Divine commission, coats of arms thrust heavenward. Waiting below, the dirty-robed, wild-eyed, swarthy Arabs. The clash of steel against steel; the grunt of powerful steeds rearing; the shriek and groan of stab and slash, of heads rolling; the throaty cheer of victory as infidel turns and runs, routed in a cloud of dust. Jerusalem taken—ours.

But it occurs to me now that there was something missing from all those heroic battle scenes. Where was all the horse shit?

You see, I was thinking the other day about my forced layover in Amman, and the tourist brochure that charming bureaucrat (now *he was* wild-eyed and swarthy) at the Ministry of the Interior used to kiss me off. One of the entries described a ruin called Kerak, an enormous Crusader castle set on top of a sharp bluff somewhere near the Dead Sea. The knight in command of this fortress at one point shortly before Saladin chased them all out of the Holy Land was a brutal little Frenchman. His name eludes me—Baron de something or other, I imagine. Anyway, his penchant was tossing captured Arabs (Saracens/Mohammedans, pick your favorite term) over the walls of the castle so he could lean across his elbows and watch them

190

splatter on the rocks a couple of hundred feet below.

Oh yes, we Euro-Christians have a long and distinguished tradition when it comes to dealing with the Semites. Trust me, I now have some firsthand experience with which to speak.

Musli was seated at his desk in his small office at the rear of the hospital, staring down at some paperwork. Actually, he appeared to be staring through it more than at it, and he must have penetrated to quite a depth because it took a racket by Geoff in the open doorway to get him to look up. Yet when he finally did, his face was implacable, an expression that said: Yes, I knew you were standing there all along.

"There were rumors that you had gone to Baalbeck today, but I see that is not so."

Geoff said nothing.

"What is that you are holding?" the surgeon asked.

"*This* is arak." Geoff shook the bottle he had purchased from the barkeep at the Commodore Hotel. "And *this* is about eighty feet of nylon rope." With his other hand, he held up the thick yellow coil he had discovered in a basement utility room of the hospital.

"Planning to get drunk and hang yourself?"

"Come on, for a woman?" Geoff answered.

This made Musli smile a little. "What are you planning, then?"

"Well, if I had a partner who knew what he was doing, I might be persuaded to try climbing one of the Raoucheh Rocks."

"You would not be afraid?" Musli leaned back in his chair. He was definitely interested.

"Yes," Geoff answered.

To get to the rocks, which rose from shallow water about one hundred feet from shore, they needed a boat. Not so much for them as for the precious bottle of arak, the rope and their shoes. After asking around Musli located a battered rowboat that sat upturned on the grounds of the closed and locked Beirut Sporting Club. The two of them cleared out the debris—sand and thriving weeds—then declared it seaworthy with a few solid kicks and thumps. They hauled it up the club driveway and along the Avenue de Gaulle to the best, closest launching area.

They paused for a christening of arak—the bottle sipped from rather than shattered–then shoved the rowboat into the sea. Because the craft was oarless when they'd found it, they had to strip down and swim along behind it, pushing as they went. The current in the small bay that half-enclosed the rocks was stronger than they'd anticipated, so every few strokes one of them had to swim forward and redirect the prow.

Finally they arrived at the base of the larger of the two rocks and hooked the boat upside down over a knob of granite. The rock was roughly the shape of Gibraltar except that the sea had cut a narrow channel right through the center of it to a height of ten feet. It was about sixty feet in length, Geoff determined with his professional eye for such details, slightly less than a third that wide, and perhaps eighty-five or ninety feet high. By day, from the Avenue de Gaulle, he had seen a cap of grass growing on the top and a fairly obvious route up the one end. By night, however, from the bottom of the rock, all he saw was dark and steep.

"I've changed my mind," he said.

Musli laughed and leaned back against the boat to put on his shoes. The surgeon grabbed the khaki rucksack that held the bottle and slung it over his shoulder.

"Wait. Can't I have a little more courage first?"

"I do not think that would be wise," Musli replied, waiting for Geoff to finish putting on his shoes. Then he started up.

"Hey. You won't forget this is a novice behind you, will you?" Geoff called after him.

"I will drop the rope to you when I find a good place to stop. Climb slowly and carefully and concentrate on what you are doing."

Because it was much better than thinking about heights, Geoff contemplated the phenomenon of male play as he squeezed the rope Musli had dropped for him and picked his way gingerly up the fissured rock face. Why was it lately that he kept voluntarily getting himself into ridiculous hillside predicaments with the members of this family? At least with Musli, though, there would be no surprises awaiting him.

"There, that was not so difficult." Musli grasped him by the elbow and yanked him up the final rise to a yard-wide ledge he had settled on. Geoff clawed his way flat to the rock face and felt the cold stone against his cheek. All he could manage was a faint nod and a grunt. The Norwegian laughed and immediately started up again. He was really enjoying this; it was close to fair payback for a hand on his wife's knee.

When Musli at last pulled him onto the top, Geoff collapsed on the grassy plateau and felt the accumulated tension wobble through his legs like vibrating current. He rolled onto his back and gazed up at the pushed-in night sky that was now so familiar to him.

"Arak," he said, holding his hand out for the bottle. Musli took a drink himself and passed it over.

"I think you're going to have to airlift me off this hunk of stone." Geoff crawled as near the edge as he dared and looked down at the white lace of the sea throwing itself against rock. He felt droplets of spray, even at this height, and he smelled salt.

"And who will handle your evacuation, the Israelis?" Musli asked, taking the bottle back.

Made braver by the anise liquor, Geoff gradually slid over next to the surgeon and likewise dangled his legs over the bluff. Content to say nothing, the two men exchanged the bottle back and forth for a while and looked across at the black jag of West Beirut's seafront. The electricity had been cut off again–the IDF playing occupier's games in the main Beirut power station they controlled–giving highrises along the Avenue de Gaulle the visual quality of movie-lot cutouts.

Musli finally spoke. "It is so quiet. Tonight, one could almost believe it has never been otherwise."

"Do you think it's over?" Geoff asked.

"There is beginning to be some opportunity for thought in that direction," Musli answered.

The few days following their return from the Bekaa Valley had been relatively subdued. What fighting there was, was sporadic and short in duration, mostly small arms fire back and forth across the Green Line and the airport frontier. There had not been an air raid in over forty-eight hours, and as a result the flow of casualties to the hospital had become almost manageable. The buzz at the moment, the reason for Geoff's question, was a rumor spreading through the city that an American-brokered accord was close, that a few smallish details were all that was left to pound out: Where would the PLO go? Who would comprise the multinational force overseeing and safeguarding their evacuation?

"What happens when it's over? For you, I mean."

"I don't know," Musli answered. He picked at the paper label on the arak bottle.

"Grete wants to go home, doesn't she?"

Musli looked at him, understanding that neither of them had secrets any longer. "She wants to return to Oslo, yes."

"You're going, aren't you?" Geoff said.

"And you? What does the end now mean for you?" The surgeon sought to evade a reply with a question.

Geoff shook his head at their shared paralysis. "Oh yes, we're quite a pair you and I." Here we sit, two emasculated crusaders, staring out at the long night and wondering what hit us. The image made him laugh.

Musli got up and walked to the other side of the rock to relieve himself. He remained there after the chore was completed, pitching stones into the sea. Geoff watched him and read anger in the strain behind each throw. Suddenly, Musli spun around and whizzed a stone past his head.

"*Hey*." A second stone ricocheted off the ground beside him. Geoff scrambled to his feet.

"She had no right telling you anything," Musli shouted, throwing a third stone in his direction. Geoff moved in towards the center of the rock.

"It's not like I'm going to print it up on leaflets and drop them all over Beirut. And it's not like it's the end of the bloody world either."

When the Norwegian's fourth stone hit him in the chest and stung, Geoff picked up one of his own and drilled it at Musli's knees. He just missed.

"Okay, Musli, you can quit the Neanderthal act anytime now. If you're that pissed off, come over here and we'll argue about it like grown men."

Considering the larger setting for this confrontation–Beirut, Lebanon, in the summer of 1982–his rebuke sounded rather silly. But it was enough to bring Musli rushing at him. He allowed himself to be grabbed, and for a few moments the two of them lunged and twisted about like a parody of sumo wrestlers. Geoff couldn't help it: he began laughing again, which further infuriated Musli. Finally freeing one hand, he took a wild, clumsy swing that glanced off Geoff's ear. Slipping to the ground to duck a second punch, Geoff wound an arm around the surgeon's calves and tripped him. They wrestled in the grass until Geoff had used his weight advantage to wriggle on top. He sat on Musli's chest, pinning the Norwegian's arms under his knees.

"Stop laughing at me and fight," Musli demanded angrily. He struggled to get out from under Geoff.

"I'm not laughing at you, fool. I'm laughing at two macho idiots trying to punch each other out on top of a cliff."

Musli struggled a bit longer, grunting with frustrated exertion, until he stopped and grinned. When he at last began laughing, Geoff got off his chest and let him up.

"I am still damn angry," he said, grabbing the arak bottle after Geoff retrieved it and held it out as a peace offering.

Geoff stared at him. "You think I'm not? But what the hell can we do about it?"

"We can drink," he said, tipping the bottle up.

"That's why I come to this bar," Geoff said, waiting his turn.

If Geoff thought going up was the most difficult part of rock climbing, he'd changed his mind before they got halfway down. The two of them now half-cut on the sickly sweet liquor, they had to devise a crazy system of descent that saw Musli climb down, then up, then down again, setting and retrieving the rope three different times so Geoff would not have to free-climb. The surgeon was exhausted by the end of it.

"Some sport," Geoff sniffed, looking back up the rock. "You go up, then you turn around and come down. What's the point?" He looked at Musli, bent over at the waist, hands on his hips and breathing hard.

"Get in the boat," Geoff offered. "I'll push you back to shore."

He was swimming along slowly, treading as much as stroking, when Musli leaned out over the squared-off stern.

"You tell me to go back to Norway, and yet you will not go to Baalbeck."

"My problem is more complicated than yours," Geoff

answered. He thrust his face underwater and began a furious kick to shore.

*   *   *

It seemed to Geoff a fitting irony that the Israelis should be the ones to save him from any further agonizing over his decision not to go to Baalbeck. The following morning, the IDF, under the orders of Defense Minister Sharon, returned in their F-15s and F-16s. They bombed the refugee camps, the impoverished southern suburbs, and even the commercial core of the city. Their gunboats opened fire, and their artillery in the East Beirut hills was greased up and loaded again. So indiscriminate and thick was the onslaught over the next three days that bombs fell even on Beirut's lone synagogue, chasing the city's remaining handful of Jewish families from their homes in the area.

On the fourth day the air raids went on for eleven continuous hours, from six in the morning till five in the afternoon. Local radio stations called it the heaviest bombardment of the war and quoted police casualty figures of 156 dead, 400-plus injured.

Two of the dead on day four were Dr. Patal and Leila al-Nouri, the Palestinian nurse he had been wooing all summer. They died, along with three patients, when the east wing of the hospital took a direct hit at a quarter to five, during the IDF's final aerial sortie. This in spite of the huge red cross painted on the roof that clearly marked the building as a medical facility. Wounded witnesses said the two of them had been standing together in a corridor–Patal no doubt entertaining Leila with a story–when the shell slammed home and a massive section of the concrete wall caved in on top of them. Another witness swore she saw them reach out and grab for each other at the last moment. Whether this was true or not, everyone chose to believe it. Picking through the blocks of smashed concrete alongside Dr. Musli and the other searchers, Geoff imagined finding them just like that: side by side and touching. Instead, what they found was meat-filled clothing. Patal was recognizable only by the deep chocolate color of his hands.

Long after the bombing was over–halted, the radio reported, by an ultimatum from dismayed apologist Reagan to Begin–the casualties were still pouring into the damaged hospital. An incredibly obese man who had lost most of both legs was brought through the doors and across the floor by two friends. Unable to support his full weight, they had to half drag him, and the bloody stumps of his limbs left streaks across the tile.

At nine o'clock in the evening, a pair of ambulance attendants rushed in carrying a cardboard box smoldering with phosphorus smoke. As they crossed the lobby, headed towards the treatment rooms, others saw the contents and began to cry. Inside were newborn triplets. The mother had given birth hiding in a cellar shelter in Bourj el-Barajneh camp that afternoon. Moments after delivery, a phosphorus shell had penetrated the shelter, blessing the mother and midwife with instant death but only wounding the babies. In the chaos of the air raids, no one had found them until five hours later. By then, one had died, *cooked,* as Musli described it, from the inside out by a piece of gel-covered shrapnel. The other two hung on long enough to die in the hospital. Even dead, the three little bodies continued to burn. In the end, the only way found to extinguish them was to submerge each in a water-filled bucket.

The next day, Friday the thirteenth of August, was said by some to be the quietest day of the war. The only reported casualty was an IDF soldier wounded by a sniper in the Bekaa Valley. Grete told Geoff to think of it as one for Jamal, who was now believed to be one of the seven thousand Lebanese and Palestinians being held at the Ansar prison camp in the south. He asked her when there'd be one for Patal. And, in any case, hadn't he himself already taken care of the one for Jamal? That evening, a BBC broadcast relayed out of Nicosia reported that General Sharon's authority had been curbed by the Israeli cabinet after American officials expressed the fear that his intention was to sabotage their accord and press the war. People around the radio in the hospital were pleased, but no one really believed for a minute that Sharon had been permanently reined in.

The ceasefire held through Saturday too, and then on Sunday came the quietly delivered announcement: the Israelis had accepted the accord. It was over. *Halas*–finished.

Perhaps, but nobody in West Beirut went out on the streets and danced. It could have been because everyone here was feeling the

same sense of manipulation that Geoff felt. Intellectually, he of
course understood that wars start and stop with suddenness, like
the turning on and off of a tap. The blood pours and then it stops.
True enough, but this suddenness was not the product of
capricious spontaneity. No, it was an option chosen–*one* of the
available options–by the hand on the top. And that hand, after
all, was still right there, lurking.

On Monday the radio reported that eighteen hundred U.S.
Marines had just set sail from Naples, preparing to join two
regiments of French paratroopers and an Italian mechanized
battalion in a multinational force that would safeguard the PLO
exodus from Lebanon.

On Tuesday the IDF agreed to withdraw their troops from
around the parliament building so that elections could take place
to choose a new Lebanese president. It was already considered a
fait accompli that Phalangist commander Bashir Gemayel would
succeed the outgoing Elias Sarkis. (Geoff wondered how Camille
and Genevieve Haddad had passed the heat of the summer in
their cool, empty villa in the hills above East Beirut.) That
afternoon the blockage around the west was eased and half a
dozen truckloads of fresh produce were allowed in through the
Museum Crossing. People, too, began to return to the city.

Others began to consider the future: it existed again. If his
mother (poor woman–he'd sent her a vague telegram from
Jerusalem, but that was a lifetime ago) could see him now, she
would undoubtedly say he was moping. A mother's verb if there
ever was one. As in: stop your moping, Geoffrey, you don't know
what true suffering is. But he did know. He continued to work at
the hospital; with Jamal missing, he'd become a regular, if
unpaid, orderly. But it was relatively mindless toil, and now he
didn't even have the horrific gallery of daily new casualties to fill
his head. He was left to think about Nadya, and he did.
Constantly.

When he was not working, Geoff passed the time in much the
same way as he had before. He went out and he wandered, the
difference being that now he merely looked at, not for. He
returned to Hamra Street, found it had survived the last Israeli
firestorm more or less unscathed, and ended up by chance on the
same corner where he'd encountered the little boy and his

terrified sheep. Someone else was operating the butcher shop now. He saw the closed cinema house and the sun-faded promotional poster with the man and woman frozen in place and staring at each other from opposite sides of a room. Ignoring the people walking past him on the sidewalk, who probably could not have cared less anyway, he pulled the poster down, folded it in half and dropped it on the pavement. There, he thought, together at last.

By week's end, a new kind of battle was underway in West Beirut, a warfare waged by cowards. Car bombs were certainly nothing original here, but they suddenly began to appear like mushrooms in the dark. It had started on the Wednesday, when a Mercedes sedan rigged with plastique blew up near the offices of the Palestine Research Center, just blocks from where Geoff was walking his misery along Hamra Street. Four people were injured. On Thursday a Lebanese Christian woman was caught parking another rigged car outside the Lebanese Information Ministry. Three more mobile bombs turned up around the Hamra on Friday, but anonymous tips saw them all discovered and defused before they could harvest flesh and mayhem on the tight streets that were gradually beginning to fill with people again.

Friday, the twentieth, was also the day that Yasser Arafat finally ordered the release of two Israeli pilots his fighters had shot down and captured early in the invasion. This was considered the last remaining impediment to a peaceful evacuation of the PLO scheduled to begin the following morning. The resulting atmosphere of wind-up, however, only drove Geoff's depression to the bottom.

"I'm going home."

The words surprised him almost as much as they surprised Grete. But only for an instant. He was up on the roof of the hospital with her at dusk that evening. A generous breeze blew late summer cool off the sea as the two of them stood and watched the heavy offshore traffic of Israeli gunboats, French and American troopships and Greek freighters that were to begin the job of scattering Palestinian fighters across the Arab world, from Algiers to Yemen.

"*Now?*" she asked.

"Yes, tomorrow."

"When did you decide this?"

"Tonight. Just now. Up here."

"Why?"

"Why?" He repeated her question to himself. Why–it was everything, but most especially the fool he suddenly felt looking at these ships and the sea through this bad light and thinking how much the tableau reminded him of the view of English Bay from Nadya's apartment that first evening, when he'd bullied her into accepting his ride home from the university. Why–it was the vividness with which he continued to remember the way they had sat on the floor and studied each other over the length of her coffeetable like the inhabitants of two different worlds, which was what they were, he had finally come to understand. Why–it was the humiliation, as ridiculously vain as that sounded after what he'd been through and seen these past weeks, if she should ever find out that he had been here at all. "I miss my mom," he told her instead.

"What about Nadya?" Grete asked.

"Who?"

"And all you have been through and done while you were here?"

"Call it a charitable donation. Maybe I can try to take it out of my taxable income for the year. What do you think?" He smiled.

Grete reached out to take his hand. She held it tightly. "I think you are caught between a rock and another place," she said, messing up the figure of speech like Nadya might have.

"Yes." And then he smiled even harder because of the sudden wet threat in his eyes if he didn't.

*   *   *

That night, the dream he had had in Amman, so long ago, about a drowning made its way into his sleep again. He woke up in the middle of it, though, realizing it was not a dream at all but rather the edge of a distant memory. The grass under his shoulder blades, the sun like a broiler element overhead, those oddly perfect cries–it was all now as graspable as fabric.

It had happened a decade earlier, during the summer of 1971, or '72. Yes, it was 1972. In those days, when he was finishing up his commerce degree between fraternity parties, he had worked his summers as a construction laborer on office towers, freeway overpasses and other large projects around the Lower Mainland. There was lots of overtime and the money was good, so for a couple of years he was wealthy enough to take the whole month of August off and head for the sunshine in Penticton. He and two friends who also had some money, or pretended to, would spend four weeks drinking beer, smoking huge quantities of dope and pursuing well-filled bikinis up and down the beaches at the Skaha or Okanagan ends of town. Occasionally, they even caught a bikini or two, and for years afterwards he counted those simple-minded squanderings as among the best days of his life.

All but one. Still, it too had soon been buried under the sheer weight of other days—most of them better, but a few even worse—to come. Given that, wasn't it a strange and improbable little incident to be so forcefully unearthing itself now? Yes, but this was Lebanon, and he'd long ago given up trying to figure out the reasons for anything that happened here.

It was a hot afternoon in a month of hot afternoons, one where the crickets in the quack grass sounded like old wooden floors underfoot, and the tinkle-tune of an ice cream truck passing by on the soft asphalt road above the beach drew small children up out of the lake and racing across the nipping sand to squeal and dance around and beg quarters from their sprawled, red parents. He and his friends, Gerry and Jerry (great jokes were made of that), were stoned and drunk, but mostly stoned, perhaps even on Lebanese hash, and pinned to the strip of grass between the beach and the road. Someone, somewhere, had a radio on, and the Doors' spooky "Riders on the Storm" was playing not quite loud enough. A lovely pointlessness was settling on everything, and then the cries began.

They went on and on for perhaps three or four minutes, and then they stopped because the lungs that had driven them up onto shore had filled with water. Though for obvious reasons he never said anything, Geoff was convinced that nobody and everybody at the same time knew that the sounds were the cries of a woman drowning. *If we'd only known* (we did). *It happened so quickly* (it had not happened that quickly). When the body was pulled from the water, limp, all those who'd been unable to make themselves move earlier got up off their backs and bellies and came to stand around with their arms crossed over their chests, talking in whispers and watching the too-late attempts to breathe life back into the young woman. That evening, he and his two friends drank so much beer they each, at one point, had to leave their orange nylon tent in the campground and throw up in the bushes. In the morning, they laughed at one another and went on with their partying.

Afterwards, Geoff was unable to go back to sleep. Giving up, he rolled off his mat on the floor and took a seat on one of the comfortless wooden benches in the waiting area. He pulled out the notes he'd written over the past month and a half–there were a dozen dog-eared pages now–and reread them. When he got to the end, he took his pen and scribbled across the bottom: The end. Then he tore the notes up, once, twice, and added them to a can full of garbage beside the central nursing station.

At dawn he went outside and began what would be his last walk around West Beirut. As a sort of parting honorarium, he supposed, Musli had arranged for a hospital driver to take him the fifty miles to the Damascus airport later that morning. From there, he could pick up a Syrian Airlines flight to Athens, and from there something else the rest of the way home. *El-hamdu lillah,* praise be to God for credit cards, he thought. But it didn't matter; by Wednesday or Thursday next, he would be back in his office selling square footage again.

He started off for the seafront and a final look at the Raoucheh Rocks, but partway there he changed his mind. It had become important to return something that did not belong to him. If he was going to give her up, he had to give all of her up.

There must come a point when further pulverization is only redundant. That was one of the thoughts that occurred to him as a lone fedayeen sentry waved him through and he crossed the road from Sabra camp into Chatila. In the three weeks since he'd been here, the refugee camps had been pounded over and over again by air raids and artillery, but the scale of the destruction was somehow no worse. Perhaps it was like this: a pile of rock can be hit and split as often as one cares to do so, but it will still be a pile of rock when one has finally given up and stopped. The only thing qualitatively more awful than before, Geoff felt, was the smell of raw sewage glistening gray-green and brown in the gutters in the middle of the narrow alleys between the huddled rows of pitiful battered huts. That was definitely worse, but the air was still not foul enough to dissuade women from hanging their laundry out to dry. There were clothes waving at him everywhere.

It took a while, some zigzagging and circling back and forth around shell craters and heaps of debris, but at last he recognized a graffitied wall that told him he was in the right part of the camp. He made a turn from there in the wrong direction, realized it and doubled back. He came upon an old woman, wrinkled and gray beneath her head-scarf. She was sitting on a low wicker stool in front of her house, and he stared at her hugely swollen ankles. She looked up and he smiled sympathetically, then he walked a few yards farther before stopping with a silly little gasp. He backed up very slowly, wanting to be absolutely sure it was the right house. It was.

"*Sabah el-khair,*" he said.

"*Sabah el-noor.*" There was a swing of surprise at the end of the woman's reply to his dry-mouthed croak of good morning. He stood in front of her, one hand self-consciously hovering over the shirt pocket that held the photograph he'd come to return.

"*Keef halak? Keef saha?*" How are you? How is your health? He was not certain what would happen next because he had just about come to the end of his useful vocabulary.

"*Mabsut el-hamdu lillah.*" Well enough, praise be to God.

"*La, la.*" No, no. Geoff shook his head as she launched into a flurry of questions of her own now. "*Ana ma bahki 'arabi,*" he apologized. I don't really speak Arabic.

The old woman laughed toothlessly, slapping her hands together in front of her.

"*Ya Sittee, meen hada?*" A voice drifted out from inside the house. Geoff recognized two words: grandmother and who. But he recognized much more than that.

The old woman twisted around towards the house and beckoned. "*Ta'a la hoon.*" Come here.

She emerged from the house a moment later, dressed in jeans and the pink sweatsuit top and chasing off sleep with a stretch of her slender arms. Geoff wished he could disappear–hide–just so he could stare for a while. He stared anyway.

Barely looking at him at all, she came and stood behind her grandmother. "*Sabah el-khair*," she said.

"Good morning, stranger," he replied.

Now she peered at him closely. He put his hand to his face and tugged at the beard on his cheeks. Suddenly, her mouth fell open and she swayed hard against her grandmother.

"Geoff?" Her voice trembled.

"Surprise."

FIFTEEN

AS PREDICAMENT, THIS WAS EXCRUCIATING. NADYA'S EYES were torrents, and yet Geoff could make no move towards her. She was spoken for. Seated quietly below both of them on the squat wicker stool, a confused old woman craned her head back and forth, looking for explanations neither one could give her. Touched by her granddaughter's tears, she too had begun to cry.

"Geoff, how?"

"Nadya, you'll have to help me out here. May I shake your hand or something?"

It was left to her to do what he could not. Stepping out from behind her grandmother, she came to him. He opened his arms and wrapped them around her and buried his face in that black hair. She did not pull away. He squeezed tightly and kissed the top of her head.

"I'm sorry," he heard himself say. "Sorry." He forced himself to shut up and let her go. Even with this small parting, though, he felt some kind of scab tearing away inside.

"When? How?" She was still talking in shocked little bits; her grandmother in insistent bursts. Nadya turned and hushed the old woman.

"I came as soon as Walid told me where you'd gone."

"But this is crazy. You are a crazy person to be here."

"You're here."

"This is where I come from. I know this place," she said. Which, of course, was not at all what he had meant, but it served as a reminder of things. He struggled into some platonic high ground and felt sick.

"When did you come back?"

"Two days ago." She gave him a strange, confused look. "How could you know where to come?"

"Your father-in-law-to-be showed me the house," Geoff said evenly. He pulled the photograph out of his pocket and handed it to her.

"Tell your grandmother I'm sorry I broke the frame for this. I cut myself and got a little blood on the edges. I'm sorry about that too."

Nadya stared at this image of her younger self for a moment, and then, without a word, returned it to her grandmother. The old woman said nothing either. Possibly, she was beginning to flesh out parts of this mystery for herself.

"Have you had your breakfast?" Nadya asked. He answered her faint and troubled smile with one of his own.

"Come inside, then." She turned and explained something to her grandmother. Geoff noticed that several neighbors had emerged from their own hovels and were watching them from a distance. He envisioned the crazed father-in-law being informed of this reunion and right this moment rushing across the camp to chase him away.

The old woman remained outside on her stool, as she had likely been asked to. Geoff followed Nadya into the dreary house. Just over the threshold, she stopped and gazed around the empty gray room. He watched her.

"A few nails in a wall for hanging clothes," she said, "two mats for sleeping and some cardboard boxes of garbage. *Halas*. This is a life?"

"Old people don't seem to need much." It was the best he could offer.

"Yes, and some day it will all of it be mine. Then I too will not need much."

"Nadya."

"Sit down," she said, pointing to one of the bed rolls. "I will make you something to eat." Her voice, he noticed, was dull. It was not unfriendly; no, much worse, it was not anything.

Nadya got down on her knees and dug through one of the

cardboard boxes, dredging up a small gas cooker. She set to work boiling a few eggs. When they were done, she placed them in a bowl and set it down on the concrete floor in front of him, along with some Arab bread and a saucer full of thickened yogurt that she had disappeared outside to get, perhaps from a neighbor. She returned to the cooker to reuse the same water for tea, and she looked up to see that he was not eating.

"Eat," she said.

Geoff shook his head. "This may be the Middle East, but I'm not going to let you *serve* me. Thank you very much for the food—now come and have it with me."

"Let me make the tea, and then I will come. You begin."

"Fine, make the tea. But I'll wait."

They chewed their food and sipped their tea in silence. Geoff was overwhelmed by missing focus, by the complete absence of palpable feeling at this moment. He had found Nadya and now, not two feet away, was separated from her by a vast emptiness blacker than anything he'd experienced in the past two months all alone.

"One would think the two of us ought to have a lot to talk about."

"Yes," she said, but that was all.

"I'm surprised your fiancé's father hasn't showed up. We had quite a first encounter, he and I."

Nadya remained quiet, and Geoff tried to cover his despair with a whitewash of congratulations.

"I'm happy for you. Truly. Tell me, when is the big day? What's his name? Where is he now?"

Nadya looked at him briefly, then she got up to clear their breakfast leavings. He reached out and grabbed for her arm. He held on gently.

"Please—talk to me, Nadya."

"There is so much you cannot understand, Geoff."

"Haven't I at least earned a chance to try?"

This stopped her, if only for an instant. She flicked her eyes past his and then straight down at the floor. "I must take breakfast to my grandmother."

He watched her from the doorway as she gave the old woman what was left of the eggs, bread and yogurt. At seeing her there without him, a handful of neighbor women hurried over with saved-up questions. She put them off with a few words, and headed back to the house. He stepped aside to let her in.

"Did you understand why I said I was sorry out there?"

"Yes."

"So you do remember some things about Vancouver?" He pursued her around this cell-like room much the same way he had pursued her that morning along the bank of Lost Lagoon, in Stanley Park.

"I remember everything," she answered.

"Everything? Including all the things I said to you?"

She stopped her agitated pacing and turned on him in exasperation. Fresh tears brimmed in her eyes. For Geoff, it was another Lost Lagoon: his own.

"What do you want from me?" she cried, the tears now freed and running.

"I want you to tell me who this man is, and when you'll marry him, and then I just want you to say goodbye because that's when I'll leave and never bother you again."

She appeared to absorb his words very slowly.

"His name is Mohammed Chauer, and we will be married soon . . . quite soon."

"Where?"

"Here."

"And where will you live?"

She shrugged.

"You don't know where you'll live?" he said impatiently.

"I am a Palestinian," she answered. "You tell me."

"You've never passed up a chance to march your flag up and down in front of me, have you?" he said quietly.

Honoring a vow that he had made less to her than to himself, he wished her luck, said goodbye and strode out of the house. He looked at the wondering face of the old woman and started up the alley that would take him to the edge of the camp. He walked hard, staring straight ahead, and willed himself to think of nothing but the ride through the mountains and across the valley to Damascus. Of nothing but a blessed end to this.

"Geoff."

At the sound of her voice, he spun around with a quickness that put the lie to his resolve. She was hurrying up the alley after him, followed in turn by the curious eyes of Chatila's refugees. He waited.

"Why did you come here?" she asked.

"You said you remembered everything."

"I do."

"Then you know why I came."

When she had nothing to offer in response, he felt sick and spun away to start walking again.

"I am not engaged to this boy, Mohammed Chauer," she said.

"What?"

"I am not marrying him."

"Nadya, I'm tired of games and riddles," he cried, not fully registering what she'd just told him.

"No, this is the truth," she said. "That which you heard before was only an invention by this man, Mohammed's father."

"An invention?"

"An invention for keeping a son alive. Mohammed is dead, you see, killed by the Israelis in the first days of the war."

"But why you?" Geoff demanded. Why me? he thought.

"Mohammed and I, we knew each other when I lived here before. He had, I think, something like a crash . . . a crush . . . on me. His father always thought we would someday be married, and—well, this place, this dying everywhere, it has made us all to go crazy."

It was Geoff's turn now to absorb the words slowly. He stared at her eyes. They no longer tried to escape his scrutinizing; they appeared to proclaim something, like a decision made. He heard giggles, belt-level giggles, and looked away from her long enough to see that the camp's small children had begun to gather round. Button-eyed, pot-bellied perpetuity.

"Do you want me to stay?" he said at last.

"Do you want to stay?" she answered.

*   *   *

That subtle, Levantine cluck of her tongue as a way of saying no; the habit she had of suddenly tossing her head to one side—always the same side–to shake out her long hair; her lithesome ability to sit cross-legged on the floor, the soles of her bare feet almost at her hips; the softly nodding sincerity whenever she listened to him speak at length; the shyness that would see her biting down on her lip if he said anything the least bit tender to her: the Nadya of Vancouver returned to him over the course of that day in the angles and expressions of her face and body. He watched and coveted them all.

They sat in the house and talked, alone with their words in spite of the constant gaze of her grandmother, who was now installed inside on the wicker stool. There was so much to explain and describe, and for Geoff, at least, to plumb and probe and decipher. He retraced his route from Amman for her. He told her about Thomas Dix, the car bombing and hospital, his venture over the Museum Crossing and up the Raoucheh Rock. She told him about a hurriedly booked flight from Vancouver to Montreal to Paris to Damascus, her own overland rush from there to Beirut, and she described the conditions they had lived under in the temporary camps at Baalbeck.

But they both knew there were much more important things to talk about than these, and Geoff fought against her unwillingness to do so. He charged at her headlong; he circled and circled, trying to make her dizzy and drop her guard, but nothing worked. Walid had been right: there were questions she simply would not answer.

"Nadya."

"Yes?"

"I'll borrow your word, invention. Why the invention of an aunt and uncle in Kuwait? A wealthy aunt and uncle in Kuwait, if I remember correctly."

"It does not matter."

"What do you mean, it doesn't matter?"

"We both of us said and did many strange things in Vancouver. Here is not there, and so it does not matter."

He scowled at her logic. "Oh, I see. Meaning that nothing that was said or done in Vancouver matters?"

"Perhaps so."

"How, then, would you explain my being here? My coming here?"

She smiled. "You are a clever man with words, Geoff. You are always setting traps. I think I am seeing why you are successful in selling real estate."

"Are you being nasty, Nadya?"

"No, I think I am being complimentary. . . . Is that not a correct word, complimentary?"

"Yes, it's fine."

"Good, I find I must be careful when I choose my words in English around you."

"Now you're being nasty."

"I am?"

"No. No, you're not. I deserve at least that, don't I?"

Late in the afternoon, they left her grandmother curled up and napping on one of the bedrolls and went for a walk. Chatila was gray: served up in its most squalid and hopeless state by this fuzzing light. Some children immediately sought to join them—it was as if they had been waiting outside the house for just such an appearance all day long—but Nadya shooed them away. Geoff teased himself with thoughts of taking and holding her hand.

"Nadya."

This, they both realized, had become the standard opening to another of his questions.

"Do you not grow tired of . . . how did you say this before? . . . of banging your head against a brick wall?" she said.

"I have a very thick skull."

"And I have very thick walls."

Geoff laughed and told her he would not be deflected.

"As you like," she shrugged. "Ask."

"Why did you play along with being engaged?"

"I thought it was best."

"Best for whom?"

She said nothing.

"But then you changed your mind."

She nodded.

"Why?" he asked.

"I do not know." She stopped walking and looked right at him. Her words were seriously spoken; they pronounced themselves as her final ones on the subject. "This is the truth, Geoff. I do not know."

When they returned to the house, they found the old woman in the midst of preparing the evening meal. There was a scant offering of boiled lentils and rice, hardened yogurt and flat bread, but she and Nadya both insisted that Geoff share it with them. He finally agreed to eat, promising himself he'd buy meat and produce for them the next day. He knew there was some available now because the Israelis had started permitting farm trucks from the Bekaa to again cross the Green Line.

This plan to buy groceries served to make him aware that he had not yet asked a most obvious question.

"Nadya."

"Ask," she said, smiling indulgently. She stooped to hand him a steaming glass of tea, then sat down beside him with one for herself.

"What are your plans?"

"I have no plans, Geoff." Her answer was matter-of-fact flat.

"You will go back to Vancouver, won't you? You have a doctorate to finish," he reminded her.

"You have been in Lebanon long enough. You have seen what they have done to our camps and our people. How can such a thing as that be important any longer?"

Geoff sighed, and then he was angry. "Forgive me, Nadya, but sometimes the martyr's tone of you Palestinians is just too much. You've got to live your life."

She glared at him. Her own anger caused her to spill piping hot tea on her thigh. She gasped at the scald, and Geoff reached out to touch her. She slapped his hand hard and he withdrew it, all the more embarrassed by the concerned stare of her grandmother.

"You know nothing at all about me—nothing. And you know almost nothing about the Palestinians," she said fiercely. "Ten thousand. That is how many people they killed here this summer, and you Americans did nothing to stop them."

"Wait, Christ, hang on here, Nadya," he said. "I'm no American. This is me you're talking to."

"You are all Americans," she said, her mouth twisting.

He kept quiet. There was no point arguing with her any

further. It was better to wait out this vitriol, to let it seep away, than stir it up and be splashed in the face.

"Please, forgive me," she said a moment later.

"It's okay. Perhaps you're right, anyway. If acquiescence is an absolute crime and not something marked by degrees, then, yes, maybe we're all Americans."

"No, not you. You are here with us," she said.

This sudden, turnabout softness in her voice caught him off-guard, and he immediately thought she was being somehow sarcastic. When he understood that her words were sincere, he could barely hold back the emotion as he nodded his head and spoke. "Yes, I am here with you. And I have no plans that matter either."

He was desperate to stay the night, and quite willing to sleep on the concrete floor if need be, but Nadya refused to let him. It would be terribly unfair to his friend Grete, she said, if he did not go back to the hospital and explain what had happened and why he had not turned up for his arranged ride to Damascus. He told her he would do that, certainly, and then come back, but she was adamant. No, he must stay there. She walked him out to the edge of the camp, and then at his insistence a little way up the deserted street beyond it. When she resisted going any farther, he took her hand and led her into the shadow at the side of a half-collapsed building. She let him press his mouth to hers, but he stopped when he realized she would not kiss him back.

"You'll still be here tomorrow?" he said.

"Where would I go?"

"Promise me that much, Nadya." He squeezed her hand.

"I promise," she said.

He let go of her hand and stepped back, trying to remember how to say good night or goodbye in Arabic. He could recall neither–perhaps he'd never learned them–but another phrase did find his lips. He had practiced it often enough alone that summer. Now it crossed the distance between them before he could stop it.

"*Ana pubik.*"

She fixed him with a soft stare but said nothing. Smiling tightly and nodding at the familiarity of this feeling, he turned away from her and walked quickly in the direction of the hospital. He had told her he was in love with her, and she had left his words rattling empty in his heart, like the dried-up seeds inside a gourd.

*   *   *

Just as Nadya had said she would be, Grete was upset by his all-day disappearance, but only for as long as it took him to tell her where he had been. Then she was upset at herself. Her eyes widened in disbelief at his news, and she took him by the arm and made him sit down beside her on a bench in the waiting room. Eventually, Musli wandered over to stand in front of them, listening.

"Geoff, I feel so guilty," Grete said.

"You couldn't have known," he told her.

"But I should have realized something was wrong. The man was completely without joy. I should have known he was making the whole thing up. And that family whose house we were in, they must have known the truth. How could they let him go on like that?" She was angry.

"It doesn't matter, not now," Geoff said. He looked up at Musli, standing there with his arms crossed. It was clear from the expression on his face that he had something to say.

"Why have you come back here?"

"What do you mean?" Geoff asked, though he knew exactly what Musli was getting at.

"You travel to Lebanon in the middle of a war to search for a woman. After some time and much difficulty, you find this woman. Now you have left her for the night?"

"I felt obliged to let you know I was all right. You had gone to some trouble for me."

"That is true," Grete agreed, but not convincingly.

"Nonsense," Musli said. "He could have sent a boy from the camp to tell us this."

"It is none of your concern, Thommie," Grete said.

"Ha," the surgeon scoffed. "There are no private concerns or secrets between we three. Are there?" He looked directly at Geoff.

Grete winced at this, and Geoff knew he had interrupted the two of them in the middle of a fight. The subject was obvious.

"He's right, Grete. You're right," he said to Musli. "No secrets. I shouldn't be here, and if it were up to me tonight I wouldn't be here."

"She does not want you?" Musli said. Geoff hated the man for the hopefulness in his voice.

"I don't have a clue what she wants," he admitted. "Which puts me one step behind you, doesn't it? You at least know what your wife wants."

"Geoff, no," Grete said desperately.

"Meaning what?"

But Geoff no longer had the stomach for cruelty. "Meaning that you know she wants you."

"Please," Grete cried.

She need not have bothered to plead for a stop; he was done. He stood up and looked at them, both with the same fine bones and straight blond hair. They could have passed as brother and sister. "I wish us all whatever we deserve," he said quietly.

"You are leaving?" Looking pained, Grete got to her feet. Her husband stepped back grudgingly to give her room near Geoff.

"Let's just say I've decided to lead by example." He looked at Musli. "I am standing on top of the Raoucheh Rock, and there is nowhere left to go. It is time to leap into the great abyss and find out what's down there."

"Happy landings," the surgeon said, ice in his words.

"Will you come back again?" Grete said.

"No." He shook his head and smiled at her. "One way or the other, no."

Their goodbyes were brief: there was nothing left to say to Musli, and little that could be said to Grete with him standing there. She handed him a scrap of paper with their address and telephone number scribbled on it, and he promised to look her up if he was ever in Norway, which seemed less than improbable. Then he hugged her, exchanged a final, dull look with her husband and walked back out into the Beirut night.

He slowly followed the same cratered streets back to Chatila and then the same cratered alleys to the house. He arrived there just past midnight and found it darkened and silent, its two occupants sleeping. Slipping quietly through the pale cotton sheet that did as a door, he scuffed about for the old woman's stool, found it, took it and set it down outside the house. Then he sat, sentry-like, and readied himself to wait for morning and the edge of the abyss.

At some point, he heard the phlegmy rattle of someone clearing his throat, and realized that he had slept. Blinking hard a few times, he pushed off the block wall of the house with his shoulderblades and sat upright, grunting at a mild kink in his neck. He checked his watch; it read a quarter to three.

"*Salam.*' A half-whispered greeting of peace lifted his gaze to the stooped figure of Mohammed Chauer's father, standing just a few feet in front of him. The ailing man cleared his throat again and leaned away to spit. He wiped his lips on the end of his khaffiyeh and stepped a little closer to repeat his hello. Geoff replied in the same guarded tone. The Arab then launched into a long speech of some sort. Too tired to stop it, Geoff let him go on until he was done before indicating that he had not understood. The old man tried again and Geoff shrugged. The Arab gave up at last with a shrug of his own. He lowered himself to a squat on the ground, displaying a flexibility in his joints that Geoff would not have guessed possible, and pulled out a packet of cigarets. Tapping the pack against the heel of his hand to loosen it, he offered it to Geoff, who declined, then lit up himself and proceeded to smoke two consecutive cigarets down to the filter.

They shared the night's silence like this for perhaps a half hour in all. Geoff, no longer able to be angry at the man, found his thoughts leaping from the barrier of language here to the barrier of language that had existed between him and his own father (for all of Geoff's adult life, they had been almost mute in each other's company), and thence to the process of grieving. There had not been any real problem between them, but Geoff remembered how little the loss of his father had affected him. He contrasted that with the way it had devastated his mother, and the way a son's death was now savaging this man, and he felt a vague shame forming itself inside him. Was he really such a cripple?

The old man got back to his feet. He started to say something but caught himself and stopped with the recognition that it was pointless. Instead, he put his hands together against his face as a gesture of sleep and motioned for Geoff to follow him.

"*Shookran*," Geoff said, thanking him but shaking his head.

The old man tried to insist, but Geoff made it clear he planned to stay right where he was. The Arab nodded and held out his hand. Geoff took it.

"*Salam*," the old man said intensely, his voice as strong as his handshake. Slowly, Geoff understood that this was the Arab's apology for what he had done.

"*Salam*," he replied, nodding. "Go in peace." He watched the old man turn and hobble away with some measure of his dignity now restored.

Not fighting it, Geoff fell asleep again. This time, it was a hand against his cheek, or perhaps only the dreaming of it, that woke him up. He saw Nadya there beside him, and he smiled at her groggily. She knelt alongside the stool and handed him a demitasse of Turkish coffee. He raised the tiny cup and saucer, both as thank-you and as question.

"Where's yours?"

"It is too early for me," she said.

Geoff looked at his watch. It was just past four. "Too early for anyone. Why are you up?"

"I heard you with Mohammed's father."

"We woke you. Sorry about that."

A quiet moment passed.

"You know something," he said. "I don't think I've ever heard you say 'never mind' or 'it's okay, Geoff' when I've apologized to you for something. And God knows, I've apologized plenty."

"When you tell me you are sorry, it would be impolite if I did not let you be sorry. Is that not so?"

"Maybe, but in the West it is a sign of graciousness to accept an apology by forgiving the offense. We consider that polite."

"We, however, would consider that insincere on the part of both people. Gestures only."

He thought about it for a moment and came to the conclusion that she was probably right. In fact, he'd come to the conclusion that she was probably right about most things she ventured an opinion on. Was she right about him too?

"Tell me, when I apologize to you, do you hear insincerity?"

"No."

Unable to stop himself, Geoff reached out to stroke the soft skin of her neck with his fingertips. She did not seem surprised; she did not appear resistant.

"What about the other things I say to you? Insincere?"

She shook her head. Touching her like this, pressing into her with his words, Geoff felt a surge of control that he had not often had in her presence.

"Then what does it do to you? What goes on inside when I tell you, for example, that I love you?"

She fought off meeting his gaze. He stopped stroking her neck and waited to hear her say something, anything.

But nothing came.

"Then I'll tell you what happens to me each time I get your blank stare."

"Geoff, if you knew me, you–"

"It feels like I'm swallowing broken glass, Nadya."

He was swallowing it right now, and he had to close his eyes and take a deep breath. He heard her choke and looked over to see that she too had taken in a mouthful of painful shards. Suddenly freed from stupid maleness in this most male place imaginable, he let go and cried. It was, he felt quite certain, the first time since childhood.

Nadya stood up. Still crying herself, she put her arms around his head and cradled him against her body. She rocked him like a baby.

"I just don't understand," he said.

"Be patient with me, Geoff. Please, be patient with me."

SIXTEEN

HE WOKE UP ON HER BEDROLL. AFTER A MOMENT OF DEEP
confusion, he remembered her insistence, just before dawn, that
he go inside and lie down for a while. He remembered something
else too: strong hands cradling the back of his head, and a soft,
warm, sweet-smelling body pressed against his face and unafraid
(finally unafraid) of him. In the calm that had followed the
surprising tears, he had been content to forgo words and stay
wrapped in her arms for as long as she could stand it. Just how
long that was he did not know; at some point, he had fallen asleep
against her belly, and then she had sent him in.

Sitting up, he saw he was alone in the room. The old woman's
bedroll was snugged in twine and standing on end in a corner.
The gas cooker was out on the floor but switched off, and there
were a couple of dirty plates and tea glasses nearby.

It was then that he saw the half sheet of paper lying on the floor
beside him. Something told him it had probably been left on the
edge of the bedroll for him, but that he had knocked it off in his
restless sleep. He picked it up.

> Into a grief without end
> What is this thing he brings
> And how might I enter, if for just one day,
> Such noble sanctuary with him

"You slept well?"
He looked up from her poem to her face, framed by Chatila

219

as he could see it through the door in the sharp light of midmorning. She dropped the cotton sheet and came into the house, accompanied by hints of the day's heat and the wretched odors of the camp.

"When did you write this?"

"After I sent you inside to rest. It is nothing, only a few lines of beginning."

"Will you finish it?"

She shrugged.

"But you must. I've never been the subject of a poem before."

"What makes you so certain you are the subject of this one?" she said, not even trying to hide the play in her voice. He smiled and patted the bedroll that she might sit down beside him. When she did so, and without hesitation, it was as if he had suddenly acquired the power to manipulate mountains.

"This last bit, the words 'noble sanctuary.' They sound familiar, like I've seen them together before."

"Jerusalem?" she guessed.

"Was it? . . . Yes, you're right, it was. Up at the Dome of the Rock."

"Al Haram Al Sharif. That is how it is known in Arabic. It is the name of the disclosure . . . no, that is not right . . . the enclosure that holds the Dome of the Rock and Al Aqsa mosque."

"It's beautiful," he said. "All the stone archways and the palm trees, the rose bushes and that incredible domed. . . ." Feeling like an idiot, he stopped and shook his head.

She smiled. "No, I am happy that one of us has been there. I know—why not pretend I am blind. Describe it for me. What would I see?"

"Nadya, I can't," he said, feeling badly. "You will see it for yourself."

"You believe that?" she said softly.

"What, you don't anymore?" He looked at her and the entire summer rolled over on top of him.

"I never have."

It was she who found a way through the gloom. She changed the subject.

"Are you hungry?"

"Not really, but I do have food on my mind."

"What do you mean?" She frowned and watched him rising to his feet. He offered her his hand, and when she took it he tugged her up beside him. She held on longer than she needed to, and in that instant Geoff knew that he was finally happening to this woman.

"Let me splash some water on my face, and then I'll tell you."

Knowing what he did about her pride, though, he was not going to tell her much. When they left the camp, walking north towards the Hamra and market center of West Beirut, he explained only that he had errands to run, taking what he realized was shameless advantage of the vestigial (in her case) remains of an Arabic upbringing that taught women not to question men too closely. At the same time, he could not resist teasing her a little on a related subject.

"Aren't you supposed to stay three paces behind me?"

"As you wish," she said, dropping back.

"Okay, okay, come back already," he laughed, after his attempts to slow down and rejoin her only slowed her down further, until they were almost not moving forward at all. They smiled at each other. Hers was somehow different now, and it excited him.

"You're a cute one," he said as she moved into step beside him. "I'm beginning to think I might have to keep you."

"And I you," she replied without missing a beat.

"What?" He gave her a long look.

"The bombs they have done harm to your hearing?" she said, those green eyes dancing.

"My hearing is excellent." He bit down hard on the corner of a creeping smile and quickened their pace.

The markets were crowded, and almost surreal in their commercial vigor. Ox-like in their resilience, Beirutis appeared determined to put the summer's horrors behind them and get on with life. Though prices were outrageously inflated, the lineups to buy were long at the produce stalls and in the butchers' shops. Nadya read Geoff's intentions quickly but did not, as he'd expected she would, issue much of a protest over his intention to buy food for her and her grandmother. Indeed, unable to stand by and watch him bumble and gesture his way through the purchase of some chicken, she took over and completed the transaction for him. If that was what she was after, she got some measure of satisfaction by embarrassing him with a coin by coin, bill by bill countback of the change as she placed it in his hand.

"I see some beef there," he said, pointing towards a dubious cut behind a butcher's smeary glass. "Should we get some?"

"Geoff, we have no refrigeration. The chicken is enough," she said firmly.

They wandered towards the produce stalls next, Geoff enjoying the first smells of fresh vegetables and ripe fruit he'd had in weeks. They reminded him of nothing quite so much as Saturday morning walks with Angela through the Chinatown market in Vancouver, a ritual that included a stop for hot-and-sour soup in the downstairs diningroom of a Chinese bakery, and less routinely but often enough an afternoon return to bed at her apartment. That sexual memory quickly dragged up another, though, the one that had been so fittingly climaxed by Nadya's phone call. He shuddered involuntarily. Nadya noticed.

"What is wrong?"

"Nothing, just someone walking on my grave." He saw her stricken look and immediately explained. "It's okay, Nadya, just a figure of speech."

"It is horrible."

"Take it easy, sweetheart." Somehow, he hoped this endearment—the first he had ever had the courage to use with her—might do something to calm the strange and sudden storm churning up inside her.

"Why would you say something so ridiculous?"

She was not ready to drop it, so he stopped walking and faced her.

"It's only a silly expression, Nadya. Why does it bother you so much?"

"I do not like joking about death," she said, slowly regaining her composure. "Yours, or anybody's."

"In a place like this, I have to joke about it." He spoke firmly.

So did she. "Then you will please do so in the company of someone else, but not me."

They were standing on a street corner, still annoyed with each other but peaceably sharing a pound of swollen green grapes when they heard a burst of machine gun fire somewhere to the northeast. Nadya collared an unconcerned passerby and was told it was only PLO fighters bidding a defiant farewell to all at the port. The evacuation had begun that morning, and the first shipload of fedayeen was preparing to sail for Cyprus. Excited by the possibility of waving her compatriots off, Nadya wanted to go to the port to watch. Geoff gave in reluctantly.

Weighted down by their groceries, they elected to travel the short distance to the port by taxi. There they pulled up in the tailings of a large crowd who had come, like them, to witness the important departure. Not even waiting for Geoff to finish paying the driver, Nadya climbed out of the cab and began pushing her way towards the front.

Initially, her rush to take part in this spectacle struck Geoff as childlike, a parade fascination, but as soon as he was in the throng and trying to catch up to her he understood it as much more. Many of those whose shoulders he bumped and brushed in passing were crying, some–women and men both–deeply sobbing, and most of the rest either cheering and chanting slogans, or trilling to the point of breathlessness between volleys of gunfire served up by guerrillas shooting heavenward from the decks of their ship.

Impassive overseers at this emotional exodus, a contingent of French marines stood fanned out in a loose cordon between the edge of the crowd and the waterfront. Not that they were trying or able to restrict the crowd. Every few moments, someone would yell and run forward with a handful of flowers or a frantic, tearful embrace for some fighter as he prepared to head up the ramp and onto the ship. Although it was nothing new to him–he'd seen wounded boy soldiers every day at the hospital–Geoff was still affected in an unsettling, perhaps even vaguely paternal, way by the sight of fourteen-year-olds among the departing:

fourteen-year-olds with heavy AK-47s resting against their thin collarbones and the lifetimes of old men locked in their fiercely dry eyes. Many of the older fedayeen felt free to weep here, but not the young ones. There was a strong possibility these children would not see their mothers again. But then that was a rather mild obscenity in this place.

Along with the French troops, there were other uniforms positioned around the area, and Geoff recognized them as Lebanese regulars. Part of the final ceasefire and withdrawal agreement had been that the Lebanese Army would take control of the port from the IDF and Phalangists, and this had apparently occurred. Just the same, he was quite certain that the IDF and the Phalangists were both well represented, in fact or by proxy, in and about this chaotic crowd. He searched the faces around him for something like a spook's glance, then saw that Nadya had at last settled on a spot from which to watch. He pushed on to join her.

"Trying to ditch me again already?" He had to lean towards her and half shout to be heard over the din. Nadya shook her head but said nothing; she was preoccupied in much the same way she had been that afternoon outside the art gallery. He, however, would handle her distraction differently this time.

It took about an hour to finish loading the ship, a converted car ferry. Though the terms of the accord prohibited the Palestinians from exiting with artillery, they appeared to be set on taking out as many of their jeeps and trucks as possible. By the time the captain of the requisitioned Greek carrier was able to stop the run of vehicles into his hold, his beleaguered vessel looked ready to sink right there at its berthing. This did not seem to concern the fedayeen, who continued to climb the ramp and jostle each other for the best spots along the railing of the twin decks.

A blast of the ship's foghorn at last signaled that the moment of leaving had come. Stevedores unslung the heavy mooring ropes from their attachments along the quay and tossed them out to the ship. With the splash of knotted loops in the gray harbor, the full meaning of this event hit everyone at once. The gunfire, the cheering and wailing: it all reached a new and fevered pitch as the sluggish vessel began to pull out. The enormous photographs of an unshaven Arafat and the flags of nonexistent Palestine were thrust that much higher in the air, and Geoff was suddenly surrounded by scores and scores of splay-fingered victory signs. One of them belonged to Nadya. Reminded of her furious rebuke that he did not know her at all, he watched and listened to her join in a swelling chorus. *Thora, thora, haut ten nas.* He had heard that chant before, and he roughly knew its meaning in English. Onward, onward, to victory.

As the ship chugged away, the crowd ignored the French soldiers and pushed their way to the edge of the quay for a last goodbye. Unable to get out of their way, Geoff and Nadya were carried along with them. Taking care not to get bumped in, Geoff leaned over the quay and looked down at the water. He saw a diesel rainbow in the subsiding wake of the ship. For a moment, he considered pointing it out to Nadya, but then he thought better of it. There were no good omens, and wrongs were not righted in the end, and nobody knew that better than a Palestinian.

At last, Nadya touched his elbow and nodded; she was back with him again. Following her through the dispersing crowd, he could only wonder what might have happened differently if he had just stuck around that last afternoon outside the art gallery in Vancouver. The hypothetical scenarios overwhelmed him, though, and he immediately shut them off.

"Hey you, Mr. Canadian journalist."

It was the word Canadian that caused Geoff to stop; he had forgotten all about his Dix-inspired ruse. Looking around for both the caller and the hailed reporter, he spotted a familiar clean-shaven face in a shadowed doorway. With his arms crossed over his thick chest, Camille Haddad smiled at him like an old friend.

"Still here and still whole?" Haddad said with a laugh and strode out of the doorway to greet him. Geoff shook the hand only because it was thrust in his way, then looked at Nadya and felt sick. He could tell she already knew who and what this man was.

"It was a summer full of stories for you, I think," Haddad said pleasantly. Casually but expensively dressed in a lime green

Lacoste sport shirt, tight-fitting white pants and polished black loafers, and smelling of too much aftershave, the Phalangist's presence here was towering arrogance.

"Out slumming, are we?" Geoff said.

"Like you, I have just come to say goodbye." Haddad glanced briefly at the distant profile of the ship, and then much less briefly at Nadya. "A lovely sight, no?"

"What, the boat or the sea?" Geoff said.

"The boat *on* the sea, and leaving us," Haddad replied fearlessly.

Geoff saw Nadya backing away from the two of them. "Yeah, well, we were just leaving ourselves."

The Phalangist feigned disappointment. "Ah, that is too bad. I had so much to tell you."

"Some other time," Geoff said, moving away. Haddad followed him.

"How about a quote for your newspaper, my friend?"

"What?" Geoff kept a careful eye on Nadya, who looked set to break into a dead run.

"Today we see the end of a very bad chapter in Lebanon's history. On Monday we will see the beginning of something much better."

"Why Monday?"

"Bashir Gemayel will be elected president. Many, many things will change. You will see."

"Right. You got it, front page tomorrow," Geoff muttered. He hurried away, bristling at the sound of Haddad's amused laughter giving chase. You bastard, he thought, I wonder if you'd be so cool if there weren't a few hundred French soldiers down here protecting your ass.

When he caught up to Nadya, Geoff tried to make nothing of the encounter, but she would have none of it. Rising from a sullen and impenetrable silence only after they had walked a long distance from the port, she turned on him. Her eyes were filled with distrust.

"You know such a man?"

"Only by accident, believe me."

Then, sensing that he must, he told her everything he could about Haddad. He recreated his naïve arrival in East Beirut and their first meeting in the St. Michel. He told her about dinner in the sprawling, empty villa and the strange scene in the library, and he even tried to explain the significance of discovering the Spanish Civil War photograph–*his* photograph by prior claim–there on the wall.

Nadya listened to all of this with a look of loathing until Geoff told of the conversation that had taken place on the terrace, where Haddad had talked with revolting nostalgia about his cognac-coated evenings of lobbing mortar shells down on the Tal al-Zaatar refugee camp. Bursting into tears, she told him to stop, and quite suddenly bolted up the road. He chased her and grabbed her arms. She struggled to get away, then gave up and leaned into him weakly, her entire body heaving with sobs.

"Nadya, what is it?"

She refused to tell him. Shaking her head furiously, she straightened up and pushed away from him, gulping air in a battle to stop crying. "Nothing. It is nothing," she insisted. "Let us just go back to the–"

"Shut up," he shouted, cutting her off. "Shut the fuck up."

He was every bit as stunned by the harshness of his words as she was, but he did not regret saying them. They had, after all, given him her complete, open-mouthed attention. "I want you to come with me now."

She did not argue. Pliantly, she got into the taxi he hailed, and quietly she listened to him instruct the driver to take them over to the beach opposite the Carlton Hotel. It was along that stretch of sand that he had seen Arafat, but he doubted she cared, so he did not bother telling her.

Leading her down the same rocky path from the point on the road where they left the cab, he detoured for a moment to duck inside the small cave where Musli and Grete had attended to Arafat's sick lieutenant that night. It was empty now, save for the rusting food tins and crumpled cigaret packets left behind by its former inhabitants. Again, he realized there was no value in trying to distract her with the story, and he continued down to the beach without a word.

"Over there," he said, pointing to a slight elevation in the sand just above the watermark. He wished she could know how little he enjoyed this bullying.

She sat down where she was told to, and he dropped to the ground beside her.

"So," he said, stupidly nudging her with his elbow. She did not react; she kept her eyes locked on the sea. He took a deep breath and got on with it. "I'm going to tell you something that isn't easy for me to say, Nadya. It's an admission that I'd really rather avoid, partly because I'm more ashamed of it than anything else I've done in my life, and partly because all it might do is hurt you. Before I go on, though, I want you to know that I'm doing it only because I've run out of ways to try to make you understand how I feel about you."

Idiotic, he thought, makes no sense at all, and I am digging a big hole.

"You know the day of the demonstration in Vancouver, when I left and then you called?" He stopped, because of course she knew. "Well, I was with Angela. I think you probably know what I mean by that."

"Angela?" It came out the voice of mild surprise, but not of great shock.

"I was stupid angry at you, and then I started drinking, and then . . ." He frowned.

"I knew you were with a woman, Geoff."

"Was I that transparent on the phone?"

She did not bother to reply. He picked up a handful of sand and let it dribble away through the hole at the bottom of his fist.

"Well, this is a bit of a disaster. I thought I'd drag you down here so we could trade secrets, but I see I shot my bolt a long time ago," he said.

"You think I have secrets?" she said.

"Nadya, I *know* you have secrets."

"And is this another Western practice, the trading of secrets, as you call it? Something like your practice of apologizing?"

"Right," he snapped. He flung away another handful of sand and jumped to his feet, prepared to storm down the beach, or perhaps even fully clothed into the surf. But then he stopped and sat back down. He rested his hand on her arm. "No. It was a nice try, but you can't drive me off this time, Nadya."

Slowly, she turned away from her stare at the sea and met his gaze. Her eyes and mouth had hardened, and she looked much older than her twenty-seven years. "I prefer to walk," she said.

"Sure." He stood up and waited for her.

When they had covered some distance, she asked, "Where would you have me start?"

"Anywhere," he said gently.

"My family does come from the village of Bekroum, to the north and west of Jerusalem, in the Galilee. We had some land there."

"I remember. Lots and lots of land, you said."

She shook her head. "No, not so much. Only a small farm with an orchard."

"I've been known to exaggerate the size of things, too." Her glance told him he was trying too hard to be ingratiating.

"The events of 1948 are much as I told you before. My family and everyone else in the village were forced from their homes by the Zionists. Most fled to Lebanon, and it was here in Lebanon that I was born."

"In 1955?"

"Yes."

"Well, you haven't lied about your age," he said, smiling.

"But I have lied."

"About Kuwait?"

She nodded. "We did not go to Kuwait and, as you have seen, my family did not become wealthy in any import-export business."

"And your parents, they did not die in a traffic accident?" he guessed.

"No."

"Where are they, then?"

"Dead," she said.

"How?"

"Go ask your friend, the fascist at the port." She stopped walking. Her face pinched up small in a spasm of pain, then dissolved beneath a new wash of tears. She began to shake. "Tal al-Zaatar," was all she could manage.

Haddad's words pitched stones into the wild darkness at the

back of Geoff's brain. *We would watch them run, we would watch them bleed, and if we were very, very fortunate, we would watch them die.*

*   *   *

Geoff would never have asked her to go on, but as soon as she had calmed down enough to speak again she insisted upon it. He then realized that the catharsis was critical. To stopper it now might be to do so forever. So he took her hand and refused to let go of it as they continued south along the beach.

"What do you really know about Tal al-Zaatar?" she asked.

"It no longer exists, I know that." He thought about the Israeli bulldozers he had seen leveling Ein Hilwie, and envisioned the same thing done to Tal al-Zaatar.

"You know it is gone, but do you know the story of how it happened?"

"No. Tell me."

"You know about the civil war here?"

"In 1975 and '76," he said. "It's never really ended."

She nodded. "In 1976 the Syrians came into Lebanon because they were afraid of what would happen to their own regime if the PLO and the Lebanese left under Kamal Jumblatt were to defeat the Maronites, as it looked like they would."

"I did know that much, yes."

"At this same time, Tal al-Zaatar, being in East Beirut, was surrounded and under siege. The main Maronite forces there were Camille Chamoun's, the Tigers. But there were many Phalangists too. All of them like packs of street dogs.

"Our fighters held the Christian militiamen off for seven months, even with the Israelis giving them all the guns and bombs they wanted to use against us. But after the Syrians came into Lebanon, there was no chance. The Syrian army prevented the PLO from getting to the camp to help. In the end, when there was no more food or bullets left, Tal al-Zaatar was invaded."

Nadya stopped talking then. Her lips pursed and trembled, but she did not permit herself to cry again. Geoff squeezed her hand hard so she would not forget he was there for her.

"They killed thousands during the seven months that the camp was cut off. There was terrible shelling every day. Another one thousand died during the final attack. And then, when that was finished and they controlled the camp, the fascists lined up and shot another thousand people. Men, women, children–it did not matter to them, so long as they were Palestinians."

With awful, prescient clarity, Geoff could sense what was coming next.

"Do you think it is God's blessing that I do not know when it was during those months that my family died?" Nadya asked. "My mother, my father, my sisters and brother?"

"Maybe." Geoff had searched for something more comforting to say, but he was spiritually unequipped for it.

"If it was a blessing, then it was a blessing of the smallest pity on someone already in hell," she continued, speaking in a tone of indictment.

"Oh, Nadya, I'm sorry," he said. But she wasn't hearing anything, anything except perhaps the sounds of the gunfire and screaming six years earlier.

"You see, I was a student then, working on my bachelor's degree at the American University, here in West Beirut. From the moment the siege of Tal al-Zaatar began, I could do nothing but listen to it and pray."

Which you did but no longer do, Geoff understood. He contemplated their separate paths to atheism.

"Now you know my secret–the important one, at least," she said stoically.

Yes, and he could probably guess the rest of it. The Kuwait story, with its orphaning car accident and rich aunt and uncle, had become the armor of choice for deflecting the curious and those who would seek to get close to her. As for the appearance of a camp refugee in a place as remote from the tortured Middle East as smugly lovely Vancouver, Geoff imagined that her considerable brains alone could have carried her there.

"I don't know what to tell you, Nadya." Which was true: he had already determined that anything from him could only trivialize. He squeezed her hand again and they walked a bit farther, neither one saying anything.

"It is getting hot," Nadya said at length. "We should return to the camp and get this food out of the sun before it spoils."

Geoff nodded. In truth, he would have tried to swallow the chicken raw right now if she had asked him to.

*   *   *

Thomas Dix and the best-known Dixism came up during dinner. It occurred to Geoff, as he tugged at some stringy thigh with his teeth, that the one other supper Nadya had cooked for him had also featured chicken. That, of course, was the night of her party—another of the nights, in other words, that he would just as soon forget. It was perverse, he thought: I run to Lebanon in the middle of a war to chase down a woman with whom I have had almost no good times at all, but what feels now like an entire marriage's share of unhappiness. Glutton for the awful.

He looked up and smiled at Nadya's grandmother, as usual plunked on the one stick of furniture in the house, her wicker stool. She had already finished her portion of the bird and was now working on some of Nadya's with her few remaining teeth.

"Aren't you hungry?" he asked.

"I have gone so long without meat that it seems I have lost my taste for it," Nadya told him.

"It's not the greatest anyway," he said. "I think this chicken must have lost its taste for grain, or whatever it is Lebanese chickens get fat on."

Nadya smiled and dabbed at some fried eggplant on her plate with a piece of bread.

"You remember the American I told you about, the journalist who helped me?" Geoff asked.

"Fix?"

"Dix."

"Yes."

"He was big on alternative philosophies. He had this one that argued that life is an orbit, not the straight course that begins with birth and ends when we get old and die." He hesitated, sorry that he had implied old age as the only partner of death.

"An interesting theory," she said.

"According to him, because it's circular, we pass the same points over and over again even if we don't always recognize them." With somebody else, he would have sought to explain it in terms of the photograph on Haddad's library wall. With her—conscious of the need to avoid that topic area altogether—he was stuck with chicken for an illustration. "Take this dinner, for example," he began.

"I can see this is going to be deep philosophy," she said solemnly.

Geoff's surprise made him laugh. Nadya was not a joke-teller. She began to laugh too, and soon even the old woman was chortling, though at what she had no idea.

"Seriously." He stared at a rare twinkle in Nadya's eyes and ached to be free to touch her. "You've made supper for me twice, and both times it's been chicken."

"This sounds silly, but go on," she said.

"Think about it. That first time turned out badly, so it became fixed in my mind. Now it's chicken again, and I trip over my memory of that first time."

"I see, so every time you eat chicken from now until you grow old and die you will think of the night you first hurt my feelings and then offended me as a Palestinian?"

"Yes, exactly," he answered without thinking it all the way through.

"Do you have any idea of the number of times you are likely to eat chicken in all those years?"

Geoff frowned. He was about to concede the point and trash Dix's stupid theory when he realized that in setting him up she had also set herself up. "You plan to serve me a lot of chicken dinners through the years, do you?" he said.

She tossed her head and laughed at him. He waited until she was done.

"That's a proposal, Nadya."

"It is what?" She was clearly startled.

"I want to marry you," he said.

*   *   *

He knew she would get back to him—after their confessionals on the beach, she was out of dark corners to flee to—so he was prepared to wait all evening if need be. Or so he thought. As

always, she refused to let him help with the clean-up and dishes
from supper. Besides, he could tell she wanted some time and
space to absorb his ambush. Accepting a glass of tea, he gave in to
her request that he go outside and take some night air. Some
cooling night air, she had said, which made him laugh.

He took up a place on the ground just outside the doorway,
pressed his back against the block wall and listened to the
murmur of the two women talking while they worked. At first, he
was certain Nadya was confiding in her grandmother; their
voices were low and he heard the subject as important. But then,
when bits of laughter gradually began to punctuate their
conversation, he started to worry. Worry that they were not
talking about him; worry even more that they were. Could it be
that Nadya was going to refuse to take this seriously too? As
quickly as he had found it, his belief that he had finally
penetrated through all the layered shell around this strange
woman began to fail him. Would nothing ever be as he wanted it
with her?

"Come."

Come. That was all she said to him when she stepped out of the
house and started up the alley. It was more than an hour after his
banishment before the talk inside slowed then stopped. The old
woman lumbered outside to wash her face in the basin left for that
purpose, and to spit a few times in preparation for sleep. Only
after she was back inside and had settled on her bedroll with a
series of contented grunts did Nadya emerge. Come. He went.

They walked to a neighbor's home and, after a ritual Arab stop
for coffee, emerged with a bedroll. Nadya informed him it was
his, so he took it from her and prepared to press her for some kind
of response during the walk back. So absorbed was he in his
wind-up for delivery that he failed to notice that they were not
headed home.

"Now where are we going?" he asked.

They'd come to a section of the camp that had been especially
heavily damaged by Israeli air strikes. All the homes in an area
the size of a full city block had been ripped apart. No one lived
here anymore; many of those who had no longer lived.

"Go there," Nadya said, pointing to one of the few hovels that was still more or less standing. It had three walls and nearly half a roof.

"Where, inside?" he asked, looking through the dark for protruding shards of metal and other sharp hazards in the debris. He watched her nodding yes, and he thought: how can a lead-up like this end in anything but an answer I don't want to hear?

Straddling mounds of rubble, he led her into the house through the gape of the missing wall. He dropped the bedroll on the floor and turned away. He was finished with being the first to speak at all the important moments.

"Geoff."

He turned towards her, and it felt as if his knees were about to give out. Nadya had picked up the bedroll where he'd dropped it and was now unfastening it. Done, she let is slide to the floor, where it uncoiled like a long tongue and lay there, waiting.

"Oh my," he said.

At first, all he wanted to do was run his fingertips up and down her arms, from the rounded edge of her shoulders to the ends of her fingers and back again. Nadya understood this need. She lifted her arms and held them straight out to the sides for him. He moved closer, brushing but just brushing against the more obvious and urgent points of contact as he stretched his arms out alongside hers. For as long as he had waited, he would wait a little longer.

Theirs was a strange dance, but theirs had always been a strange dance. Facing each other and arm to arm like mirror images of the same crucifixion, they grasped hands and traveled through a slow circle, listening to the shuffle of their feet through the grit and broken stone on the floor. The night sky beyond the jagged hole in the roof was choked with stars.

"You are mine now," he heard himself telling or warning her.

"Is this the noble sanctuary?" she asked.

They kissed, and their tongues met, his the bold first caller. At Geoff's gentle insistence, Nadya lifted her arms over her head, and he pulled her blouse up and off. Then he lifted his arms and invited her to do the same. She did. Next, unhooking her bra and tugging it away, he cupped the blades of her shoulders and pressed her bare breasts to his chest.

Leaving her lips with regret, he dropped to his knees in front of her. He unzipped the fly of her jeans and carefully dragged them down over her hips and thighs. She quivered, and he leaned in to kiss her dark warmth with reassurance. He felt her fingers dance along his jawline, soft but urging him to stand up. He did, and she surprised him by going to her knees in his place, intent apparently on keeping pace with this undressing.

They stood naked now. Caressing with his hands and his mouth, Geoff circled and circled, spiraling down her slender body from earlobe to ankle. He tongued back up the inside of her thighs, pausing to tug and tease. She moaned. He bobbed his lips over her erect nipples. She moaned.

And then he could wait no longer. Reaching out, he swung one hand around her knees and hoisted her into his arms. Why? He did not really know–they were barely a full step away from the bedroll–but perhaps he needed that sense of strength, an illusion of control over her. With his mouth on hers all the way there, he at last lowered her to the floor.

"I love you, Geoff," she said. "I love you."

And then the time and need for words was over.

SEVENTEEN

MORE SHOCKED BY THE SWOLLEN FORCES OF HER OWN physicality than she was by his–at least it appeared that way to Geoff–Nadya initially refused to make a return visit to the bombed-out house the next evening. This retreat of hers back toward chastity did not last, however. It could not last. Tapped into once, love would not be denied. *Now*, he whispered at her after the old woman had said good night to them and gone inside to bed. Nadya shook her head a bit too vehemently. Now, he repeated a little later, with a patience born of certainty. Now. Until at last, when the old woman was sure to be asleep, she got up to fetch a bedroll from inside and went with him to the other side of the camp.

Afterwards, as they lay on the moonlit floor of the roofless house, Geoff wanted to tell her that a sniper could shoot him dead and a shortened life would be worth it just to have seen the look of amazement in her eyes when she reached the edge of pleasure that first time and tumbled over it beneath him. Instead, he asked her a peculiar question.

"Have you had many lovers?"

Nadya eyed him closely. "Do you ask this because I am an Arab woman, and you have certain ideas about the behavior of Arab women?"

Leaning on his elbow, Geoff traced his fingertips along the faint line of down running from her navel to the base of her breasts. She was gradually becoming more comfortable with this intimacy, with a kind of talking done nowhere else and the most

237

vulnerable nakedness of all, but that first night she had sought to cover herself in every way–physically and emotionally–as soon as the act was completed.

"In part, I suppose," he said.

"No is the answer to your question. Not many."

He wondered if his smile told her that he was just a bit pleased.

"But you, you have had many lovers?" she said, her tone one of broad surmise.

"Scores of women."

"Yes?"

He laughed. "See, you've bought as many myths about the West as I have about the Middle East."

"But you have had many sexual partners?"

"No, I've had *some* partners," he said.

"Strangers?"

"One or two. Alcohol tends to hurry friendships along. But of course you wouldn't know that."

"I have observed it," she said with a wry smile of her own. "And I am a biochemist. I do know what ethanol is capable of."

"Yes, I'm sure you do, *Beaker*," he said, affixing a little nickname to her. He was feeling playful now and would soon want to make love again. "So, let me guess."

"Guess? At what?"

"At who your partners might have been."

"*No.*"

But her howl of protest did not stop him. "The phantom fiancé. Did you ever sleep with Mohammed Chauer?"

"No, I did not. I told you he was just a boy when I knew him. You are a terrible, awful man, Geoff." She knocked him off his elbow. Then she tried to push him right off the bedroll and onto the rough, cold floor. He fought his way back on and pinned her gently under his weight. They lay like that for a moment, staring, listening to each other breathe. Suddenly, Nadya lifted her head and bit the end of his nose hard enough to fill his eyes with water.

"How about Wawid?" he persisted through the pain.

"Who?" She had to let go of his nose in order to speak.

"Walid. The hairdresser."

"No, not him either. Now go away," she said, a little angrily.

"You really want me to go away?"

"Yes, go away."

"Fine." He shrugged and began to get up off the bedroll.

"No." She threw her arms around his neck to keep him there. He fell forward and kissed her. She was a novice, as well, in the kind of games that made up the warring of love as he had learned to fight it. Yes, she might be his beautiful primitive, but he would forever be the brute.

This time they made love with her on top, a position that enabled Geoff not just to play with her breasts but to bury his hands in her hair as it spilled down over her shoulders. Just as that night out on her balcony, it smelled once more of lemons. When he came, they were lying on soft meadow grass at the edge of an orchard. He assumed it must be Palestine.

"I've been to your village, Beaker," he told her afterward while they rested. She lifted her cheek off his chest and gave him a quizzical look. Her hair fell across her face. He reached up to tuck it behind her ears.

"When?"

"Just now, while we made love."

She smiled and eased herself onto her side. She leaned on her elbow as he had on his. "What did you see?"

"Well, not a lot—I was kind of busy," he said. "But there was grass, fruit trees, a very blue sky. I was wearing a khaffiyeh, if you can picture it."

Nadya laughed. "You? *Ibn Arabiya*—a son of Arabia. What was I wearing?"

"Nothing, actually."

"Tell me about *your* partners," she said after a moment. "The important ones. Angela and your wife."

"My *first* wife," he said, drawing her attention to last night's still-unanswered question. He was beginning to think her quite sly. As a diversion, this provision of regular sex would probably give her considerable breathing space for a while. He had certainly been put off less pleasantly than this in his time.

Predictably, Nadya ignored his remark.

"What's to tell?"

"I will trade secrets with you," she offered, poking fun at him.

Still curious about her past relationships, he weakened. "Names?"

"Yes, but you must talk first."

"With you, I nearly always do," he pointed out. "Okay, what do you want to know about them? How they performed in bed?"

Nadya looked embarrassed. Geoff thought: why is it so often that my bent towards the crude best illustrates the differences between the two of us?

"Tell me about them as women. Why did they not make you happy?"

"You never ask simple questions, do you? I don't know why, Nadya, I honestly don't. I mean, does anybody ever really know?"

"You ask the wrong person. I have not been in love with anyone before," she said.

"Nor have I."

He shook his head hard at her frown of doubt. "No, I mean it. And maybe that is the *why* you're after here–I didn't love them. Couldn't."

"Why not?"

"Linda wasn't nice enough. Angela was too nice. How's that for ten words or less?"

Nadya shook her head and slapped him loudly on the belly. "You are a most hopeless man."

"But it's true. Linda was a very hard case. She wouldn't bend at all on her notion of what I ought to be. I wouldn't bend either; I guess I was not the thoroughly modern male she had in mind. It's just that at some point, some very early point, I decided that I was not going to be the modern male if she was the modern female. She was shitty to me, and I was shitty to her. End of story, end of marriage."

Nadya, the orphaned refugee, looked at him as if this were so much trivial nonsense. "And Angela?"

"Poor Ange. She only seemed to be happy when she was forgiving me for something." He laughed at that.

"What is so funny?" Nadya asked.

"When I think about it, Angela was usually pretty happy. I guess there were always fresh heel marks on her back."

Nadya was puzzled. "I do not understand?"

"From me walking all over her. Angela was convinced that I would hurt her, and you might say I didn't disappoint her. We had a very complete relationship in that sense." He was struck by how ugly he sounded.

Nadya immediately sought to take this particular mirror away from him. "I do not believe you," she said.

"Believe me what? That I abused Angela intentionally, or that she invited me to?"

"None of it. I do not believe that she wanted to be hurt, and I do not believe that you would ever be cruel on purpose." She leaned across his chest and looked very closely at him.

He thought: Oh Nadya, I love you for many things, not the least of which your remarkable naivete. "There, I've fulfilled my side of the bargain," he said. "Your turn."

Nadya scowled at him and slipped back onto her elbow. "But you have not told me anything," she complained.

"I'm waiting," he said.

Her expression was an appeal for reprieve.

"Uh-uh. No way. A deal is a deal, Nadya. Even here in the Middle East.

Finally she told him. "Seamus."

"You're kidding," he said. He thought about the small, bearded Irishman. "And there I was thinking he hated me for my politics. How did that happen?"

"It happened. That is all I am going to tell you."

"Yeah, but Seamus?"

"He is a good man, Geoff. His ideas on many things are right."

"Left, you mean. . . . The way you talk about him, he sounds like the guy you might pick for a job, not to be a lover."

"He did do a job," she said quietly.

"What job?" But then he understood. "You *asked* him to sleep with you?"

"I was twenty-six years old. I wanted to be done with it."

"A tough job but someone had to do it, eh?" Geoff cracked.

"Do not laugh at me."

He stopped instantly and reached out to pull her close to him. He took her chin in one hand and stroked the side of her face with his other.

"Nadya, I'm not really laughing. Not at all. Don't you know what this is?"

She waited for him to tell her.

"I'm jealous as hell of Seamus."

"But why? You have me–he does not."

"Do I really?"

"Yes, you do."

"And tomorrow? What about tomorrow?"

"If you want tomorrow."

"You know I do. Is that a *yes*?"

She nodded, and then quite suddenly she was sobbing into his hands. He felt himself melting.

"Will you cry like this at our wedding too, Beaker?"

"I am so afraid, Geoff," she said.

"Afraid–of what?"

"Afraid that now that I love you, I will lose you too."

"What? You won't lose me, Nadya." And then he understood what she was talking about. "No, no, no. Didn't I tell you? I'm immortal."

*   *   *

Dramas of a different sort were played out during the day and reported over the radio stations and in the newspapers. The close of August and opening days of September were both hot and superheated: the summer swelter gave no indication of letting up (orchard fruit and undiscovered bodies ripened fast and did not remain unpicked or undiscovered for long), while the friction of Lebanese political flux burned at the touch. As Camille Haddad had vowed, his friend Bashir Gemayel, at thirty-four just one year older than Geoff, was elected president by parliamentary ballot–this in spite of the fact that a full third of the eligible deputies refused to vote–sparking furious denunciations by

Muslim and Druze leaders, and more violent reactions among their followers. All over West Beirut, the homes and offices of deputies who had voted for Gemayel flamed under fire bombs. Meanwhile, Ronald Reagan called the Lebanese election a positive development, and Menachem Begin was reported to have sent a congratulatory telegram to the leader of the goose-stepping Phalangists that began with the expansive greeting, "My dear friend."

Out at the port, the ships full of exiled Palestinian fighters continued to steam away: to Tartus in Syria, to Iraq, Algeria, Tunisia, Egypt and Greece. On September first, Yasser Arafat arrived in Athens to a sympathetic welcome by Greek president Papandreou. That same day, the last boatload of seven hundred fedayeen left Beirut for North Yemen, led out by Arafat's senior lieutenants, Abu Walid and Abu Iyad. Meanwhile, the Sunni Muslim Mourabitoun militia, the PLO's main Lebanese allies, reluctantly agreed to begin turning over their positions and weaponry to the Lebanese Army, as demanded in the final ceasefire accord. Among their surrendered positions, it was noted in passing by the media, was guardianship over West Beirut's three refugee camps.

On September second, the news was less Lebanon's than Washington's. In a letter to Prime Minister Begin and a television address to the American people, President Reagan outlined his own Middle East peace plan. He called for Palestinian self-rule, linked in some fashion to Jordan, and asked for an end to the building of Jewish settlements on the West Bank and Gaza Strip. The Israeli response was immediate–a flat no. Foreign Minister Yitzhak Shamir said that Israel would never give up the territory it had captured in the Six-Day War, and Deputy Premier David Levy reiterated government intentions of settling a hundred thousand more Jews in the West Bank by 1992.

On September third, the news was loudly Lebanon's again. Insisting that they had done so only for purposes of clearing away land mines and unexploded shells, the IDF ignored the terms of the accord they had signed and advanced into West Beirut to new positions in the Bir Hassan neighborhood adjacent to Chatila. This development was quickly forgotten when someone in the Israeli Defense Ministry leaked news of a September 1 secret meeting between Begin and president-elect Gemayel in the Israeli border town of Nahariya. The subject and details of the meeting were not disclosed, but that it had taken place at all set West Beirut to howling again. There were more fire bombs.

By September fourth, and in spite of the nights with Nadya, Geoff could not stand the do-nothing days any longer. He had discovered that there was something almost as bad as living through siege: living through the days after the lifting of siege and being left to watch people poke through the physical and mental wreckage around them. When the brief euphoria at war's end ends, war's damage remains. No longer filling graves and hospitals, the inhabitants of West Beirut bled only through the eyes now, but their perpetually half-open mouths formed an unspoken *what next?*

What next for Geoff was obvious. With two of three personal quests now over, his one remaining obstacle was to convince Nadya to leave this awful place and return to Vancouver with him. It should have been easy, he thought (nothing next to finding her, and then finding a way inside her mysteries), especially now that she'd said she would marry him. But he had not counted on the illness of a tired old woman.

It began with simple dysentery, a common affliction here all summer with the lack of sanitary drinking water, but then a second infection took hold of her chest. After three days of wracking cough, breathlessness and bloody sputum, Nadya convinced her grandmother that she must see a doctor. Geoff convinced Nadya that the doctor ought to be Musli, and Musli informed them both that it was a serious case of pneumonia.

"She must stay here in hospital until the congestion in her lungs clears. I am concerned about complications. The build-up of fluid is affecting her heart," the Norwegian explained. He stood with Geoff and Nadya in the corridor. It was starkly quiet against Geoff's memories of July and August.

"How long will it take?" Nadya asked.

"Possibly a few days, but a pneumonia like this is very dangerous for someone as old and generally unwell as she is."

"Could she die?" Nadya asked bluntly. This invitation for honesty made an impression on Musli.

"She will either get well, or she will not," he said. "And a good part of it depends on how much she wants to get well."

"Did you tell her this?"

"I wanted to speak to you first. I will."

"Then, please, let me be the one to talk to her," Nadya said.

Musli nodded his consent. Nadya thanked him, then slipped away to the treatment room. The surgeon watched her go.

"Very pretty," he said dully. "Lucky you."

Geoff looked at him, at his underfed frame and pasty face, and doubted that the man had left this gloomy building even once since the last time he'd seen him. Geoff could also tell that was once, at least, not often enough.

"She left, didn't she?"

"Less than one hour after you did," Musli answered. "As you said, you wanted to lead by example. Besides," he went on bitterly, "why should she want to stay after you left?"

"What, now you'd like me to take the blame?"

Musli glared at Geoff but said nothing. He was about to walk away, then stopped. "Why are you here? Gaza Hospital is much closer to Chatila than this one."

"I guess I came to see your wife. Wasted trip, eh?"

"You are a damn and stinking bastard," Musli sputtered.

"And you swear about as well as you fight," Geoff replied. "About as well as you fight for anything, I should say."

The Norwegian's face tightened down even further. "All summer long I have been here in this hospital watching the maimed children come in, but believe it or not I do not think I despise the Israelis as much as I have come to despise you," he said.

"If that's true, then you're an even bigger fool than I thought."

"A fool to hate you? I do not think so," the surgeon said.

"No, but you are if your hatred of me is greater than this need you feel to still be here."

"Why?"

"Because if it's true, you made the wrong decision, didn't you?"

"I had to stay." But the man looked caught.

"Bullshit. You're a good doctor, Doctor, but you're not that good."

"I–" Musli stopped. Nadya had come out of the treatment room and was headed back towards them. The surgeon stared at her with a lost and hopeless expression, and it was almost enough to move Geoff to pity.

"She understands the need for it," Nadya said. "She will stay in the hospital."

"Good," Musli replied, trying hard to smile. But then he looked at Geoff and the effort died.

While they were walking back to Chatila some hours later, Nadya asked Geoff about him. "He does not like you. Why is that?"

"I remind him of something, something unpleasant," Geoff said.

And then quite suddenly, it struck him: Musli believed he had gone to bed with Grete. There was no other explanation possible. What the hell had Grete told her husband before she left, Geoff wondered. Could she really have used him as a weapon against Musli? Needing the physical contact, he put his arm across the back of Nadya's shoulders.

"And where was your friend, the nurse? I had hoped I would meet her."

"She has gone back to Norway. Apparently, she'd had enough of dealing with damaged people."

"Oh, that is sad," Nadya said.

"Yes," Geoff agreed. "It is."

*   *   *

Meaning to tease, Geoff had taken to calling their secret place on the other side of the camp "the noble sanctuary." With the old woman in hospital, though, they no longer had to go there to be together at night. Now, early in the evening, when Nadya returned from her daylong sitting at her grandmother's bedside, they would prepare and eat a simple supper, rarely talking much as they did so, and then go straight to bed.

But bed was different here and now, and Geoff was quite sure he was not alone in noticing a change in his lovemaking. At times, the tenderness that should have been there was missing, supplanted by a rawness that was not so far from violent. More often than not too, he was interested only in riding on top of her, and he recognized that as baldly symbolic. He was fucking her more than he was making love to her: fucking her for having a sick grandmother, for choosing to spend her days with that sick grandmother and not with him, fucking her for having a grandmother at all. Succumbing to the blackest thoughts, he sometimes lay in the dark afterwards, while she dozed on and off out of exhaustion from trying to make a rhythm of his thrashings, and wondered where the old woman had been during the massacre of Tal al-Zaatar.

"I feel like one of Samuel Beckett's hobos, waiting for Godot," he said one night, sensing her wakefulness in the dark beside him. "Waiting, and waiting, and waiting."

"It is the full Palestinian experience you are having, then," she replied. "Many of us have spent our whole lives waiting."

"And up goes that damned flag again," he snapped.

She was silent.

"Sorry," he mumbled.

"Never mind," she told him. But straight away, he thought about her opinion of easy Western apologies and fast Western forgiveness.

Except to buy food for their meals, Geoff rarely left that miserable single room during the day. Every morning, Nadya asked him to come with her to the hospital, but he never went. He could do nothing here every bit as easily as he could do nothing there, and without the depressing presence of Musli. In her absence, his companion was a battered transistor radio that, along with a handful of cheap batteries, she had managed to scrounge up for him. Lolling on a bedroll for hours at a time, he tuned it back and forth between the stolid BBC relay out of Cyprus and a manic East Beirut station that played Western pop music and featured hourly news breaks in English.

September 14. It was around the time of Nadya's usual return from the hospital that somber classical music inexplicably began to play on the East Beirut station. Because it went on and on, uninterrupted by either DJ chatter or the next regular news spot,

Geoff assumed some sort of transmission difficulty and switched it over to the BBC. The news there was already half over, so it was not until the broadcaster closed the segment with a recap of the headlines that he learned of a massive late-afternoon bomb blast at the Phalange Party offices in East Beirut. At last report, the broadcaster concluded, there was still no confirmation of whether President Bashir Gemayel was in the building at the time of the explosion.

Ah, but there was confirmation as far as Geoff was concerned. The music on the other station was enough to convince him that Gemayel was laid out blue beneath three stories of rubble. There, payback for Dr. Patal. Much amused, he thought about Camille Haddad and laughed out loud. A miserable week and a half had just about been salvaged for him.

This perverse euphoria was gone by the time Nadya arrived home. She was almost two hours late and not the least bit apologetic about it. Geoff paced around the room—his cell—and watched her casually light the gas cooker to start supper.

"I was worried about you," he said. In truth, he was mostly resentful.

"No need to worry." She smiled up at him from her knees and blew out the match she'd struck. The flame on the cooker wavered then held. She placed a pot of water on the burner and began to cut up potatoes. Geoff listened to her humming.

"How was she today?" he asked, expecting to hear a word of improvement.

"The same."

He frowned. Just yesterday, Nadya had returned home upset because Musli had told her the congestion was not clearing as he'd hoped. If her condition today was exactly the same, why then this strange ebullience? Perhaps—"You heard about the bombing at Gemayel's office?"

"Yes," she said, dropping a handful of potato into the water. "Do you think he was inside?"

"Beirut Radio has been running nothing but Beethoven symphonies for the last three hours."

"This is what he gets for dealing with the Israelis," she said.

"Maybe it was the Israelis who did it," he suggested. Ending his sulk, he squatted beside her to help with the preparation. She handed him a tomato and a knife.

"That could be, but I do not think it likely. I would guess it to be the work of Syrian agents, or a rival Maronite group like the Franjieh family, or maybe both working together. A man like Bashir Gemayel makes many kinds of enemies."

"Among them the Palestinians."

"Yes, and you can be certain his people will blame us first."

"Possible?"

She shrugged. "All things are possible in Beirut. But that building would be very carefully guarded. For a Palestinian to get inside with a bomb. . . . No, I am quite sure it was not one of us."

"Too bad. I'd like to think your people had done it," Geoff said. This made him smile a little. Even old Seamus might be pleased with him now. How did that chant go again? *Thora, thora, haut ten nas.* Onward, onward, to victory.

Nadya had stopped chopping an onion. She looked miles, whole continents, away.

"What are you thinking about?" he asked. She gazed up at him and her eyes were as soft as he had ever seen them. He thought she might be about to tell him someting tender. In anticipation, he leaned over to kiss her. What she said made him stop.

"Do you think Gemayel has children?"

"*Had* . . . and I don't really give a damn."

"If he has . . . had . . . I feel a sadness for them. No child should lose a father," she went on. Then, flushing with embarrassment at what she had just said, at this strange show of remorse for a man who himself may have pulled the trigger on her family in Tal al-Zaatar, she looked away and returned to chopping her onion.

"Yes, I should say," Geoff scolded her. "What the hell happened to you today?"

"Oh—these stupid, stupid onions," she said, weeping.

EIGHTEEN

SHE TOLD HIM AT BEDTIME. AS IT WAS, SHE HAD LITTLE CHOICE given the ferocious way she'd just fended off his efforts to draw her into making love. Geoff's reaction was every man's first one to this piece of news–a question.

"Are you sure?"

"Dr. Musli ran the test this afternoon. That is why I was so late," she said.

He was naked; she was still fully-clothed. They lay facing each other on the bedroll. She stroked the coarse hair on the knuckles of his hand, while he rubbed his foot up and down the inside of her ankles. He realized that it should not have come as any great surprise to him. The odds were pretty good after nearly three weeks. Still. . . .

"You know I'm ecstatic, don't you?"

"But we're not married," she fretted.

He couldn't help laughing at her Old Worldness. "That's right, and now that you're knocked up maybe I'll just slip on out of town, eh."

He made her smile, but as much as he tried he could not convince her–Nadya the scientist–that some celebratory sex at this point would not dislodge their baby in the making. But that was all right, her naïveté was appealing, so he settled instead for the kind of talking expectant parents do.

"What would we name our child?" she asked.

"What *will* we name our child. Sweetheart, you've got to get your verb tenses straight. Bashir Gemayel *had* children. You and

I *will have* children. Dozens of them, and all black-haired beauties like you."

"And all with the brains of their father?"

"I hope not. You're the PhD candidate."

"You will give them nothing?"

"Oh, I will contribute something to the mix all right," he said. "They will have my tenacity."

"Tenacity? I do not know this word?"

"It means they won't give up pursuing the things they really want."

Understanding this, Nadya bit down on her lip. Geoff almost bit down on his in turn; this innocent habit of hers never failed to fill him with a sudden need to protect her, with an immediate want to cup her face in his hands.

"That would be a wonderful gift to give them." She reached out to touch his cheek with her fingertips. He pulled them into his mouth and sucked on them for a moment. As he stared at her face–at the unmarked olive skin, the dark eyebrows, the thick eyelashes–the name he wanted came to him.

"Duncan."

"That is the name you choose?" she said.

"For a boy. Duncan means dark warrior in Gaelic. It was my father's name. He was a black Scot. Before it turned, his hair was nearly the color of yours. One time, he told me about this theory, some historian's attempt to explain the origins of black hair and olive skin in a place as pale as the British Isles."

"I think I know this theory," Nadya said.

"About the Moors sailing out of Spain and periodically getting themselves shipwrecked along the Irish and Scottish coasts?"

"Yes, something like that."

"So maybe I have some Arab blood in me after all," he said. "Just much diluted after all these centuries."

"Much."

"But there, you see, that tells all about my wanting you from the first instant I saw you in the park. We were fated to be together. From across the sands of time, spun into each other's arms by a desert sirocco–" He spun right into her laughter, and then her arms.

"You are a lovely idiot, Geoff Andrews."

*   *   *

Midnight, with a decision made. Gently lifting Nadya's head off the inside of his shoulder, Geoff slipped out from beneath her and sat up. He scooped the blackness at his feet in search of the transistor radio. He found it and switched it on, picking up static and then, shortly, the sounds of her stirring behind him.

"Geoff?"

"Hush," he said. Fiddling with drifting reception, he got as close to the BBC as he could only to have it fade out again. He fiddled some more, and an Arabic station punched through clear and loud. There was a male voice, grim and monotonous.

"No, wait, leave it." Nadya sat up and slipped her hand over his so he would not move the tuner. "It is Shafik Wazzan, the prime minister. . . . He is talking about Gemayel. . . . Yes, it is official now. They have found his body in the Phalangists' building. . . . Gemayel is dead."

Geoff tugged the radio away from her and switched it off. It had served its wake-up function.

"What does your name mean, Nadya? Do you know?"

She squinted at him as if he had just mumbled something unintelligible in his sleep.

"When I was lying here a while ago, I remembered what mine meant. Geoffrey–seeker of peace. If Duncan, my dark warrior father, having hand-picked the names of all his children, wanted to plot destiny, what do you suppose he had in mind? What kind of peace am I seeking?"

But Nadya was not really listening to him. "It is late, Geoff, and you seem very tired. We should sleep."

"*No.*" He was tired, and because of it he spoke more sharply than he intended to. "No, what we're going to do is get up and pack whatever it is you need to take with you."

"Take with me?"

"We're leaving Lebanon," he said.

"We cannot," she protested, stiffening. "My grand-mother . . ."

"Don't worry. She's leaving with us. We'll collect her first thing in the morning after I find a driver to take us to Damascus." He rolled forward to his feet and reached back to take Nadya by the hand, meaning to pull her up from the floor with him. She refused to be moved. He let go and stood over her, slack from arm to jaw.

"She is sick and in the hospital. She must remain there. The doctor has said this."

"Nadya, you don't know how Musli feels about me. I'm telling you that man would keep your grandmother in his hospital with a hangnail if he thought it might be a way to get back at me for something he believes I did."

"What?" she cried. "That is craziness, Geoff. She is an old woman and she is ill. These other things you talk about, they are nonsense."

"They are not nonsense. You haven't the first bloody clue what it's all about," he said, growing angry. "Now come on, or I'll pack for you."

"No, we will stay," she insisted. Then, retreating forwards with words carefully measured: "At least, I will stay."

"Hey." He was almost shouting now. "You're pregnant with my child. Let's not forget that. I am not going to let you stay here in this fucking sewer for one more day. Jesus, I'm sick to death of this place."

"*You* are sick of this place. Listen to yourself, Geoff. You want to leave, but it is not because of concern for me."

"Of course I'm concerned about you. About you and our baby," he said. "This camp is full of garbage and disease. It's no place for a pregnant woman."

Nadya's laugh was harsh. "This camp has many pregnant women. Women have been getting pregnant and giving birth here in Chatila for more than thirty years. I am somehow different?"

"Yes, damn it, you are different. You're *my* pregnant woman."

His declaration settled heavily and lay there between them.

"I belong to no one," she said quietly.

"That's not what I meant. It's just that—"

"You are not my master, Geoff. You are not even my husband. I will not be told what to do."

"I'm not telling you what to do."

"No? What, then? What are you telling me?"

"I can't stay."

"And I cannot leave."

"I don't belong here, Nadya," he said. "I'm not a doctor, I'm not a fighter, I sell real estate for Christ's sake."

She nodded. She nodded, and then they both fell silent, unable even to look at each other for a time. Geoff felt an overwhelming sadness.

"So Walid was right. When you left Vancouver, it was for good."

"I did not ever imagine you would come looking for me."

"But I did come."

"Yes, and I fell in love with you because of it."

"And now you're pregnant. Unmarried and pregnant."

Nadya's eyes welled up. "I did not plan for any of this to happen, Geoff. I did not want to fall in love with you, and I had no wish to get pregnant. All I wanted was to come back here, to stop running away from who I am."

"Oh, and just who are you?"

"I am a camp refugee whose family, all but one of them, were butchered in this city."

"No, that's your past. What you are now is a young woman named Nadya Karameh who's just found out she's going to be a mother, who could be my wife, who could be a brilliant and influential scholar doing good things for herself and her people in a place a hundred times happier than this place will ever be."

"I don't deserve happiness."

Geoff stared at her. "That might be the most ridiculous thing I've ever heard anyone say. You don't *deserve* happiness?"

"I cannot have happiness," she corrected herself. "Perhaps I do not even want it."

He stifled his urge to scoff at her. "Fine, but what about me? You say you love me. Does my happiness not matter to you?"

She looked away.

"Nadya, I know I can't begin to understand the depth of your pain. All I know is that from where I stand there are no other options for us. Do you think I could leave you now? Never. But I can't stay here either. Nadya, don't you see–you have to come with me."

Geoff waited for her to say something. Slowly, she got to her feet and pulled on her clothes. She stepped into a pair of plastic slippers and headed towards the door.

"Where are you going?"

All he got as reply was the scuff and shuffle of hard plastic across gritty concrete.

"Nadya," he said.

"I am going for a walk."

"Can I come?"

"I would like to be alone for a while. I need some time to think."

"I'll wait up."

"No, don't," she told him firmly. "I will come back when I know what it is I want to do."

"God," he said, badly losing the struggle to keep his voice even. "You mean to say you really have to think that hard about it?"

She stopped in the doorway and looked at him. With eyes glistening, she forced a smile. "Into a grief without end, what is this thing he brings, and how might I enter, if for just one day, such noble sanctuary with him."

"Nadya, I've been sitting here in this house for three weeks doing absolutely nothing. I know you know how miserable I've become, and how miserable I've started to be to you. I don't like it. I don't like me."

She nodded and stepped through the door. Geoff climbed into his pants and followed her outside, and stood watching her disappear into the darkness of the camp.

"I'll be waiting up for you," he called, hearing the words fall far short.

An hour and a half later, she had not returned. Knowing nowhere else to look, Geoff walked to the ruined house on the far side of the camp. But she was not there. He waited, peering up the roadway through the missing wall in case she came, finally knowing she was not going to come. He walked back to the grandmother's house. Banging pots and dragging boxes across the floor, he piled the two women's belongings in the center of the room. When he was done, he stood and stared at the pathetic assemblage, feeling cold and shriveled-up inside.

At dawn, having sat a numb vigil through the rest of the night, he got up from the wicker stool, boiled some water and made himself a cup of tea. He stood in the doorway sipping it and listened to the sound of tanks on the move in the streets beyond the camp. It had to be the IDF, but what were they doing this deep into West Beirut?

When the clatter of grinding gears and rolling tread grew so loud as to sound right outside the south entrance to Chatila, he had to investigate. Walking through the narrow alleys, self-consciously alone, it struck him as odd that nobody else appeared as curious to find out what was going on.

But the curious were already there. A small group of worried old men and agitated adolescent boys milled about a wary distance back from the abandoned sandbag bunker that had served as the camp's sentry post. One of the boys had a battered AK-47 slung over his shoulder on a strap of string and shoelace, but that somehow only made the whole lot of them appear more vulnerable. They looked surprised at the sight of Geoff moving on past them.

He stopped at the side of the road beyond the camp perimeter and watched an Israeli officer standing near a tank call up directions to some soldiers on top of the two-story Kuwaiti Embassy. The embassy was a strangely placed building–strange in that it was alone in one corner of an otherwise empty field–whose flat roof provided a deep look into Chatila. The IDF soldiers were building up a sandbag wall for themselves. Behind it was a heavy fixed-mount machine gun.

"Do you speak English?"

"Wha– Who are you? Where did you come from just now?"

"I'm a Canadian journalist, *Vancouver Sun*, and I want to know why you've come here. This is a complete violation of the ceasefire accord."

Confronted by Geoff's tough posture, the young officer's own tone softened a little. The hard etch on his face eased, and his thick shoulders relaxed. "We are only here to prevent the shedding of blood. You know that the president of Lebanon has been assassinated?"

"Yes. Are you telling me you're here to protect these people?" Geoff said, waving his arm in the direction of the camp.

"Of course we will protect them," the Israeli replied.

"And who's going to protect them from you?"

"They have nothing to fear from us."

Geoff's short laugh was provocation.

"I am not going to debate our war with you," the soldier snapped back. "You asked and I have now told you why we are here." He shouted something else at his men on the roof, then swung his attention to Geoff again. His gaze tightened down and narrowed. Geoff could tell what was coming. "You know, sir, I think I should like to see your documents as a journalist."

"That makes two of us with doubts, then, doesn't it?" Geoff said. He walked away. The Israeli let him go.

Instead of returning to the camp, Geoff went the other direction, onto Avenue Camille Chamoun. It had just then occurred to him to go to the hospital. Nadya might be there even now, but if she wasn't she would be eventually. He thought it would perhaps be better if she was not there when he arrived because it would give him the time he needed to reason or, if pushed, to shame Musli into discharging the old woman. Becoming keen on the idea as it settled in his mind, he broke into a jog and hurried north up streets that were now full of IDF armor and troops dressed in full combat gear.

As it was, neither Musli nor Nadya was there at the hospital.

"Where is Dr. Musli?"

An Arab nurse whom he did not recognize looked up from her charting behind the admissions desk and stared at him blankly. He had found nobody else on duty, here or up in the second-floor ward where the old woman lay sleeping with the aid of an oxygen mask.

"*Wain* Dr. Musli?" he tried.

"He is not here," the nurse said, returning to her charting.

"I need to talk to him."

"You have a medical problem?" she asked with annoyance.

258

Scot Morison

"I have a problem, yes." Geoff decided he had better change his tack. "Listen, I used to help out here as a volunteer orderly. Won't you please tell me where he is? If he's sleeping, he won't mind being woken up for an old friend."

The nurse sighed and took a look at her watch.

"At this time, you can probably find him at the rocks," she said.

"The rocks?"

"The Raoucheh Rocks. He has gone there to climb every morning this week."

"What time will he return to the hospital?"

The nurse shrugged. "Sometimes he is gone an hour, sometimes two or three. There is not so much to be done here right now. Many of the wounded have gone home."

Frowning, Geoff thumped the top of the desk and pivoted away to leave. He stopped. "Would you do me a large favor?" he asked. "You have an old woman up on the second floor with pneumonia."

"Yes."

"There is a young woman who comes to see her every day–her granddaughter."

"I know her, yes."

"If she shows up here before I get back, please, *please* keep her here. Don't let her leave under any circumstances."

"Why not?"

"I can't explain it to you. If you have to tell her something, tell her . . . tell her that a certain Moorish sailor is feeling very lost at sea."

The nurse gave him a baffled look.

"Never mind," he said quietly. "Please, just ask her to wait here for Geoff."

*   *   *

And so here we are again, both of us edging a private abyss. This was the thought that came to Geoff as he stood on the bluff overlooking the bay and stared across the short stretch of water to the top of the smaller Raoucheh Rock where Musli stood, at roughly the same height of land, staring back at him. With the sun still low in the sky behind him, the fully shaded bay was a cold deep blue. The early morning rays struck Musli square in the face, though, and lit him up in all his blondness until he appeared to be translucent.

Geoff had cupped his hands around his mouth and was set to call out once more, but he changed his mind. It was plain that the Norwegian was either not understanding him or was simply choosing not to answer. Fine, he decided, have it your way, you miserable bastard. I'll go down below and wait until you row ashore, and if you don't climb off and come ashore soon enough I will swim out there and drag you back.

Halfway down the steep path to the spot where he and Musli had launched the rowboat that night, he noticed the gulls gathered at the base of the rock. Scores of them rode like a loosely tethered raft on the surface of the sea, bobbing up and down on a gentle swell. He'd begun to wonder why they were there in such odd concentration when he saw Musli tossing something down to them. Pieces of bread?

Another time, different place: he was in Stanley Park again, moments and yards from their first words, watching her feed the geese. . . .

And back further still, to his father quoting verse. Cast they bread upon the waters: for thou shalt find it after many days. . . .

When Musli stepped off the rock, his arms reaching out as if to embrace the sun, it was with the arc of a diver, not the sprawl of one who had simply jumped. But this was no dive. Geoff closed his eyes because he could not watch the end, and he kept them tightly shut until the silence was filled with an awful half splash and the cries of gulls rising up alarmed from the water.

He forced himself to look. To look at Musli floating face-down, the back of his white shirt (perhaps the same shirt Grete had worn that day above the orchards) pillowed full of air, his body buffeted against the descending flare of the rock by the same benign sea that had rolled beneath the gulls.

Those gulls. Their angry shrieks, as they swung and hovered over the site of a rudely ended feed, brought Geoff back to himself. He had tripped and fallen to the ground and was now clutching at the hard clay of the path with his fingers. He

remembered his dream about the drowning. Just a bird, I tell
you. And then his dream within a dream of a naked shoulder so
familiar that he could describe exactly the taste of its salt on his
tongue. Now, unlike before, he could put a face to that shoulder.
It was Nadya's face, Nadya's shoulder. Nadya. . . .

*   *   *

There were other uniforms out front of the Kuwaiti Embassy
when he got back: dark green Phalangist fatigues scattered
amongst the drabber olive of the Israelis. Geoff paid no heed to
them. Drenched in sour sweat and aching for breath from his long
run, he had only the one thing in mind: to get to the house. He
sprinted towards the camp.

"*Stop!*"

He stopped, halted not by the shouted word but by the click of
rifles being readied behind it. Turning around slowly, he
watched the same IDF officer he'd confronted earlier come
bristling across the road.

"Where are you going?" the Israeli demanded.

"Excuse me?"

"Where are you going?"

"What does it look like?" Geoff said peevishly.

"The camp is closed to nonresidents."

"I am a resident. I have been living in Chatila for the past three
weeks."

"The camp is closed to non-Palestinians," the Israeli corrected
himself.

"Why?"

"We have new orders. We are soon to begin an operation."

"What operation?"

"We have received reports of enemy activity inside. We have
orders to search the camp for terrorists."

"*Terrorists.*" Geoff exploded. "The only terrorists here are you
and your drooling friends over there," he shouted, pointing at a
group of Phalangists. "You people saw the ships leave. You know
there's nobody in there but women, children, old men and
cripples."

"Enough." The officer shook his head and took firm hold of Geoff's arm. "Enough talk. You are to evacuate this area now."

"The hell I will," Geoff said, twisting free. But before he could take two steps towards the camp entrance, the Israeli had whipped out a side arm and pressed its cold muzzle into the flesh at the side of his throat. The pistol was lowered only after Geoff had raised his hands in exchange.

"*Now.*"

"Twenty minutes—I only want twenty minutes to collect my belongings," he pleaded. "I won't make any trouble."

"Give me your passport and press identification."

"All right, all right." Geoff hurriedly unbuttoned the top of his shirt and removed them from the cloth pouch strung around his neck.

"You have *ten* minutes," the Israeli said after a quick study of the documents. He held them aloft and motioned as if to toss them away over his shoulder. "If you do not come back in that time, I will destroy these, and then your troubles in this place will be very serious. Do I make myself clear to you?"

Geoff nodded.

He had barely crossed into the camp when the frightened inhabitants living closest to the entrance spilled out of their houses. Wide-eyed, they surrounded him. He pushed his way through their wall of frantic questions—*Shu fee? Laish?*—and their wildly gesturing arms. I don't know what's going on. . . . I don't know why. . . . Just go back inside your homes and leave me alone. Free of their clutching at last, he put his back to them and ran, ran until the air was roaring in his ears.

Shoving aside the sheet across the door, he burst into the house, then dropped to his knees and slammed his hands on the concrete floor. He slammed them again and again, not stopping until the sting on his skin had become a throb in his bones. She was not there, but she had been there. The boxes he had carefully packed and deliberately placed in the center of the room were now unpacked, the contents returned to their places around the room. Slumping forward onto his cheek, he had nothing left to summon up but a groan.

Remembering the sledgehammer of time, he struggled back to his feet and searched for something, anything with which to leave a message. If she had gone on to the hospital from here it wouldn't matter, but if she had not yet left he must leave a note for her. He found a nub of pencil but nothing to write on, then remembered the half sheet of paper with the poem she had begun to him. He took it out of his pocket, unfolded it and scribbled across the back.

Nadya–please stay here and wait for me. Please.
G.

The gauntlet of drawn faces watching him leave; the dull eyes of the camp subtly casting him into the *other camp*, as they followed him out to the road, out to the IDF officer who stood waiting with his hostage documents, waiting with a black frown at his empty-handed return from inside.

But Geoff was a long way from Chatila, and much nearer the hospital, before the lingering image of his silent departure from them sunk in with its true meaning. Nadya would not be at the hospital because she could not be at the hospital. The Israeli had lied to him. Chatila was not so much closed to non-Palestinians wanting to enter as it was closed to Palestinians wanting to exit.

No less troubling was the next level of comprehension. If Nadya was still in the camp, as she must therefore be, she would have been aware that he was there too. The reliable grapevine would have quickly located her and told her as much. Could it be that from behind some low wall or around some alley corner she had watched him come back to the house? Had hidden and watched and kept silent, their just-planted seed already drying up and dying in her belly?

*   *   *

There was a rear stairwell on the second floor of the hospital. During the summer, its thick and windowless walls had seen occasional service as an extra bomb shelter when the basement became too crowded with people scrambling in from the street.

Geoff used it now to sneak the old woman outside. Shawled in a blanket draped over her backless dressing gown, she allowed him to support her by the elbow as they picked their way down the unlit stairs. The pace of this descent made Geoff want to scream and throw her over his shoulder, but the rasp of her breathing told him she was doing as well as she could. She truly was sick.

At last they emerged into hot, bright sunlight at the back of the hospital. Geoff steadied the old woman against the wall, and indicated that she was to stay there and wait for him. He ran around to the front and jumped into one of two ambulances left parked by the emergency entrance. The keys were in the ignition (Geoff gave a silent thanks for Musli's fast-response policy), and he pumped the gas a couple of times to be sure of a clean start. The engine roared to life. The fuel gauge registered half-full; it was enough, certainly, to get them to Damascus. Punching the stick into first gear, he glanced back to see that no one was coming out of the hospital to give chase, then wheeled the ambulance into the driveway and pulled away.

Out in front of Chatila, the olive-colored fatigues had disappeared, taking their tanks with them. At the slow approach of an ambulance, the forest of dark Phalange green that now stood in their place opened up. But it opened up to swallow, not to let pass. Geoff heard the old woman mumbling under her breath as he pressed the brakes to a full stop and watched the Christian militiamen swarm in around the vehicle. They peered in through the windows, palmed and fingered the glass. Some of them grinned. One of them standing next to the passenger door made a rolling motion with his hand, and the old woman undid her window. He asked her something and she answered. There was laughter.

Someone tapped on the glass for Geoff now, and he rolled his window down a crack. He smelled burning hashish and recognized the glazed expression of stoned young men. There was a question for him as well, also delivered in Arabic. He shook his head and called out for someone who spoke English. There was further laughter, some of it more like giggling, but no English.

The sound of the passenger door being unlocked and opened

snapped Geoff's head back the other way. A Phalangist had taken hold of the old woman's arm and was leading her out of the ambulance.

"Stay here," Geoff shouted, too late. Popping up his own lock, he threw open the door, banging a couple of militiamen with it, and jumped out. There was angry murmuring around him.

"*Presentez votre passeport*," someone demanded.

"Piss off," Geoff said, pushing through bodies to get to the other side of the ambulance. He stepped between the old woman and her escort and swung her gently back towards the vehicle. An arm reached out and shoved him hard. He fired an elbow backwards in retaliation but struck nothing. There was more laughter.

And then, through a hole in this jostling forest, he saw Camille Haddad.

Dressed in the same loud uniform as all these others, the wealthy hotelier had assumed a casual pose on the hood of somebody's powder blue Mercedes sedan. He sat with his legs dangled over the edge. At the sight of Geoff coming towards him, the old woman in tow, he yawned and crossed his ankles. Unlike the others with their heavy combat boots, he was wearing the same meticulously polished black loafers he'd had on at the port. Geoff recognized them by their short country-club tassels. Apparel for the consummate weekend warrior.

"Good morning," he said, flashing his cracked-ice smile.

"Where did your masters go?" Geoff said, foolishly he knew. Haddad merely chuckled.

"The Israelis feel that we are better than they at this sort of thing."

"What sort of thing?"

Haddad scratched his chin and grinned. "I told you once, I believe, that I gain much pleasure from play with these people."

"How can you do this?" Geoff asked weakly. Through the heaviest bombardment from air, land and sea, in the face of all that other imagery of violence and death during the summer, he had never been half as filled with fear as he was that night out on the terrace, overlooking the black hole that had been Tal al-Zaatar, as he was right now.

"It is easy," the fascist assured him. "Especially now that Bashir is dead."

"They didn't kill him and you know that," Geoff said.

Haddad did not argue the point.

"I want you to let me go into the camp and bring someone out," Geoff said.

"Yes, I know who it is you want to bring out."

"And you'll let me do it?"

"What do you think?" the Phalangist smirked.

"Damn it. I know your name, and I know the name of your wife, your brother and father. I know the name of your hotel. I can make sure you're smeared across the front page of every newspaper in Europe and North America tomorrow."

Haddad's face hardened. "I do not know quite what you are, my friend, but you are certainly no journalist. Perhaps you are an agent for somebody, a spy? Should I suggest that possibility to my men?"

"I'm no spy, Haddad."

"No–no, you are not careful enough to be a spy," he agreed. "Your feelings about things are much too obvious."

Most of Haddad's men had gathered round this little meeting. They were getting impatient. Laughing amongst themselves, they pushed and slapped at each other's faces. Two of them fenced with the barrels of their automatic rifles, while another began to tug at the blanket wrapped around the old woman's shoulders. Geoff pushed her tormentor away, then he turned back to his own.

"Do you want me to get down on my knees and beg for this?" he said.

"That might be enjoyable to watch."

"Please?"

"Try harder."

"*Please.* She's pregnant." Immediately, Geoff realized that this disclosure was going to gain him nothing at all.

Haddad smiled and said something to the militiamen. There was uproarious laughter. The old woman looked at Geoff and began to mumble again. She was terrified. Someone pushed her towards the camp.

"What did you tell them?" Geoff demanded, watching her go.

"I told them that you are a man with a Palestinian whore as your lover, and that you are prepared to get down on your knees and suck my cock if I let you into Chatila to get her. I told them that I would tell you a polite no thank you." He grinned. "But I also told them that I will be happy to personally deliver very special greetings on your behalf when I see her. What is her name, if I might?"

Haddad was caught unprepared for the speed of the attack. His eyes widened as he flopped onto the car hood with Geoff sprawled on top of him. But the Phalangist was a strong man. Reacting to Geoff's fingers tightening around his throat, he twisted hard, this way then that, and pitched them both off one side of the hood and onto the pavement.

Less winded by his fall, Geoff got back up first and managed one hard kick at Haddad's head before the militiamen set upon him with the butts and barrels of their guns. Their terrible rain of wood and steel fell upon his skull, his stomach, his back, his face and ribs. Screaming in pain, he collapsed on the ground and turtled. He could taste, smell, the spill of his blood. His last conscious images were of bayonets fixed above him, of the pooling of evil in men's eyes, of frantic shouting in the distance and then a sudden parting in the crowd around him and the reappearance of olive green uniforms—and, finally, of the sharp glint of binoculars trained down on all of this from the roof of the Kuwaiti Embassy. The voyeurs were back. You're back, he thought. And then it all went blessed black.

NINETEEN

THE BOY DID NOT SPEAK AND HE HARDLY SMILED, BUT GEOFF was fond of him immediately, and for a while stood watching him from the other side of the chain link fence that surrounded the townhouse complex. He looked a bit smaller or younger than the other boys wrestling in the grass next to a sandpit playground—with its geodesic monkey bars and tubular plastic obstacle course—and that, perhaps, was why he shied away from their roughhousing.

He might have been physically timid, but those who watch are almost always the most curious, and eventually the presence of a stranger hanging about just beyond the fence could not go uninvestigated any longer. He hiked up his pants and cut a path across the lawn between a pair of hissing sprinklers. Geoff was now looking at the trees: an apple, two pears and an olive that had been planted close together. They were old trees, which was what he wanted, and the reason why he had pulled his rented car over to the side of the road when he saw them there.

"What are you doing, mister?" The boy stuck his fingers between holes in the fence and swung his body against what little give there was in the wire mesh.

"I'm trying to decide where to leave something for someone." Geoff answered. The boy spoke with a North American nonaccent, but Geoff had long ago stopped being surprised by any implied origins he encountered in this part of the world.

"What are you gonna leave?"

"A deed."

"What's that?" the boy pestered.

"It's kind of hard to explain. Ask your dad."

"He isn't here. He's up fighting the Arabs."

"In Lebanon?"

The boy nodded importantly. "I think so, yeah."

An official statement read out by a spokesman for the Cabinet said that the Israel Defense Forces had taken up positions in West Beirut to prevent the danger of violence, bloodshed and anarchy following the bomb assassination of Bashir Gemayel.

"Well, then, go ask your mom."

"Okay," Thus dismissed, the boy turned away to leave. After a couple of steps, he came back. "I could help you if I climbed over the fence," he suggested brightly.

"Do you think I need your help?"

The boy shrugged, but the cloud on his face showed he knew that the answer to the question was no.

"Maybe I could use an assistant at that," Geoff said. "Do you think you can get over the fence? It looks pretty high to me."

"Sure I can." He scrambled up to the top, then wavered. "Will you catch me if I fall?"

Geoff took the hint and moved over. "Try not to fall though, okay? My body is kind of sore."

When the boy got down, Geoff let him hold the Swiss Army knife he had purchased in a souvenir shop near Jaffa Gate, inside the Old City, before driving out here. He had bought the expensive knife, even though it was far better than he needed, after the Arab merchant refused to accept any money for the map of pre-1948 Palestine he produced from the rear of his shop and gave to Geoff.

"We need to pick a tree," he told the boy. "Which one shall it be?"

Following a close inspection of each of the four possibilities, a choice was made.

"This."

"The olive tree?" Geoff said.

"It's the nicest one," the boy argued.

"And maybe the best for leaving a deed like this one too."

The boy appeared to be pondering. "What does a deed look like?" he asked.

"They can look like just about anything, I guess. This one, though, is a set of initials. Do you want to carve them for me?"

"Sure."

Among the victims—men, women and children slaughtered without prejudice—were a large number with crosses carved into their chests, a well-known Phalangist signature.

Really, when you got down to it, how hard could killing be? Geoff wanted to know as he stood behind the boy, this little Jewish boy whose pants refused to stay up on his hips, and watched him working at the rough bark with the sharp knife. He could do it right here in the cover of these old Palestinian trees, be gone in the car, and in six hours be safely aboard his flight to London. The authorities would still be down on their hands and knees combing a thirty-foot-square strung-off grid for clues. No one would ever know.

No one, of course, but him. Without being aware of it coming, he had been possessed once again by the game of imagining that had ruled his waking hours, and so often more than just his waking hours, during the past week's stay in an uncrowded, well-equipped Jerusalem hospital, the place the voyeurs had taken him to after they'd saved his non-Arab skin from Haddad's men.

The very fortunate ones were shot, often execution-style in groups. The less fortunate were strangled, had their throats slashed, were buried alive, or worse. Breasts and male genitalia were hacked off, the latter sometimes stuffed into the mouths of their owners, or others. Pregnant women had their bellies slit open, the fetuses ripped out and mutilated.

He was testing the limits in his mind and discovering that limits did not exist there. It was a game that had begun after the drug dosages were reduced and the news reports on the television set slung above his roommate's bed began to get through the morphine clot in his brain.

Initially inhibited by some sort of veneer of moral conditioning, he started with safely impossible scenarios. The appearance on the screen of Ariel Sharon or Menachem Begin, sounding shrill in their claims to innocence at what had taken place during those seventy-two hours of massacre in the camps of West Beirut, led him to such silly fantasies as grenades smuggled into the Knesset and requests for an exclusive private interview by a correspondent from the *Vancouver Sun.*

But then the game evolved. He was quite lucid and not in so much pain anymore on the night when it was reported that a gang of ultra-Zionist Jewish settlers had marched through the Arab quarters of the Old City, banging on doors and shouting at residents to flee before the events of Sabra and Chatila were repeated there. From his roommate, a middle-aged gall bladder sufferer from whom all this inhumanity was distressing, he solicited the names and locations of several of these ultra-nationalist enclaves. A rented car, a knife, an unarmed settler (surely there must be a few of them who did not have Uzis slung over their shoulders) walking alone along a back road—something like that was possible. A different sort of deed to leave behind.

But no, he was just too well conditioned; it could be nothing other than a game for him. In the end, he'd been forced to acknowledge that there was never a real chance of anything otherwise.

The final confirmation of this had come that morning, after he checked himself out of the hospital and made his flight arrangements home. He had his knife and his map—the Palestinian village of Bekroum circled in ink for him along with the name, printed in the margin, of the kibbutz and town that now occupied that place on this land—and had gone up to the Noble Sanctuary for a last look at the Dome of the Rock, and a last touch of the smooth, cool marble beneath that golden crown. Afterwards, down below the enclosure, he had spent some time watching a group of black-clad Orthodox Jews at their wall. Then, all the while playing with the short sharp blade in his pocket, he'd followed an aged Hasidic out through the winding, narrow cobblestone streets to the Damascus Gate and up Jaffa Road into an Orthodox neighborhood of West Jerusalem. He followed the old man for blocks and blocks, edging a little closer all the time, but when his victim left the open street and slowly started up the darkened staircase of a decrepit apartment block— a perfect place in which to kill—he'd simply walked on. . . .

"There," the boy said. He stepped away from the olive tree now deeply etched with a crooked *N* and a slightly smaller *K*.

Geoff stared at the letters. "Something is missing, don't you think?" he said.

The boy squinted at his handiwork for a moment before nodding. "It needs to have a heart around it."

"Yes. Yes, a heart would be good. Do you want to—"

The boy had already started. With more creative energy than artistic ability, he carved the wobbly borders of Nadya's deed. Knowing how such things should look, he made a heart large enough for company: the expected, second set of initials.

"*Joshua.*"

A woman called out sharply from the edge of the sandpit playground.

"My mother," the boy said.

"Joshua, what are you doing over there?"

Geoff heard the voice of a parent from a place where the chinless molesters of children lurked behind every bush. He watched her hurry over and knew that the first thing she'd do would be glance down to see if his fly was open. He checked just in case.

"You're not supposed to be over on that side of the fence." She rose up on tiptoes and leaned over the top of it to scold—and to glance.

"I'm helping this man. He's leavin' a deed for someone."

"What are you talking about? No, never mind . . . just get yourself back in here right now."

"Wait till I'm finished."

"You're finished, Joshua," Geoff told him. "Better do as your mother says." He took back his knife and gave the boy a little nudge in the right direction. "My fault," he explained to the woman, but without apology.

"He should know better," she said, catching her son as he stumbled after leaping from the top of the fence. "Anyhow, what is this he tells me you're doing?"

"He's leavin' a deed, I tol' ya."

"Hush up, Josh."

"You could say I'm looking for the home of a woman I knew," Geoff said.

"Oh?" she said suspiciously. "What's her name? Maybe I can help you."

"No, you can't help me. It was before your time," he said.

"We've only been in Israel for a couple of years, it's true, but we do know almost everyone in this town."

"Where did you come from?" Geoff asked.

"Chicago."

"You're immigrants, then?" he said.

"Well, yes, aren't you?"

"No."

With her son now back on the safe side of the fence, the woman pointed to his face. "You have a car accident or something?"

"I was in Beirut."

"You got hurt like that in the fighting?" she said, her voice immediately rising with concern.

"Not the main fighting."

"My husband is serving in the army near Beirut. I'm so worried about him I can hardly sleep at night."

"I don't think you need to worry. He's about as safe as anyone could be there," Geoff told her.

"Safe? My God, look at you," she said.

"Yes, why don't you do that." Geoff shook his head and struggled to control himself. "Listen, he and I hung out with different crowds. Believe me, I'm quite sure he's okay."

"Oh God, I hope you're right. Do you really think so—I mean really?" But Geoff had already turned back to the olive tree. Without looking up, he listened to mother and son walking off.

"What's a deed, Mom?"

"*What* are you talking about, Josh?"

Geoff stared at the empty space beneath Nadya's initials for a long time before making up his mind what to do. He pulled the blade out of its housing and drew his fingers slowly along the cool steel. He leaned in close to the tree and carefully carved an *M* and then a *C*. Mohammed Chauer. Snapping the knife shut, he dropped it in the dirt beneath the tree for curious Joshua to find some day, then straightened up and walked away, believing that this was where an old man who had once lived in a place called Chatila—a place that should never have been at all—would have liked to see it finish. He ducked in behind the wheel of his car, started the engine and pulled away from the curb. He thought about the only line he could still remember from the only piece of poetry that had ever been written for him—

Into a grief without end